"What'd you come here for? To find a husband?"

If looks could slap, his face would have been stinging.

"No, I am not looking for a husband. I could have had one back in Pennsylvania. That is, if I didn't mind being a workhorse, raising six stepchildren under the age of twelve." Her tone was uncharacteristically biting.

She reddened. "I didn't resent the children, honestly, but if I'd felt any love for their father… Or sensed that he might ever…" Her jaw tensed. "I like to do business, but marriage should be a matter of the heart, not something akin to a business contract. Doesn't thee agree?"

A matter of the heart. His jaw clenched and his unruly mind brought up Lorena's face. Miss Rachel wanted to be loved, not just needed. And he'd found out that his beloved one could let him down, turn her back and walk away.

Wrenching his mind back to the present, he held up both hands. "I get it. I ain't looking for a wife."

"That suits me."

USA TODAY Bestselling Author

Lyn Cote
and
Allie Pleiter

Heartland Courtship
&
Homefront Hero

LOVE INSPIRED
INSPIRATIONAL ROMANCE

LOVE INSPIRED®

INSPIRATIONAL ROMANCE

ISBN-13: 978-1-335-97195-1

Heartland Courtship & Homefront Hero

Copyright © 2021 by Harlequin Books S.A.

Heartland Courtship
First published in 2014. This edition published in 2021.
Copyright © 2014 by Lyn Cote

Homefront Hero
First published in 2012. This edition published in 2021.
Copyright © 2012 by Alyse Stanko Pleiter

Recycling programs for this product may not exist in your area.

This edition published by arrangement with Harlequin Books S.A.

For questions and comments about the quality of this book, please contact us at CustomerService@Harlequin.com.

Love Inspired
22 Adelaide St. West, 40th Floor
Toronto, Ontario M5H 4E3, Canada
www.Harlequin.com

Printed in U.S.A.

CONTENTS

A *USA TODAY* bestselling author of over forty novels, **Lyn Cote** lives in the north woods of Wisconsin with her husband in a lakeside cottage. She knits, loves cats (and dogs), likes to cook (and eat), never misses *Wheel of Fortune* and enjoys hearing from her readers. Visit her website, booksbylyncote.com, to learn more about her books that feature "Strong Women, Brave Stories."

Books by Lyn Cote

Love Inspired Historical

Wilderness Brides

Their Frontier Family
The Baby Bequest
Heartland Courtship
Frontier Want Ad Bride
Suddenly a Frontier Father

The Gabriel Sisters

Her Captain's Heart
Her Patchwork Family
Her Healing Ways

Visit the Author Profile page
at Harlequin.com for more titles.

HEARTLAND COURTSHIP

Lyn Cote

For my thoughts are not your thoughts,
neither are your ways my ways, saith the Lord.
For as the heavens are higher than the earth,
so are my ways higher than your ways,
and my thoughts than your thoughts.
—*Isaiah* 55:8–9

Are not two sparrows sold for a farthing? and one of
them shall not fall on the ground without your Father.
But the very hairs of your head are all numbered.
Fear ye not therefore, ye are of more value
than many sparrows.
—*Matthew* 10:29–31

To my PA and dear friend, Sara Scholten

Chapter One

Pepin, Wisconsin
June 2, 1871

In the dazzling sunshine, Rachel Woolsey stood on the deck of the riverboat, gazing at her new home, its wharf and huddle of rustic buildings. After all the lonely miles, she'd accomplished her journey. Relief flooded her when she recognized her cousin Noah standing near the dock, his wife and children at his side.

But she stiffened herself against this warm, weakening rush. She didn't want to dissolve in tears at the sight of family. She would make a life for herself here, fulfill her ambition of independence, start her own business, own a home—no matter what anyone said.

Her empty stomach churning, she smoothed her skirt, calming herself outwardly, and prayed silently for the strength to accomplish all she hoped. *With God's help, I will. Otherwise why did I leave my father's house in Pennsylvania?*

Finally, at the rear, the paddle wheel stilled, dripping and running with water. Porters carried her luggage onto shore where she tipped them and turned to her cousin. When she told him all her unusual—for a woman—plans, would he be a help or hindrance?

Holding his daughter, Noah enveloped her in a one-armed embrace. "Cousin Rachel!"

The intensity in his joyful welcome wrapped itself around her like a warm blanket and went straight to her lonesome heart. "Cousin!" She could say no more without tears.

Then he released her and his pretty blonde wife handed their little son to him and hugged her close. "We're so happy you have come. It's good to have family near."

Rachel sensed a breath of hesitation in Sunny's welcome. And Rachel guessed it must be because she knew of Sunny's unhappy past. How could she let Sunny know she would never, never reveal what she knew? She wouldn't tell anyone here that before marrying Noah, Sunny had borne a child out of wedlock.

"I'm so happy, Cousin Sunny," she said with heartfelt sincerity. "I'm so happy thee and Noah look…good together."

And they did. The two children looked happy and well fed. Noah looked healed, content and Sunny touched his arm with obvious affection. Then tears did come.

Maybe this place would be good for her, too. She realized that she did feel welcome, more than in her stepmother's home where she'd been an unpaid servant instead of a beloved daughter. She tried to shake off the bittering thought.

At sounds behind Rachel, Noah looked up and frowned. Speaking past her, he asked sharply, "What are you men doing?"

"The captain say bring this man on shore to the doctor," the black porter said.

Rachel swung around and saw that two porters were carrying an unconscious man, one holding his shoulders and one his ankles. A third porter followed with what looked like a bulging soldier's knapsack.

"We don't have a doctor here," Sunny said, sounding worried.

"Well, then we suppose to leave him anyway," the porter said, appearing abashed. "We got no one to nurse or doctor him and his fare run out two stops south."

Rachel's sense of right balked. "So thee's just going to abandon him?"

The porters looked ashamed, helpless. "That's what the captain order us to do."

Rachel struggled with herself. She couldn't take out her umbrage on these innocent men. She would tell the captain what she thought—

The boat whistle squealed. The porters gently laid down the shabby man and his travel-worn knapsack and then hustled onto the boat, which was already being cast free.

Within moments the boat was far from shore, heading north, the paddle wheel turning again. Rachel fumed at the departing craft as she dropped to her knees beside the man.

Thin, with a new beard and shaggy chestnut hair, he appeared around Noah's age, in his thirties, and would have been handsome if not so haggard looking. Drawn to help him, Rachel touched his perspiring forehead. Anxiety prodded her. "He's burning up, Noah."

Her cousin knelt on the man's other side. "We can't leave him."

"Of course we can't," Sunny agreed, holding her little girl back from going to her father.

Rachel rose with new purpose. "I'll help thee carry him, Noah." She bent and lifted the man's ankles and Noah quickly grasped his shoulders. They carried him to the wagon and managed to arrange him on a blanket Sunny kept under the wagon seat. Rachel should have had a harder time carrying a man's weight, but he must have lost pounds already, not a good sign.

Some of the shopkeepers and customers had come out to watch and a few helped wedge Rachel's luggage on the other side of the wagon bed along with the man's knapsack. They kept a safe distance from the feverish, unconscious man, evidently fearing contagion.

A man whom Sunny addressed as Mr. Ashford said, "He doesn't look good. Be sure you don't catch this from him."

Rachel understood this sentiment, but didn't let it sway her. Her father hadn't raised a coward.

Noah voiced what she was thinking, "We'll do what we can for him. It's shameful to just drop a man off to die."

"Irresponsible," Ashford agreed, though he backed away. "But not every river man is to be trusted."

Rachel couldn't decide if the man was speaking of the captain who'd abandoned the man or warning them that this man might do them harm—if he lived. Indignation stirred within her.

Noah helped Rachel up onto the wagon bench to sit beside Sunny. Rachel accepted Sunny's sweet little girl to sit on her lap. Noah turned the wagon and headed them home.

Rachel's attention was torn between the beautiful thick forest they drove into and the man moaning softly behind her. As they rolled into and over each rut and bump, she hurt for him. After traveling alone for weeks, she was moved by the man's plight. If she had become sick, would this have happened to her? "What does thee think he might be ill with?" she asked Sunny.

"I don't know. I have some skill in nursing the sick, but he might be…" Sunny's voice faltered.

Beyond our help, Rachel finished silently. A pall hung over them and the miles to Noah's homestead crawled by. Rachel mentally went over the medicines she'd brought with her and where they were packed. She questioned Sunny and found that her stock of medicines was meager, too.

Rachel closed her eyes, praying for this stranger, for all traveling strangers. The man's dire situation overlaid her joy at arriving here. Pepin was her new beginning. Would it be this man's ending?

Brennan Merriday groaned and the sound wakened him. He heard footsteps. Someone knelt beside him. A cool hand touched his brow. "I have broth and medicine. Open thy mouth, please." A woman's voice.

His every joint ached, excruciating. His body burned with fever. He couldn't speak, didn't have the strength to shake his head no. A spoon touched his lips. The only act he could manage was letting his mouth fall open. Warm, salty broth moistened his dry throat. Then something bitter. And then more broth. He let it flow into his mouth and swallowed.

He moaned, trying to lift his eyelids. Couldn't. Swallowed. He began to drift again. A face flickered in his mind—Lorena's oval face, beautiful as ever with black ringlets around it, a painful memory that lanced his heart. He groaned again.

The same firm voice summoned him back. "A few more mouthfuls, that's all I ask."

The gentle words fell soft on his ears. He made the effort to swallow again. Again. And then he felt himself slipping away.

Half asleep, Rachel sat in the rocking chair, the fire very low on the hearth, keeping a small pot of chicken broth warm. Every time the stranger surfaced, she spooned as much into him as she could, along with willow bark tea for his fever. She was trying to keep him alive till his fever broke.

Still he looked emaciated and beneath his eyes dark patches showed signs of his decline. Would she succeed? Or would they bury him without a name? The thought lowered her spirits.

She had cared for him around the clock for nearly a week. Weariness had seeped in as deep as her bones, but her overall worry, that they might bury this man never knowing his name, pressed in on her more. Noah had gone through the man's knapsack but had found nothing marked with a name.

Even sick, the stranger beckoned. Something about him drew her—more than merely the handsome face obscured by a wild, newly grown beard and mustache and the ravages of the fever. He looked lost somehow. Would he remain a mystery? Who was he? Why had he boarded the same riverboat as she? Was some woman pacing, worrying about him?

She'd thought she would quickly put her plans for her business into motion. But once again the needs of others took precedence. *Just a little longer. I don't begrudge helping this man, Father.* Her chin lowered and she slipped into that fuzzy world of half sleep.

A loud groan woke her fully. Pushing away the dregs of a dream about home, she sat up straighter and looked down. In the light from the hearth, she saw that the stranger was awake. And this time he opened his eyes. She quickly moved into her routine. She knelt by his pallet and felt his forehead. She pressed her hand there again. Was she imagining that he seemed cooler?

With the top of her wrist, she touched her own forehead and then his. She stared down into his dull eyes. "The fever has finally broken." Cold relief coursed through her.

The man tried to talk, his dry lips stuck together.

She held up a hand. "I'll get the broth." Soon she spooned more into his mouth. This time he didn't fall asleep while she was feeding him. His dark eyes followed her and for the first time she knew he was seeing her. This made her uncomfortable, being so close to a man, a stranger, performing an intimate task for him. Finally, the bowl was empty. "More?"

His head shook yes fractionally.

She quickly fetched more and fed him a second bowl, very aware of her disheveled appearance—though in his state he wouldn't have noticed even crossed eyes. And their being very much alone, even though Noah and Sunny slept in the next room, affected her oddly, too.

When done drinking, he closed his eyes and drew in a long breath. "How long have I been delirious?" A Southern accent slurred the words.

"Nearly a week."

"Where am I?" His voice sounded rusty, forced. His *I* sounded like *Ah*.

"In the home of my cousin Noah Whitmore in Pepin, Wisconsin."

His face screwed up as if the news were unwelcome. Then it relaxed as if he'd given up some struggle.

He might still die. She must know who he was. She couldn't explain the urgency, but she couldn't deny it. "What is thy name?"

His eyelids fluttered open. He had the thickest dark lashes she'd ever seen on a man. She held back a finger that errantly wanted to stroke their lush upward curve. "I'm Brennan Merriday."

She smiled down at him, relieved.

"What's your name, miss?"

"I am Rachel Woolsey," she said.

"Rachel," he murmured, rolling her name around his tongue. "You're a good woman, Miss Rachel."

Words of praise, so rare, warmed her with satisfaction.

She thought again of a woman, looking for him, a hitch in her breath. "Does thee have family we can contact?"

"No."

The way he said the word saddened her. She'd been without family since her mother died and her father had remarried.

She touched his forehead again, more to connect with him than out of necessity. Was her compassion carrying her off to more than it should?

"Miss Rachel," he repeated. Then he closed his eyes.

She didn't think he had fallen back to sleep. He'd closed his eyes to shut her out. Was it her question that prompted this or was he too weak to talk further? Though his fever had broken, he would need careful nursing before he recovered fully. She sighed long, not letting herself dwell on her own plans, already much delayed.

A man's life was worth more than her business. And this man hadn't chosen to be sick. She pulled the blanket up around his neck and smoothed it. Why had this desire to touch him come?

Finally she pushed herself up onto her feet before she gave in to temptation and did something like touch those thick lashes and embarrassed herself.

She settled back into the rocking chair with her feet on a three-legged stool. She pulled the shawl up onto her shoulders like a blanket and almost fell asleep. One thought lingered—the man did not seem very happy to wake from a fever. That could be due to his weakness. But from his few words, she didn't think so. The lonely recognized the lonely.

Brennan lay on the pallet, still aching, feeling as flat as a blank sheet of foolscap. For the first time, he was aware of what was going on around him. The family who lived in this roomy log cabin had just risen and was getting ready to start its day. He hadn't been this close to such a family for a long time—by choice. Too painful for him.

A tall husband sat at the table, bouncing a little girl on one knee and a baby on the other, saying nursery rhymes and teasing them. The children giggled; the sound made him feel forlorn. A pretty wife in a fresh white apron was tending the fire and making breakfast. Bacon sizzled in a pan, whetting Brennan's once-dormant appetite. How long before he could get away from this homey place that reminded him too much of what he'd lost a decade ago? When he reached Canada, maybe then he could forget. When would he be able to travel again?

The woman who'd nursed him…what was her name?

His wooly mind groped around, seeking it. Miss Rachel, that was it. She still slept in a rocking chair near him. He could see only the side of her face since her head had fallen against the high back of the chair. Light golden freckles dotted her nose. Straight, light brown hair had slipped from a bun, unfurling around her cheek and nape. From what he could see, she was not blatantly pretty but not homely either. There was something about her, an innocence that frightened him for her.

The smell of bacon insisted on his full attention. He opened his eyes wider and turned his head. His stomach rumbled loudly.

As they heard it, both the husband and wife turned to him. Miss Rachel's eyes popped open. "Thee is awake?"

He nodded, his mouth too dry to speak. *Thee? Quakers to boot?*

"I'll get you a cup of coffee," the wife said.

Miss Rachel stretched gracefully and fully like a cat awakening from a nap and rose from the rocking chair, throwing off a shawl, revealing a trim figure in a plain dark dress. She knelt beside him and tested his forehead. "No fever." She beamed.

He gazed up into the largest gray eyes he'd ever seen. They were serene, making him feel his disreputable appearance. Yet her gaze wouldn't release him. He resisted. *I'm just weak, that's all.*

The husband walked over and looked down. "Thank God. You had us worried."

At the mention of God, Brennan felt the familiar tightening. God's notice was not something he wanted. The wife handed Miss Rachel a steaming mug of what smelled like fresh-brewed coffee. She lifted his head and shoulders. Lilac scent floated in the air.

"I can sit up," he protested, forcing out the words

in a burst through cracked lips. Yet when he tried, he found that he could not sit up, his bones as soft as boiled noodles.

"Thy strength will return," Miss Rachel said, nudging his lips with the mug rim.

He opened his mouth to insist that he'd be up before the day was out. But instead he let the strong, hot, creamy coffee flow in. His thirst sprang to life and he drank till the mug was empty. Then he inhaled, exhausted by the act and hating that. Everyone stared down at him, pity in their eyes.

The old bitterness reared. *Enjoyin' the show?* he nearly snarled. His heart beat fast at the inappropriate fury that coursed through him. These innocent people didn't deserve the sharp edge of his rough tongue.

"You'll feel better," the wife said, "when you've been able to eat more and get your strength back."

"How did I end up here?" he asked, the thought suddenly occurring to him. Hadn't he been on a riverboat?

"The captain put you off the same boat I arrived on," Miss Rachel replied, sounding indignant.

Brennan couldn't summon up any outrage. What had the captain owed him? But now he owed these good people, the kind who usually avoided him. The debt rankled.

"You're from the South?" the husband asked.

There it came again. Most Northerners commented about his Southern drawl. Brennan caught his tongue just before his usual biting answer came out. "Yes." He clenched his teeth.

The husband nodded. "We're not still fighting the war here. I'm Noah Whitmore. This is my wife, Sunny, and our children, Dawn and Adam. And Rachel is my first cousin."

Brennan tried to fix the names to the faces and drew in air. "My brain is mush," he admitted, giving up the struggle.

Noah chuckled. "We'll get you back on your feet. Never fear."

The immense, unasked-for debt that he owed this couple and this Miss Rachel rolled over Brennan. Words seemed paltry, but they must be spoken. "You have my thanks."

"We were glad to help," the wife, Sunny, said. "We all need help sometime."

Her last phrase should have eased him but his reaction was the opposite. Her last phrase raised his all-too-easy-to-rile hackles, increasing his discomfort. How could he ever pay what he owed these people? And he'd be forced to linger here to do that. Canada was still a long ways away. This stung like bitter gall.

Three days had inched past since Brennan had surfaced from the fever that had almost killed him. Noah had bathed him. And humming to herself, Miss Rachel had washed, pressed and ironed his clothing. The way she hummed when she worked, as if she was enjoying herself, made him 'specially fractious. Each day he lay at ease under their roof added another notch to his debt.

From his pallet now, he saw the sun barely lighting the window, and today he'd planned to get up and walk or know the reason why. He made himself roll onto his knees and then, bracing his hands against the wall, he pushed up onto his feet.

For a moment the world whirled around. He bent his head and waited out the vertigo. Then he sat in the chair and pulled on his battered boots. His heart pounded and that scared him. Had this fever affected his heart?

Visions of old men sitting on steps in the shade shook him, moved him.

He straightened up and waited out a momentary wooziness. He shuffled toward the door and opened it. The family's dog lay just outside. Brennan held a finger up to his mouth and the dog didn't bark, gave just a little yip of greeting. Brennan stepped outside and began shuffling slowly down the track toward the trail that he knew must lead to town. The dog walked beside him companionably.

Brennan tried not to think, just to put one foot in front of the other. A notion of walking to the road played through his mind. But each step announced clearly that this would not be possible.

About twenty feet down the track, his legs began to wobble. He turned, suddenly wishing he'd never tried this stunt.

"Brennan Merriday!" The petite spinster was running toward him, a long housecoat nearly tangling around her ankles.

He tried to stand straight, but his spine began to soften.

She reached him just as he began to crumple and caught him, her arm over his chest, her hand under his arm. "Oof!"

Slowly she also crumpled. They fell together onto the barely bedewed grass, he facedown, she faceup. She was breathing hard from running.

"Brennan Merriday," the little Quaker scolded, "what was thee thinking?"

"Why do you always use both my names?" he snapped, breathing hard too and saying the first thing that came to mind that didn't smack of rudeness.

"That is the Quaker way, our plain speech. Titles

such as mister and sir are used to give distinction, and all are equal before God."

She lay beside him, her arm lodged under his chest, much too close to suit him.

"God and Quakers may think that but hardly anybody else does," he panted. He rolled away to stand but halted when he'd gained his knees. He had to get his breath before trying to stand to his feet, get away from this soft, sweet-smelling woman.

The Quaker sprang up with—he grumbled silently— a disgusting show of energy. "I'll help thee."

"I prefer to get up by my lonesome, thank you," he retorted, his temper at his own weakness leaking out. He glanced at her from the corner of his eye.

Her hair had come loose from a single braid and flared around her shoulders. Her skin glowed like a ripe peach in the dawn light. He took a deep breath and tried to turn his thoughts from her womanliness.

"Why did thee do this without discussing it first, Brennan Merriday?"

"I reckon," he drawled, "I overestimated my strength, Miss Rachel."

"I don't think thee understands just how ill…" She pursed her lips. "A little patience is what is needed now. I had planned to help thee take a short walk today. It is exactly what is needed."

"Well, I saved you the trouble and took my own walk." He couldn't stop the ridiculous words.

She gave him a look that mimicked ones his sour aunt Martha had used often when he was little.

"I'm not a child," he muttered.

A moment of silence. Miss Rachel pressed her lips together, staring at him. Then she glanced away. "I know that," she murmured.

Slowly he made it onto one foot and then he rose, woozy but standing.

She waited nearby, both arms outstretched as if to catch him. "Should I call Noah to help?"

"I can do it myself. Just let me take my time."

The family dog stayed nearby, watching as if trying to figure out what they were doing.

"You can go on in," he said, waving one hand.

She studied him. "Very well, but since thee has so much energy, thee can help me today. I am going to try a new recipe and I need the walnuts I bought in Saint Louis shelled and chopped."

"I'll look forward to it, Miss Rachel," he said with a sardonic twist and bow of his head.

She walked away and he had to close his eyes in order not to watch her womanly sway. Even a shapeless housecoat couldn't completely hide her feminine curves. Why hadn't some man in Pennsylvania married her? She wasn't ugly or anything. And why was he, Brennan Merriday, drifter, thinking such thoughts?

He was the last one to speak about getting married. His wife had betrayed him, but perhaps from her point of view he'd betrayed her. Either way, Lorena was dead and he had no business wondering why someone was or wasn't married.

After breakfast, Noah went outside to work on some wood project. Brennan watched him leave, wishing he had the strength to do man's work. The pretty wife and children were off to visit friends and that left him alone with the spinster.

Miss Rachel began setting out bowls, eggs, flour, sugar and such. "I am baking rolled walnut yeast logs today. I recalled that it's one of Noah's favorites and I want to thank him for his kindness to me."

Her remark caught Brennan's attention. So she felt beholden to the Whitmores, too? And then he recalled that she had said she'd arrived on the same riverboat as he had. "What'd you come here for? To find a husband?"

If looks could slap, his face would have been stinging.

"No, I am not looking for a husband. I could have had one back in Pennsylvania. That is, if I didn't mind being a workhorse, raising six stepchildren under the age of twelve." Her tone was uncharacteristically biting.

She reddened. "I didn't resent the children, honestly, but if I'd felt any love for their father…or sensed that he might ever…" Her jaw tensed. "I like to do business but marriage should be a matter of the heart, not something akin to a business contract. Doesn't thee agree?"

A matter of the heart. His jaw clenched and his unruly mind brought up Lorena's face. Miss Rachel wanted to be loved, not just needed. And he'd found out that his beloved one could let him down, turn her back and walk away.

Wrenching his mind back to the present, he held up both hands. "I get it. I ain't looking for a wife."

"That suits me." She lifted her chin. "I've come to set up in business here."

He couldn't mask his shock. "You plan to have your own business?"

"I intend to open a bakery and sweet shop. And Pepin is just the kind of town that can support one."

"Are you out of your mind?" he blurted. "A bakery in this little half-horse town?"

"No," she said, dismissing his opinion. "I am not

out of my mind. Pepin's a river town. Boats stop daily, dropping off and picking up passengers and goods. I will sell my confections to the river boatmen and passengers. Candies and baked goods. I've rarely met a man without a sweet tooth."

He glanced directly at her for the first time. "You good at makin' candy and such?"

He glimpsed a flash of pleased pride in her eyes. "People have said I have a gift for creating sweet things."

"Well, when am I gonna taste some?" he asked with a sly glance.

He'd made her smile. "Well, if you start shelling these walnuts, that would be today."

She set a cloth bag of nuts, a small hammer and a slender, pointed nutpick in front of him. "Take thy time. I must mix the dough and it must rise once before I'll need to roll it out, then spread the filling of honey, cinnamon and crushed walnuts and roll it back up to rise again."

He usually spent his days sweeping out liveries or saloons or lifting and carrying at docks. It had been a very long time since he'd sat in a kitchen with a woman while she baked. There was something cozy about it. Then memories of shelling pecans for his aunt Martha came back to him. He shook out a few walnuts from the bag and stared at them.

Many minutes passed as Miss Rachel measured and mixed.

"I've been thinking about a proposition for you, Brennan Merriday." She took a deep breath and plunged on, "I also intend to stake a claim for myself here."

The few words shocked Brennan again. He'd never

conceived of a woman doing something like this. "A single woman homesteadin'? Is that allowed?"

"It is. I am determined to have my own place."

Unheard of. "You couldn't do it. You wouldn't have the strength to prove up, to do all the work."

Proving up meant fulfilling the government requirements of building and clearing the land within the five year time limit. She went on, "That is where my proposition comes in. I was wondering if I could hire thee to help me out for a few weeks." She wouldn't meet his eyes, concentrating on her mixing and measuring.

He gaped at her. Work for a woman?

"Around here, men only work for others upon need or when their own chores are done," she explained what he could already guess. "And this is the growing season. Men are plowing and planting…" Her voice faded away.

Work for a woman, he repeated silently. When he'd been without funds in the past, he'd done chores for women in payment for meals. But *work* for one like a hired hand? The idea sent prickles through him. He swallowed down the mortification.

"So?" she prompted.

"Even if I accepted this employment, I can't build a cabin all by myself, not even with Noah's help," he pointed out.

"Noah says there is an abandoned homestead near town." Her voice had brightened. "There is already a cabin. So that would mean just fixing it up. But I'll also need someone to dig me a garden and so on." She looked him in the eye, her expression beseeching. "Is thee interested in such employment?"

Brennan's mind struggled to take this in. A woman stake a claim? A woman run her own business? Preposterous. And him work for a woman? An outlandish idea.

Men didn't do that. He could hear the kind of comments he'd get from other men about working for this spinster.

And Miss Rachel was just the kind of woman—respectable and straightlaced—he generally steered clear of. And he never stayed in one place long and this suggestion would interfere with that—mightily. Canada was calling him.

But then he recalled his debt to her and picking up the little hammer, he whacked the nearest walnut so hard it cannonaded off the table and hit the wall.

Miss Rachel's finely arched eyebrows rose toward her hairline. She walked over and picked up the walnut. "Try it again, Brennan Merriday. If thee doesn't wish to work for a woman, I will understand." She turned her head away.

He could tell from the mifftiness of her tone that he'd insulted her. He hadn't meant to. But Miss Rachel was going against the flow and probably knew what was in store for her, probably knew what people would say to him for working for her.

Why would she do this? He looked down at the returned walnut. He remembered Aunt Martha, his father's unmarried sister, who'd lived with them. He'd just accepted that unmarried women spent their days looking after other women's children and washing other people's clothes. Had that made his aunt so crusty? Had she hidden blighted dreams of her own?

He couldn't actually work for a woman, could he? He looked up. Did he have a choice? He owed this Quakeress his life. "I can't take the job formal-like, Miss Rachel. But I will help you get set up."

"Thank thee, Brennan Merriday. I'd shake thy hand but..." She nodded to her hands, already kneading the large bowl of dough. Her face was rosy from the oven and from their talk no doubt. He wondered why this woman kept catching him by surprise, causing him to want to shield her. She was not like any other woman he'd ever met.

He expertly tapped another walnut and it opened in two clean-cut halves. He felt a glimmer of satisfaction and began digging out the nuts, breathing in the scent of yeast and walnut oil.

He'd help this woman get started and then he could leave, his conscience clear. He'd start north to Canada again—Canada, where no one had fought in the war and held no grudge nor memory. Where he might finally forget.

Chapter Two

A week later, Rachel climbed up on the bench of the wagon with Brennan's help. He had insisted that if he was accompanying her, he would do the driving. She'd given in. Men hated being thought weak and this man had been forced to swallow that for over a fortnight now.

Finally she'd be able to get started doing what she'd come to do, create her new life. A fear niggled at her. What if someone had gotten the jump on her and already claimed the property? Well, she'd deal with it if she had to, not before.

Another worry pinched her. The homestead might need a lot of work, more than Noah and Brennan could do. "Did Noah tell thee where to find the abandoned homestead?" she asked, keyed up.

"Yes, Miss Rachel, you know Noah explained where it was. What you're asking me is, do I remember how to drive there."

She grinned at him, ignoring the barely disguised aggravation in his tone. "Thee must be feeling better if thee can joke."

He looked disgruntled at her levity but said nothing, just slapped the reins and started the horses moving.

They rode in silence for the first mile. Against her own will, she studied his profile, a strong one.

Freshly shaven and with his face no longer drawn with fever, he was an exceptionally handsome man. She brushed a fly away from her face. She turned her gaze forward. Handsome men never looked at her. Why should she look at this one?

Brennan spoke to the horses as he slowed them over a deep rut. His Southern accent made her wonder once more. The horrible war had ended slavery, yet tensions between the North and South had not eased one bit. And after four years of war, the South was devastated. What had brought this Southerner north?

She watched his jaw work. She wondered what he was getting up the nerve to say to her. She hoped he wasn't about to repeat the usual words of discouragement.

"Are you sure you're ready to set up a place all by yourself?" he asked finally.

Rachel did not sigh as loudly as she felt like doing. Her stepmother's voice played in her mind. *An unmarried woman doesn't live alone. Or run a business on her own. It's unnatural. What will people say?*

"Brennan Merriday," Rachel said, "if thee only knew how many times that has been asked of me. I am quite certain that I can homestead on my own land." Her tone was wry, trying to pass his concern off lightly—even though it chafed her. She had become accustomed to being an oddity—a woman who didn't marry and who wanted to do things no woman should want.

"Why do you say thee and thy and your cousin doesn't?"

This question took her by surprise. "I don't really know except there isn't a Quaker meeting here."

"I take it that Noah's the preacher hereabout, but not a Quaker."

She barely listened to his words, still surveying him. His body still needed feeding, but he had broad shoulders and long limbs. Most of all, the sense of his deep inner pain drew her even though she knew he didn't want that. She turned her wayward eyes forward again. "Yes, he seems to have reconnected with God."

"Don't it bother you that he's not a Quaker no more?"

"We were both raised Quaker but I don't consider other Christians to be less than we are. Each Christian has a right to go his own path to God."

"And what about those who don't want to have nothin' to do with any church?"

She heard the edge in the man's voice and wondered how to reply. She decided frankness should be continued. "When he enlisted in the Union Army, Noah was put out of meeting."

The man beside her said nothing but she felt that he absorbed this like a blow to himself. She recalled praying for God to keep her cousin safe and reading the lists of the wounded and fallen after every battle, hoping not to see his name listed. The horrible war had made a dreadful impact on all their lives. Still did.

She brushed away another fly as if sweeping away the sadness of the war, sweeping away her desire to hold him close and soothe him as she would a wounded bird.

Brennan remained silent. His hands were large and showed that he had worked hard all his life.

Just as she had. "I know that people will think me odd when I stake a homestead," she said briskly, bypassing his digression. "But I intend to make my own way. I've worked for others and saved money enough to start out on my own."

Any money a woman earned belonged to her husband or father. Still, in the face of her stepmother's disapproval, her father had decided that Rachel should keep what she earned. No doubt he thought she might never marry. His wife would inherit everything and leave Rachel with nothing. This had been her father's one demonstration of concern for her. How was it that when she'd lost her mother, she'd also in effect lost her father?

Except for Brennan murmuring to the team, silence again greeted her comment. Finally he admitted, "I see you got your mind made up."

They rode in silence then. The homestead Noah had told her about lay north of town within a mile and had been abandoned just before deep winter the previous year. Rachel gazed at the thick forest and listened to the birdsong, trying to identify the different calls.

Her mother had taught her bird lore. She heard a bobwhite and then a robin and smiled. A pair of eagles swooped and soared overhead. She realized she already loved this place, the wildness of it, the newness.

Another mile or so and Brennan drove through town and then turned the horses onto a faint track and into an overgrown clearing. A small log cabin and a shed sat in the middle of it. Stumps poked out of tall grass, dried from weeks without rain. Only deer had grazed here earlier this spring. The sight of the almost cozy clearing wound warmly around her heart. Would this be her home?

Brennan halted the team with a word and set the brake.

She started to climb down.

"Miss Rachel," he ordered, "ya'll will wait till I get there to help you down. I may be riffraff but I know enough to do that."

She froze. "Thee is not riffraff."

He made no reply but helped her down without meeting her eyes. Again, she longed to touch him, offer comfort, but could not.

So this man had also been weighed by society and found wanting. She recalled all the times people had baldly pointed out her lack of beauty or wondered why she wasn't married yet—as if either was any of their business. And of course, she couldn't answer back without being as rude as they.

Lifting her skirts a few inches, she waded through the tall, dry grass, which flattened under her feet. Noah had been praying for rain. The cabin's door was shut tight. A good sign. She stepped back and bumped into Brennan, nearly losing her balance. He steadied her. She was shocked at the rampant and unusual sensations that flooded her. She pulled away. "My thanks."

He reached around her and tried to push open the door. It stuck. With his shoulder, he had to force it. Looking down, he said, "Mud washed up against the door and under it and grass grew on it."

She stepped into the dim interior and let her eyes adjust. Brennan entered and waited behind her. Finally she could see a hearth on the back wall, cobwebs high up in the corners and a broken chair lying on its side. Otherwise only dust covered the floor. "It just needs cleaning."

"Look up."

She obeyed. "What am I looking for?"

"I see stains from a few roof leaks."

She turned to him. "Is that hard to make right?"

"No, I just need to bring a ladder to get up there and see where the shingles have blown loose or cracked."

She considered this. "Thee can do that?"

"Sure." He looked disgruntled at her question.

"Let's look at the shed then."

They did. Just an empty building but in good order. *Excellent.* Mentally she began listing the new structures she'd need. She noted how Brennan looked around as if tallying something, too. Finally she asked, "What's thy opinion? Will this be a good homestead for me to claim?"

"Well, it's fortunate to already have a cabin and shed on it."

She pointed to a mound between the cabin and the shed. "Could that be a well covered over?"

"Might be." He strode over to it and stooped down. "You're right. They were good enough to cover the well and mud got washed onto the boards and then grass sprouted." He rose. "Do you know why the family left the claim?"

"Sunny said the wife died."

The bleak reply silenced them for a moment.

"Life is so fragile," she murmured. Then she took herself in hand. "But we are alive and I need a home."

"I do, too."

She took this to mean that he'd decided to accept her position, but couldn't bring himself to say so. And he would know he couldn't live anywhere on the property of a single woman.

Tactfully she said, "I'm glad making this livable will not take long. It's important I get my business up soon because the prime season for making a reputation for my sweets up and down the river is summer, when the boat traffic will be at its peak. This far north the Mississippi freezes, according to Noah."

"You make good sense," he allowed grudgingly.

She moved to look directly into his eyes. After a

mental calculation she said, "I could afford to pay you
two dollars a week. That would include meals."

"I won't take anythin' for my work, but I'll need to
pay for a room." He left it open that he'd need her to
cover that.

"Where will you live?" she asked finally.

"I thought I'd ask in town who has room for me."

She offered him her hand. "It's a deal then. Let's go
to town and stake this claim."

"Yes, Miss Rachel." His words were polite but she
caught just the slight edge of irony under them. What
had made this man so mocking of himself and others?
She would just take him as he was. Until he moved on.

And she ignored the sensitive currents that raced
up her arm when he gripped her hand and shook it as
if she were another man. Were foolish schoolgirl feelings going to pop up now when she least needed them?
And when to show them would embarrass both her and
this complex man?

Brennan halted the team outside the narrow storefront. In the window, a small white placard read simply
Government Office and beneath that a smaller placard—Agent Present. He went around and helped Miss
Rachel down. She looked sturdier than she felt as he
assisted her. She was such a little bit of a woman—with
such big ideas.

He seriously doubted she would be allowed to regis-
ter for a homestead. The idea was crazy. Still, he asked,
"Do you want me to come in with you?"

She looked up at him with a determined expression,
her large gray eyes flashing and direct. "No, I can handle this myself."

He listened for any sign she might want him to accompany her. But he caught only a shade of tartness in her tone. He accepted her decision. He didn't like people hovering over him either. "Then I'll be going to find me a room."

"Very well. If I am not here when you need me, look for me at the General Store." Without waiting for his reply, she marched to the door and went inside. He wondered idly why she never wore any lace or pretty geegaws. And she skimmed her hair back so severely. Didn't she want to look pretty?

He stood a moment, staring after her. Northern women were different all right and up to now, Miss Rachel stood out as the most different he'd met. Lorena's biddable face flickered in his mind, stinging as it always did. He walked resolutely away from the starchy Yankee and his own taunting memories.

He paused, scanning the lone dusty street for a likely place to ask for a room. This little dot on the shore of the Mississippi hadn't progressed to having a boardinghouse yet.

Whom could he ask? Then he noticed the saloon at the end of the street, the kind of place where he always found an easy welcome—as long as he had money in his pocket.

No doubt it would irritate Miss Rachel if he went in there. So he strode toward it, reveling in the ability to walk down a street healthy once again. He pushed through swinging doors into the saloon, almost empty in the late morning. A pudgy older man leaned back behind the bar.

"Mornin'," Brennan greeted him.

"What can I do for you?" the man replied genially.

Brennan approached the bar. "I'm new in town, need

a room. You know any place that'd be good for me to ask at?"

They exchanged names and shook hands.

"You're from the South?" Sam, the barkeep, commented.

"Yeah." Though bristling, Brennan swallowed a snide reply.

After eyeing him for a few moments, Sam rubbed his chin. "Most shopkeepers have family above their place or build a cabin behind their business. Got a blacksmith-farrier in town. Single. Think he's got a loft empty. Can't think of anybody else that has room."

"Don't have many businesses in this bump in the road," Brennan drawled, leaning against the bar, suddenly glad to have someone more like him to talk to. The Whitmores were good folk, but he had to watch his errant tongue around them.

Sam smirked. "You got that right."

A look of understanding passed between them. Brennan drew in a deep breath. "Thanks for your advice about the room."

"Glad to help. Drop in some evening and we'll have a tongue wag."

After nodding, Brennan headed outside. Miss Rachel probably hadn't finished in the government office yet. So under the hot sun, he ambled toward the log-constructed blacksmith shop. The clang of metal on metal announced a smithy hard at work. Would the blacksmith be anti-Southerner, too?

He entered the shady interior and fierce heat rushed into his face. A broad-shouldered man in a leather apron pounded an oblong of iron, shaping it into some long-handled tool, sparks flying. Finally, after plunging the tool into a barrel of water, the sweating blacksmith stepped back from his forge. Over the sizzling of the molten iron meeting cold water, he asked, "What can I do for you, stranger?"

Brennan moved forward and offered his hand. "Name's Merriday. Ah'm lookin' to rent a room."

Pulling off leather gloves, the blacksmith gripped his hand briefly. Brennan felt the power of the man in that grip.

"You sound like you're from the South," the man observed.

"I am." Brennan said no more, though smoldering.

"Comstock's my name. Levi Comstock," the tall man said. "How long you staying here?"

"A few months maybe." These few words cost him. He never spent a month in any place anymore. The disorienting flashes of memory and restlessness always hit him after a few weeks. He hoped in Canada he could finally settle down. *But I owe Miss Rachel.* "You got room for me?"

The blacksmith studied Brennan.

Brennan didn't like it and pressed his lips together to keep back a nervy comment that itched to be said.

The man finally nodded toward a ladder. "I built me a lean-to to sleep in for the summer. Get the breeze off the river. Not using my loft now. It'll be hot up there. I've been meaning to cut out two small windows for some air. Maybe you could do that."

"How much do you want a week?"

"Four bits?" Comstock asked.

"That's all?"

The man's blackened face split into a grin. "You ain't seen the loft yet. No bed. Just a dusty floor."

"And two windows when we cut them." Brennan knew he'd just taken a liking to this practical man and dampened down the lift it sparked in him. He'd be here only as long as Miss Rachel needed him. Then he'd move north and get settled before winter. The two men shook hands.

"When you moving in?"

Brennan considered this. "Soon. Maybe tomorrow."

"See you then." The smith turned back to his forge.

Brennan stepped outside and gazed around at the nearly vacant main street and sighed. What would he do in this little berg for a few weeks? And how was Miss Rachel faring with the land agent? He headed toward the office. Maybe Miss Rachel needed some backup by now.

Just inside the door of the government office, Rachel paused to gird herself for battle, quelling her dislike of contention. She knew she faced one of the the biggest battles of her life, here and now.

The small, middle-aged man in a nondescript suit behind a small desk rose politely. "Miss?"

She smiled her sweetest smile and went swiftly forward. "Good day, sir. I am Miss Rachel Woolsey." She never used sir. Quakers didn't use titles. But she couldn't afford to be Quaker today. After she told him what she'd come for, she was going to brand herself odd enough as it was. Their hands clasped briefly.

"Please take a seat and tell me what I can do for you, Miss Woolsey."

She sat primly on the chair he had set for her and braced herself. "I'm here to stake a claim."

Shock widened the man's pinched face. "I beg your pardon."

"I am here to stake a claim," she repeated, stubborn determination rearing up inside.

"Your husband is ill?" he asked after a pause.

Hadn't she introduced herself as Miss? "No, I am unmarried."

"Then you can't stake a homestead claim." Each of his words stabbed at her. "It isn't done."

She'd expected this reaction and she had come prepared. "Excuse me, please, but it can be done." She tried to keep triumph from her smile. "And quite legally. My father consulted our state representative to the U.S. Congress before I left Pennsylvania." She pulled out the creased envelope. "Here is the letter."

The man did not reach for the envelope. "I know the law, miss. But a single woman homesteading, while legal, is ridiculous. You will never prove up your claim. Why put yourself through that?" His last sentence oozed condescension.

Her irritation simmered. So many sharp replies frothed on her tongue, but she swallowed them. "I have already hired a workman and the claim I want is the one that the Ryersons left last winter. May I please begin the paperwork?" She gazed at him, giving the impression that she would sit here all day if need be. And she would.

He glared at her.

Seconds, minutes passed.

She cleared her throat and pinned the man with her gaze. "Is there a problem?"

"I think it's shameful that your father would let you leave home and homestead on your own. What will people think of you—a single woman without a male protector? Have you thought of that?"

Rachel shook off this measly objection. "Sir, I cannot think that anyone here would take me for a woman of easy virtue. And—" she didn't let him interject the retort that must be reddening his face "—my cousin Noah Whitmore is here to watch over me."

"You're Noah Whitmore's cousin?"

"Our mothers were sisters."

He stared at her again, chewing the inside of his cheek—no doubt trying to come up with another objection.

She kept her steady gaze on him. The door behind her opened. Glancing over her shoulder, she glimpsed Brennan enter. She lifted one eyebrow.

"Miss Rachel, aren't you about done here?" he asked, hat in hand, but the willingness to dispute with the agent plain on his face.

"I still need to fill out the claim form," she replied evenly and then turned to face the government official who should be earning his money by doing his job and not wasting her time.

With a glance at Mr. Merriday, the man whipped out a form and jumped to his feet. "I need to walk a bit."

She didn't reply. Outside sea gulls squawked; the sound mimicked her reaction to this officious little man.

After he exited with a huff in each step, she moved to his side of the desk and, using his pen and ink, neatly and precisely filled out the form. All the things she wished she could say to the agent streamed through her mind. She wore skirts—why did that make her incompetent, inferior?

She knew all the various restrictions society placed on women and knew that many quoted scripture as their justification. But she never knew why submitting to a husband or not speaking in the church had anything to do with regard to a woman without one. And the Quakers didn't believe in either anyway.

Soon she finished filling out the form and read it

over carefully to make sure she hadn't omitted any-thing. When satisfied, she rose.

"Miss Rachel, why don't you go on to the store and I'll find that government agent and give him your claim?"

She paused to study Brennan's face. Then she under-stood him. Oh, she hadn't thought of that. Papers could go astray so easily. Though this goaded her, she said nothing, merely handed him the paper and walked out the door, thanking him for his help. Brennan might not approve of her intentions but he wasn't treating her like a female who couldn't know her own mind. A definite point in his favor. And no doubt why he'd begun pop-ping into her mind at odd moments. She must be wary of that. He would be gone soon. She tried to ignore the shaft of startling loneliness this brought her.

Brennan accepted the paper, accepted that once again he was going against the grain by backing the unpopu-lar horse, his curse it seemed. He let the lady go, deter-mined to get her what she wanted. As little as Brennan approved of Miss Rachel's filing for her homestead, he wasn't going to let some scrawny government weasel gyp this fine lady. Not on his watch.

Outside the office, he scanned the street for the man. When he didn't see him, he headed for the sa-loon. Maybe the barkeep would know where the agent stayed when in town.

He stepped inside and found the man he was look-ing for, pouring out the affront he'd just suffered in his office. "I don't know what this country is coming to. Giving black men the vote and now a woman thinks she can stake a claim like a man. Next they'll want the vote, too! A woman homesteading—I ask you!"

"I know it's not the usual," Brennan drawled. "But it's a free country. For women, too." He didn't like meddlesome little squirts like this man who liked to throw around their half ounce of power.

The land agent glared at him. "Who are you?"

Brennan eyed the man with distaste. Suddenly he felt proud to say, "I'm the one who's workin' for the lady."

"Then you're as crazy as she is," the agent declared.

Sam moved back and leaned against the wall behind the bar as if enjoying a show.

"I been called worse than crazy." Leaning against the bar, Brennan began enjoying this rumpus. He didn't cotton to the fact that he had to stay in this little town. So why did this man think he could have everything his way?

The agent turned away from him, venting his spleen by muttering to himself.

"I brought Miss Rachel's paper." Brennan said the words with a barely concealed challenge in his voice. "I want to make sure it gets into the mail today and marked in your records nice and legal." Brennan had never staked a claim or done anything else with any government except enlist in the army. But he figured the agent should keep a record of the transaction and send one to Washington. That sounded right to him.

The man swung around, glaring at him. "Nobody tells me how to do my job. Least of all some Johnny Reb."

Sam's amused gaze swiveled back and forth from one to the other.

Brennan did not respond to the derogatory Yankee nickname for Confederate soldiers. "I'm not tellin' you how to do your job. Just…helpin' you do it. After you." Emphasizing the final two words, Brennan swept one hand, gesturing toward the door. Brennan itched to grab the man's collar and drag him out.

The man glared at him.

So Brennan waited him out—not changing anything in his expression or stance, barely blinking.

The land agent finally caved in, growled something under his breath about stinking Southerners, and stalked past Brennan out the door.

Hiding a grin, Brennan nodded politely to the barkeep and followed the man to his office. Lounging against the doorjamb, he said nothing as the man sat at his desk, filled out a ledger. Brennan moved to look over his shoulder.

The agent then slapped Miss Rachel's application into a mailing pouch. "There! Are you satisfied?" the man snapped.

"Anything else need doin'?" Brennan asked in a mild tone.

"No!"

"Then after you write me out one of those receipts—" Brennan gestured toward a pad of receipts on the desk "—I'll just help you by taking this mailbag to Ashford's store. I seen the notice in the window that he's the postmaster hereabout."

The agent resembled a volcano about to blow, but he merely chewed viciously the inside of his cheek. Then he dashed off the receipt, ripped it from the pad and shoved the mail pouch at Brennan.

"I'll bid you good day then," Brennan said drolly and strolled outside.

A stream of epithets followed him, including "Confederate cur."

He ignored them and crossed the street, his boots sending up puffs of dust with each step. The drought filled his nose with dust, too. His destination in sight, he moved forward. He'd been inside Ashford's store only once before on a trip to town with Noah. But he nodded politely at Ashford's hesitant greeting and handed him the leather pouch, which read Official U.S. Documents. "I brought this over for the land agent. Do you think the mail will go out today?"

Ashford, middle-aged with thinning hair, consulted a notice on the wall. "Yes, if the *Delta Queen* arrives on schedule." The storekeeper cocked an eyebrow at Brennan. "It's odd that the agent let you bring this over."

"Oh, I just told him I was on my way here. Now you watch over the mail pouches, don't you? You don't let *anybody* mess with the letters, right?" Brennan asked.

"I certainly do not let anybody interfere with the mail. I took an oath." Ashford starched up.

"Excellent. Glad to hear it." Brennan turned to Miss Rachel. "Here is your receipt for the land transaction."

"Thank thee, Mr. Merriday." She accepted the paper and slid it into her pocket, then dazzled Brennan with a smile that cast her as, well, pretty.

At this realization, Brennan stepped backward. Whoa, he had no business thinking that. Why had he thought her plain? Was it the way she hid behind that plain Quaker bonnet?

"I just staked my claim, Mr. Ashford," Miss Rachel explained, "on the Ryersons' abandoned claim."

Ashford goggled at her. "Indeed?" he finally said.

"Yes, Miss Rachel's makin' her own way in the world." Brennan regained his aplomb. "An independent woman." Brennan relished setting another pillar of society on edge.

"And Mr. Merriday will help me as my hired hand," Miss Rachel agreed. "Mr. Ashford, I will be back next week to pick up the flour, sugar and other items I've ordered. And please let it be known that I want to buy a cow and chickens from anyone who has any to spare. I'll pay what's fair."

"Yes, Miss, but I still think you should have ordered much less flour to begin with," the storekeeper said.

"I appreciate thy concern," she replied, but this didn't show in her tone. "Mr. Merriday, I think our town business is done now."

He was back to himself. So he did find the lady pretty—what did that have to do with the likes of him? "Yes, Miss Rachel," Brennan said, grinning with sass as he followed her to the door, opened it for her and let her step outside. He glanced over his shoulder to catch Ashford frowning. And mocked the man with a grin.

Back on the wagon bench beside Miss Rachel, Brennan slapped the reins and piloted the team toward home. A rare feeling of satisfaction suffused him. And he was beginning to like Miss Rachel. That was all. "You called me Mr. Merriday," he teased. "Thrice."

"Yes, I thought if I called thee by thy first name as Quakers do, the storekeeper might misunderstand our relationship. I think it will be best if I use Mr. Merriday so everyone understands...." Her voice faltered.

"I take your meaning, *Miss* Rachel." He couldn't stop his grin from widening. Working for Miss Rachel would certainly bring zest into his life for a time.

From the corner of his eye, he gazed at her profile. She sat so prim and proper, her back straight and her gloved hands folded in her lap. What would she do if he turned and kissed her? A startling, disturbing thought.

Then she glanced at him out of the corner of her eye. "My thanks, Mr. Merriday, for thy support today."

"Just part of my job, miss," he said, taking control of his unruly mind. He owed this lady a debt, that was all.

And then the two of them rode in outward silence toward the Whitmore claim. But one sentence ran through Brennan's mind—*What have I gotten myself into this time?*

Chapter Three

On the dusty drive home, Rachel felt unsettled again. She tried not to think of those first few days on the journey here when nothing had seemed right and she hadn't been able to eat. And sitting beside this handsome man who'd stood up for her added more confusion.

"How soon could I move into my cabin?" she asked, forcing herself to stop musing.

"Just need a day or two to get it cleaned out and fix the roof."

"I will do the cleaning so thee can concentrate on the fixing." She had succeeded in staking her homestead claim. She should be experiencing relief but she wasn't. Her stomach churned. *What's wrong with me?*

The ride home passed much more quickly than the ride to the homestead and then to town. The hot sun beat down on Rachel's shoulders and bonnet. But she found herself more aware of Mr. Merriday with every mile. She hadn't expected him to abet her in town. Also she'd seen in Mr. Ashford's expression that having the Southerner work for her would be frowned on. *Well, so be it.*

When Noah's cabin came into view, Rachel's heart started jumping oddly. She stiffened her self-control and tried to remain unmoved as Brennan helped her down from the wagon with his usual courtesy, which was not usual to her.

Noah hailed them from outside his woodshop. With their little boy in her arms, Sunny opened the door and greeted her warmly.

Rachel burst into tears.

Everyone rushed forward as if she'd fallen, which shamed her. She turned away, trying to hide her face.

Sunny came to her and grasped her elbow. "Come. I'll make you some tea."

When Rachel looked up, the two men had disappeared with little Dawn and only she and Sunny went to the bench outside the cabin. Rachel sat while Sunny went inside. The toddler in his dress rolled in the grass, playing with his toes. Tears dripping down her face, Rachel watched him, envying his innocence.

Soon Sunny handed her a cup of tea and sat beside her. "Was the land agent very rude?" Sunny asked conversationally.

"Of course he was." Wiping her eyes with her hankie, Rachel tried to keep bitterness from her tone, but failed. "Why are men so…?" Words failed her.

Sunny made a sound of agreement. "They certainly can be."

Rachel sipped the sweet, tangy tea. "Life would be easier if I just went along with what's expected of me," she finally admitted.

More tea. "Yes, but would that be easier on you?"

"No!" Rachel's reply flew from her lips.

"Then you will just have to thicken your skin."

Rachel sighed. "I thought I had."

"It's just this starting out part. Everyone here will get to know you, begin to see that you're a good person.

You'll become part of the town and then they'll resent anybody who disparages you."

Rachel turned to Sunny. "Really?"

"Yes, that's how it happened with us."

"Really?"

Sunny beamed at her. "Noah's the preacher now."

For some reason, Rachel couldn't swallow a chuckle. Then the two of them were laughing out loud.

In a while, no doubt drawn by the sounds of mirth, the men approached, looking as if the women's behavior mystified them. And that only caused Rachel and Sunny to shake with more laughter.

The next day Brennan climbed the ladder onto the roof of Rachel's cabin, no clouds masking the hot sun. He crawled across the rough surface till he reached the spot where he thought the leak was. Three wooden shakes or shingles had blown loose.

His lady boss was humming below, sweeping out her cabin. And soon Noah would arrive to start work on the large oven Miss Rachel needed for her business. The question over whether to add a kitchen to the cabin had been debated completely. Finally a summer kitchen connected by a covered walkway to the cabin had been deemed best.

Thinking of Noah, Brennan found himself filled with potent envy. Noah Whitmore had it all—a place of his own, a pretty wife and two great kids.

Reminiscence of a time when he'd thought Noah's kind of life would always be his life goaded him. Lorena's slender arms slipped around his neck and her soft voice—

Then the worst happened—one of his infrequent spells hit him. The past flooded him. Waves of darkness engulfed him. That awful day before the war? Or all the awful days of war after it rolled into one? He was surrounded. Fists pounding him, the stench of stale sweat, curses bombarded him. He tried to keep his eyes open, tried to keep in touch with his surroundings—which way was up and which was down. He lost.

He felt himself sliding, the rough shingles hitting his spine as he slid. He wrenched his eyes open and at the last minute jammed his heels into another space where shingles had been blown away. His hands scrabbled for something to cling to. He stopped and then he lay back, gasping for air.

"Is thee all right?" Miss Rachel called up.

Brennan couldn't answer. The world still tilted and swayed around him. Then he heard Miss Rachel climbing up the ladder.

He had to stop her, couldn't let her see him like this. Brennan wanted to send her away with a flea in her ear, anything to prevent her from asking what the matter was. Upon the rare occasion when he had one of these spells, he just left town.

But I can't leave this town. And Noah saved my life as much as the little spinster. Brennan waited for the inevitable questions.

But Miss Rachel asked none.

Brennan finally could sit up. His slide had taken him within a foot of the ladder and there stood Miss Rachel near his boots. Still she didn't speak. Brennan's heartbeat and breathing slowed to normal. He didn't know what to say. Better to let her think he just slid. "Sorry to give you a scare, Miss Rachel."

She tilted her head like one of the robins nesting in the tree nearby. She reached out her hand to him.

And surprising himself, he took it.

"Please be careful, Brennan Merriday. I wouldn't want to see thee laid low again."

He tried to ignore the softness of the hand in his. Tried to ignore the fact that the sun glinted off the threads of gold in her hair and that her expression drew him like bees to honey. In any other woman, he would have interpreted her comment as selfish, as indicating that she wanted him to keep well and in working condition. But did this woman have a selfish bone in her body?

The moment was broken when they heard Noah's whistling.

Their hands pulled apart. She blushed and he looked away.

"Morning, Rachel. Brennan, I was thinking," Noah called out as he approached them, "it makes more sense for us to work together. I think we'll get more done. Why don't I hand you the shakes we cut? You can be nailing new ones in place and I'll go over the roof, checking every shake to make sure none are loose. I don't think Ryerson did a very good job on his roof. Then you can help me with the oven."

"Sounds good to me," Brennan said, forcing out the words.

Miss Rachel slowly disappeared from view as she climbed back down the ladder. Brennan felt the loss of her and hardened himself. What had they been thinking? Holding hands in broad daylight?

About two weeks later Rachel tried to calm her fluttering nerves. Tonight she'd stay alone in her cabin for the first time. As the shadows darkened, Noah's family, who had helped her move in today with her new table and chairs and bed Noah had made her, was leaving.

Sunny had helped her prepare the first meal in her new home. The day had been busy and happy. A nearby farmer had delivered her young cow, chickens and a rooster. Now she would have cream and eggs for her baking. But Brennan's distant behavior had pruned her enjoyment of the occasion.

Noah's wagon had just turned the bend out of sight when Brennan ambled over to help her carry the last of the chairs inside.

"Thee didn't join in much today," she said.

"Didn't feel sociable."

She sensed that he was about to lay out the last chores he would be doing for her and then announce he'd be leaving. His restlessness over the past few days had not gone unnoticed. She didn't like the gloom that realization opened inside her. Yet she'd wanted to be on her own and now she would be.

Three strangers appeared on the track to her cabin. This was an odd occurrence. "Hello, may I help thee?" Rachel called out, though as they came closer she recognized that the three looked disreputable.

"We're looking for the lousy Confederate you got here!" one declared, slurring his words from drink, no doubt.

"Yeah, we don't want any scurvy dogs like that hanging around," another added belligerently.

To her dismay, Brennan picked up a tree limb lying on the ground and moved to confront the men.

"The war is over," Rachel said, trying to stem the confrontation.

Brennan ignored her. "There is a lady present here. From your voices, I'd say you men have been imbibing today. Too liberally."

The men glowered at her. Even in their inebriated

state, Brennan saw, they realized that fighting with a proper lady present would be roundly condemned.

Rachel stepped forward, hoping her presence would send the strangers away.

Instead, a fist shot past her.

Brennan dodged it easily. Then he slammed his fist into his attacker's nose. Blood spurted.

Rachel cried out. Brennan pushed her out of the fray. She stumbled and fell to the grass.

The other stranger rushed Brennan. He dealt with him. The third one turned and bolted. The two who had been bested followed suit, cursing as they ran.

Rachel put her hands to her ears, shocked to silence. "Oh!"

Just as they disappeared from view, the first one, his hand pressed over his bleeding nose, shouted, "This isn't over!"

"Yes, it is," Brennan muttered, rubbing his knuckles.

Rachel began to weep, trembling.

Brennan gripped her hands and pulled her up and into his arms. "There, there," he said, holding her against him. "You're safe now. I wouldn't let anyone hurt you."

The temptation proved too great to resist. She let herself lean against him, feeling the strength of him supporting her. She tried to stop her tears. "I'm sorry to be so weak."

"I'm sorry you had to witness such behavior." As he said this, his lips actually touched her ear. "You're not weak."

The last of the weeping swept through her like a wind gust and left her gasping against him. "I've never been near violence before."

"Then you're a lucky woman." He patted her back clumsily.

She wiped her face with her fingertips and looked up into Brennan's face. His expression of concern moved her and she reached up and stroked his cheek.

What am I doing?

Rachel straightened and stepped back. She must break contact before he did. An unwelcome thought lowered her mood more. Tonight would be her first night sleeping alone in her own house. She'd never spent a night alone in her life. And these violent men had come tonight.

"Maybe I should sleep in the shed tonight," Brennan said, his gaze going to the trail to town.

The idea had appeal. But she would be here alone every night, perhaps for the rest of her life.

In the clearing, Rachel and Brennan faced each other. "Thee doesn't think I am really in danger of them coming here again tonight?"

Brennan bumped the toe of his boot into a tussock of wild, dry grass. "No, not because the three show any sense, but they're probably all passed out from drink by now."

Rachel stared at the ground, listening to the frogs in the nearby creek.

"I'll bar my door," she said with a lift of her chin, which belied her inner trembling.

"Maybe you'd be better off if I didn't hang around any longer."

"Brennan Merriday, in case thee has not noticed by now, I am not a woman who gives way to pressure from others. I have hired thee and I expect thee will show up for breakfast tomorrow and continue the work that still needs doing here."

He looked up.

And suddenly she was very aware of how alone they were here just outside her door. Funny sensations jiggled in her stomach. "You were very brave," she murmured.

He started digging at the tussock of grass again with the toe of his boot.

Her mind flashed back to her schoolgirl days. She'd watched boys do this when they talked to girls they liked but didn't want to show it. Did he like her that way?

She turned abruptly. "I bid thee good night."

"Okay, Miss Rachel, I'll head to my place then. See you in the mornin'."

She didn't trust herself to reply. The desire to hold him here and the residual fear had worsened and she was afraid her voice would give her away. She entered, shut the door and lifted the bar into place. Few cabins had such. But Noah had insisted on this and now she understood why.

Once inside, she scanned the inside of her new home. Sunny had helped her wash the dishes so there was nothing to do. Noah had made her a rocking chair as a gift. She sat in it now and tried not to feel her lonely state. She picked up the socks she'd started to knit for Brennan as a going away thank-you. The thought hit her as unwelcome.

For just a second, she imagined Brennan Merriday sitting on a chair across from her, whittling the way he always did. She was knitting and the two of them enjoyed that companionable quiet that happily married couples sometimes shared.

Where did that come from?

She shook off this foolishness, put down her knitting and lifted her small portable desk. She began working again on a recipe she'd thought of, something with chocolate and nuts no man could resist. Except Brennan Merriday in one of his touchy moods.

She would have to be very careful around him—he was too handsome for his own good—and hers—and he was staying to help her. She thought of his courtesies. Brennan Merriday treated her like an attractive woman, not a spinster. This alone must be working on her, drawing her to him.

But he carried some deep wound and would be leaving very soon. Even if he was momentarily attracted to her, nothing would come of it. Nothing ever had. And she'd accepted being alone, hadn't she?

Brennan marched to town, boiling for a fight. Cold reason halted him a few yards from the saloon. Only a fool barged into to a three-to-one fight. He planned his strategy and sidled to a side window. What he saw flummoxed him.

He entered the saloon and Sam was alone, wiping down the bar. "What's wrong? Customers find out you were watering the whiskey?"

Sam gave him the eye. "That's an unfounded accusation. It might have been better if I had tonight. Some people just don't know when to stop."

Brennan leaned against the bar. "What happened?"

"Had to kick out a bunch earlier. They drank too much too fast and wanted to pick a fight with anybody who came near."

"I know the type." He described the three and Sam nodded. Brennan continued, "Someone must have told them that a Southerner lived around here. And they wanted to run me out of town. They actually started a fight in front of the lady I work for."

The barkeep rubbed his face with his big hands. "That's not right, fighting in front of a decent woman. Had to show my rifle to get rid of them. Most locals left. Tame crowd lives around here. The troublemakers are probably on the boat that brought them by now."

Brennan chewed on this. "Okay. Thanks." He offered his hand to the man.

"When you coming in just for that tongue wag?"

"Soon." Brennan left with a wave, not satisfied. What if after he left town, rowdies came looking for him and bothered Miss Rachel? He felt her again in his arms, so petite and slight. A fierce protectiveness reared inside him. He couldn't leave her unprotected. How could he make sure no one would bother her?

The next morning, Rachel hadn't experienced such quaking since the morning she'd left her father's home in Pennsylvania. Under the clear, late-June sky, she drew in a deep breath and let Mr. Merriday help her down from the two-wheeled pony cart she'd borrowed from Noah's neighbors. The blue sky did not sport even one cloud. When would the rain come?

Brennan's strong, steady hand contrasted with her shakiness. After he'd held her close last night, now she had trouble looking him in the eye. She felt herself blush and turned her face away.

She'd filled several large trays with baked goods and Brennan had set them in the back of the cart. Today she would launch Rachel's Sweets, what she'd come here to do, what her future hinged upon.

"I still think you should call it *Miss* Rachel's Sweets," Brennan grumbled.

She realized then that she still held his strong, calloused hand, not for aid but for comfort. This jolted her. Was she going to start having foolish ideas? No.

Scolding herself for this lapse, she quickly smoothed her skirts. "But Miss might imply to some that I cannot cook since no man married me." She repeated her objection with an attempt at humor. Why was she so nervous? No one was going to arrest her for selling sweets.

"The name of your business needs some swank. That's all I'm sayin'."

She had to admit that having this man with her bolstered her and she didn't like that, couldn't let herself depend on him. Brennan Merriday had made it clear he was staying just so long and then heading north.

She turned from him. "Well, I'm a Quaker and we don't go for 'swank.' And my baked goods don't need that to sell. Just a lot of creamy butter and sweet sugar." She walked briskly toward the rear of the cart.

There her products lay on tin trays, covered with spotless, crisply starched white dishcloths. Yesterday Brennan had rigged up a sling that would support the tray and then go around her neck to help her carry it.

Now as he arranged the sling on her, his nearness flooded her senses. She could smell the soap she'd given him. He'd also shaved this morning and his clean chin beckoned her to stroke it. She jerked herself back into her right mind.

Then she wished he wouldn't frown so. His negativity prompted her stomach to flip up and down. And she noticed he'd worn a hole in one elbow of his blue shirt. She'd need to mend that before it dissected the sleeve completely. It was a wifely thought that she resisted. He was her hired hand, not her responsibility.

When he finished, she smiled bravely to boost her resolve and strode toward a boat that had just docked. She had sold her baked goods before, but never to strangers and all by herself. Brennan had come only because he was paid to, not because he was part of her venture. *But I've always been by myself. And I'll likely always be so.* She shook her head as if sending the thought away. *I like being alone.*

"Are you sure you want to do this?" Brennan asked from behind her.

"Quite sure," she said, denying that what she really wanted to do was run home, denying that she'd like him to come along for support. Speaking to strangers always tested her.

She lifted her mouth into a firmer smile. She marched toward the dock, repeating silently, *I will not run from my future. My plan will succeed.*

She expected Mr. Merriday to stay and watch her. However, when she glanced over her shoulder, she saw that he'd walked away from the wagon and was heading toward the saloon. This nearly halted her in her tracks. What? Did the man drink? And in daylight?

The fact that she had reached the pier, her goal, shut down this line of thought. She reinforced her thinning smile. "Good day!" she called out to the men standing or working on the boat, tied to the pier. "I'm Miss Rachel." She had intended to say her full name but Brennan's voice had somehow seeped into her mind. "I have baked goods for sale."

She had expected smiles. People always smiled when she offered them her treats. The men merely looked wary.

Finally one man asked, "What kind of baked goods?"

"I have apple fastnachts and sugar cookies." Fastnachts, yeast doughnuts filled with fruit jam or creamy custard and sprinkled with sugar, were popular in Pennsylvania.

"Got any bear claws?" one man asked.

"No, I don't."

The faint hope in many faces looking toward her fell. And so did her own hope. Then a thought bobbed up in her mind. She walked past the workmen on the pier and stepped onto the moored boat. "May I speak to the captain, please?"

Soon Rachel smiled up into the captain's face. "I'm offering a sample of my baked goods."

The tall, trim man with dark sideburns and harsh features did not look friendly. But then he glanced down. "Fastnachts?" His voice echoed with surprise.

"Yes, with apple jam and cinnamon. Please help thyself." And he did. And with his first bite, a powerful smile transformed his unwelcoming expression. "Just like my grandma used to make. You must be from Pennsylvania."

She nodded, her heart calming. "Yes, I'm homesteading here and plan to sell baked goods and sweets to the river trade. I'm Miss Rachel Woolsey."

"Pleased to meet you, miss. Do you have more of these? I know they won't keep for more than a day, but I'd love to have one with my coffee later."

"I fried three dozen this morning." Then she turned to the crew hovering nearby. Her spirits were rising like dough on a warm, humid day. "I'd like each of thee to have a sample, too. Please." She motioned toward them.

The men lined up and cleaned off her tray in seconds. One black porter gushed, "Best I eat since I was in New Orleans and had beignets, miss. And I thank you."

"Beignets?" Rachel echoed. "Are they similar?"

"Yes, miss, but with powdered sugar."

"Was it the same dough?"

"I'm no cook, miss." The man shook his head and then grinned. "But you certainly are!"

The other men agreed heartily. And her spirit soared.

"Miss Rachel, thank you for letting us sample your wares. I'd like to buy another two dozen for me and my crew," the captain announced.

Rachel thrilled with pleasure. "Wonderful. Thee is my first customer."

"But not your last," the captain said, smiling down at her.

Elated, she scurried back to her cart and Brennan met her there. "We need to bag up two dozen for this boat." She busied herself wrapping each doughnut in waxed paper and filled two paper sacks. She delivered them to the captain.

He bowed. "Thank you, miss. You brought me sweet memories I had long forgotten."

"My pleasure, captain. Please, I'd appreciate thy letting others know I'll be here with fresh baked goods daily. I also plan on making fudge and other candy."

A happy murmur from the crew greeted this.

Grinning and promising to see her the next time they docked in Pepin, the captain bowed again and then called cheerfully to his crew to get busy or they wouldn't get another doughnut.

Buoyant with her success, Rachel walked back to the cart. Brennan lounged against it.

"We goin' home now? That's the only boat here today," he asked.

She sensed now he was worried about something. What? "Let's fill up the tray with the remaining goods."

Rachel glanced up the street. "And please help me with the strap again."

He did so, arranging it around her neck once more. Their nearness once again distracted her, stirred odd sensations. She brushed aside their brief embrace the night before.

"What are you up to, Miss Rachel?"

"I need to make the mouths of my neighbors water, too." She grinned at him. She'd learned today that while generosity should be its own reward, it also made good business sense.

Soon she entered Ashford's store, jingling the bell. Brennan followed her in as if curious. Near the chairs by the cold stove sat only an older man in a wheelchair. He nodded to her politely. Had she met him?

Rachel nodded to him in case she had, then turned. "Good day, Mr. Ashford," she greeted brightly.

The storekeeper looked dubious. "How may I help you, Miss Woolsey?"

"I am here to offer samples of my baked goods." She stopped right across the counter from him.

He looked at her and then at the tray. He reached for one just as his wife walked down the stairs into the store. His hand halted in midair.

"Miss Woolsey," Mrs. Ashford said disapprovingly, "I saw you just now talking to men on that boat."

"Yes, I am starting my business. Today I'm giving away samples of my baked goods."

Mrs. Ashford studied the tray of cookies and dough-nuts. "I wonder that your cousin will abet you in this. You will find yourself in the company of all sorts of vulgar men." Then the woman glanced pointedly past her and frowned deeply at Mr. Merriday.

Rachel guessed that she was suggesting Mr. Merriday was one of these low men. That goaded Rachel. She bit her lower lip to keep back a quick defense of the man. She must not insult so prominent a wife and perhaps start gossip.

And after a moment's reflection, Rachel realized that Mrs. Ashford was the kind of woman who wanted to be consulted, to be the arbiter of others' conduct. She'd met her ilk before.

This too grated on Rachel's nerves. But nothing would be gained by telling the woman to mind her own business. "No doubt thee is right," Rachel said demurely. "But even vulgar men will not insult a woman offering sweets."

Brennan chuckled softly.

Discreetly enjoying his humor, she masked this with her most endearing smile. "Please, Mrs. Ashford, taste one of my wares and tell me thy opinion. I hear that thy baked goods are notable." She did not like to be less than genuine, but the old dictum, that one attracted more flies with honey than vinegar, held true even in Wisconsin.

Mrs. Ashford picked up a fastnacht and tore it in two, the fragrance of apple and cinnamon filling permeated the air. The storekeeper's wife handed half to her husband. They both chewed thoughtfully as if weighing and measuring with each chew. They looked at each other and then her.

"Very tasty," the woman said, dusting the sugar from her fingers. Her husband nodded in agreement, almost grinning. "But most women here do their own baking," Mrs. Ashford pointed out discouragingly.

"That's why I'm courting the river trade," Rachel assented. "And single men hereabout. And occasionally a woman might want to purchase something for a special occasion like a wedding."

Mrs. Ashford listened seriously as if she were a senator engaging in a debate in Congress. "True."

"Then I'll be going on. Good day—"

"I'd like a sample too, miss," the older man by the cold stove piped up.

Rachel turned and offered him her tray. He scooped up one sugar cookie and chewed it with ceremony. After swallowing his first bite, the older man announced, "I'm Old Saul, Miss Rachel. I heard from Noah you would be arriving this month. Much obliged for the cookie. I foresee success in your endeavor."

His puckish style of speaking made Rachel chuckle. It was as if he had enjoyed her parrying Mrs. Ashford, too. "My thanks, Old Saul. Nice to meet thee." She walked outside, feeling another lift in her spirits. She could do this. She walked toward the blacksmith shop, ready to offer another free sample.

Mr. Merriday walked a step behind her. She felt his brooding presence hanging over her spurt of victory. Why did people always have to make rude comments to him? Or stare at him with unfriendly expressions? The war had been over for better than six years. Wasn't it time to let the old animosity go? And once again, the unwise attraction that drew her to him surged within.

He helped her restore the tray to the rear of the cart and then helped her up onto the seat. She had never been shown these politenesses before. Her father of course performed them for her stepmother, but Rachel was left to help her smaller stepbrothers and sisters. That must be why it touched her so every time he did this for her.

But I mustn't become accustomed to his courtesies. I will be on my own soon enough. Too soon.

* * *

Brennan rolled over, half asleep, in the dark loft. Something had wakened him. What? Fire? The grass was tinder-dry and that had been a worry for the past few days. He listened, alert, to the sounds in the warm, humid summer night. More times than he wanted to recall, his acute hearing had saved his life. Then he heard the faintest tinkle of breaking glass.

Probably high spirits at the saloon. He rolled over. Still, sleep didn't come. Why would there be a fight at the saloon? That usually happened only when several riverboats moored at the same time for a night.

He rolled away from his pallet. Since he couldn't stand up in the low attic loft, he crawled to the open window draped with cheesecloth to keep out the mosquitoes. From his high vantage point, he scanned the street. The half-moon radiated little light.

Just as he was about to go back to lie on his pallet, he glimpsed movement down on the street. Three men were creeping around the stores. One had a large, full sack thrown over one shoulder. A man didn't have to have much imagination to come to a quick conclusion.

Thieves.

The three men were slinking toward the front of Ashford's. Better to access the store on the side away from where the storekeeper slept.

The uppity face of the owner's wife came to Brennan's mind. Her expression a few days ago—as she'd weighed and measured him and pronounced him wanting—had been burned into him. If she'd had the power, she would have caused him to vanish from her prissy sight that day. It rankled. Yet that he cared what she thought of him rankled more.

He watched as the shadowy men paused as if waiting for something.

Their plan unfolded in his mind. These river "rats" were using the saloon's loud voices to mask the sounds of the thievery. He let out a breath. These little river towns were without any presence of the law and were easy pickings for thieves.

The thought suddenly rolled like thunder in his mind. He didn't want this little bump on the river to become a target for unlawful types. Not with Miss Rachel living just outside town. The memory of the ruffians who'd come to her place to find him goaded him. The thought of the innocent Miss Rachel being accosted sent icy shivers through him. *Never.* He had to make sure the reputation of this town stayed strong—for her sake.

He crawled over to his knapsack, retrieved his two Colt 45s and checked to be sure both were loaded and ready. He scooted to the ladder and slipped down to the blacksmith shop. He paused, thinking of who could provide him backup. He crept to the lean-to and roused the blacksmith. Seeing Brennan's index finger to his lips, Levi swallowed a waking exclamation.

Brennan leaned close to the man's ear. "Thieves." He motioned toward the rifle hung on the wall and then for the blacksmith to get up.

Soon, the two men stood side by side in the lean-to. Brennan outlined a plan and the smith nodded. They crept along in the shadows and took their places— Brennan across from the front of the General Store, closest to the river, and the smith slipped along another store behind Ashford's. The familiar sensations of preparing for battle prickled through Brennan, keenly heightening his awareness of every sound and sight.

Laughter echoed from the saloon and then one of

the thieves raised his hand to break the glass next to Ashford's door.

"Hold!" Brennan roared, hidden in the shadows.

The three men started and glanced around frantically.

"Hold!" Brennan repeated.

The three scampered toward the rear as if to hide themselves.

Brennan let loose a warning shot over their heads. The smith let his rifle roar from the rear. The three men stopped, not knowing which way to run. Two had drawn pistols.

"Drop that bag and empty your pockets!" Brennan ordered.

The three started to run toward the river. One shot toward Brennan, but the bullet went wide. *Idiots!*

Brennan shot into the dirt in front of them, halting them in the middle of the street. "Drop your guns and that bag, then empty your pockets! Do it! Or this time I'll shoot one of you!"

The man with the bag put it down and raised his hands. The other two put their pistols on the ground, yanked out their pockets and raised their hands, too.

"All your pockets!" Brennan commanded.

The bagman pulled out his pockets.

"Run!" Brennan bellowed.

The three obeyed, racing toward the river.

Just then Ashford ran out the front door, dressed hastily and holding a rifle. "What's happening?"

Before Brennan could reply, more men armed with rifles bounded into the street. Brennan wondered if they had any sense. It was crazy to show themselves so plainly before they knew who was shooting whom. Some, he noted, did cling to the shadows, probably veterans like him.

Not wanting to be the center of attention or suffer being thanked, he slipped away, back to the blacksmith shop and up to his loft. Still his heart pounded with the excitement. He listened to the buzz of voices below. Levi explained, loud enough for him to hear, what had happened.

The town men shouted and ran toward the river. Brennan looked out his riverside window and saw a rude boat sliding out into the current. The town men shouted and shot toward the craft, their bullets sizzling as they hit the water. But the night had only half-moon light and soon the craft became invisible, lost in the dark.

Brennan lay down on his blanket, his heart still racing. The thieves had gotten away, which was best. What would the town have done with them if they'd been caught? Pepin didn't have a jail and somebody might have gotten hurt trying to corral them. Better they escaped. They wouldn't come back anytime soon. But what about others like them?

This staying in one place was costing him. He lay listening to the men talking, and hoped no one would disturb him. He hadn't done this for any of them. He'd done it for Miss Rachel, but if he said that, they would think something was going on between them. Better to lay low.

How long would they have to hash over this minor dustup? People here didn't cotton to him. And he generally didn't cotton to people so they were even. That suited him. But what else could he do to keep Miss Rachel safe after he left town?

Just after dawn the next morning, Brennan freshened up down at the river as usual, glad to wash away last night's sweat. He then set out toward Miss Rachel's place, his stomach rumbling for the breakfast she'd provide. The heat was already climbing high and not a hint of a cloud showed on the horizon.

As he passed Ashford's store, the proprietor burst out and ran toward him. Brennan halted. What did the man want?

Mr. Ashford panted. "I just came out to thank you." The man's face looked tired from lack of sleep. "For last night. All the storekeepers are grateful. The smithy told us you woke him up and were the one who ran off the thieves."

Brennan hadn't expected appreciation. And didn't want their gratitude. He looked at the man, giving nothing of himself away. "Didn't do it for your thanks."

"We owe you."

Brennan shrugged. "Don't mention it," he said with finality and tucked in an edge that promised unpleasantness if the man went on thanking him.

The man's wife came running out of the store and offered him a folded new shirt and trousers. "Just a token of our thanks."

Brennan didn't take the clothing. "Thank you, ma'am, but I'm expected at Miss Rachel's for breakfast." He hurried on.

Brennan spent the morning building a chicken coop strong and high enough to outfox any fox or other varmint. To start with, he'd logged the needed wood and dug postholes. This afternoon he'd set posts.

With a rumbling stomach and sharp anticipation of another tasty meal, at noon he sat down at Miss Rachel's table. When she carried in the steaming crock from the outdoor kitchen, he noted she did not look happy. What was the bee in her Quaker bonnet?

"Mr. Merriday, why didn't thee tell me what happened last night?" She made it sound like a scold.

He bristled. Why did she sound mad? After all, he'd done it for her. "Because I didn't think it was worth mentionin'. That's why," he replied, eyeing the bowls of stew she was dishing up.

She set the crock on the table and sat down.

He waited quietly for her to finish silently blessing the meal as she always did. When the amen came, he picked up his fork and dug into her stew. The woman could cook as well as she could bake.

"The Ashfords told me all about it. And about thy graceless behavior this morning." She motioned toward the chair by the cold hearth. The dratted new clothing the storekeeper's wife had offered him sat there, evidently drying after being washed. This aggravated him but he kept eating.

"We have something in common," she said, also beginning to eat. "We are different from everyone else here. I'm the pitiful and eccentric Quaker spinster."

Brennan suddenly felt ashamed of thinking of her with this less than flattering term. But he hadn't meant it in a bad way. And Miss Rachel was unusual, who could argue that?

"And Mr. Merriday is thought of as a shiftless wanderer. And ex-Confederate," she finished.

He chewed, trying to focus on the rich taste of the wild onions in the stew. After all, she wasn't saying anything he didn't already know.

"Last night thy quick action saved the town from thievery. They wish to show their thanks. Why refuse it?"

Annoyed suddenly, he barked, "Because I don't care what they think of me!"

She gazed up at him, unperturbed. "Everyone, even we, put labels on people. No doubt thee thinks Mr. Ashford is a prosy storekeeper and his wife, a know-it-all busybody."

Her apt descriptions of the two hit his funny bone. His heat turned to laughter. Chuckling, he picked up his fork once more.

"But we all have worth to God."

His grip on the fork tightened. Easy for Miss Rachel to say. She hadn't seen what he'd seen in the war. And what he'd seen he sensed was the root of his spells and nightmares, the horror of bloodshed and needless loss of life.

"Thankfully God doesn't judge by our outward appearance but looks into our hearts." Before he could respond, she reached over and tugged his cuff, ripping half the sleeve loose.

He drew in a sharp breath.

"Thankfully I think Mrs. Ashford guessed the size correctly," Miss Rachel continued in an even tone, "but I'll have to hem the trousers of course."

He gawked at her in disbelief. "You tore my shirt."

"It didn't take much," she said in a matter-of-fact tone. "I think the polite thing to do on the way home after supper is to stop and thank Mrs. Ashford." Then she sent him one of her managing, very determined, gray-eyes-flashing looks.

He didn't respond, but returned to eating in silence, trying to hold his temper. Soft-spoken Lorena would never have ripped his shirt to make a point.

Then he recalled Miss Rachel's description of herself as a pathetic spinster. He didn't think that about her now, but he struggled again with guilt over originally disparaging Miss Rachel—just like everybody else. The memory of holding her in his arms… He had to stop thinking about that. He was leaving for Canada as soon as he'd done everything to get Miss Rachel set up here.

He didn't care what other people thought of him. But Miss Rachel thought more of him than the others did. That was dangerous. He'd let down everyone in his life. Would he let down Miss Rachel, too?

Chapter Four

Brennan did not want to do this, did not want to go to the Ashfords', hat in hand, and thank them for the unwanted, unasked-for new clothes. Wearing his new clothes now, he didn't even feel like himself. Earlier, after the new clothing had dried, Miss Rachel had hemmed his pants and pressed everything up nice. The new clothes felt stiff and thick, not thin and shaped to him like his old clothes. Made him feel strange. As strange as pausing here, looking to go somewhere he was not welcome.

He stood, looking at the store. The closed sign sat in the window, granting him a reprieve. He turned to head to the blacksmith shop to jaw with the smithy.

"Mr. Merriday!" a woman's voice called from above. "Did you need anything?"

Irritation ground inside him. Mrs. Ashford with her windows overlooking Main Street didn't miss a thing. He looked up, pinning a smile on his face. "Yes, ma'am, I came to thank you."

"Come to the rear and we'll let you in," she ordered.

He wanted to decline but Miss Rachel didn't want him to be rude to this busybo…this good woman. So he walked around to the rear and Mr. Ashford let him in. "I just came to thank you—"

"Ned, ask Mr. Merriday to come up!" Mrs. Ashford called down.

Ned dutifully motioned to Brennan to precede him up the stairs.

Brennan gritted his teeth and climbed to the living quarters. As he topped the stairs, he snatched his hat off and schooled his face into a smile. "Evenin', ma'am."

"Mr. Merriday, so glad to see you accepted our gift of thanks." The storekeeper's wife sat in the dining area that took up half the large, open room overlooking the river. There were several people around the long table, two he'd never seen in town.

"Cousin, this is Brennan Merriday, a workman in our village," Mrs. Ashford said. "He saved our store from thievery last night. Mr. Merriday, my cousin, Mrs. Almeria Brown, and her granddaughter Miss Posey Brown. They arrived today by boat."

Brennan glanced at the plump older woman who lifted an eyeglass on a string to study him like a bug on a pin. He bowed his head to her, his neck stiff. "Ma'am." And then to the younger lady who looked about seventeen, too slender but pretty in a common way with brown hair and eyes. "Miss."

"Are you homesteading hereabouts?" the older woman asked, piercing him with her gaze, her eye magnified by the glass. Some of her iron-gray hair had slipped from its bun.

"No, ma'am, just working to help set up Miss Rachel, the preacher's cousin, on her homestead."

Two other young people, one a young girl and one a young blond man, also sat at the table, looking at him.

"This is our daughter Amanda and her friend Gunther Lang," the storekeeper said.

Brennan nodded, feeling beyond awkward. These were not the kind of people he associated with. He knew where he belonged—down the street at the saloon.

"You did very good last night," the young man said with the trace of a foreign accent.

"Yes," the young girl agreed, "you were so brave."

"I didn't do much. They weren't too dangerous, just sneak thieves."

"Please sit down, Merriday," Ashford invited, coming up behind him. "I'm sure Miss Rachel has fed you, but would you take a cup of coffee with us?"

From the shopkeeper's tone, Brennan knew these people were experiencing the same disorientation. They weren't comfortable with his sort in their dining room. And the old biddy with the eyeglass on a string was staring bullets at him. "No, thanks. You're right, Miss Rachel fed me to the brim. I just wanted to say thanks. This morning I wasn't ready to accept anything." *Anything from you people.*

"We wanted you to know that we appreciated your quick action," Ashford said.

Brennan nodded, his head bobbing like a toy. "Just did what anybody would."

"I think you did more," the young man said.

Brennan nodded once more. "I'll bid you good evening then." He waved Ashford back into his seat and tried not to jog down the stairs.

Unwillingly he overheard the old woman say, "What kind of man works for some woman when he could stake his own claim? Must be shiftless."

Insulted yet irritated that a stranger's opinion could

get to him, he let himself out and breathed with relief. And headed straight for the saloon.

He walked through the doors and let out a big breath. The saloon didn't have a piano player and the atmosphere was more drowsy than raucous, but nobody here would make him wonder if his shoes were shined bright enough.

He headed straight for the long bar and ordered an ale.

Sam poured his drink and then leaned his pudgy elbows on the bar. "So you're the man of the day now?"

Brennan snorted. "Right. Me?"

"From what I hear, you rousted them robbers efficient-like."

"They were just a few paltry sneak thieves. No big effort needed."

A man came up and clapped Brennan on the back. "The town hero!"

Brennan recoiled. "I didn't do nothing special, okay?"

"Ah, does not the laurel rest easy upon thy brow?" the man asked grandiloquently.

Brennan picked up his glass and tried to ignore the man. "Thought we'd finally have that tongue wag, Sam."

But it was not to be. More men crowded around, asking Brennan for the whole story. He bridled.

Sam leaned forward and muttered, "Play along. They don't get much excitement in this bump on the river. Tell them the story and they'll leave you alone."

So Brennan did, forcing himself to tell the story in full to prevent questions. He had a rapt audience. These people really didn't get much excitement. "So that's how it happened," he concluded.

Brennan suffered through a few more minutes of felicitations and gratitude and then, finally interpreting his silence as a desire to be left in peace, the men moved away, discussing the occurrence among themselves. Brennan refused all offers to buy him a real drink. He just wanted a refreshing mug of ale, nothing strong. Strong drink brought him nightmares and he didn't want that.

Brennan swallowed deeply of his drink, his mouth dry.

One man, middle-aged, better dressed and polished looking, stayed near him. "This place needs a sheriff. You might think about running in the fall election."

"Won't be here then," Brennan said.

"A pity." The stranger tipped his hat and walked out.

Sam swabbed the bar and then looked up from under his bushy eyebrows at Brennan. "You know who that is?"

"No." *And I don't care either.*

"That man sits in the state legislature. He's traveling around, drumming up support for the November election."

Brennan shrugged and repeated, "I won't be here then."

"Why not?" Sam asked. "You got a good reputation here now. Why leave?"

Even the barkeep had an opinion? Brennan stifled the urge to yell his frustration. "I'm just staying long enough to help Miss Rachel get set up and then I'm leavin'." He downed his drink and stalked outside.

In the hot evening, he marched to the blacksmith shop, looking for a place to get shut of all this attention. Once there, instead of resting, he paced up and down along the riverbank. Everything within him wanted to

pack up his knapsack and catch the first boat north.
But he couldn't.

His mind racing, he recalled sitting at Miss Rachel's
table, watching her serve up another tasty meal, something she seemed to do as easily as breathing. Her bis-
cuits were the lightest, the best he'd ever eaten. And her
soft cheeks had been flushed pretty pink from making
them for him. The thought of stroking one froze him
in place.

He growled at the bullfrogs bellowing along shore,
trying to attract females of their own kind. He wasn't
trying to have anythin' to do with females. He had nothing to give any woman, not a home or a heart.

Miss Rachel was upsetting him by making him think
about her that way. Why did she have to be such a good
cook? And so honest and open? She was always so
good-hearted, not a mean bone in her.

She made him think of settling down here, not Canada—far from all the war did to him, to everyone. Canada would let him forget all that, start over fresh.

He tried to focus on how she'd torn off his sleeve.
Managing woman. His unhappy thoughts twisted
around into a rat's nest. But one thought stood out
clear. He owed Miss Rachel and he wouldn't leave her,
couldn't leave her still needing help.

Two weeks later, nearing the beginning of August,
Brennan fidgeted in the bright summer sun near Miss
Rachel, who stood at the dock watching her brand
spanking new stove be carried off the boat. She glowed
with evident satisfaction over her major purchase while
he shifted from one foot to the other. He wished he were
waiting to get on this boat and go.

Irritating Ashford stood nearby, saying he wanted to

make sure that the purchase matched all that the firm had advertised. *What a fuss about a stove.*

Brennan stayed near the lady, but felt miles and miles away already. Tomorrow he'd dig her future garden plot. Then he would be gone on the next riverboat that docked here. Restlessness consumed him. At times the itch to leave became physical, as if he wanted to jump out of his skin. But how to tell Miss Rachel? Something about her kept him confused, unsettled, making it hard to leave, and this was the first time in memory this had happened. *But I'm goin'.*

The boatmen pushed the stove, supported on a wooden skid, off the boat onto the pier. Noah had come to help Brennan and held his team unhitched from the wagon.

Though the boatmen moved as slow as molasses on a very cold January day, Brennan held himself in check. *Move it along, why don't you?*

"Miss Rachel Woolsey?" a boatman asked, looking down at an invoice.

"Yes."

Brennan noted she could barely speak, she was so happy.

"Sign here, please."

"Miss Woolsey must examine the stove first," Mr. Ashford said, holding up a hand.

The boatman looked chagrined but motioned for another two men to crowbar off the sides of the wooden box.

Brennan held his tongue between his teeth. He'd been ready to say that. Of course Ashford would butt in. And take his time about it, too.

Rachel examined each side, looking for any imperfection. "It looks fine."

"Open and close the doors. Check to see if the latches fit tight," Mr. Ashford suggested.

She did so and then signed the invoice. The boatman had the men nail the crate back together.

Brennan noted her convoluted signature revealed her excitement. *All over a stove.* Miss Rachel, pink with pleasure, made a pretty picture. He looked away.

"My cousin Noah and Mr. Merriday will attach the horses to the skid. Isn't that right, Noah?" Miss Rachel asked.

Brennan held tight to the ragged fringe of his temper. Couldn't they just get this going?

"Rachel's place is just a half mile up the road," Noah said, gesturing toward the other end of town. "I'll bring the skid right back to you."

"Sure. Fine." The boatman handed Rachel her copy of the invoice and then turned away.

Finally. Now they could get this home and in place and then he could begin to lay out the garden. And if all went right, he'd be off tomorrow. Somewhere inside him, deep down, a voice whispered, *Stay. Why leave?*

Stonewalling the thought, Brennan helped Noah secure the team to the skid. The horses began to drag the heavy iron stove up the road. The progress was excruciatingly slow, with a lot of creaking. Brennan's nerves tangled into knots, but he kept from showing it. Miss Rachel had become a trap for him. He'd escaped other orchestrated marriage traps. But Miss Rachel had set no trap for him—that made it harder. He knew he was making no sense.

Finally they reached Miss Rachel's cabin door.

Noah and Brennan had already prepared a row of short logs of similar size, stripped of branches and bark, to use to roll the stove inside. The hard part would be getting it up over the threshold. They contrived a little ramp for this. Now the two of them painstakingly shifted the stove in its crate off the boat's skid and onto the logs and steadied it.

"I need to take the skid back first. Wait for me. I'll be quick." Noah turned the team around and headed back to town at a run.

Miss Rachel came near Brennan or rather her new stove. She stroked it the way another woman might have stroked a fur coat. Her nearness made his stomach twist. Her soft cheek tantalized him, beckoning him to press his lips...

Unable to brook further delay and needing to distance himself, Brennan started to roll the stove ponderously away from this woman. The stove picked up momentum—off balance because only one man had started it.

"Brennan Merriday, please wait for Noah. Thee might hurt—"

Unsettled, the stove began to tip and rock on the logs, rolling forward. Brennan tried to dodge the out-of-control iron beast, but—

Rachel cried out.

Stifling a curse, Brennan gasped with pain. His arm had become pinned between the cockeyed stove and the doorjamb of her cabin. Backed up against the log wall and half sitting, he struggled to keep outwardly calm but inside he was kicking himself down the road. And fighting to keep on top of the pain, ride it out, keep it in.

She hurried forward, voicing her upset. She moved as if to try to shift the stove, half on the logs, half off.

"Don't!" he thundered. "It might come off completely and crush me."

She stared down at him, wringing her hands. "Going for Noah won't help. He will not delay in returning."

Brennan couldn't meet her eyes so he focused on her chin. If he hadn't given in to his own haste, this wouldn't have happened. He waited for the lady to point this out.

Instead her mouth moved as if she were chewing tough meat. Finally, she said, "Thee has been behaving like a fly caught in flypaper. What drives thee, Brennan Merriday, to chafe so?"

The pain goading him, he almost bit off her head, but now *his* mouth chewed on that imaginary tough meat. He had no answer for her. Why did he get so restless?

But now all his concentration was tied up in not showing how much he suffered. He could not shift the unwieldy weight of the stove pressing on his wrist and upended forearm. Had he broken his arm? Inwardly he called himself every name he could think of, venting the pain.

Rachel stood over Brennan, folding her hands, murmuring a prayer for help.

The minutes spent waiting, bearing the brunt of the iron stove on his hand and wrist, depleted Brennan like hours spent working in the sun.

Within minutes Noah, accompanied by the young man Brennan had met at the Ashfords', entered the clearing.

"The stove rolled!" Rachel called out the obvious. But she didn't add the fact that Brennan had caused this by his haste. Brennan nearly gagged on the fact that it was all his own fault. That admission and the pain were nauseating him. But still Miss Rachel protected him.

Noah and Gunther hurried to Brennan. Without wasting any time asking questions, the men surveyed the situation and with quick commands, they hefted the stove back squarely onto the logs, releasing Brennan.

At the sudden deliverance, Brennan could not suppress a long moan. The two men rolled the stove inside.

Rachel dropped to her knees beside Brennan.

At first he resisted Rachel's efforts, holding his painful arm close to his chest, shielding it with his other arm. Finally he let her support his injured arm. He sent her an anguished look, their eyes at a level.

"How bad does his arm look?" Noah asked in his unruffled voice, standing over them.

Rachel gently probed the arm from the shoulder downward. When she prodded Brennan's wrist, he sucked in air sharply, not only from the pain but from her touch.

"Bend the wrist, please," Rachel instructed.

Brennan tucked his lower lip under his front teeth and bent his wrist, stifling a groan. Sweat popped up on his forehead but he did as she asked, knowing a broken wrist wouldn't bend.

"Rotate it?" she pressed

Again Brennan suppressed any show of pain and obeyed, watching his wrist move.

"Well, that's a relief," Rachel pronounced.

"Easy for you to say," Brennan gasped. Her prodding and instructions had aggravated the pain of the injury. Her soft shoulder was so near his cheek. He imagined resting his head there. He closed his eyes, willing away the image, the temptation.

"It's a relief that the bone isn't broken," Rachel said with force. "The wrist is sprained, I think."

"Take a week to ten days to heal," Noah added.

"It's good I'm right-handed," Brennan said through gritted teeth. He looked to the young man. "Glad you came along to help Noah." Though Noah wouldn't talk, this lad probably would. Everybody in town would soon hear about his foolishness.

"I am Gunther Lang," the young man introduced himself to Rachel. Then he glanced down at Brennan. "Sorry you are hurt."

"I think soaking the wrist in cold water may help," Miss Rachel said, rising. "I'll get a basin. Brennan, come sit inside." She nodded toward the door.

"I must go," the young man said and hurried away.

Noah reached for Brennan's good hand. "I'll help you up and then I'll hook up the stove."

Looking away, Brennan accepted the hand, managed to get to his feet and followed Noah inside where he sank into the rocker by the cold hearth. The pain was weakening him.

Rachel entered with a basin of water from the well and set it on her small sewing table. She reached to lift his hand in.

"I can move my hand," he said gracelessly. He folded up his sleeve and lowered the hand into the cool water. His gaze met hers over the basin. The concern he saw there chastened him.

"Very well." Rachel turned away. "Noah, is there anything I can do to help thee?"

Brennan toughed it out, the cold water making his bones ache more.

"Yes." Noah and she worked together, connecting the stovepipe sections and sliding it through the hole Brennan had cut for it this morning. Noah accepted Rachel's thanks, commiserated briefly with Brennan and headed home with his wagon and team.

Rachel retrieved her jar of arnica, pulled the bench

over and sat down near him. She opened the jar and began tenderly rubbing the ointment into his wrist.

Even her gentle touch caused him pain and he didn't like her having to care for him again. Her nearness worked its way through him—even in his pain. Her tender touch awakened something within that he didn't want to acknowledge. He lowered his eyes, not wanting to let her know her effect on him. Finally she brought out a large white dishcloth and folded it into a triangle.

"I don't need a sling," he objected irritably, knowing that he sounded like a boy.

She just stared at him, waiting.

"Oh, all right," he finally conceded and rose, cradling his arm.

Their faces a hairbreadth apart, Miss Rachel efficiently looped the sling around his arm and tied it behind his neck.

The scent of the lilac soap she always used filled his head and again he yearned to lean his head on her soft shoulder.

Obviously unaware, Miss Rachel adjusted the sling. "I know why thee couldn't wait for Noah." Her tone did not scold, merely informed. "Why are thee so fretful and champing at the bit to leave?"

Brennan wouldn't meet her gaze.

"Rest. I'll make some willow bark tea for the pain." She went to her new stove.

He sat down, watching her from under his lashes. Was she unscathed from contact with him? Her cheeks glowed pink—from touching him, from imagining his touch?

He turned his mind from this foolishness. How could something like this sprain take so much out of him? He closed his eyes and leaned back against the rocker. His wrist throbbed. He'd been so close to leaving, and now this. In his mind, old Aunt Martha's voice hectored him. *Worthless, thoughtless boy.* He couldn't argue with her.

And why *was* he so fretful and champing at the bit to leave? For the first time in a long time, he had a place to stay, a job, good food, new clothes… But he didn't belong here. He needed a new start far from…everything, especially this woman who continued to surprise him, to pull him to stay.

The next morning, Miss Rachel hummed to herself as she scattered chicken feed. Brennan sat in the shade against a maple, resting his arm in his sling, trying to think of some chore he could do with one hand. His wrist was swollen and painful. He'd felt guilty over eating breakfast at Miss Rachel's table when he couldn't work.

From the corner of his eye, he noted the young woman who looked to be seventeen or so, the one he'd met at the Ashfords' that evening when he'd gone to thank them. She was edging closer to them through the trees, as cautious as a doe. Fine, just what they needed—company. And what did she want?

"Good morning," Miss Rachel called out in a cheery voice that grated against his temper.

The young woman entered the clearing. Her clothing looked as if it had been refurbished to look new, but was in fact an old dress. And her manner was cautious. "Good morning. I'm Posey Brown. I was taking a walk and I saw your clearing—"

The distinctive call of a robin interrupted their conversation. The Quaker lady looked up and then imitated the birdcall. The robin hopped farther down the branch, moving in the breeze toward Miss Rachel, and sounded its call again. Miss Rachel replied, going to get the full water bucket. She then filled up a large wooden bowl attached to a stump. The bird flew down, perched on the side of the bowl and began drinking.

Brennan watched and listened, reluctantly fascinated by the interaction of the bird and the lady. Finally the bird sang its thanks and then flew and hopped back to the crook of the oak tree to its nest.

"That was like you were actually talking to each other." Posey's words radiated with wonder.

He'd almost said the same words aloud. And suddenly he was more aware than before of his sour mood. He hoisted himself up onto his feet.

"You put out water for the birds?" the girl asked as if this were the first birdbath she'd seen.

"It's been so very dry and several birds have nested nearby. I do it so they don't have far to go."

"Cousin Ned says if we don't get rain, one spark could burn the whole town," the girl said in a voice that spoke of living in the South.

Brennan thought Ned Ashford was right.

Miss Rachel turned to the girl and smiled. "My mother taught me birdsong. She spoke to birds. And they seemed almost to understand her."

The way Miss Rachel said these words he knew that her mother had died and what was more, that she had been a beloved mother. His own ma had died young. He didn't want to feel the connection to Miss Rachel this brought.

"How old were you when she died?" Brennan asked gruffly in spite of himself.

"I was nearly thirteen." Miss Rachel turned back to scattering chicken feed.

Posey edged closer. "My mother died during the war.

That's when Grandmother came to live with me," Posey paused. "And Pa died in the war. He was in the Kentucky Militia."

At this Brennan looked at her sharply.

Rachel motioned for the young girl to come forward. Rachel held open the bag of chicken feed, encouraging Posey to help her.

Though sorry for the young woman and uneasy that she hailed from Kentucky, Brennan moved away from the tree, his unabated restlessness goading him.

"It's just my grandmother and me now," Posey said, scattering the feed.

"I'm glad thee has her."

"Yes," Posey said, not looking up and not sounding happy.

Sensing the girl had come to tell Miss Rachel her sad story, like females did, Brennan turned and started toward town. He had to get away from this homey scene, from hearing how the war had torn this girl's world into shreds. He found that unfortunately he couldn't walk fast without jarring his wrist.

"I'm finishing cinnamon rolls this morning, Posey. Perhaps you'd like to help me get them ready to take into town. A boat is expected today."

"I heard how you sell baked goods. You must be good at that."

"I do my poor best," Rachel admitted.

Brennan walked carefully across the uneven ground through the wild grass, trying to get away.

Miss Rachel made the best sweets he'd ever eaten and that's all the credit she'd own up to. Yes, Miss Rachel was too nice. Didn't she know such goodness only invited trouble? This was a nasty world and it destroyed niceness.

The two females turned toward the cabin.

Though he'd begun to walk away, some curiosity prompted Brennan to ask, "Your father remarried, Miss Rachel?"

"Yes" was all she said.

And that told him more about this lady and why she'd come West than she'd probably ever put into words.

His wrist was aching so he couldn't be of help to this good woman. What could he do with one hand? "I'm heading to town!" he called out. Maybe he could have that quiet tongue wag with Sam the barkeep at last and think of something else. Maybe that would take the edge off his keen craving to leave.

He had to get away from this woman who made him remember things like family and belonging, things he'd long kept sleeping in the back of his mind. Miss Rachel was waking him up to…to feeling, caring. *I've got to get away—soon.*

Chapter Five

On the next morning, yet another steamy summer day, Brennan did not show up for breakfast. Rachel stood at her door, looking for him. Concern needled her.

Had he left town?

Or had he been hurt worse than she thought?

Or since he couldn't work, was he lying in bed, moping?

The idea of going into town and finding him to put a flea in his ear tempted her. But she turned from it and went inside. If the man didn't want his breakfast, so be it.

She cracked an egg in the skillet, listened to its lonely sizzle and then toasted a single slice of bread for her breakfast. She sat down to eat alone. Well, she wanted to be on her own and now she was.

Recalling Brennan's edginess over the past week didn't diminish her uneasiness. This morning he might have just up and left town. Men like him did that: drifters drifted.

But she'd become accustomed to his laconic wit. And in his company, she never felt judged and found wanting. She now recognized that this feeling was something she'd lived with daily since her father remarried. She stared at the solid walls of her snug cabin, her own home, grateful for it yet feeling so isolated, set apart.

She snapped off this self-pitying train of thought and began her day. Soon she loaded her dishcloth-covered trays of just-out-of-the-oven, fragrant cinnamon rolls onto the narrow shelves of the two-wheeled pushcart Noah and Brennan had built for her. Mr. Merriday didn't like her meeting boats without him. But she had to start doing that. If he weren't gone already, Brennan Merriday would be soon.

At this thought a weight settled over her lungs. She shoved against it but it refused to budge. The feeling would pass, she told herself. Perhaps it would be better if Brennan had left. Then she could face her solitary life starting today and make peace with it.

A boat's whistle prompted her to hurry along so she wouldn't miss one that might just be stopping to pick up the mail.

Soon she rolled the cart into town. She forced herself to smile despite the stubborn weight that was making it hard to breathe. She was rolling her cart past Ashford's store when she saw Posey hurry out from it.

"Hello, Miss Rachel!" she greeted her.

Rachel smiled but didn't stop. Posey joined her and kept in step at her side.

Out of the corner of her eye, Rachel noted Brennan Merriday coming out of the blacksmith shop. So he hadn't left town. The weight she'd carried vanished. *That is not good. I must not depend on him.*

He was hurrying as if to catch up with her.

She picked up her pace, letting him know she wasn't waiting around for him.

"Posey Brown!" a strong, shrill female voice called out across the main street.

Posey halted. Now it appeared that the girl might have been escaping from the store. Posey turned. "Yes, Grandmother?"

"I was not done with our conversation. Please come here."

Posey did not look happy but she obeyed.

Rachel continued on, reaching the boat dock. Brennan trailed her. Somehow she sensed him scowling behind her back.

She smiled with professional cheer. "Good morning!" she called to the boatmen. "I have cinnamon rolls and sponge candy for sale today!"

Boatmen, who'd evidently heard of her business, swarmed onto the dock and surrounded her.

A wiry man with a young boy around ten pushed past the men, coming toward Rachel on land. She was handing out rolls in wax paper as fast as she could and men were dropping coins into a small bucket at her feet.

As the wiry man passed, she noted the stormy look on his face as if he was spoiling for a fight and the shuttered expression on the boy beside him. And how he hung back. The man reached behind and yanked him forward. *So unkind.* But Rachel was keeping up with business.

"Brennan Merriday!" the wiry man bellowed. "So you are here in this little backwater town!"

Everyone within hearing distance went silent. Rachel's hand faltered. The man's bellow had clearly been a challenge. The boatmen still snatched pastries from her hands and dropped in their coins, but they did it with haste and then crowded onto the shore as if they didn't want to miss the show…or fight.

And this man had called out Brennan's name. Who was he? She glanced over her shoulder but stayed where she was.

When the cook from the boat arrived with a tray and scooped up the rest of her fare, she was sold out. Her pulse jumping, she accepted his payment, offered her thanks and turned around, trundling her empty cart through the crowd at the dock.

In the center of the town's street, Brennan and the stranger and boy stood, confronting each other. The two men glared as if about to battle. Would there be fisticuffs?

Rachel parked her cart and unable to stop herself, moved closer.

"What're ya'll doing here, Jean Pierre?" Brennan asked, his voice low with an edge of menace.

Aware that Brennan would not appreciate any interference from her, Rachel halted, keeping her distance, but remained watchful.

"I never thought I'd be forced to set eyes on your worthless face again," Jean Pierre sneered with obvious relish. "But it's time you took responsibility for your get."

The man's last word, a vulgar term for *child,* sent a spike of ice through Rachel. Brennan's "get"? The shock forced a gasp from her. "Oh."

Brennan looked confused. "What are ya'll saying?"

"I'm saying this is your son, Lorena's child, Jacque."

Brennan appeared speechless.

"Your own kin and Lorena's were glad to be rid of a coward like you," Jean Pierre continued. "Then I read about you in the Saint Louis paper." He pulled a folded newspaper from his back pocket. He slapped it into

Brennan's hand. "Guess you aren't the coward we all thought you were."

Brennan looked at the paper, but still reacted only with mute shock.

"Everybody in both our families in Mississippi and across in Louisiana is dead or scattered. I'm headin' West. I was going to drop your boy off at an orphanage run by some Quaker woman near Saint Louis when I seen this paper and read about you running off the thieves here. So here's your son. You take care of him." With that, Jean Pierre turned on his heel and stalked back to the riverboat.

Rachel tried to take this all in, but had trouble grasping what had just taken place. *Brennan—a son?*

Brennan didn't move or speak, just stood staring after the man heading toward the boat.

Then the boy took action. He turned and ran after the stranger. "Don't leave me here, cousin! Take me with you!"

At this, Brennan woke up. He chased the boy and grasped him by the shoulder, halting his flight. "Jean Pierre! Are you tellin' me that Lorena had my son and never told me?"

"Why would she tell you? She was well shut of you. Boy, stay with your father. He's all you got!"

The boy jerked away from Brennan and ran after his cousin. "Don't leave me!"

Jean Pierre ignored his calls and boarded along with the boatmen. A river porter, carrying the mailbag, hurried back toward the dock. When he reached the deck, the whistle sounded, the few boatmen left on land scurried on deck, and the riverboat began pulling away.

"Come back!" the boy at river's edge shouted, a rending hysteria in his voice.

The riverboat swept into the current and steamed away.

Tears sprang to the boy's eyes and he swiped at them with his tattered sleeve.

The sight wrenched Rachel's heart. She instinctively drew nearer Brennan and his son. *His son.* Was this Brennan's son? The idea of his having a child startled her, shook her—in a way she hadn't expected. She resisted it and didn't have time to examine the wave of emotion now.

Brennan stood a few paces behind the boy, obviously still in the grip of his own bewilderment.

His lips quivering, the boy appeared about to burst into sobs. Rachel knew that would crush his spirit. Men and boys didn't cry. She glanced once more at Brennan's frozen expression and decided she must act. *Father, help me. I must do something but I don't know what.*

"Hello," she said, coming close to the boy, trying to behave as normally as she could. "I'm Miss Rachel Woolsey. I am thy father's… Mr. Merriday's employer."

With dirt-smeared cheeks, the boy looked into her eyes without much comprehension.

His naked anguish hit her like a broadside. She offered him her hand. "Welcome to Pepin. We are a small town but we have a school and a general store," she babbled, very aware that everyone in town was listening to her every syllable. She looked to Brennan once more.

"Mr. Merriday hurt his wrist recently and has been resting in town." She prayed again for guidance. She saw that she could do nothing but try to proceed as if nothing unusual had happened. "I need a few things at the store before we head back to my homestead."

She looked at the boy and his basic needs were too plain. He needed clothing, food and a bath. The first was a good place to start. "Mr. Merriday, I think I should stop and purchase some fabric for new clothes for your…for Jacque." The last words were more an order than information.

Brennan stared at her as if she were speaking Chinese.

She sent him a silent message with her expression, telling him to command himself. Now. She resisted the impulse to draw near and touch his good arm.

"That's right, boy. Go with Miss Rachel," he said and turned away.

Rachel watched him head for the saloon and sighed deeply but quietly. *Not the best choice, Brennan Merriday.*

Touching the boy's thin, boney shoulder, she urged him to follow her into the store. There she tried to behave as if suddenly having a boy with her was an everyday occurrence. All three of the Ashfords, as well as Posey and her grandmother, stood behind the counter, gawking impolitely. This stiffened her instinct to protect the child.

"Mr. Ashford, I need some cloth to make this boy a new shirt and pants." Mr. Ashford helped her choose suitable dark fabric and Mrs. Ashford helped her figure out how much she would need for the new garments.

Then Rachel ordered more flour and sugar as she had planned. On the way out, she noted the boy looking at the candy display. "Don't worry, Jacque. I have sponge candy at home. Needs somebody to eat it."

She handed him the brown paper wrapped package of fabric and walked him to her cart. She motioned for him to put the package on the empty, cloth-covered trays. "Will thee push the cart? Home isn't far."

As they passed the saloon, the urge to march inside and collar Brennan Merriday nearly turned her from her path. Instead, she faced forward and guided Jacque toward home. Some food, some gentle conversation, some candy—that was all she could provide for this child. She hoped it would be enough to help. *Mr. Merriday, is this your son?*

Brennan stood at the bar, staring at Sam, unable to talk.

"What is it, Merriday?" Sam asked with concern. "You look like you seen a ghost."

Brennan's mind felt like scrambled eggs. He braced his good palm against the bar, trying to get hold of himself. He'd sought this place to hide while he dealt with this turn of events. The expression on Miss Rachel's face when she heard Jean Pierre... He shook his head as if that would shake it loose.

"Is that kid really yours?" Levi in his leather apron asked the words before he even cleared the doorway.

"What kid?" Sam asked. "What did I miss?"

Brennan stared at the blacksmith he'd come to like and shook his head as if coming up from underwater. Was this boy his? "Gotta go."

He started up the road toward Miss Rachel's at full steam but faltered, his mind dragging him back in time. Something like the Gulf surf roared in his ears. His senses reeled. As from far away he glimpsed familiar faces, then the blows began falling on him, forcing him to fight...

He shouted aloud, "No!"

The present sounds returned to normal, birds in the trees, squirrels chattering. The roaring in his ears receded. He bent and braced his good hand on his knee, panting for air. The urge to turn and run and keep running rolled over him. He stood his ground.

Could it be possible? Had Lorena borne him a son

before she died? When he'd gone back to Mississippi after the war, why hadn't anybody told him? He recalled the bitter words and the sneering faces he'd encountered while trying to find out if his wife still lived and if she needed anything. They'd told him Lorena had died and they had literally run him out of town at gunpoint.

And now he must face this child who—if he was really his son—probably hated him, too. And what did Miss Rachel think about him and this boy?

Wondering when Mr. Merriday would appear, Rachel halted Jacque at her door, seizing upon everyday needs to show her concern. Brennan must face this problem, but would he?

"Jacque, please wash thy hands before entering." She gestured toward the outdoor washbasin with its bar of yellow soap and linen towel on the peg.

"Why?"

"Because I promised thee sponge candy and one must eat only with clean hands."

The boy began to wash his hands that appeared to have several layers of dirt on them.

When he reached for the towel before he'd worked his way through all the layers, she shook her head. "Keep washing till they are completely clean."

He glared at her but obeyed, his stomach growling. Finally clean skin appeared.

Rachel nodded.

He dried his hands and stalked into her cabin.

"Come back and toss the water onto my flowers," she said, standing patiently outside.

He did so, glaring more, his stomach growling more.

Then she motioned him inside. "I think more than

just candy would be good for thee. Nibble on this while I fry some eggs." She handed him a cinnamon roll.

He ate it in two bites, standing.

"Sit at the table, please." Then she set her cast-iron skillet back on her stove, stirred up the fire and began cracking eggs. She stopped at four, not wanting to make him sick. The boy looked starved. "Hard or soft?"

"Hard."

She soon set a plate with the four fried eggs and another cinnamon roll in front of him. She added a glass of fresh milk from deep in her root cellar.

Before she finished her silent grace, Jacque began to gobble the food.

She studied his face, trying to discern any resemblance to Mr. Merriday. "Slow down, please. There will be two more meals today and snacks if thee needs them."

"You talk funny."

"Thee do also," she replied, alluding to his thick Southern accent. "Slow down and chew the food. Don't make thyself sick."

"You're not my aunt or anythin'." He sent her an aggrieved look.

Rachel reached over and pulled the plate from him. "I am the one who cooked breakfast. Sitting at my table means obeying the rules of this house. Clean hands to eat with and chew the food."

The boy glared at her, then muttered, "Yes, miss."

She slid the plate back to him.

He began eating again, but marginally slower.

She wanted to ask him questions but decided not to. She needed to talk to Brennan first and find out where this boy had come from.

As if he heard her thoughts, Brennan appeared in her doorway, his hat in hand. "Miss Rachel."

"Has thee eaten breakfast, Mr. Merriday?" she asked, hiding how her heart sped up at the sight of him.

Her question evidently prompted his stomach to growl. "No, miss."

She set another two cinnamon rolls on a plate and poured some coffee that had been keeping warm and then sat down at the table again.

Brennan stepped outside and she could hear him washing his hands. Then he entered, hung his hat and sat down beside Jacque.

"You gotta wash yer hands, too?" Jacque asked, sounding put out.

"That's her rule. You eat at Miss Rachel's table, you wash your hands."

Rachel stifled a grin, but her pulse still beat faster, though she couldn't say why it should. "Jacque, done with breakfast?"

"Yes, ma'am, I mean, Miss Rachel."

"Come here then." She motioned for him to come around to her. "As promised" she offered him a piece of sponge candy, which disappeared instantly. "Now I need to measure thee for thy new clothes." Rising, she began measuring the boy's skinny arms, then scrawny chest, waist and legs with a tape measure from her sewing box. Since she'd be fattening him up—she hoped— she'd make the seam allowances wider than usual to be let out later.

Mr. Merriday's gaze followed her every move. She forced herself not to look back at him. "The clothing should be done by Sunday for church." Suddenly she needed time to sort all this out, figure out how she should feel about this.

She turned to Brennan, who rose. "I know thy wrist

is still swollen, but why not take Jacque and mark off my garden? He could begin turning over the sod."

Brennan gazed at her. Miss Rachel had fed the boy and was sewing for him. But now she had informed him it was his turn to deal with the boy. He sucked it up. "Sounds right. Boy, why don't you go out to the lean-to and find the shovel there?"

Jacque looked disgruntled but obeyed, his hands shoved in his pockets.

When they were alone, Brennan looked across the table. Miss Rachel sat again and gestured for him to sit also. He obeyed reluctantly.

"Evidently thee wished to speak to me alone?" she asked coolly.

No, he didn't really want to speak to her alone, not about this. Brennan didn't know what to say so he said the first thing that came to mind. "I didn't mean to burden you more. My wrist is sprained and now the boy…"

She gazed across to him. "Is it likely that this boy is thy blood?"

Leave it to Miss Rachel to cut to the marrow. "Could be." He knew he should tell her about Lorena, about what had happened to tear them apart. He couldn't. He had no words to express that dark time.

"It is really none of my business. But a child complicates…"

He looked at her, willing her to be silent. *Don't tell me what I already know.*

She tightened her lips. "Very well. I will not press thee now."

He heard the remaining sentence she did not voice—*but we will talk about this, and soon.*

He rose, grabbed his hat from the peg and headed outside, nearly running.

"Come on, Jacque!" he called in the yard, feeling something near hysteria building in his stomach. Why hadn't the past stayed in the past? But it wasn't the child's fault, none of this was. "We'll pace off the garden and start you diggin'."

The two of them began walking to the back of the clearing.

"Isn't it late to be planting?" the boy asked, sounding annoyed. "She should have planted in March."

"She didn't live here in March. She came in June like I did. We're just going to start turning up the soil for next year." Was this silly conversation real?

"This ain't gonna be much of a garden," the boy said, looking at the trees surrounding them. "And everything looks burned up, dry."

"True." Brennan cradled his aching wrist close to his chest, holding in his agitation. "Let's pace out the boundaries and get started."

The boy stood, leaning on the shovel handle. "What did you do to your hand?"

"I sprained my wrist." He stared at the boy, his curiosity sparking. "What's your whole name?"

"Jacque Louis Charpentier."

Charpentier had been Lorena's maiden name. "Who was your mother?"

"You heard who my ma was."

"Do you remember her?"

"No."

"When'd she die?"

"During the war."

"So what year were you born?"

The boy gave him a sarcastic look. "Fall of '61, the year the war started."

Brennan stared at him, searching for something of himself in the boy's face.

"Do ya'll want me to dig this or not?" the boy demanded.

"Dig." Brennan experienced a sudden weakness that had more to do with shock over this new revelation than anything else. He moved into the shade of a nearby oak and settled onto the rough, wild grass. That Lorena had taken back her maiden name didn't surprise him. And perhaps he shouldn't be surprised that she'd borne him a son and never tried to let him know.

But if they hadn't wanted the boy when Brennan returned after the war, why wait till now? Had Jean Pierre brought him someone else's child who didn't remember his mother as a final kick in the gut, a final insult?

What did Miss Rachel think of this? And why did that matter so much to him?

Rachel had smoothed out the heavy cotton fabric for Jacque's new clothing on her table and was calmly fashioning a pattern from brown wrapping paper. Inwardly she roiled, trying to come up with an explanation for what had happened in town. Was Jacque really Brennan's son? Why did she keep asking herself that question?

"Hello the house!" said a feminine voice that sounded familiar as she voiced the usual frontier greeting.

Rachel rose and peered out the open door and saw Posey, the new girl in town, had come again to call. "Oh, hello," she said, trying to hide her lack of welcome.

"A letter came for you today so I told Cousin Ned I'd be happy to bring it." Posey held up the letter as she approached.

The joy of receiving a letter zinged through Rachel. She beamed. "Come in, Posey."

The young woman did so and handed her the letter.

"Please be seated." Rachel didn't apologize, just slit open the letter with a kitchen knife and read it.

July 1871

Dear Daughter,
We were relieved thee reached Cousin Noah's family in Pepin safely. Thy stepmother and I are in good health as are thy sisters. We are going to be blessed again near the end of the year with another child, God willing. Here are notes from thy younger sisters.

Then she read the notes written in childish printing:

Our dog misses thee. The cats looked all over for thee.
Love,
Hannah

I cried for two days when thee left.
Love,
Elizabeth

I MISS THEE AND SO DOES SARA.
LOVE,
MARTHA

Then her father's script resumed.

Your obedient servant,
Jeremiah Woolsey

A pang of homesickness tangled around Rachel's lungs. *I miss thee, too.* "It's from my family. I have four younger stepsisters." And perhaps another on the way. Her father sounded as if he missed her, too.

"A letter from home is always good. What are your sisters' names?"

"They are Hannah, Elizabeth, Martha and baby Sara." Each name pinched her heart. *I do love them, Father. Keep them safe.*

"Those are pretty names."

Wanting to get some distance from this emotional topic, she said, "Posey is a pretty name. Who chose it?"

"When I was born, my pa said I was as pretty as a posey." The young woman grinned shyly.

"Very true." Smiling politely, Rachel folded her letter and slid it into her writing box that sat on a shelf near the window. She suddenly felt tired.

"Where is the new boy?" Posey asked, looking around.

Ah, gossip. Was that Posey's true purpose in coming? "Jacque and Mr. Merriday are out making me a small garden." Rachel began working on the pattern for the pants again.

"Is that for the boy?"

Rachel only nodded, discouraging talk about Jacque.

"If you like, I can make a pattern for the shirt. At home I often sewed for boys. I took in sewing with my mother."

"How kind." Rachel pushed a sheet of brown paper and another pencil to the girl. "If thee has the time?" *But I won't give thee any information to spread around. I don't have any.*

Posey sighed. "I'm not needed at the store or above it. Four women in one house." She shook her head.

Rachel read more in the tone of the girl's voice than the actual words. Had Posey delivered the letter as a way to get out of the store? Rachel didn't blame her. Mrs. Ashford and the girl's grandmother would be a daunting pair.

Wondering how Brennan was doing behind the house, Rachel opened her roomy sewing box and removed a paper of straight pins. "Is thee going to be visiting the Ashfords for long?"

Posey stared down at the brown paper and began measuring with a tape and drawing the outline of a shirt, glancing at the dimensions Rachel had jotted in one corner. "We aren't visiting. We've come to stay."

"Really?" Rachel tried to keep sympathy out of her tone. She wouldn't want to have to move in with the Ashfords. Rachel borrowed the tape measure and checked the dimensions of the pants. Mr. Merriday's shocked face kept coming to mind. The public scene had stirred up something troubling him. She wished she didn't feel as much concern as she did. *He's leaving.*

"We lived in northern Tennessee but when the war started, we moved to Kentucky." Posey glanced up. "We didn't own slaves, and we were against secession. My father settled us in a boardinghouse and joined the Kentucky Militia. My mother and I made a living sewing and helping the lady who ran the boardinghouse. We were hoping to go back to our home after the war."

"But that didn't happen?" Rachel had heard variations of this story at home and on her way here, her sympathy caught. Had the war spared anybody? Again her mind thought of Mr. Merriday's ravaged expression.

"Father was killed in the war. Afterward, we were afraid to go back to Tennessee. We heard Northern sympathizers were lynched. And Pa fought for the Union so…"

"I'm so sorry." And Rachel truly was. The war had brought so much suffering and death. The two out back digging her garden included. She measured a yard and then two by holding the fabric from her nose to her outstretched hand.

"My mother died earlier this year and that ended my father's army pension."

Though grieved by Posey's story, Rachel found her mind laboring over how to help Mr. Merriday. But perhaps this was beyond her power. She sighed and began pinning the paper pattern to the cotton.

"Grandmother decided that we should come north to our cousins and hope that they could help me find a husband. Grandmother said that many men are moving north and west to homestead on free land, make a new start, and would need a wife."

Rachel heard the shame and worry wrapped around each of the girl's words. Heaven knew she had enough to keep her busy with her business and now this unexpected child, but she would try to help Posey discover how to make her way in the world.

Perhaps marriage would be the best solution for Posey, but certainly not marriage solely out of necessity. Rachel had escaped the latter and wouldn't let it happen to this young woman.

"Mr. Merriday's given name is Brennan?" Posey asked, a sudden departure from the topic.

"Yes, Brennan Merriday." Rachel looked at the girl. Did she think to marry Brennan Merriday? She pricked her finger with a straight pin.

"His name is an unusual one. It sounds familiar somehow."

Rachel glanced at the young woman who in turn was busy sketching in marks for buttonholes on the brown wrapping paper. Her mind wandered. If Brennan hadn't sprained his wrist, he would have departed by now. Would Brennan leave and take the boy with him? A totally new feeling rolled through her, a kind of dread mixed with hope. She didn't want Brennan to leave and now that Jacque had come perhaps he wouldn't.

With a burst of insight, she admitted this to herself. A startling revelation. And she acknowledged that this was more than just about her losing his help. She didn't want to lose Brennan Merriday. *I have feelings for him.* She stood stock-still as waves of shock rolled over her.

Rachel experienced a kind of swirling in her head. Too much had happened and everything had been up-ended. She gasped, trying to catch her breath. She couldn't. She was breathing too fast.

Suddenly Posey came very close. "Miss Rachel." Then the girl blew into her face. "You're not getting enough air. Miss Rachel!" The girl grabbed Rachel's wrists and pulled her to sit. "Miss Rachel!"

Rachel inhaled deeply and then coughed, shuddered. Posey patted her on the back. "Are you all right?"

Rachel nodded, far from all right.

She did not want Brennan Merriday out of her life. That much had come clear—disturbing but clear. "I'm fine. Sorry."

"Mama breathed too fast like that when we got word of my father's death," Posey said sadly. "I was afraid you'd faint."

"I never faint." *I've never become attached to a man either.*

Finally Rachel persuaded Posey to go home.

Rachel sat outside on a chair in the shade of one of

the tall maples on the edge of her clearing, fretting. She forced herself to go on slipping her fine needle in and out of the stiff cloth, trying not to think of Mr. Merriday, yet straining to hear the sound of his voice from behind the cabin. Would he stay now that the boy had come? She tried to control how her heart lifted at this thought. *I must not let myself hope that.*

Chapter Six

The sun had lowered when she heard Mr. Merriday and the boy join her in the shade. She kept her gaze on her sewing, afraid Brennan might read her feelings for him in her expression. She couldn't imagine the humiliation of caring for a man uninterested in her. Whatever happened, he must never know.

"Jacque, I should have thy new clothing done soon," she said mildly, her heart thrumming in her ears. Mr. Merriday's presence stirred her, waking her somehow. She clung to her self-control.

"Yes, miss," Jacque said in a tone that showed no interest.

Brennan slid his back down the tree.

Her awareness of him slid higher.

"We dug some of the garden—" Brennan started.

"*I* dug some of the garden," Jacque interrupted Brennan.

"Don't correct thy elders," Rachel said out of habit, a scold she'd used on her younger sisters. Tension crackled between the two males. It added to her own. She changed topics, as keeping words flowing provided her some cover. "I received a letter from home today."

"Oh," Brennan said flatly.

His attitude doused her like cold water. She was never one to ignore matters—why should she now? "Jacque," she said, setting down her sewing, "I am going to give thee a towel and soap. Go to the creek and take a bath."

"I'd like a swim," Jacque said, eyeing her.

"The creek is shallow but do thy best." She went inside and came out with the towel and soap. "Don't lose the soap in the creek. And don't forget to wash behind the ears, the back of the neck, and hair."

"I won't." He grabbed the towel and took off running in the direction Brennan had told him.

Brennan had risen when she had. Not meeting his gaze, she returned to her place on her chair and he eased back onto the wild grass and leaned against the tree trunk.

His nearness still affected her, but she bolstered her resolve. "Is Jacque thy son?" she pressed him again, taking up her needle and thread again, voicing the question perhaps uppermost in both their minds.

Brennan stared forward and did not reply with even a change of expression. The lowering sun glinted on the highlights in his hair. He needed a trim and she nearly reached out to lift the hair hanging over his collar.

"What business is it of yours?" he grumbled.

Instead of biting off his head, she bit off a thread. "I am merely concerned." Not the truth, she admitted to herself. "I am not a gossip." That much was true.

"He could be my son," Brennan allowed grudgingly. "The time works out right."

"I see." That was all he was going to say? Obviously Brennan Merriday didn't want to tell her—now. And did she want him to open up to her? Wouldn't it be better to try to go back to where they had been—if possible?

* * *

She made a cold supper for them. Jacque ate his fill and then fell asleep, his damp head buried on his arms at the table. In the stillness broken by the sound of frogs at the nearby creek, Rachel tried not to stare at Mr. Merriday across the table from her. And failed.

Worry lines bisected his forehead and his shoulders looked tense. Again she resisted the impulse to touch his arm, speak comfort to him. She would have to fight these foolish tendencies or he might leave that much sooner just to get away from her. She endured a sharp twinge around her heart.

"I don't know what to think," he said out of the blue.

She didn't pretend to misunderstand him. "Today was a shock. But remember it was a shock to Jacque, as well." She frowned deeply, feeling the hard lines in her face. "That man, that Jean Pierre, will reap a bitter harvest from his unkindness. Such public cruelty."

"He did it to shame me."

"And without a thought for the child." The unkindness sliced Rachel to the heart. She knew Brennan would never abandon a child or treat anyone so thoughtlessly. Under his gruff exterior, Brennan had an innate honor. "This boy has lost much and he's so young."

"I get your meanin'." Brennan rose. "I'll take him to my loft."

Rachel nearly objected. She had room for the boy, but he wasn't hers. The chasm between her feelings for this man and what was appropriate in this situation spread further apart. "I'll loan a pillow and blanket for him."

"Much obliged." Brennan shook the boy's shoulder.

Jacque looked up, blinking.

"Take the pillow from Miss Rachel. We'll head home now."

"Don't you live here?" the boy said, knuckling his eyes.

"No, that wouldn't be proper. I live above the blacksmith shop," Brennan said, accepting the light cotton blanket she offered him.

Rachel watched them walk down the track to town till they vanished from her sight. She wished to help but Brennan plainly had told her to keep her nose out of his business. Until he left town, though, he was her business. How did one stop having feelings for a man? He was a totally unsuitable man yet that didn't make any difference to her heart.

Brennan's nerves still stuttered from the scene earlier that day on Main Street. He led this boy he didn't know, but who might be his only family, through the trees and the deserted town to the silent blacksmith shop. They found Levi sitting on his one chair, looking out over the river.

A refreshing breeze blew over them, dissipating the heat from the forge. But Brennan's stomach felt loaded with lead. What would come next? And for some reason he couldn't stop thinking about Miss Rachel.

Levi sat forward. "Well, hello. I'm Levi Comstock."

Brennan appreciated Levi's uncomplicated greeting. Both Levi and Miss Rachel could be counted on for kindness. Miss Rachel's face, surrounded by delicate wisps of her light hair, came to mind, drawing him back. He hadn't wanted to leave her, hadn't wanted to take full charge of this child tonight. After fighting in the war and drifting for years, he was completely unprepared to be a father.

Jacque merely nodded to Levi.

"Boy, when a man introduces himself, you say your name and call him sir," Brennan said sternly.

Jacque threw Brennan a scalding look. "I'm Jacque Charpentier, sir."

Levi offered his hand and shook the boy's. "Nice to meet you, Jacque."

Brennan noted Levi raised a quizzical eyebrow, more than Miss Rachel had done. She'd been mighty cool about everything. That stuck in his craw.

"Jacque, I'll show you where we bed down." Brennan walked him inside and waved him up the ladder to the loft. "You'll see my bedroll up there. There's a good breeze so you'll do okay. Be up later."

Jacque raised a shoulder in reply and with his bedding over his other shoulder climbed the ladder. At that moment, Brennan recalled what Miss Rachel had said. *This boy has lost much and he's so young.*

His conscience clipped him hard. "Jacque," Brennan said, making his voice kinder, "everything will work out."

The boy didn't even pause on his way up the ladder.

Brennan didn't blame Jacque for doubting him. *What does he know of me but what's been told him, and none of it good?* Brennan's stomach burned, as he thought about all the lies this boy had probably heard about the man who might be his father. Or had they told him nothing except that Brennan was a coward? Miss Rachel's face kept coming to mind. The good woman she was, she'd been concerned for the boy. Her sweet voice played in his mind.

Outside again, Brennan stooped with his back propped against the rough log wall.

"Charpentier?" Levi asked.

"My wife's maiden name."

Levi looked at him, expecting more.

Brennan stared at the wide river. He could not speak

of this now. Again, he wished he could speak frankly to Miss Rachel. She saw human nature clearly, but Jacque wasn't her responsibility.

"You see that new gal in town?" Levi asked finally.

Brennan thought for a moment, his mind a jumble. "You mean Posey?"

"Yeah, she's a pretty little thing."

Brennan looked sideways at the man, relieved to discuss something else. "You lonely?"

"I have been hoping some young ladies would move here, but so far it's only been little girls, couples or single men. If I'd stayed in Illinois, I could have found a wife easy."

Brennan went along, a welcome distraction. "Why didn't you stay in Illinois then?"

Levi frowned. "I wanted to have my own shop. Too many blacksmiths in Illinois."

"And a lot of women." Brennan eased his own mind by teasing the blacksmith.

"But most of them are too hoity-toity to move to the frontier. They want board sidewalks and hat shops."

This forced a laugh from Brennan, a release of tension.

"It's not funny. I want a regular cabin and a wife to snuggle up to in the long winter ahead."

Brennan shrugged. "I wish you luck."

"You don't think your Miss Rachel is interested in getting married, do you?"

Brennan snorted in response; unreasonable irritation sparked within. "Told me she's not getting married," he said, warning the man away.

"Women say that, but do they mean that? She's a great cook and as neat as wax. Pretty, too. She just don't take pains to look it."

This aggravated Brennan. He had no right but it irked him to have another man notice how quietly pretty she was. "You can try, but I doubt she'll come around. She... she sounds like some man insulted her by offering marriage...for *his* convenience. Had a passel of kids he needed a ma for."

"Ah." The sound conveyed that Levi had no idea what Brennan was talking about and Brennan didn't feel like telling more. Miss Rachel's business was hers alone.

"Women don't like it if you start paying attention to one woman and then switch to another," Levi commented. "You know what I mean?"

Brennan did, but had bigger problems of his own.

"I think I'll start trying to get to know Miss Posey Brown. She's younger and tries to look pretty. That's a sign she's not adverse to marriage." Levi glanced at Brennan. "Wouldn't you say?"

Brennan let out a long breath. Levi was never this talkative. "What've you got to lose?" Brennan asked.

He'd once been so in love and look how it had all turned out. If there hadn't been slavery, abolition, secession, would he and Lorena have done better? The sad truth was in this fiery world, love lasted as long as tissue paper. So letting himself begin to care at all for the Quakeress was more than foolish.

When Brennan woke the next morning, he found a thin small body pressed against his right side. He jerked more wide awake, hurt his sprained wrist and cursed under his breath.

Jacque rolled away from him with a stifled yelp of surprise. For a moment the boy looked as if he didn't know where he was.

The panic in his eyes stabbed Brennan; he regretted disturbing the child. "You're in Wisconsin with me, Jacque," he said in a voice he wished sounded more comforting.

The boy lost the panicked look but did not appear very reassured.

"Now, we get up and wash in the river and then go to Miss Rachel's for breakfast."

Jacque nodded. "She cooks good."

"You don't know the half of it yet," he said with deep sincerity. He cradled his aching wrist to himself. After a sleepless night, he felt like a limp piece of rag, and what unexpected unpleasantness might come today?

Soon, the two of them walked through town. Brennan tried not to notice how people, sweeping the steps of their cabins, stopped to gawk. What did he care? What were they to him? He'd be gone before long.

Brennan stumbled on a rock that had rolled onto the path. The false step jiggled his sore wrist. He gritted his teeth. His wrist would heal in its own good time and this matter with the child would have to work its own way out. But how?

After eating a breakfast of scrambled eggs with fried salt pork and buttered toast, Brennan rose to thank Miss Rachel for another good meal.

"How is the wrist?" she replied, already turning to her stove.

He glanced down at his hand. "Still stiff."

She came to him and slid his arm from the sling. Her touch was gentle, nonetheless it rocked him to his core.

"It's mending," he muttered, withdrawing abruptly from her touch. A moment of strained silence passed.

She looked to Jacque. "I'll do the milking again, but I could use this young man to collect the eggs this morning and then scatter chicken feed. Why doesn't thee go rest in the shade, Mr. Merriday? Rest will make the wrist heal quicker."

And then what? he asked silently. This is what happened when a man stayed in one place too long and got comfortable. He pulled back mentally from this cozy woman.

Jacque accepted the basket she handed him and headed out for the chicken coop and yard to look for eggs. Hens could be foolish and lay eggs outside, too.

Brennan put on his hat and followed the boy into the summer day. He sat on the grass under a shade tree, watching the boy gather eggs. The sun was rising and the heat was, too. His eyelids felt heavy and sleep would keep him from thinking thoughts of Miss Rachel he had no right to think.

"Mr. Merriday!" Miss Rachel's voice cut through Brennan's morning nap.

He jolted awake and bumped the back of his head against the rough tree trunk and rubbed it. "Miss?"

"Where is Jacque?"

Blinking at the bright sun beyond the shade, Brennan scanned the clearing. "I musta fell asleep."

"Thee looked exhausted at breakfast. Healing takes energy, too."

And last night I didn't sleep worth a Confederate dollar. He got up quicker than he should have and jiggled his wrist again. He clamped his lips together to keep in an exclamation of pain and refused to look at her. "When did you see him last?"

"He brought in the egg basket full. Then I gave him the feed to scatter for the chickens. I'm about to make lunch so I came out and I've looked all over the clearing and haven't been able to find him."

Brennan stared at her. Was this just kid folly or had the boy run off? In either case, he couldn't think what to do.

Miss Rachel looked skyward. "He might have gone looking for someone to play with."

"I'll go into town and look for him," Brennan said.

She frowned at him and didn't move, just tapped her cheek with one finger.

For some reason this irritated him. "Do ya'll want the boy back or not?"

She looked at him, chin down, almost frowning, that finger still tapping.

He read her look as her repeating his question back at him—did he want the boy? He had a strong urge to yell in frustration.

"Perhaps I'll go into town—" she began.

"I'll go. He's my…responsibility." With that Brennan turned and headed down the trail to town. His insides bubbled like a pot of grits. Whether Jacque was his blood or not, he couldn't just let the boy run into trouble.

Rachel watched him go, holding herself back from giving advice or tagging along. Mr. Merriday would have to come to terms with this child himself. Still, as she walked inside to start her next chore, she fretted and couldn't think of anything else but Mr. Merriday and Jacque.

In a few minutes a voice came through the open door. "Miss Rachel?"

Rachel moved to peer outside. The storekeeper's teenage daughter stood there. "Come in," Rachel said, trying to sound sincerely welcoming.

"I'm Amanda Ashford, Miss Rachel," the girl re-minded her.

"Yes, hello, Amanda," Rachel said, hoping the girl would come to the point of her visit. She'd decided to work on her sewing. No use making lunch till Brennan came back with the boy.

"My pa sent me to tell you a boat has come in and people are asking for the sweets lady."

"I didn't hear a whistle."

The girl shrugged. "The boat is stopping long enough for you to come. They are delivering a shipment to my father's store."

Rachel didn't answer with words. She dropped her sewing and turned to the kitchen and began wrapping the fresh-cut caramel squares in wax paper.

"I'll help."

"Wash thy hands first," Rachel said out of habit.

Soon Amanda stood beside her and without asking for instructions, she began to mimic Rachel, rolling the caramel into small squares of wax paper and then twisting the ends.

Soon they filled a basket and headed out the door, striding briskly to town. "I overslept so I don't have any rolls ready," Rachel admitted.

Amanda fiddled with her apron pocket, looking as if she had something to say.

Rachel asked finally, "Is there something I can help thee with, Amanda?"

"I heard about how good your baked goods and can-dies are."

"Yes," Rachel prompted.

Amanda glanced up. "Would you teach me how to make some?"

Rachel hesitated. Mrs. Ashford might take her

daughter coming to Rachel as an insult. "Does thy mother know thee has come to ask me this?"

"No." Amanda looked down at her feet.

So Amanda had the same worry about her mother's reaction. Fortunately, they had reached town and she was able to sidestep the issue. Ahead boatmen unloaded sacks and boxes at the side door of the General Store. Mr. Ashford stood over them with a ledger where he was making notes. And milling in front of the store was what appeared to be a group of passengers.

"This is Miss Rachel!" Amanda called out. "She has fresh caramels for sale!"

The passengers met them in the street in front of the store. "Is your stuff as good as we've heard?" one sour-looking woman asked.

Rachel smiled. "Thee will have to find out. A penny a piece."

A man held out a coin. "A nickel's worth please, miss."

Rachel slipped the coin into her pocket and then handed the man the caramels.

He unwrapped one immediately and popped it into his mouth. He moaned a sound of pleasure. "It's still warm in the center."

At this, everyone was pressing coins on her. Without being asked, Amanda began collecting the money and Rachel doled out the candy. The basket emptied completely within minutes.

The people moved away and she glanced at Amanda. "I thank thee. It is obvious thee is the daughter of a storekeeper."

Amanda blushed with pleasure. In a low voice, she asked, "Will you think about teaching me to bake? I want to be a really good baker."

Rachel thought of how the girl's know-it-all mother would respond to clandestine lessons. But of course, she couldn't say that. "I will give it thought." She smiled her thanks again and then looked around.

Now that the rush was over, her concern over Jacque returned. "I'm looking for Mr. Merriday and Jacque."

"I saw Jacque and Johann go toward the schoolyard."

"Johann?"

"Johann Lang. He's Gunther Lang's nephew."

"Oh." Rachel recognized the family mentioned. "I wonder if Mr. Merriday found Jacque there."

"Did the boy run away?" Amanda asked, sounding shocked and a little interested, reminding Rachel of her mother.

Trying to protect Brennan and Jacque from gossip, Rachel chuckled. "Most likely Jacque did his chores and then decided he deserved some fun." She waved to Amanda and then set off toward the schoolyard. She should have headed home, but couldn't bring herself to turn around. She wanted to see if this simple solution was correct.

Before she reached the edge of town, she heard Jacque's voice. "Let me go!"

"You're going home to apologize to Miss Rachel for runnin' off like that. You finish a chore and then you ask if the lady needs anything more before you run off to find fun." Appearing on the trail south of town, Brennan gripped the boy by the upper arm and was tugging him away from the direction of the schoolyard.

"I don't have to do what you tell me! You're not my pa!"

Rachel froze in place. This was not something she wanted aired on the main street of town.

She hurried forward to the two. "Jacque, we were

looking for you! It's time we go home for some lunch."
She formed a completely false smile with her lips.

Both males glared at her. Brennan's face was beet-
red. Jacque's face defined the term *stormy*.

"Well, come along," she prompted and waved them
forward.

The two didn't budge.

She tried to come up with a way to get them moving
toward home. People were staring. She glanced down
and saw that one caramel had been overlooked even by
her. She held it up. "I have a caramel for a boy to eat
after lunch," she coaxed.

Jacque's sweet tooth won the day. He hurried forward
and Brennan followed. She sighed with relief as she led
the two through town feeling a bit like the Pied Piper.

Jacque's words—*I don't have to do what you tell me!
You're not my pa!*—echoed in her mind.

I don't have to do what you tell me! You're not my pa!
rang in Brennan's mind. Was it the truth or just a retort?
He doubted the child even knew the truth.

The three of them sat at Miss Rachel's table, eating
a generous lunch of canned beef sandwiches on thick,
delicious bread. At first, he didn't even taste what he
was eating, but then he realized the sandwich had been
made with the best spicy mustard he'd ever tried. Finally this came to the surface of his mind. "Did you
make this mustard?"

"Yes, I brought one jar with me. We need to find if
there's any wild mustard growing nearby so I can make
more. In fact, you and Jacque might go looking for some
today. There is a meadow north of town, I've heard."

Was there anything good to eat this woman couldn't
make? He realized again that he respected Miss Rachel

Woolsey, not just for her considerable cooking talent but for herself. She was a fine woman.

As she explained to Jacque what a wild mustard plant looked like, he found himself studying her face. Her gray eyes opened wide to the world. He found a small mole by her right ear he hadn't noticed before and a few tiny golden freckles that had popped up on her nose.

"Mr. Merriday, I think we'll all rest a bit till the sun lowers. The heat today is too high for much work. It's not healthy."

"What do I have to do then?" the boy asked, still sounding disgruntled.

"Rest in the shade. That is my plan."

Jacque looked as if he might protest but then he just shrugged. He rose.

"Jacque, you should ask to be excused before you leave the table," Brennan ordered.

Jacque glared at the reminder. "Miss Rachel, will you excuse me?"

"Thee may leave the table and find a tree to rest under." She rose and stacked the few dishes and carried them outside to wash.

Brennan felt bad he wasn't able to carry them for her. He lingered beside her, unable to leave. Somehow being near Miss Rachel made life feel easier. While he felt torn up inside, she possessed a deep peace. It drew him.

She glanced up from the washbasin. "Thee is troubled?" Her voice was a whisper.

He nodded, his tongue like a board.

"I do not think there is any way we can know for certain that this child is thy blood. Thee must make the decision to accept him or not." She said the words plainly, gently, but uncompromisingly.

He wanted to look away from her, knew he should

but found he couldn't. He nodded. "I'm going to go sit in the shade."

"I will finish this and do likewise. I thought that Wisconsin would be cooler in the summer than Pennsylvania."

He shrugged. "Feels 'most like home to me." The bitter thoughts of home pushed him away from her. He found the tree he'd patronized lately and settled under it, resting against the trunk. The dried grass crunched under him, reminding him of the rainless summer.

Jacque had chosen a tree near the springhouse and looked to be playing with twigs and pebbles as if fighting a play battle.

Brennan closed his eyes. He didn't want to think but the ideas from the past days swirled in his head. What was he to believe? And what was he to do about it? And how could he stop himself from drawing closer to Miss Rachel? She didn't need him or deserve his troubles.

Chapter Seven

After a late supper Brennan walked Jacque back to town to get the boy to bed. Jaqcue had washed up in the creek and was already rubbing his eyes and dragging his feet. Brennan's midsection still roiled with confusion and his mind was a tornado of conflicting thoughts. Was Miss Rachel right? Would he just have to accept the child as his? Was there no way to find out the truth about this young'un?

They found the forge empty. With relief Brennan sent Jacque up the ladder with only a wave of his good arm. Then tired but restless, he went outside to gaze at the wide river, hoping for some easing of his turmoil. The Mississippi was his old friend. He'd fished and swam in it as a boy. In the end it had saved his life that awful day in '61.

Forcing out the past and his own confusion, he concentrated on the blue water, now shadowed by the trees on the bank, the eddies swirling near the shore around rocks and driftwood—mesmerizing. A sandbar stretched in a long oval near the middle, and gulls hopped there, eating insects.

Still worry pecked its way in. If it weren't for his

wrist and the boy, he'd leave town tonight and head north on foot if he had to. Brennan paced back and forth, telling himself he could not leave, not now, not without a word to Miss Rachel.

The faint sound of a female laugh lifted Brennan from his thoughts. He looked for the source of this interruption and glimpsed Levi and Miss Posey Brown farther up the shore, walking together. At the romantic sight, a sour taste rolled over Brennan's tongue, his agitation leaping higher, sharper.

So Levi was making up to Miss Posey. Brennan watched them; the way they moved, careful not to brush against each other, her head bent coyly. He could almost imagine their conversation, a lot of words with not much said. Just words to be spoken so they could stay together because being near one another was what it was all about.

Miss Rachel came to mind and Brennan thrust her image away, again facing the river, focusing on its steady current. His mounting tension wouldn't be denied. He began to scratch his arm at the edge of his sling. He began pacing again.

Gripping his arm so he wouldn't scratch it anymore, Brennan noted that the couple said their goodbyes at the riverside, not near the store; Levi had not yet reached the point of launching the formal courtship. That would officially start when Levi approached Mr. Ashford and asked permission to court Posey. Bitterness from the past came up, more of the sour taste on Brennan's tongue.

Brennan kept walking, gripping his arm, trying to release the tension goading him.

As Levi neared the forge with a silly grin on his face, Brennan felt one hundred, maybe two hundred years old. No part of him wanted to talk to Levi, a man who didn't realize he was like a burly lamb being led to the slaughter. Brennan swung away to go in.

Levi hailed him.

With a supreme effort, Brennan turned back, trying to ease his edgy mood with a deep breath. "Levi."

Levi grinned, obviously bursting to tell Brennan about walking with Miss Posey.

"I seen you two," Brennan said out of friendship. That surprised Brennan. He hadn't known anyone he considered a friend since the war ended and his militia company had broken up to head home. He halted.

Levi's silly grin broadened. "I saw her walking down the bank and I decided to take a chance and greet her."

Brennan reckoned the girl had probably come out for just that purpose. He knew now that men thought *they* did the courting. *Ha.* "How did it go?" Brennan forced himself to ask.

Levi sank onto his chair. "She's kind of shy and I'm not much of a talker. But she told me about her home in Tennessee and how sad she was that they couldn't go back. I guess somebody seized their place during the war since they considered her father, who fought for the Union, a traitor to the South."

With a pang Brennan wondered who had taken over his own father's land. Had Jean Pierre told the truth? Was everyone in his and Lorena's families truly dead or scattered? He shoved his good hand through his hair. "That's too bad," Brennan said, manfully keeping up his part of the conversation.

"She sure is pretty and she has a sweet way of speaking."

Brennan thought a nod of the head would suffice for this. Then he felt an easing in his chest. Somehow speaking to this man with an uncomplicated life helped Brennan. He looked at Levi, who was staring at his sling.

"How's the wrist?" Levi asked.

Brennan had been so tangled in his inner worries, he'd forgotten all about the sprain. He moved the wrist. "Better. It's healing."

"Good. Where's the boy?"

"In the loft."

Levi looked at him, his mouth shut holding back something.

"Go ahead and spit it out," Brennan grumbled, afraid to trust the way his stress was leaking out. He stooped down, pressing his back against the wall, breathing almost normally.

"Maybe I'm talking out of turn," Levi said with reluctance, "but I was thinking. Where the boy was born, would anybody have kept a record of his birth?"

Brennan stopped just short of rebuffing this suggestion—when it occurred to him that Lorena's family had all births and deaths recorded in the local parish church records. He knew the names of the church and the priest. "Why didn't I think of that?" He couldn't hide the rise in his voice.

Levi looked surprised but pleased that his suggestion had found favor. "You think it'll work?"

"I do." The momentary lift evaporated and fatigue from the heat and worry nearly pushed him over onto the ground. "I'm goin' up to bed." *While I can.*

"'Night."

Brennan started up the ladder and then paused. He heard something—a whimpering sound. Was some small animal caught in a trap nearby? Then he realized it was the boy in the loft, crying. The sound caught him around the chest like a chain. Brennan looked at their situation from the boy's point of view: abandoned by family and stuck with a man he thought a coward. *Poor kid.*

Finding out one way or the other what was really true would help both him and the boy. If he found out the boy was his, he'd deal with that. If the boy wasn't his, he'd make sure the boy got a good home. Maybe with Miss Rachel?

Very, very early the next morning, Rachel stared at Amanda and Posey. The rooster had barely announced dawn. Rachel had just finished dressing and needed to start a batch of ladyfingers, a light little cake for which she'd had a few requests. And she wanted this all done before Mr. Merriday came.

She needed company now like she needed salt in her sugar.

With a fixed, intent gaze, she silently prompted the storekeeper's daughter to state her reason for coming at such an early hour. Emotion rolled inside her as she thought of Brennan and Jacque and what they'd gone through in the past few days. Would Brennan appear this morning or not?

Amanda finally broached the reason for their untimely arrival. "I was thinking we could help you this morning fixing your baked goods."

Posey stepped forward. "Miss Rachel, I come to ask if you'd teach me to bake, too."

Rachel gazed at the two hopeful faces. Though Rachel did not think Mrs. Ashford would like this, she couldn't turn the girls away.

She waved them toward the outside basin. "Always wash hands before baking."

Soon the two girls hurried inside. Each donned an apron she'd brought along.

Rachel glanced at the wall clock her grandfather had given her when she turned sixteen. She must get this batch done before the heat of the day made whipping the egg whites impossible. She showed them how to use a wire whisk and all three began beating egg whites into white glossy peaks.

Brennan and Jacque appeared at the door, earlier than expected, of course.

Immediately Rachel noted the man had something on his mind. She had come to know his moods, a dangerous realization.

If the girls hadn't been here, she'd have tried to find out immediately what concerned him. "I'm sorry, Mr. Merriday. Breakfast will be a little late—"

"Not to worry, Miss Rachel," Brennan replied. "The boy will milk the cow and get busy with chores. Call us when yer ready."

"Please check the outdoor oven and see if it's getting hot."

Brennan nodded and headed toward the back.

The egg whites whipped up pretty well though sweat beaded on the white mounds. "I must move quickly. Just watch." Rachel swiftly folded the egg whites into the dry ingredients and then loaded a pastry cloth and began piping the batter into "fingers" on baking sheets. Soon the batter had been piped onto all six pans. "Please pick up two sheets each and follow me."

The three of them marched out the back door, through the covered walkway to the outdoor oven. There the three of them shoved the sheets inside and Rachel secured the door.

Then the brusque voice of Mrs. Ashford sounded.

"Where is Miss Rachel? I'm looking for my daughter and her cousin."

Rachel's stomach suffered a sudden jolt.

"Oh, no," Amanda breathed, sending Miss Rachel an imploring glance. "How did she find out where we went?"

Rachel waved for the girls to follow her and she marched back inside and began clearing away the mess from the table. If Mrs. Ashford wanted to talk to her, she would have to find her.

"Miss Woolsey," Mrs. Ashford said, standing in the doorway, "I'm looking— Oh, there you are, girls. What possessed you to come here before breakfast? I didn't know where you'd gone, but the blacksmith saw you walking this way."

Rachel couldn't come up with anything but the truth. Social prevarication was not her strong point.

"We took a walk," Posey offered.

"And then we realized Miss Woolsey was probably baking—" Amanda continued.

"So we asked if we could help," Posey finished. "She let us help her whisk egg whites for ladyfingers."

Rachel could see the woman's mind working—Mrs. Ashford eyed the aprons the girls were wearing. They were evidence of planning to come here. And the hour was much too early for a social call, as the girls well knew. Well, this was not Rachel's doing.

"I'll bring some to the store in thanks for their help," Rachel said, hoping the three would leave—now. "I must prepare breakfast and make sure I don't let my ladyfingers burn." With that, she swept the bowls and implements from the table and set them outside in the washbasin for later.

What could Mrs. Ashford do but leave? Amanda and

Posey went with her and Rachel sighed in silent relief. Dustup on her doorstep averted. She noticed that on her way through the yard, Posey said something to Brennan and he didn't look pleased. What had the girl said?

Leaving behind speculation, she cut strips of salt pork and laid them in the frying pan. Their fragrance drew in the two males. "Mr. Merriday, will thee watch these? I must go and fetch my ladyfingers before they become too brown." She hurried outside, even surer the man had something on his mind.

She returned, slid the slender little cakes onto cooling racks. Mr. Merriday brought the other trays back in two quick trips. She then finished making breakfast and asked them to be seated.

Brennan's mouth watered as he watched Miss Rachel slide four slices of crisp pork onto his plate and then add three soft fried eggs and two slices of golden toast. The boy got a smaller version for his breakfast. Brennan heard the tiny moan of pleasure the boy made. Brennan knew just how he felt. Miss Rachel had a way of making even simple food more than regular tasty. Sitting down, Miss Rachel said grace and they began to eat.

As his hunger became satisfied, Brennan went back to ruminating about the request he must broach to this lady today. He'd have to get the boy busy doing something while he talked to her alone.

He didn't want to ask her, but his command of written English was minimal. There had been no town schools anywhere near him in Mississippi. His aunt Martha had taught him his letters and numbers and how to print them and do simple arithmetic—enough for a Mississippi farm boy.

Jacque finished his meal first and at Miss Rachel's silent prompt, wiped his face with his napkin.

"Jacque, you can go outside and start looking for eggs," Brennan instructed.

Miss Rachel raised her eyebrows but said nothing.

"Thank you, Miss Rachel, for the good eats," the boy said.

Brennan felt a tingle of pride at this show of unprompted good manners.

"Thank thee, Jacque."

The boy left, obediently carrying his plate and mug out to the basin.

"So, Mr. Merriday, while thee tells me what is on thy mind, I will take a look at that wrist."

She was a knowing woman all right. But he didn't want her fussing over him. She did anyway.

She sat on the bench beside him. She drew his arm from the sling and held his hand in both of hers.

He tried to ignore the reaction he had to her gentle but sure touch. *It's just because nobody ever touches me,* he told himself. *Especially not a pretty woman with soft hands.*

She probed carefully with both thumbs over and around his wrist, sweet agony. The scent of bacon still hung in the air but he also detected just a breath of some floral scent. Her head bent over his wrist, her soft hair grazed his nose.

"So you done fiddlin' yet?" he asked, goaded.

"The wrist appears to be healing well," she announced. "But thee hasn't told me what is on thy mind."

The time had come. He gathered his gumption. "I need," he began, "to get a letter to the parish priest in my…wife's hometown in Louisiana. The priest would have a record of the boy's birth and parentage." The words had come out in a rush and he burned with embarrassment.

She gazed at him steadily in that way of hers. "I see, and with your wrist compromised it's difficult to write."

Did she believe that or was she offering him a plausible excuse for his not writing the letter? Miss Rachel was thoughtful that way.

"I'd appreciate it," he said, not saying yea or nay about his reason for asking.

"What is the name of the priest, church and town?" she asked briskly. She rose and reached for a pad of paper and pencil she kept on a shelf. She jotted down his answers. "I'll write it today and send it off. This is an excellent idea. The truth shall set us free."

He'd heard that but didn't really agree. He'd told the truth once and had nearly died for it. He stood up, galvanized. "I'm going to look for downed branches and the like with the boy. Good kindling for the winter."

She hopped up too as he'd moved the bench. "Excellent. I must be busy with my ladyfingers."

They rarely stood so close to each other and the air between them appeared to waver, an odd feeling of connection. He tried to move but was captured by the sight of little beads of perspiration on her upper lip, which drew his gaze down to her mouth as pretty as a rosebud, soft pink and…

Abruptly, he nodded in assent and headed straight for the door. Outside he pulled on his hat and scanned the yard. The boy was carrying a full basket of eggs toward the cabin. "Let's go. We'll gather some downed wood."

He walked rapidly toward the road and headed north of town, Jacque soon at his heels. Again he wished he'd been able to leave town when he wanted to. Without the boy here, last night he would have bolted for sure.

Staying around a special woman like Miss Rachel was giving him foolish ideas.

And now he'd just asked Miss Rachel to contact Lorena's home place. This could stir up the past. Already his stomach wanted to reject his breakfast. He forced down the sensation.

He had to know if the boy was his and the boy needed to know it, too. Another worry niggled. Did Miss Rachel think him completely illiterate? Shame burned his cheeks and he lengthened his strides, hurrying the boy.

A week later Miss Rachel and Jacque stood outside, she washing and he drying the breakfast dishes.

She found herself chewing her bottom lip. This morning, First Day or what most called Sunday, she would as usual attend worship at the schoolhouse and this afternoon go to the church picnic, a social occasion where she could get to know more of her neighbors. She was trying to come up with a way to persuade Jacque and Brennan to come, too. Her earlier invitation had been met with silence. She glanced over her shoulder to where he lounged against a tree in its shade.

Brennan cleared his throat. "Jacque, I decided you're going to church and the picnic with Miss Rachel like she asked. You mind your manners. You'll like it. I remember church picnics. Lots of good food and kids playin' tag."

Jacque didn't reply, merely stared at him, looking confused.

Rachel was just as surprised. She hadn't expected him to allow Jacque to go. "Perhaps thee would like to come, too?" she asked, her heart suddenly speeding up.

"My wrist's healed and I got plans for today," he said,

rising. "I'm going to take a walk. Maybe fish a bit." Then he turned and headed up the road away from town.

Unhappy with this response, Rachel handed Jacque the final spoon to dry. She looked down at him. He looked more than usually cheerful and she guessed it was because he wore his new clothing and she'd cut his hair. Worry nipped her. The scene on the main street, when that awful man had so rudely abandoned him, and Jacque's thick Southern accent, would not be ignored.

After Jacque handed her the dried spoon and emptied the dishwater onto her flowers, Rachel and he carried the clean dishware inside and set the stack on the shelf and covered it with a clean cloth.

Rachel rested a hand on Jacque's shoulder. "We will have a good day," she said more to bolster her confidence than his. "I'll get my Bible." Then the two of them walked down the track toward town.

She sighed. "Let me be frank, Jacque. Thee knows how children—and grownups, too, unfortunately—can be to strangers."

Jacque looked up and frowned.

"I remember how children always pick on anyone new or different."

Jacque shrugged. "I can take care of myself."

"Thee intends to fight anybody who is rude?" she asked without rancor.

Jacque repeated the shrug.

"I understand thee might have to…defend thyself, *but*—" to emphasize her point, she gripped his shoulder "—don't start the fight." She had been raised to turn the other cheek, but even Quaker boys fought with each other. "Does thee understand me, Jacque?"

He considered this. "I can fight back, but I better not take the first swing?"

"Well stated." The schoolhouse lay on the other side of the village. As they walked through town, Levi came out of his shop and joined them. Rachel nodded in reply to his greeting and noted that Levi looked as if he'd taken special care with his appearance today. She wondered why. All the while, the fact that Mr. Merriday had not come also prodded her, drawing down her mood. Why had she even hoped he'd come?

At the door of the log schoolhouse community church, Noah waited to greet them. Rachel said, "Jacque, this is my cousin Noah Whitmore. Noah, this is Jacque."

"Hello, sir," Jacque said, but refused to look into Noah's face.

Noah gripped the boy's shoulder. "You are welcome here, Jacque."

This caused the boy to glance up at the man. Then the press of others arriving moved the two of them into the church.

Just inside the door sat Old Saul in his wheelchair. Rachel had met him again in town with Noah, who obviously held the older man in high regard and affection. So she stopped to greet him and introduce Jacque.

The older man took the boy's hand gently. "Jacque, we are happy to have you with us. Just remember God never forgets us even when it feels like He has."

"Yes, sir," Jacque said obediently.

Old Saul smiled and nodded. "You'll understand that when you're older, I pray."

More people wanted to greet Old Saul. Rachel headed straight for her cousin's wife near the front. Jacque sat beside her, craning his neck and swinging his legs.

She noted the attention, some surreptitious and some

blatant, that Jacque was receiving. She hoped no one would ruin the day with rudeness. She would make certain to steer clear of certain people, most notably Mrs. Ashford.

Noah went to the front. The service went as usual, hymn singing, prayers for the nation, state and town, and one of Noah's bracing sermons on loving one's neighbor. Rachel hoped it would actually penetrate a few stubborn hearts here. Loving others always brought blessings.

Soon everyone was outside in the blazing summer sun. Sons helped fathers set up tables in the shade of trees and daughters helped mothers set out tablecloths and bowls of food. Families laid down blankets for the children to sit on while the adults sat at the tables.

Rachel enjoyed the festive excitement but Jacque stayed close by her side, which saddened her a little. He should be off making friends, but his situation and history worked against him. Evidently he didn't even trust Johann to be his friend in the presence of others. When Mr. Merriday had ordered Jacque to come with her, had he given this any thought? Probably not.

Then a younger boy with dark hair and eyes approached them. "Hello, Miss Rachel."

She smiled. Everyone had adopted Brennan's form of address. She liked it. She'd seen this boy before. "Thee is Gunther Lang's nephew?"

"Yes, miss. I'm Johann." He turned to Jacque. "You want to play tag with us, Jacque?"

Jacque looked up at her, asking silent permission.

She nodded with a smile.

Jacque's face lightened. The two boys hurried off together.

Ellen Lang, Johann's new aunt and a former schoolteacher in Pepin, had come behind Johann. She was a tall, elegant woman in a lovely dress of blue cambric and a fashionable hat. "I was happy to see you brought Jacque with you. He needs to start making friends."

"It was kind of Johann to invite him."

"Johann understands being the new boy in town." Then Noah called everyone to quiet for grace. A few solemn moments, then a loud Amen and the buzz of happy voices, young and old.

Rachel smiled. Memories of childhood meetinghouse gatherings came back to her with a pang of homesickness. Then she noted how Levi had managed to get himself seated at the table where Posey Brown sat with her imposing grandmother and the Ashfords. *Brave man.*

Rachel found herself at the next table, sitting with Noah, Sunny and their children and other neighbors, Martin and Ophelia Steward and Nan and Gordy Osbourne. Rachel contented herself with listening to the chatter though her eyes kept straying to the edges of the clearing, hoping to see Mr. Merriday appear.

From the corner of her eye, she also kept track of Levi's shy pursuit of Posey and of Jacque's behavior. He had been invited to sit with Johann at another table. She had never seen the boy happier than when he'd run over to ask her permission to sit with the Langs. *God bless Johann.*

Posey kept looking over at Jacque and Rachel wondered why.

After everyone had eaten their fill, they rose and began putting food away in the shade or in the springhouse. Posey passed by Rachel. "Mr. Merriday didn't come?"

Rachel merely shrugged, wondering why the girl asked.

"That day we helped you whip up ladyfingers,

I asked him if he ever was in Kentucky. He said he doubted we'd met before. But his name just sounds so familiar. I wish I could place it."

Rachel didn't know what to say and then Mrs. Ashford called Posey.

The quiet, friendly afternoon passed pleasantly. Rachel sat on a blanket near Sunny, whose two children were napping in the shade. Rachel noticed that Levi and Posey were nowhere to be seen. The young woman's grandmother Almeria sat dozing against a tree and Mrs. Ashford was talking to another woman. Rachel told Sunny to lie down and nap, too. She'd watch the babies.

Rachel relaxed against the tree behind her, watching the sun and shadows play over the dry grass of the schoolyard, hearing the clink of the horseshoes and the voices of children playing as quietly as they could manage since it was the Sabbath.

Breathing in the heavy August air, she wished Mr. Merriday had come and was here tossing horseshoes with the other men. She now knew that something bad must have happened to separate him from his wife, but what? Why had Jean Pierre called him a coward?

Then a strident woman's voice snapped Rachel completely alert again. "You should show more sense."

Rachel, along with almost everyone else, turned to see a sad-looking Posey being reluctantly led by the hand back to the clearing.

Red-faced, Levi followed a few paces behind.

"But Grandmother—" Posey started.

"Do not bother to argue. I will not change my mind."

Posey sent Levi an agonized glance over her shoulder. Her grandmother kept pulling Posey through the gathering toward town. Levi turned away into the trees, evidently aware of how everyone was staring.

Rachel was embarrassed for Levi and the girl and as she glanced around she saw she wasn't the only one. Rachel's gaze met Sunny's.

Sunny shook her head, frowning. "Levi is well liked in town and Almeria is a newcomer," she whispered. "Why make such a ruckus in front of everyone? This will not be appreciated."

Rachel sighed in agreement.

And then she heard raised voices. She glimpsed the corner of the schoolhouse where Jacque was taking a swing at a bigger boy. She leaped up and ran toward the boys.

When she reached them, she halted. The two boys were fully engaged. Swinging punches. Yelling. At the sight of her, the other children, except for Johann, scattered. Noah hurried to catch up with her.

Before she could even speak, Noah grabbed Jacque by the collar, dragging him away from the fight.

Another man yanked the bigger boy away, saying that the child should have known better than to pick a fight on Sunday in front of the whole town.

Rachel thought the man had missed the point.

"It is not Jacque's fault," Johann insisted. "Clayton always starts fights. He called Jacque's father a…a name."

"That was very wrong," Noah cut in, "but fighting never solves anything."

Jacque looked up resentfully.

"That takes time to learn," Noah said. "And some never do. Jacque, why don't you wash your hands and face at the pump?"

"Come on," Johann encouraged Jacque. "I'll go with you."

Jacque allowed Johann to lead him toward the pump

at the other end of the school building. Clayton and his father stalked away in the opposite direction.

Rachel looked to her cousin. "Thank thee, Noah." She didn't know what else to say.

Noah touched her arm. "Sunny and I pray faithfully for you, Mr. Merriday and Jacque."

For some reason, this comment brought moisture to her eyes. She pressed her hand over his and then turned, noticing Mr. Merriday at the edge of the clearing.

Rachel nearly called out his name, but stopped herself. She didn't want to bring attention to him. They'd both had enough of that. How could she smooth matters for Jacque after the fight? She couldn't of course. But she could prompt them to leave.

She lifted a hand and motioned toward the basket she'd brought, still resting beside Sunny in the shade. He obviously saw her silent request and moved to get it, sliding through the others also gathering up their goods. A few stopped to look at him; a few shook their heads in silent judgment, raising her hackles.

Jacque returned to her side, looking downhearted. A bruise under his left eye was just beginning to show. "Johann has to go home now."

"Perhaps when his family comes to town, he will be able to drop in for a visit."

Jacque hid his reaction to this, but pointedly did not look toward his father...toward Mr. Merriday, even when he joined them walking home.

Rachel naturally wanted to ask Jacque what the other boy had called his father, but she did not give in to curiosity. Still, she did not miss the glares Jacque was sending Mr. Merriday. Whatever Brennan Merriday had done to cut himself off from his family was still bearing bitter fruit. The strife between the two had not abated in the least.

And why had Brennan come at the end of the picnic? "I didn't expect to see you till supper," she murmured.

"Fishin' was a bust." Then he glanced toward the saloon, but like everything else, it was closed on Sundays. She couldn't believe plain boredom brought him to the schoolyard.

Rachel drew in a deep breath as she walked between two unhappy males. She ached to help both of them, but how? And was it her place? Within her power?

Chapter Eight

Back at Levi's that evening, Brennan sent the boy up to bed. Thoroughly disgruntled from a lonely and tedious and empty day, he was filled with thoughts of Miss Rachel, thoughts he shouldn't be having.

Grumpily he sank down beside Levi outside to watch the river flow by and the setting red sun dip into the blue water. Gulls swooped and screeched, tightening Brennan's nerves. The grass under Brennan had been seared by the sun. A green line of watered grass edged the river. Levi sat in a chair propped back against the wall. The silence was not their usual companionable one.

Finally Brennan hazarded a glance at his friend, whose glum face shouted a dark mood. Once again his regard for this big man prompted his sympathy. "You don't look very happy," he said quietly.

Levi humphed in a disgruntled way.

"How was the picnic?" Brennan didn't want to pry but he couldn't leave it for some reason.

"That grandmother of hers caught us…talking by a tree."

Many responses popped into Brennan's mind, but he

chose his words with care. "What's wrong with a man talking to a girl?"

"I don't know. The way she acted you'd-a thought I was a convicted felon or something. We were *just talking.* Posey… Miss Brown has a way of making conversation easy."

The blacksmith had it bad all right. Old hurt and resentment gathered in Brennan's throat, but he refused to voice it. "She seems like a sweet young gal. But you got to look at the big picture. Maybe you're better off without her. I mean, if you married Miss Brown, the old tartar might come live with you."

Levi thumped his chair forward, full on the ground.

Brennan looked up, startled.

"If the old tartar doesn't even want me talking to her, how am I going to get to court her, much less marry her?"

With that Levi left him, stalking down the riverbank.

Brennan sighed, happy that he wasn't interested in courting. Then Miss Rachel's face came to mind yet again. She'd looked worried on the way home today and hadn't said much at supper. Usually nothing much rattled her. He recalled her singing with that robin not long ago. She was too good for this town. Irritation gathered in his middle. Who had upset Miss Rachel? And what could he do about it?

At the cock's crow, Rachel woke the next morning not her usual cheerful self. She hadn't slept soundly as usual. And upon waking, she instantly began to worry about Jacque and what had been said to hurt him yesterday.

And on top of this, today already felt as if it would be a scorcher. Still she had a business to run. She quickly dressed and started a fire in her outdoor oven—grateful it was away from her dwelling. Then she mixed up a double batch of cinnamon muffin batter. Soon she was filling muffin tins.

"Good morning, Miss Rachel."

Rachel turned to find Posey at her open door yet again, looking unhappy. "Good morning," Rachel said curtly and discouragingly. "I don't have time to talk. I'm about to put these muffin tins into the oven."

"Can I help?" Posey asked, looking ready to cry.

"No, I'm sorry." Rachel softened her voice, but she couldn't help this young girl and was not about to interfere. "I'm trying to get these into the oven before Mr. Merriday and Jacque arrive for their breakfast. Pardon me."

She turned and carried two muffin tins outside. When she reached the oven, she turned to find that Posey had carried out two tins also. Irritation pinched her. *Please go home, Posey.* "My thanks," Rachel said in a tight tone.

The girl slid the tins into the oven. Waves of heat flooded against their faces. Then Posey trailed her back inside, wiping her eyes with a lace hanky.

Rachel swallowed her pity for the girl. Butting into other people's affairs was not her chosen course.

"Will you be making candy later?" Posey asked. The girl sounded…lachrymose, a word Rachel had heard but never used. Then she recalled when Posey's grandmother had caused a scene yesterday. *Poor girl.*

Rachel drew in a deep breath, reminding herself she had no business prying into what wasn't her affair. "No, I think it's going to be much too hot today to make anything more." She glanced at the wall clock so she would time the muffins correctly and nearly shooed the girl from her kitchen. "I must start breakfast."

The girl nodded, looking disappointed, downhearted.

It tugged at Rachel's heart and she relented. "I may be making candy early tomorrow morning," Rachel said, unable to help herself. "Perhaps you could come then?"

Posey burst into tears. "You saw what happened yesterday at the picnic, Miss Rachel."

Yes, she had. She'd tried not to comment, get involved. She now failed. "I noted Mr. Comstock's interest in you," she said.

"Mr. Comstock is so…" Posey began and then tears overcame her again. She shook with their power.

Rachel patted Posey's arm. She didn't want to become enmeshed in this girl's difficulties, but she was a stranger here, too. That was probably why the girl had sought out Rachel as a confidant. "What is the problem, Posey?"

"Grandmother says she won't let me marry a man without land. She says a blacksmith's widow is left with a forge and some tools. What good does that do her? If a farmer dies, at least he leaves his wife with land, something that lasts, something of value."

Rachel moved a step closer. She understood instantly why the grandmother would take that stand. Their family had been dispossessed and forced to depend on other family. She didn't know what to say, so she merely murmured some comforting sounds.

Posey continued crying.

Through the open door, Rachel was relieved to see Mr. Merriday and Jacque coming toward her cabin. Or at least she was till she saw their grim expressions. *Oh, dear.*

Posey left then, sniffling. And though Rachel tried to resist it, the girl's mood had affected her. As did the scowls on the two males who would be eating breakfast at her table.

Halfway through breakfast, Rachel finally lost patience. "Isn't my breakfast well prepared? Why so glum this morning?"

Both males looked up from their plates and frowned at her.

In that instant she did catch a likeness between them, the way their brows wrinkled when troubled. Could that be a family trait or just coincidence?

"Jacque, I'm sorry our pleasant Sunday afternoon ended in a fight," she said. "I don't think my cousin scolded thee too harshly."

Jacque slammed down his fork. "That's not what's wrong."

Rachel pulled back in the face of such a hostile answer.

"Keep a civil tongue in your head, boy," Brennan insisted.

"I told you—you ain't my father, but people think you are. They think you fought for the Confederate army. That's why that kid called you a stinkin' Reb. But I know the truth. You're a coward. You didn't fight for the Cause, for the South." With that, the boy leaped from his place and bolted outside.

Mr. Merriday rose, looking ghastly white.

"Perhaps," Rachel said uncertainly, "it would be best to let him cool off."

Brennan sank back down. Several minutes passed before he could speak.

She didn't know what to say so she said nothing.

"How long do you think that letter will take to get to Louisiana?" he asked.

"As little as a week, as long as a month. One never knows."

"And we don't know how long it will take to get an answer." Merriday lifted his mug of coffee. "I wanted to be in Canada before the end of summer."

"Canada?" Somehow the country sounded farther away to Rachel than it really was.

Draining his cup, Mr. Merriday rose. "Yes, I'm sick of the war. And nobody here can forget it." Though he spoke quietly, each word vibrated with deep emotion. "I want to go where nobody fought in it and nobody cares about it."

"But thee fought in it and thee cares about it."

He glared at her. "What's that supposed to mean?"

"Thee can leave America and the war, but can thee take them out of thyself? Both had a part in who thee has become."

"But nobody would keep bringin' the war up to me."

Rachel tried to think of how to explain what she meant to him but couldn't bring up the words. She changed her approach. "If Jacque is thy son, he is a gift, not a penance. And thee is Brennan Merriday, and a good man, a worthy man."

"To you, maybe. Not to anybody else—least of all, this boy. And you don't know what happened between my wife and me…" He bowed his head.

Well, that stopped her. She didn't know and he didn't look like he was going to tell her.

He stood. "You're a good woman, Miss Rachel. But you can't make this world all nice and sweet like one of your cakes. It doesn't work that way. I'll go to Canada. It can't be any worse than here."

"That day when thee fixed my roof," she began hesitantly, but this needed to be addressed, "something happened, something inside thee…"

"I don't want to talk about it." And he left.

She sighed, lifting her coffee mug to her lips. So that's where he planned to go. The only problem with his plan was that he carried the war with him. Anybody could see that. And if the child proved to be his blood, he'd be taking with him a child scarred by the war to Canada, too.

She sipped her coffee though it had gone cold. Running away from problems never solved them. Perhaps someone might say she ran away from her problems in Pennsylvania, too. But they'd be wrong.

Brennan tried to focus on the day's chores. He was milking the cow when he heard the sound of a boat whistle. Not usual this early in the morning, but he finished milking and helped Miss Rachel load her trays of cinnamon muffins and rolled her cart into town.

Jacque shadowed them, but stayed out of reach. The boy's words from breakfast mocked Brennan. His son, or this boy, hated him because he was a coward who hadn't fought for the Cause. If he only knew the truth… But no one here knew the truth and he would never speak it. It was nobody's business.

Dockside, Miss Rachel quickly sold out. Counting the coins from her bucket, she smiled. "I'll have to make some candy in case another boat comes through. I never want to disappoint customers. Product excellence and consistent supply are necessary to success," she recited as if reading from a book.

He grumbled and steered the empty cart for home.

The young gal Posey came running out of the store.

"Mr. Merriday! Mr. Merriday!" she called out, waving a letter.

Instead of slowing so Posey could catch up with them, he picked up his pace. There was nothing she had to say he wanted to hear.

"Be polite," Rachel hissed into his ear. She tugged on his arm, insisting wordlessly that he stop.

He paused, grumbling into her ear, "What now?"

"I knew I'd heard your name before, Mr. Merriday!" Posey exclaimed for all the world to hear.

Brennan steamed as he watched people coming out of stores, stopping to listen to the fool girl. Did she have to choose the main street of town to blab her mouth off? He began to push the cart, hurrying away from her.

"I recalled this morning on the way home that I had read your name in my father's letters while he was in the Union Army. And I found it!" She waved the sheet of stationery again. "You knew my father! You were in the Kentucky Militia with him and fought for the Union! Mr. Merriday, you're not a Confederate at all!"

Brennan did not imagine the upset this pronouncement released. But his inner outcry overwhelmed the noise and sudden commotion around him. He had eyes for only one person—the boy. He glimpsed him through the people who gathered around. The boy looked stunned and then bolted. Apparently he'd known only that Brennan hadn't fought for the South—not that he'd fought for the North.

No! Brennan dropped the cart handles and raced after him, ignoring the people who tried to speak to him. This town was just bad news all around. He'd never been recognized as more than a drifter, a Southerner. He'd kept the truth hidden. Too much to explain. Too much to expose.

He tried to catch the boy but Jacque was fleet of foot and soon disappeared into the trees. Brennan's heart pumped blood and he ran full out. "Jacque! Wait!" And then thinking of the vast forest around them, he shouted, "Jacque, stop! You'll get lost!"

Rachel stood frozen beside the abandoned cart, watching Mr. Merriday and Jacque vanish from sight.

"Why did they run away?" Posey asked, sounding dumbfounded. "This is good news, isn't it?"

Released from her shock, Rachel turned to face the young innocent. "Matters about the war that tore our nation in two are never easy." She picked up the push handles of the cart and started in the direction Mr. Merriday and the boy had run. "Thee of all people should know that."

Posey kept up with her. "But I wanted to read him the letter. Father said—"

Heat went through Rachel in waves as she thought of Mr. Merriday's shock at having his private affairs shouted on Main Street. Rachel lifted a shoulder. "I think thee should stop now. Mr. Merriday is a very private man and just days ago, his son... Jacque was abandoned here in a very public scene. Thee should have gone to him privately." People hearing her words began to drift away as if caught eavesdropping.

Posey blushed. "I'm sorry... I didn't think..." She stopped keeping pace with Rachel. "It's just everybody thinks he was a Confederate, looks down on him and..."

Rachel shook her head and kept walking. The news that Mr. Merriday had not fought for the South surprised her and didn't surprise her.

Something awful had happened to him in his home place, something that had torn him from his family and turned them against him. Posey's revelation could explain what that had been. Had Mr. Merriday been cast out because he didn't believe in secession?

But this eye-opener would make matters even more difficult between the man and his son. Jacque had berated him for being a coward and not fighting for the South. What did he think of his father fighting for the enemy, the North? That was no mystery. His reaction had been clear and swift.

Brennan raced after the boy, frantic. He must explain what had happened, how he'd come to fight for the North. The dark head disappeared into the mass of trees north of town.

Brennan ran on, branches slapping him in the face, grazing his hands. The boy disappeared from sight. Children could get lost in the thick forest and never be found—alive. He ran, though his mind tried to tell him to stop and listen—think.

He stumbled over a tree root and fell hard, flat on his chest. Hitting more tree roots knocked the air from his lungs. For a moment he was breathless. The strength flew out of him and he was weak again. "Jacque!" he tried to cry out over and over. "Jacque!" Then he fell silent, gasping for air and hurting with each gasp.

Finally he listened and heard nothing except his own breathing. Failure closed in around him like an impenetrable smoke, choking him. Would he ever have the chance to explain? And now he knew he wanted this child to be his. Then he heard her voice, not shouting, just saying his name.

"Mr. Merriday," Miss Rachel summoned him. "Mr. Merriday."

At first he didn't reply. Then he dragged himself to

his feet. "Here," he said, suddenly feeling a sharp jab as he said the word. He pressed a hand to a rib, a tender spot he hadn't pinpointed before.

Miss Rachel stepped out from the surrounding trees. "Did thee catch him?"

Do you see him? he snapped silently. Brennan hung his head, hiding his frustration, and rubbed his side.

"Did thee fall?" she asked in so calm a voice.

Her question irritated him. "Of course *I fell*." The outburst cost him another, sharper, deeper jab of pain.

"Thee must have hurt thyself." She approached him and put out her hands to touch his chest.

He grabbed her hands to stop her. Then the need to be near this woman swept away all sense. He folded her in his arms and held her close. Bending his head, he buried his face in the crook of her neck, reveling in the sweet scent of lilac. In this unpredictable and hard and dreadful world, this woman stood in stark contrast—steady and soft and kind. He couldn't push himself away; he held her.

"Brennan," she whispered at last.

The sound of his given name in her gentle voice jerked him back to propriety. He released her and stepped back. "I beg pardon." He couldn't meet her eyes.

"Thee has just experienced an upsetting…incident. Posey should have shown more…discretion. But the milk is spilled and it can't be hidden."

Her now matter-of-fact voice contrasted with her soft voice as it had said his given name. Night and day. He felt like kicking himself. He might have misled this fine lady into thinking he had feelings for her. He didn't have feelings for her, for anyone. "I'm sorry," he mumbled, ignoring a whisper asking why he'd just held her in his arms—if he didn't have affection for her.

"Thee was distressed," she said briskly. "Now let's get back to the road."

"What about the boy?" he asked, not moving.

"Blundering about in the woods will not bring him home," she said in a reasonable tone.

The reasonable tone rasped his tender nerves. The child was his responsibility, not hers. "He could get lost—"

"He is able to climb a tree and when he does, he will see the smoke from a chimney and find his way back. He will come home when he gets hungry enough."

How could she be so calm? The urge to shake her nearly overcame him. Instead he followed her out of the woods to the road to her cabin. The two of them walked home, not speaking. He let her push the cart because his side was paining him. Frustration smoldered within. He'd just got the use of his wrist back and now this?

She rolled the cart near the cabin and then waved him inside. "Please sit at the table."

He did so with ill grace. He wanted to yell at someone, Posey Brown for instance, but he couldn't yell at Miss Rachel.

She gently moved away the hand he had pressed to his side and then even more gently pressed the area. When she hit the right spot, he gasped.

Then she straightened and stared at him, barely taller than he was sitting down. "I think thee has cracked or sprained a rib."

He groaned deeply and then regretted it. Shallow breathing was the less painful course.

"Take off thy shirt," she said, turning toward her linen trunk.

"What?" Again he regretted speaking sharply.

"My father fell once and I will do for thee what my

stepmother did for him." She brought out a length of muslin, a wide bandage it appeared. "I will bind thy chest firmly. Please remove the shirt."

Brennan couldn't meet her gaze, but obeyed her reluctantly. It felt improper for him to be shirtless here alone with her.

Rachel most certainly did not want Mr. Merriday to sit in her cabin shirtless. She still reeled from the sensations and emotions his embrace had released inside her. "Raise thy arms level so I can bind this around."

She tried to tightly wrap his chest without touching or looking at him. An impossible task. An unnerving task. He had a fine chest and shoulders, so smooth to the touch. Her eyes followed the line dividing his tanned neck and untanned skin of his chest and upper arms. She chastised herself for noticing. Why had he drawn her into his arms?

No doubt it had been a moment of anguish and he merely had needed the comfort of another human being. A deflating thought. She finished binding his chest tightly. She tied the bandage neatly and securely. "That should help thee breathe with less discomfort."

He nodded and lowered his arm and drew on his shirt quickly, as if embarrassed and pained. He stared down at the table. "You really think he'll come back by himself?"

"Yes, but not until he's exhausted himself and is hungry and thirsty. He will not be happy and will probably be rude to us."

He looked up at her then, just a slight tilting of his chin. "He thought I was a coward. They all did when I wouldn't enlist in the local militia. My wife left me over it and they... I left town."

His explanation did not feel complete. She could imagine the commotion, the fury his refusal may have caused. Secession had stirred the whole nation to a fever pitch. "Thee didn't believe in secession?"

"Or slavery. I was against slavery."

This startled her. Most Southerners who fought for the North had been against secession, not against slavery. Indeed Mr. Lincoln had not advanced emancipation till well into the conflict in order to keep the border states, the states that still held slaves but fought for the Union. Men like Posey Brown's father.

Rachel looked at Brennan Merriday with new eyes. And she couldn't stop herself. She leaned over and kissed his forehead. "Bless thee," she whispered. Shocked at herself, she pulled back and bustled over to the chest to return the length of wide bandage she hadn't used, chastising herself with every step.

"I don't think he'll come back," Mr. Merriday said.

"We will see if I'm right. I hope I am." *Please, Father, let me be right. Bring Jacque home soon.*

Chapter Nine

Second by second, the endless day passed. A day of watching, waiting to see a thin boy with black hair walk into her clearing. But Rachel and Brennan waited in vain. Now Rachel watched the sun's rays glimmer through the trees. The last of her energy faded with the day.

"It's late. Thee must go," Rachel said at last, not wanting to send him away but knowing she must. She didn't want to think of the gossip that would come if townspeople didn't see him return to the blacksmith shop before dark.

She struggled with herself. She wanted to fold him in her arms and comfort him.

Brennan stared at her. "I shoulda kept going on after him."

She shook her head. She even imagined kissing Brennan's face and smoothing back his hair… She stopped her unruly mind there. *Such thoughts.* "Thee lost sight of him. Stumbling around in the forest could injure thy rib more and probably not find Jacque anyway."

He exhaled with visible pain and left without a further word.

She watched him go, his head down, his step slow. Her feelings for him were increasing, causing her to think about him when she should not. And she knew she stood in danger of being deeply hurt when he left town. But that didn't seem to matter to her heart.

Brennan tried to come up for air from the gloom smothering him, but could not. Now he realized that the boy meant something to him. He couldn't think why. Jacque might not even be his son, his blood. *But he's from home. He's my responsibility. And he's been treated bad and I can help make that up to him—if he'll let me.*

Again he felt Rachel in his arms. He'd forgotten how soft a woman felt. Grimly he shut down his mind. He'd been foolish beyond measure to reach for her when he had no intention of staying and was unworthy of her. He'd behaved like a cad.

When Brennan reached town, he was glad to see the street deserted. The saloon was quiet but held no attraction for him. He didn't want to talk to anybody. He slipped into the blacksmith shop, hoping Levi wouldn't hear him.

But Levi had evidently been watching for him. The big man stood in the doorway, his back to the river.

Brennan halted, staring at him, suddenly breathing faster.

"The boy didn't come back?" Levi asked.

"No." Brennan hid the deep heart spasm this caused him. He pressed a hand to his side as if that was where he hurt.

"Come through and sit out riverside," Levi invited. "I heard about you serving for the Union, but I won't talk you to death."

Relief rolled over Brennan. Levi had sense. Brennan realized then that while he didn't want to talk, he didn't want to be alone either. Imagining the boy alone in the coming darkness clawed at him. *I should have told him myself, told him all what happened. He deserves the truth.*

Levi waved Brennan outside into the breeze by the river.

Brennan joined his friend there, sitting as they usually did, watching the final flickers of the sunset and the blue water turning to ink. Brennan cradled his side and tried to banish Jacque's tortured face from his mind, banish the touch of Rachel's hair against his face.

"At least it's not cold or storming," Levi commented after a while.

"Yeah." No, the storm churned inside the boy.

"And Miss Rachel's been feeding up the boy. Won't hurt him to go a night without supper."

Brennan nodded, his throat too tight for words.

"You move like you hurt yourself."

"Tripped. Might have cracked a rib."

Levi bowed his head. "I still don't know why Posey's grandmother won't let me talk to her."

Brennan shook his head. He had no answer for the man. He leaned against the wall and tried not to think of a little boy huddled against a tree in the forest. There were bears in those woods. He moved and then stifled a moan, rubbing his side slowly, cautiously.

Finally, the night wrapped around them, fireflies flickering green in the blackness, and Levi got up. "See you in the morning."

Rising painfully, Brennan reached over and touched the big man's shoulder, grateful for the company and understanding. Then he turned inside to climb the ladder to the empty loft.

Would the boy make it back? Had he failed the boy, too? Or had the final break with home come at last? If so, then he could leave Miss Rachel before he misled her. The thought clogged his throat. He wanted to stay; he must leave.

Rachel had remained dressed, sitting outside fanning away the few mosquitoes. The dry weather had reduced the numbers of the annoying little bloodsuckers, probably the only advantage of the drought. She listened to the encroaching night, filled with the sounds of frogs and crickets. She hoped to hear the boy's voice, tried to forget resting her head against Brennan's chest and hearing his heart pound.

Finally she gave up and went inside. Her hearth was cold but she'd left the outdoor oven burning very low, hoping the faint smoke could still be seen in the moonlight.

She had just let down her hair when she heard the tap on the door. She hurried to open it.

Jacque stood in the scant light with a grimy face and a torn sleeve.

She nearly cried out with relief. She controlled herself and didn't throw her arms around him. She had to remember who she was to him, just his father's employer. Since Brennan had stated he would be leaving and no doubt taking Jacque with him, she shouldn't let the child form an attachment to her. And now she should scold him but she couldn't do that. She focused on the practical. "Come in. Thee must be starved."

He stumbled inside.

"Sit down at the table," she said, heading toward her pie safe to fetch bread and cheese.

She turned to find the boy outside washing his hands. For some reason this brought moisture to her eyes.

He came in and slumped onto the bench, obviously exhausted and downhearted.

She set the plate down with a glass of water. She touched his head with her hand and for once—unable to completely hide her emotion—said grace, thanking God for bringing him home safely.

He devoured two plates of food before he paused to look at her.

She waited to hear what he said, but he said nothing, just looked at her. His eyes spoke pages and pages of pain, sorrow and distrust. She ached to fold him in her arms to comfort and reassure him. But she wasn't his blood. He belonged to Brennan. She hoped.

Finally she broke the silence. "I think thee will spend the night here." She rose and went to the linen chest and drew out her last pillow, just a small square, and a worn quilt her mother had made as a girl. She handed these to him.

Without a word, he lay down on the floor and rolled up into the quilt and went to sleep almost instantly.

She stood over him, both glad and worried. She wished she could let Mr. Merriday know he'd come home safe, but walking in the dark alone would not be wise or safe for her or Jacque. Bears roamed the area. And Mr. Merriday would come for breakfast. She would face him then and banish once and for all the pull he exerted over her.

In the dark, she dressed for bed and then slid between the sheets. The multitude of emotions she'd experienced today had left her depleted. But one part of the day refused to bow to sleep—Mr. Merriday pressed against her. He'd needed her comfort and had seized it.

No man but her father, and only when she was little, had held her like that. Just one day ago, she'd realized that she didn't want Mr. Merriday to leave and now she realized that she wanted him to hold her again—often. Oh, how could she hide these unsuitable feelings?

Rachel woke with Jacque standing over her.

"I don't want to have nothin' to do with that man."

Rachel sat up and considered the boy and his words. "He may be thy father."

"I don't care. I don't want nothin' to do with a Mississippi man who up and fought for the Union."

So it fell to her to soothe the troubled waters. She sighed silently. "Jacque, there is much I could say. But this is all I will tell thee. There are always two sides to everything. Mr. Merriday deserves to have his side of the story heard."

The boy stared at her, chewing his lip. "I don't want to have nothin' to do with that man," he repeated.

"That will be difficult. Where will thee stay?"

"Why can't I stay here? I'll work for you."

She tilted her head to one side. The boy was stubborn just like his father. She did not say this, not wishing to set a spark to straw, so to speak. "If thee stays here and works for me, thee will still be with Mr. Merriday."

He glared at her.

"Is that not true?"

He glared more narrowly.

"Staring at me will not change the facts."

He shrugged in obvious capitulation. "I ain't gotta talk to him."

Arguing would not solve this here and now. "Please

go outside and wash up at the creek. I must get up and need my privacy."

He stomped outside, banging the door behind him.

What a pleasant day this was going to be. But thank heaven the boy had returned. Part of her wanted to race into town to let Mr. Merriday know. She knew, though, that like her, he expected that if the boy returned he'd come to her place. He would arrive soon enough to face the angry child.

So she brushed and bound her long hair, dressed and began her morning routine. Today she decided to make molasses cookies instead of candy as she'd planned. An easy drop dough and no standing over the stove inside. And who could refuse one of her dark, spicy cookies?

Before the first cookie sheets were in the oven, she heard through the open door Mr. Merriday approaching.

She stepped just outside.

Jacque was returning from his "swim" in the creek, damp and clean and very pointedly ignoring the man.

"You're here," Brennan said, folding his arms—to keep from reaching for the child? And Brennan looked as if he hadn't slept all night, worrying about Jacque.

Whatever Mr. Merriday said, he had affection for this child. She remained where she was and tried not to let her concern for the man show. "Thee might say good morning to Jacque," she prompted.

"Good mornin'," Brennan muttered. "Glad you found your way back."

Jacque looked away from Brennan and folded his arms over his scrawny chest—just like the man who might be his father.

"Jacque, when an elder speaks, thee will answer." She kept her voice pleasant and gentle and implacable.

Glancing over his shoulder, Jacque sent his father a scathing look. "I'm back. I'm staying here, not with you."

Brennan sent her a grim look in response, but did not scold the child.

She shrugged slightly. "We will all be civil to one another. Please come in. I have enough eggs left from yesterday to make breakfast before chores."

She turned inside and the two followed her. Soon she served up three plates and the trio ate breakfast in silence. She gazed at Brennan's hands, so tanned, strong, capable. She closed her eyes, dismissing her foolishness.

When Jacque finished, he rose. "Good eats. I'll go gather more eggs." He carried his plate and mug outside and set them on the table by the basin.

That left Rachel and Brennan facing each other. What was the man thinking?

Brennan looked at the lady, then as he recalled the way he'd overstepped the bounds of propriety yesterday, he lowered his gaze. He really did not want to talk about Jacque or anything.

"I suppose thee doesn't wish to discuss this?"

Glancing up, he frowned, confused once again by Miss Rachel's perception and no-nonsense approach to life. *She never flutters or gets flustered.*

She looked at the clock on the wall and turned, stood and headed toward her outdoor oven. "I must take my cookies out before they burn." She stopped and assessed him with a stern expression he didn't appreciate. "I told Jacque every man deserves to have his side of a story heard." With that pronouncement, she turned to leave.

Her cool attitude further disconcerted him. Any other woman would be jabbering, bending his ear about this. Miss Rachel was one unusual woman. "You're right."

Before she could reply, Brennan walked out and looked around. He didn't want to face Jacque, but he hadn't been given a choice. Posey Brown had seen to that.

He walked over to Jacque. "Come with me. We'll go look for wild mustard for Miss Rachel."

"I'm not going anywhere with—"

Brennan stooped and stared into the boy's eyes. "It's time you and me talked and that's what we're going to do. A man has a right to be heard." That woman was getting into his head.

Jacque stared back and then nodded. He quickly gathered two more eggs and then set the basket inside. He came out with another empty basket and set off, walking north on the road away from town.

Still breathing with pain, Brennan caught up with him. At first they just walked, Brennan trying to come up with a way to tell the boy all that had happened in Mississippi before he'd been born. Jacque was just ten. Could he understand it?

From his own childhood, Brennan recalled a wrinkled, dried-up old farmer who'd lived nearby. He'd learned a lot from the man, who was nearly ninety and who'd come to Mississippi when the Choctaw still roamed there. Brennan remembered how the man taught him—with questions, letting him figure things out for himself.

"I want to ask you a question, boy." He waited.

Finally, Jacque cast him a resentful look.

"I was born 'n' raised along the Mississippi and lived there till I was over twenty. Everybody I knew said slavery was good, the way things should be. What would cause a man to go agin everybody he ever knew? What would cause a man to do something so bad that his wife left him and never even told him she was carrying his son?"

Jacque merely tossed him another more resentful look.

"You don't have to like me, but it's important you figure this out. In not too many years, you'll be a man and you'll be faced with choices. Will you just go the easy way, be like everybody else—even if you think different in your heart? Or will you stand up for what you believe is right?"

Each of the words jabbed Brennan painfully in his rib and in his heart. Life would have been so much easier if his pa hadn't taken him on that trip downriver to New Orleans.

Still Jacque said nothing. They walked in silence till they reached a meadow, a natural clearing in the forest. A doe and her fawns glimpsed them and then the three bolted for the trees.

He watched them flee, wishing he could, too. Pepin had been bad luck for him since the get-go. Then he thought of Miss Rachel and saw her lips curve into one of her smiles. Her smile made her shine so pretty.

Brennan barricaded his mind against Miss Rachel and bent to look for yellow wild mustard plants that Jacque said he could recognize. The meadow should have been thick with them. But it was dry and burned up. Just like he felt.

Bending hurt his side, so he sat down, futilely moving his hand through the dry, lifeless grass searching for any green shoot. Time passed; the hot sun rose higher. They moved closer to the edge of the clearing where some green hid in the shade. They kept searching. Waves of heat wafted into the shade, nearly suf-focating them.

"Why'd you do it? Go agin everybody?" the boy fi-nally asked, not looking at him.

Brennan nearly drew in a deep breath but stopped himself. Instead he took several shallow breaths, mini-mizing the rib pain.

The words came easily, as if they had been waiting to be spoken. "When I was only a few years older than you, my pa and I went downriver to New Orleans. My pa had been savin' up and had enough money to buy a slave to work the land with him. I was real excited 'cause I'd never been all the way to New Orleans before. It was a big city with boats from the ocean." Brennan recalled that trip downriver, the last truly uncompli-cated time of his life.

"Yeah," Jacque prompted.

"We went to the slave auction down by the docks. And that was what changed me." He recalled the gag-ging revulsion he'd instantly felt. "It was the worst place I'd ever been." He reached over and grasped Jacque's chin, turning his face to him. "It was the look in their eyes, the black slaves' eyes."

Jacque stared at him, looking confused.

"I'd been to horse sales. Pa acted like it was just like that. It wasn't. I never seen a horse being sold look that way. They were suffering. They were people and they were being treated like horses, worse than horses. No lady ever went to see the auctions. It was too…"

Words failed him. He couldn't speak what he'd seen that day even though the sights and sounds had been burned into his heart. He dropped the boy's chin and then stared at the dried, cracked ground.

The shadow of an eagle soaring on the hot winds passed over them. A cicada shrieked and shrieked again.

"That's why you wouldn't fight for the South?" the boy muttered finally, the heat gone out of his tone.

"Yes, I couldn't fight for slavery after that."

"Did your pa buy a slave?"

"No, the bidding went too high for him." *I was glad.* Jacque kept running his hands through the dried grass though there was nothing green to pick.

Brennan had done his best to explain. But the boy had been turned against him since the day he was born. This hurt as much as the jab he felt with each breath.

"I want you to know one thing, though," Brennan continued, taking advantage of this rare, private time. "After the war, I came home even though I knew nobody wanted me back. I had to make sure your ma was all right."

Jacque's hands stilled.

"Even if she didn't want me no more, I was still her husband and I would have supported her till the day she died. But nobody told me anything except that she was dead. Nobody told me about you. I wouldn't have left you there with Jean Pierre if I'd known you had been born. But I couldn't stay to find out anything. They run me out of town at gunpoint—a second time." He hadn't meant to add that.

Jacque looked up then. "You didn't leave me on purpose?"

"No, I never knew you'd been born. Nobody told me."

Jacque only nodded in reply.

Brennan surveyed the cloudless blue sky overhead. "We might as well go home. Maybe there's some wild mustard near the creek."

Jacque rose and walked with him, but said nothing.

So much for honesty. And Brennan didn't like it at all when he realized that he was calling Miss Rachel's place "home."

When they arrived at Miss Rachel's clearing, he heard another familiar feminine voice. He didn't want to talk to anybody save Miss Rachel or Levi. Certainly not Posey Brown.

Jacque halted and looked up.

"Let's mosey down by the river," Brennan mumbled. "We'll try to catch Miss Rachel a few catfish for supper."

"Good idea." Jacque nodded and the two headed toward town.

Posey had come to Rachel's to apologize to Mr. Merriday for blurting out his private business in town. Listening, Rachel had just slid the last of her molasses cookies onto the racks to cool when the new school bell rang wildly. Now both of them looked toward the door.

"What? Why are they ringing the bell? School's out for the summer," Rachel asked.

Posey rushed to the open door. "Smoke! Toward town! We've got to go! They'll need us for the bucket brigade!"

"Here." Rachel thrust a spare bucket into Posey's hands.

The girl raced ahead of Rachel, who shut and latched the door behind her and snatched up her own water bucket as she ran.

The smell of smoke billowed, intensified, filling Rachel with gut-wrenching panic. The drought and the fear of wildfire had hung over them all. Had it come true?

The two of them burst through the forest onto the river flat of town. Orange flames danced with the wind like little wisps, dangerous wisps, catching every blade of dried grass on the dirt street and river flat, leaping onto anything dry.

"It's heading to the grass behind Ashford's!" Posey shrieked.

Rachel shuddered. The wind whipped the fire with every gust, driving it toward the trees. A forest in flame! Death and destruction. *God, help us! Now!*

Already a bucket brigade had formed across the main street from the river to the fire. The two of them joined the line, filling in wider gaps. Their toil began—passing heavy buckets forward and empty ones back.

Rachel saw Brennan run toward the front of the brigade.

"If it gets to the trees, we'll never stop it!" Brennan shouted in a strangled voice, pointing toward the forest. "Follow me, men! Grab shovels! Anything! We'll try to smother the flames as they leap toward the trees! The rest of you, keep the water comin'!"

These urgent orders from a man who never showed excitement and rarely talked magnified their effect. Men raced to join him. Frantic activity suspended every thought except—*fire, fire!* Rachel was aware only of the wet bucket handles passing through her hands. Terror raced through her like the wind, water splashing, worry mounting.

"We finished it!" Gunther Lang shouted in his distinctive voice. "It's out!"

Having trouble catching her breath, Rachel straightened to see for herself that he spoke the truth. Then the bucket brigade members staggered forward to view the effects of the fire.

The path of the fire was plain from the river's edge to

patches of dry grass on Main Street, scorching the front of Ashford's store to the open clearing behind the stores.

"How did this happen?" Rachel asked.

"Merriday saw it first," the blacksmith said, panting, swiping his forehead with his sleeve. "Sparks from the riverboat smokestack caught dry grass on shore. The wind—you'd a-thought it would blow out the fire—instead it just spread it faster than Merriday and I could keep up with it."

Rachel's gaze sought out Brennan. He'd slipped to the rear with Jacque. He held his arm against his side. Her thoughts went immediately to his painful rib. *The poor man.*

"I saw...them trying to put out the fire," Gunther joined in, motioning toward the blacksmith and Brennan, "and ran to...the school to ring the bell." The young man spoke between gasps for air, leaning forward with his hands on his soaked knees. "Then I came back to help."

Everyone stared at the few feet separating the blackened grass from the surrounding forest. Rachel had a hard time believing they'd caught it in time. *Thank Thee, Father.*

"A close call," Mr. Ashford said, wiping his sooty brow with a handkerchief. "What's bothering you, Merriday?"

Nearly doubled over, Brennan was holding his side.

Rachel went to him and gently probed, seeing if he'd done more harm to himself.

"I got so excited I forgot I was hurt," he murmured.

She realized then that everyone had stopped talking and was staring at her touching Brennan's chest in public. Heat suffused her face, which she kept lowered.

She dropped her hand and turned to face the town.

"Mr. Merriday cracked or sprained a rib yesterday. I don't feel any further injury." Rachel wished her face would cool and return to normal.

"Well, looks like we need to thank you again, Merriday," Mr. Ashford said. "First you run off thieves and now this."

Everyone began to agree. Brennan's expression darkened and he edged farther away. "Just did what everybody else did."

His gruff tone warned everybody—not only her—away, the last thing she wanted him to do.

She decided to ease matters by deflecting attention. "Jacque, is thee all right? No burns?"

"I'm fine, Miss Rachel," the boy said, staying close to Brennan. "We couldn't find any wild mustard. Too dry."

"Indeed it is."

"We were gonna catch some catfish for supper," Jacque went on.

Rachel wondered what had caused the boy to be so chatty. He appeared to have lost the chip on his shoulder. Had Brennan's side of the story changed how Jacque felt? Or perhaps the excitement or exhilaration of fighting a fire and winning?

"That sounds like an excellent idea," Rachel said. "I have a taste for catfish."

Then a loud groan interrupted. Everyone looked over.

Posey's grandmother was clutching her chest, uttering short gasps. As Rachel watched, she crumpled to the ground.

"Grandmother!" Posey called and ran toward her.

Rachel and Brennan reached her first; both dropped to their knees, one on either side.

"What is it?" Rachel asked in a clear, firm voice.

The woman tried to answer but could not.

"Maybe her heart," Brennan muttered.

Rachel looked at him. Moments before he was backing away. But he'd come forward to help now as he had in the fire. What conflicted inside the man? He responded to any who needed help, but wanted no help or anything from anybody else.

"All the excitement," Mrs. Ashford said, sounding distracted, "must have brought on a spasm."

Or heart failure, Rachel said silently.

Rising also, Brennan met her eyes and she glimpsed that he too realized this was more than just a fainting spell.

"Will someone help Ned carry her upstairs?" Mrs. Ashford asked.

Soon the blacksmith and Gunther were carrying the plump woman on a makeshift stretcher. Mr. Ashford went ahead and held open the door.

Posey's eyes ran with tears. Rachel slipped an arm around her as they followed. Mrs. Ashford hurried past her husband to turn down the bed. "We'll take good care of her," Mrs. Ashford said over her shoulder to Posey. "Don't you worry."

The girl broke free of whatever held her in place and rushed toward the store.

Rachel wished the woman hadn't said those words, "Don't worry." They always seemed to ignite more anxiety.

At the sound of a strange voice, she glanced around.

A boatman who'd helped fight the fire was coming toward her. "Somebody say you are the lady, Miss Rachel, who sells sweets?"

Rachel looked at him and nodded, observing Brennan and Jacque heading toward the blacksmith shop. She saw them leave the shop with fishing gear.

"Do you have any sweets for sale?" the boatman asked.

"Molasses cookies." She began to hurry toward home, not willing to lose any business. "I'll be back in five minutes!"

"The captain say we wait!" he called after her. "We'll buy all you bring!"

And after she sold her cookies, she'd keep busy till Brennan brought catfish for supper.

She wanted to know what had transpired between Brennan and the boy. But would he tell her? Oh, the man was maddening. Admirable, but maddening.

Chapter Ten

In town selling her cookies, Rachel simmered with the frustration that stemmed from not knowing what had happened between Jacque and Brennan and more from the fact that she couldn't pursue the answer right now. She didn't see them at the riverside. How far downriver had they gone to fish?

After the cookies had been bought, she trundled home the cart, all the while wondering what had changed Jacque and Brennan's relationship. In the morning, they'd left with Jacque hostile to Brennan, whom the boy considered a turncoat to the South. And later they ended up going fishing together along the river—as if yesterday and Jacque's running away had never happened. Why? How?

The orange sun lowered and she kept herself busy with chores, churning butter for tomorrow's recipe and milking the cow in the late afternoon. Waiting to see the man and the boy bring home their catch, she paced in front of the door.

Restless, she baked a large cake of cornbread and with a pop, opened a jar of piccalilli Sunny had given her. And waited. What was keeping the two?

As the red melting sun finally dipped behind the treetops, the two males wandered up the trail. Brennan carried a stringer with three huge catfish on it, held out in front of him, the end hooked over his index finger.

Since she had nothing else ready to serve, Rachel was relieved to see the fish. Yet she noted that Brennan was holding the fish with the hand opposite his compromised rib and was walking slightly bent over. That meant he was still aching.

She hurried forward to relieve him of the catfish. "Well done!"

The shocked expressions on the two males' faces halted her in her tracks. "What's wrong?"

"You don't look in the mirror enough, Miss Rachel," Brennan drawled.

"You look funny," Jacque said, pointing at her face, grinning.

She whirled around and ran inside to the small mirror on the wall. When she saw her reflection, she gasped. Smoke from the fire had blackened her face with grimy soot. "Oh, dear!"

She hung the fish stringer on a peg by the door and hurried outside to wash her face in the basin there.

When she was done, she looked up and Jacque handed her a linen towel. "How mortifying. I went into town and sold cookies looking like this!"

Brennan held his side as he tried not to laugh.

Jacque grinned at her. "We swam in the river to cool off and get rid of the smoke smell."

"And soot," Brennan added.

Rachel contemplated how good it would feel to be a girl again and go swimming in the nearby river. "I'm afraid I would scandalize the town if I did that."

"I'm glad I was born a boy," Jacque said, going inside.

"How is thy rib?" she asked, drying her hands.

Brennan rubbed his side. "Not much better."

"Putting out a fire probably aggravated everything. Thee must rest tomorrow. Just fish or nap in the shade."

"I can't do that."

"Why not? I'm thy employer and that's what I want thee to do." She looked at him more closely. "Where is the bandage I bound thee with?" she asked though she noted the bulge around his waist.

He tugged up the hem of his shirt and showed her that the bandage had slipped to his belt. "It got wet when we swam."

She swallowed a sigh of irritation. "Come. I need to bind that again." She waved him to the bench beside the door.

He shrugged out of his shirt and she bent to untie and then to rewrap the stout muslin around his chest. Again this brought her so close to him. Only a breath separated their cheeks as she worked wrapping and pulling the cloth tight.

For just a moment she was tempted to rest her cheek against his. The thought of this released such an explosion of feeling that she braced herself physically and mentally against it. She finished the last loop around him and then tied the bandage and stepped back. She turned away so he wouldn't note how her cheeks had warmed. This attraction to Mr. Merriday was so…lowering to her sense of self control. Where had her good sense gone?

Rachel hurried inside, running away from him. "I have to see to the fish."

Brennan followed her more slowly. Once inside he sank onto the rocking chair, leaning against its high back for support, and sighed with audible relief.

Ignoring him as best she could, Rachel quickly breaded the cleaned fish and laid one and then the next into a large cast-iron skillet to deep fry.

"We didn't find any wild mustard. It's too dry for anything to grow," Jacque reminded her, continuing his grumbling from the bench, elbows propped on the table.

Rachel sighed. "No doubt. And I was hoping for wild mustard and for wild berries to put up for next year. It is good that my business is taking, for it will be a long winter."

When she thought of the coming months, she wondered what winter all alone in this cabin would be like. An empty, hollow feeling tried to lower her spirits. Brushing this aside, she quickly eased the catfish onto its other side in the bubbling oil.

She looked over at Brennan, wondering if he would tell her what he'd done or said to cause this change in Jacque. She hesitated even to broach the subject for fear she would tip the delicate balance between the two of them and regret it.

"Hello the house!" a friendly voice called.

"Jacque," Brennan said, nodding toward the door, "welcome Levi in."

Though Rachel concentrated on the catfish sizzling in the pan, she too welcomed the blacksmith. Though why he had come? He never had before. "Just in time for supper," she said, smiling over her shoulder at him.

"I didn't come expecting to be fed, miss," he said, his hat in his hands.

"You loaned us your fishin' poles and hooks and stringer," Jacque said.

"We have plenty, Mr. Comstock." Rachel waved him toward the table and set another place there. She had an inkling what he'd come about and wished he hadn't.

Before long they were eating the golden catfish, buttery cornbread and spicy piccalilli. Then for dessert, Rachel set out the last dozen of her molasses cookies she'd saved and they vanished.

"Mighty good supper, miss." Levi looked at her shyly.

She noted that Brennan sent him a suspicious look and she wondered what that was about.

"Jacque, make sure the chickens are safe in their coop," Rachel said, feeling what Levi had come to say might be something Jacque didn't need to hear. She didn't want to hear it herself.

As soon as the boy moved outside of earshot, Levi appeared to gather himself. "Miss Rachel, I come to ask a favor."

She looked at him, unable to stop the flow of where this conversation was headed. "I see."

"I've taken a shine to Miss Posey Brown and I think she is not averse to me." The big man blushed.

"I had noticed," Rachel said without any encouragement. She noticed that Brennan Merriday had relaxed, now sitting at ease again in the rocking chair. *Odd.*

Levi looked everywhere but at her. "I was wondering if you could find out why Miss Posey's grandmother doesn't want me to court her."

This was what Rachel had expected, but was it her place to reveal Posey's confidences? "I don't know what I can do," she said in earnest.

"I don't either, but I don't have a sister or mother here to…to ask. I asked Mr. Ashford and he said it wasn't his business to say."

Rachel wanted to say the same. Even ill, Almeria would daunt anybody.

"I'm concerned for Miss Brown," Levi continued.

"I mean, what if her grandmother doesn't recover from this spell? She'll be alone."

Rachel doubted the Ashfords would put Posey out on the street but understood Levi's awkward situation. After all, she had allowed herself to begin to care for a man with whom she had no possible future. This alone prompted her to say, "I'll see what I can find out, Mr. Comstock. But I have no influence over events here."

"I know that." Still the man looked relieved.

She wished she felt the same. The visit ended soon.

Jacque finished helping her wash and dry the supper dishes. Then he reminded her about her needing a bath. Rachel could have crawled under the cabin in embarrassment but when Brennan lifted her water bucket, she intervened. After the afternoon's exertion, Brennan couldn't haul water. Then over both Rachel's and Brennan's protestations, Levi insisted on helping Jacque fill a tub for her. Then the three males went off together, leaving her to wash away the lingering scent of smoke on her person.

Alone, she barred the door and prepared to bathe with her one indulgence, lilac-scented soap.

As she relaxed in the cool, refreshing water, she couldn't fight the flashes of Brennan's face—his sadness this morning, the flush from the urgency amidst fighting the fire, his evident fatigue and pain at supper. How did a person stop caring about someone?

The next day Rachel had her cinnamon rolls rising the second time before her two "hired hands" arrived for breakfast. She steeled herself to welcome Mr. Merriday without feeling anything beyond courtesy. She failed miserably.

As soon as she could after breakfast, she sent them

outside. Brennan to rest and Jacque to gather fallen wood for winter. She needed the wood and she needed Brennan away from her.

As if on cue, just as she finished slathering buttercream frosting over the cinnamon rolls, a boat whistle summoned her. She peered outside and saw that Mr. Merriday was sleeping under his tree. A relief.

She reached town within minutes, rolling her cart toward the boat. Passengers and boatmen clustered around her, buying cinnamon rolls, bagged or wrapped individually in wax paper. Levi stepped outside his forge and sent her a pointed look. She concentrated on business, trying to come up with a plan to help Levi.

The cook bought what remained on her tray. "You probably don't 'member me but I'm from that first boat you gave samples to of those fast-somethings."

"My fastnachts?"

"Yeah, that's it. We gone down to New Orleans and back twice since then. The captain tell all the other captains about you and how good your stuff is. You don't got any fastnachts today?"

"No, but when will you be back?"

"We gone on up to Minneapolis. Be back by in three days."

"Tell your captain I'll have a couple dozen ready for him."

The man beamed at her and nodded twice.

Flushed with pleasure, Rachel sighed and then turned to face the storefront. Her promise to Levi couldn't wait. She pushed her cart into the shade and went into the General Store.

Mr. Ashford was alone. When he saw her, he brightened. "I see you sold out again. Your business is doing well."

Rachel felt herself expand with his praise and chastised herself. God was blessing her, prospering her—no need for vain pride. "I came to see if I could visit Posey's grandmother. Is she receiving visitors?"

"Oh, please come up," Posey said from the rear staircase. "She is not well enough to get up yet, but…"

Rachel nodded, taking polite leave of Mr. Ashford, and headed toward the woebegone-looking young woman. "I understand. It is hard to be idle, especially in this late-summer heat." When she reached Posey, the girl leaned close and pressed a folded paper into her hands.

"This is the letter," Posey whispered, "where my father mentions Mr. Merriday. I want him to see it. But I didn't know…"

Rachel wondered how she had become everybody's confidant or go-between, roles she hadn't wished for. Yet what could she do but accept the letter? Nodding, she slipped it into her pocket and followed Posey upstairs.

She had gained access. Now all she had to do was come up with a way to introduce the topic of Levi Comstock to Mrs. Brown. A touchy subject, no doubt. No touchier, however, than the letter in her pocket for Mr. Merriday.

Mrs. Ashford greeted her with evident gratitude. "Oh, Miss Woolsey, would you sit with my cousin for a while? Amanda is helping Mrs. Whitmore today. Posey and I must get busy with laundry and we didn't want to leave Almeria alone."

"Of course, I have time. Perhaps I could read scripture to her?"

"An excellent idea." Mrs. Ashford handed Rachel the family Bible. "There is sweet iced coffee in the icebox.

Help yourself." And the two of them disappeared down the rear staircase.

Before Rachel went into the guest room, she stopped in the kitchen to look over the Ashfords' icebox. She'd heard that in winter men cut ice from the frozen Mississippi. Mr. Ashford had built a commodious ice house and sold blocks of ice. She liked the new, metal-lined box with shelves and a thick door with a tight latch. She saw immediately that when she could afford it, she wanted one for herself.

Bidding farewell to enjoyment, she went down the short hall to the guest room. She halted at the doorway and looked in. "Good day, Mrs. Brown."

The older woman turned toward her. "Oh, it's the Quakeress."

Ignoring the listlessness of the welcome, Rachel responded, "Yes, it is. I have come to keep thee company. Would thee like me to read? Perhaps the Psalms?"

The woman shook her head. "Just talk to me. I'm afraid I'm not in good spirits."

Rachel thought secretly that hearing the Psalms would lift the woman's spirits more than anything Rachel could think to say, but she kept that to herself.

"I'm sorry thee isn't feeling well." Rachel thought about a topic that might interest the woman. "I just received a letter from my family. My stepmother is expecting another child later this year."

"You lost your mother?"

"Yes, when I was just about to finish eighth grade."

"I've lost everyone but my Posey." The woman blinked away sudden tears.

Rachel had attempted to begin a happy conversation and here they were talking about death. She tried again.

"I think my father may hope for a son at last. He has just me and my four young stepsisters."

"Your mother only had one child?" Almeria asked.

"Yes, just me."

"What do you think of the blacksmith?" Almeria sent her a penetrating look.

This abrupt turn startled Rachel. "He seems honest and hardworking."

"Humph. Everyone says so. Katharine and Ned can't understand why I oppose him courting my granddaughter."

Should she feign ignorance? No, of course not. "Posey confided that thee preferred she marry a man with property."

"Exactly." The woman managed to add some starch to her voice. "I don't want her left with nothing again and when I may not be here to help guide her." The woman's face puckered but she kept control, brushing away a stray teardrop.

Rachel was moved. "I think the Ashfords would do their best for her."

"Yes, but they have a daughter of their own to marry off and grandchildren in other states. They've been very kind to us. But this town isn't filled with eligible young men as I had hoped."

Rachel considered the situation. And insight came. "If I may, I'd like to point out that there is no reason Mr. Comstock couldn't stake a homestead claim. Why can't a blacksmith own land, too?"

The older woman glanced at her sharply. "Would he have time to prove up? That man works sunup to sundown six days a week as it is."

Rachel considered. "I have staked a homestead claim and I could not do the work myself to prove up. Mr.

Merriday has refurbished my cabin and built a small, snug barn and cleared some more land for me. My claim is nearly proved up."

Rachel experienced a hitch of pain in her breath. The boy had complicated matters but she had no doubt Brennan would go soon. "Perhaps Mr. Merriday would help Mr. Comstock, as well." *And stay longer in town?*

The woman looked Rachel full in the face. "An excellent suggestion. Do you think Mr. Comstock would stake a claim?"

"I think so." Rachel lowered her eyes. "He seems very taken with thy granddaughter and I have no doubt he would make an excellent husband to her. He's lived here several years and I've heard nothing but good of him."

And suddenly Rachel envied Posey Brown. She might be able to marry the man she had become attracted to. *I will not.*

The day went by with the usual chores but her tension over Brennan and Jacque mounted. Why didn't Mr. Merriday tell her what had happened between them? And when should she show him Posey's letter from her father?

Finally, the day neared its close. Jacque ran off to "swim" in the creek, leaving Rachel and Brennan sitting in the shade on the bench outside her door.

She decided directness was her only hope. "Jacque changed yesterday toward you. What did you say or do—"

"I don't want to talk about it."

She heard more than his words. She heard the lingering pain from the war. Twice now she'd tended to Mr. Merriday's physical injuries. How she longed to minister to his unseen wounds.

"I'm sorry," he said with regret. "I said that more sharp than I meant to."

She nodded, accepting his apology.

"And I should just go ahead and tell you," Brennan admitted. "I'm so used to hiding my past. But you deserve to know."

Rachel was afraid to even nod. *Lord, give me wisdom and understanding.*

"I told Jacque that going to a slave auction when I was near his age turned me against slavery."

"I heard an account of one from a runaway slave," she murmured solemnly. The account had horrified her.

"Then I don't got to spell it out for you. When Lincoln was elected and Mississippi seceded, all my neighbors formed a militia unit. I wouldn't join. I had kept my feelings to myself till then. But I told them I couldn't fight for slavery or for secession."

She heard more than the words; she heard the enormity of the day when he'd had to stand against his neighbors.

"The only thing that saved my life was jumping in the Mississippi and swimming away."

A simple sentence and so much more behind it.

"Thee has suffered much. Why did thee hide the truth from people here? From me?"

He shook his head as if warning away a deerfly. "I get back bad memories—sometimes nightmares and sometimes in daylight even. Talking about it stirs them up I think. Besides, it wasn't anybody's business."

She heard what each of these words cost him. So she'd been right. He did have spells like other soldiers she'd met. "Thank thee for telling me."

"I want to ask you a favor, Miss Rachel."

Not another one. It seemed like everyone wanted a favor from her. She waited, saying, encouraging nothing.

"I can't stay here. I'm getting restless again…like before I hurt my wrist. Jacque would be better off with you. I'm not fit to raise a boy."

Caught by surprise, she felt her spine tighten as if touched by ice. "Mr. Merriday—" she began.

And then the blacksmith walked into her clearing. "Good evening!"

Rachel leaned back against the log wall, disgruntled at the interruption. "Good evening, Mr. Comstock," she said with a sigh. "Why doesn't thee pull the rocking chair out here and be comfortable?"

The man evidently took this as a good sign because he beamed at her. Within moments, he had intimidated Brennan into taking the rocker for his rib's sake and was sitting beside her.

"I did speak to Posey's grandmother today," she said.

Turning sideways, Levi looked intently into her face.

"We discussed her objection to Posey marrying a blacksmith—"

"She doesn't like my trade?" Levi asked, looking startled. "Why?"

"She doesn't object to thy trade, merely that thee doesn't own land. She does not want Posey in the future to be left with nothing but a forge—if anything would happen to thee."

The blacksmith seemed to take this as a blow. "That's why she won't let me court Posey?" He sounded mystified.

Rachel touched his sleeve. "Thee must take this in context."

"What do you mean?"

"Because of the war, Mrs. Brown has witnessed her

granddaughter lose everything her father had worked to provide for the security of his family. She doesn't want Posey to find herself unprovided for again."

The big man chewed the inside of his cheek and pondered this.

"I made a suggestion to Mrs. Brown," Rachel continued. "I told her that thee could claim a homestead here if that's what she required."

Levi turned sharply to her. "What did she say?"

"She said that was a good idea. She said everyone vouches for thy sound character. It's just a matter of owning land."

"I intended to stake a claim," Levi said with audible relief, "just haven't gotten around to it. And I'd have five years to prove up."

"I suggested to Mrs. Brown that Brennan helped me prove up my claim." Realizing that she had used Brennan's given name, abashed, Rachel did not look in Brennan's direction. "And perhaps he might be persuaded to help thee raise a cabin before winter. And begin cutting winter wood." She looked at him then.

Mr. Merriday glared at her.

Levi swung to him. "I know you're healing, but it wouldn't take us long to put up a snug cabin before fall even."

Brennan did not appreciate being put on the spot. But gazing into Levi's hopeful face, he knew he couldn't let down a friend. Friends were too rare in this hard world. "Sure. As soon as I can swing an ax again."

Levi leaped up. "Should I go tell Mrs. Brown that I'm going to stake a claim?"

"I think," Miss Rachel said, "thee should find a good claim nearby and stake it. Then go and show the paperwork to Mrs. Brown and Mr. Ashford and ask permission to court Posey."

Levi pulled Miss Rachel up and threw his arms around her, lifting her off her feet. "Thank you, Miss Rachel! You've made me so happy!"

Brennan fumed at the man's taking such liberties.

Miss Rachel looked startled, but chuckled. "I think thee should say these words to Miss Brown, not me!"

The big man laughed out loud.

"What's the blacksmith hugging Miss Rachel for?" Jacque asked, arriving in the clearing.

"Miss Rachel did me a favor." Putting her down, Levi looked like a different man as he thanked her again and started away.

"Jacque, you go along with Levi and get up to bed," Brennan said. "We probably got another busy day tomorrow."

Jacque looked as if he might object, but Levi scooped him up and tossed him onto his broad shoulder. "I'll give you a ride!"

Jacque objected but only a little as Levi began teasing him and asking him about fishing.

Brennan, still resting in her rocker, watched Miss Rachel sit again.

"Why did you volunteer me to work for Levi?" he asked, nearly snarling. "I just told you I'm restless."

She smiled at him in that way he didn't like. "Restless or not, thee must stay till the letter comes from Louisiana. And I'm sure Levi will pay thee and thee can use the money to set up in Canada. Isn't that right?"

He fumed. The woman always had an answer and she was usually right. He hated that.

"Mr. Merriday, I apologize."

Her gentle tone shamed him. She was so good, so

kind, so special. He nearly leaned forward but his rib stabbed him. And he held back.

A few moments of silence passed. He brushed away a stray mosquito.

He looked at her then. He ached to tell her how he thought of her. But his mouth wouldn't open.

The golden cast of twilight bathed her. She was such a pretty woman. A man didn't notice it right off because she...protected herself. Why was she so cautious? Didn't she think a man could love her? Count himself lucky to win her?

He shot up out of the seat, hurting his side. "I gotta git to bed."

She rose, too. "Thee must be very tired. Would thee like a cup of willow bark tea before—"

"No, thanks." He held up one hand. "See you in the morning."

"Stop." She drew a folded paper from her pocket. "Take this." She shoved it into his hand and moved out of reach. "Posey wants you to read it."

He tried to hand it back but she hurried into her cabin. "Good night," she called and shut the door.

Fuming at her managing ways, he shoved the letter into his pocket. Then he tried to walk as fast as he could without jarring his rib cage. He had indeed worsened his condition when fighting the fire. The toll of another day of pain hit him fully as he glimpsed the blacksmith shop.

He slipped inside and up to his loft where Jacque was already sleeping soundly. Brennan stifled a groan as he lay down. His mind spun with thoughts of the day, of Miss Rachel, but thankfully his fatigue was mightier. His last thought was *I must leave soon.*

* * *

Brennan woke hours before dawn and turned over. Pain and his persistent regret hit him simultaneously. His side ached worse than before the fire. Something felt odd in his pocket. The letter. The letter Posey's father had written that mentioned him.

A sudden curiosity sparked. He looked around. There was enough moonlight to see to go down the ladder. He didn't want to get up. Yet he couldn't stop himself.

Moonlight led him to the shelf near the door where the box of matches and candles sat. He felt around, removed a match, struck it, the sound loud against the night cries of frogs, toads and insects. He lit one fat candle, setting it on the corner of the shelf. He sat in the chair beside the open door to the river. He slid the letter out and opened it.

July 4, 1864

Dearest Wife and Daughter,
I write to you on this Independence Day wishing that we could be together to celebrate the birth of our nation. I cannot believe the war to preserve the Union has gone on this long. I thought we'd be home in Tennessee long before this. I do not wish to complain. I am in a band of brothers. Most of us are outcasts because of our love for our nation, our whole nation.

A welcome distraction comes. Brennan Merriday, the Mississippi man I've told you about previously, has managed to trap a few rabbits. And he is busily preparing them for the spit over our fire. Merriday's a good man, run out of his town because he wouldn't enlist in the local militia. He's a stalwart fellow who speaks little but I don't know anybody I'd want more at my back in a fight.

Brennan's eyes swam with sudden tears. He pressed his thumb and index finger to the bridge of his nose and willed away the outpouring. Now he remembered Posey's father. He began to hear in his mind Clyde Brown's voice speaking the words of this letter. The sorrow of lost comrades rolled over Brennan—names and faces of men who'd taken him in—let him be a part of them when he was an outcast.

Of course, Clyde had spoken the truth—they'd all been outcasts in some way. He'd told them of the day in '61 when he'd been attacked by his own outraged homefolk.

His fingers wet from his tears, Brennan pinched the candle flame, extinguishing it. If only he could extinguish the memories that kept him from peace, from putting it all behind him. He sat in the dark many more minutes, then rose and climbed the ladder.

Clyde Brown's letter had shifted something inside him. He began to think of what he might do for a friend here and now. But was it the letter? Or was it the petite Quaker lady who had kept him here and who beckoned him even when he knew he could never be worthy of a woman like her?

Chapter Eleven

Brennan greeted Levi at another warm, sticky dawn and started to put into motion the half-formed plan that had come to him in the early hours of the morning. After all, he must do something while his rib healed. "I was thinking that I might look around for an unclaimed tract of land for you to stake."

Levi beamed. "I've been thinking about that, too. I was going to try to take off a few days, but..." The blacksmith raised both his hands.

"That's why I thought I could look for you. Miss Rachel just needs me to cut winter wood for her but with this rib, I can't do that." And he needed to keep away from Miss Rachel. He felt vulnerable to her in a new way he didn't understand and didn't want to examine.

Levi nodded eagerly. "There's some land near Noah Whitmore's place. That's not too far from town and my wife..." The man blushed. "If I find one, my wife would be near some nice women, Mrs. Whitmore and Mrs. Steward. That's important to women. They need somebody to talk to."

Brennan felt his face break into a grin he couldn't hide. Younger than he, Levi had not been old enough to fight and Brennan was glad the war hadn't touched him. Levi would make Posey a good husband. A momentary twinge reminded him that he wouldn't make anybody a good husband, least of all…

Levi pointed out the trail near the Ashfords' toward the northeast where Noah lived.

Behind them Jacque splashed, wading out of the river, his face, bare feet and hands washed. "We going to breakfast?"

Brennan almost said no. He really didn't want to see Miss Rachel today, but not to show up for breakfast at her house would shout to the surrounding village that something had changed. And not going when expected would be impolite to the fine lady. So Brennan nodded, but he must give some thought to how things were now and might be in the future. What exactly had changed he didn't understand yet. But change had come, wanted or not.

Brennan walked beside Jacque into Miss Rachel's tidy clearing. She stood outside, singing to a little brown bird. The bird was singing back to her. He stopped, riveted, and laid a hand on Jacque's shoulder. The two waited and watched. Brennan half expected the bird to fly down and light on her hand like in a story. But the exchange lasted only a few more moments and then the bird flew away.

"You were singing to that bird!" Jacque exclaimed, running toward her flat out.

Miss Rachel smiled at him and the sun shone brighter. Brennan firmly took himself in hand. He must not let whatever had opened up inside him last night, when he was reading that letter, spill over on to Miss Rachel. He must not mislead the lady.

"It was a humble thrush, but they can sing so prettily," Miss Rachel said, leaning down and talking to Jacque in much the same way she'd sung to the bird.

"Can you teach me that? How to sing to birds?"

She looked to Brennan. "What does thee think, Mr. Merriday?"

"I think he could—easy."

The boy looked up at him shyly. "You think so?"

Brennan nodded, feeling a stirring around his heart.

"How do I learn to do it, Miss Rachel?"

"It is a skill that one must learn by himself. Thee must listen and then try to make the sounds. The younger the better, if thee wants to sing to the birds." She chuckled. "My mother started me listening and trying to imitate the birds when I was much younger than thee."

Brennan patted the boy's shoulder while he tried to stop looking at her but it was like trying to ignore the sun. The place where iron gates had stood inside him was now melting. He stiffened himself.

She looked up then and caught him gazing at her. She lifted an eyebrow but smiled. "Come! Griddle cakes for breakfast! And I have some syrup my cousin Sunny gave me. She and Noah tapped sugar maple trees this March."

His mouth watered. Griddle cakes with syrup. *What a woman.* And for so much more than just her delicious meals…

Later Rachel watched Brennan and Jacque head off to scout land for Levi. She had packed them a lunch in case they couldn't get back to her at noon. Something had changed about him, but she couldn't put her finger on it.

Did this have to do with Posey's letter from her father? She had hoped he would talk about the letter, but no, not a word. *That man.*

She turned back to her day's work. Before long, she heard a boat whistle. She had made more caramels and sponge candy earlier and headed to town to sell several trays of it.

"Miss Rachel!" Levi hailed her from his doorway.

She waved and then had a thought. "Mr. Comstock, when Mr. Merriday returns, please accompany him and Jacque to my place for the evening meal."

He looked surprised and pleased. "Thank you, miss! I'll do that."

She hurried on with only a nod in reply.

People from two boats vied for her candy, some pushing forward like children. A tall man in a suit bought a bag and one individual portion and then stood in the shade, eating it and observing her. His attention caused her to be wary. Why was he watching her so intently?

She sold out and then began to turn.

"Miss Rachel?" The man who'd been looking at her moved closer.

She sized him up. Dressed in a neat, dark suit with a stiff white collar and a gold pocket watch, she guessed from the elaborate fob, he didn't incite anything beyond polite interest. "My full name is Rachel Woolsey."

"Is there somewhere we could discuss a matter of business?"

This stopped her in her tracks. "Business?"

"Yes," he said, smiling.

After a few moments of surprised indecision, she led him to the wide front porch of the Ashfords' store and invited him to sit beside her on the long bench there. No one could make anything of that.

The man drew a small ivory calling card from a gold case in his inner pocket. "I'm the owner of several concerns in Dubuque, Iowa. I am interested in adding an exclusive candy counter to my food emporium. Have you ever considered selling in bulk?"

She stared at him and then read the card. "James Benson, proprietor and owner of the Benson Food Emporium. Office Second Street, Dubuque, Iowa."

"I must confess that I am surprised at this question," she murmured at last. *And that a man will talk to a woman about business.*

"The news of your fine candies has traveled down the river. A friend brought me a few not long ago and, Miss Woolsey, I have never tasted a better caramel. And your sponge candy—" he held up a piece "—is excellent, too. I always like to meet the person I do business with if I can. So I decided to come up and see if you'd like to supply my stores with your caramels and perhaps sponge candy."

She blushed at his praise. "I never thought of selling in bulk," she admitted. "I work alone."

"Then perhaps it's time to expand your operation," he replied, smiling. "I hope you will write to me soon and let me know if you could supply me with several dozen caramels a week—until the river freezes. I have an open account with certain riverboat lines to convey products to my warehouse. I would of course expect exclusivity in your distribution to Iowa."

"I will… I'll think about it," she stammered.

"We will need to discuss pricing and my percentage of each sale, but we can do that by mail after you've had time to consider my suggestion."

She managed to nod.

He rose. "Thank you. I look forward to hearing from you, Miss Woolsey."

She shook his hand and he strode away toward the boat landing. Her mind whirled with this news. The man had spoken to her as one businessperson to another, a revelation.

Mrs. Ashford whipped outside, her skirts snapping with her haste. "Miss Rachel, Ned told me you were talking to a man on our porch."

The woman's nosiness acted on Rachel like a spring tonic. She rose and held out his card. No use sparking speculation by withholding the facts. "He wants to order my candies in bulk."

Mrs. Ashford snatched the card and read it. "Benson Food Emporiums. Oh, my. That is a large concern. How did he hear of you?"

Rachel recounted what she could recall of the interesting yet surprising encounter with Mr. Benson.

"Well!" Mrs. Ashford exclaimed. "Well!"

Rachel couldn't decide whether the woman was happy for her or disgruntled or just surprised. "I must be getting back to my place. I have a lot to do today." *And a lot to think and pray about.*

As she hurried homeward, rolling her cart through town, she felt Mrs. Ashford's curiosity-filled gaze burn into her back. When she reached her place, she rolled the cart into the shade and then sat down on the bench near her door. *Sell in bulk? What an idea.*

She wished suddenly that Mr. Merriday were here. She'd become accustomed to his being available…but perhaps that wouldn't last much longer. He still wanted to go to Canada.

She'd have time to observe him again at supper.

Maybe then she could figure out what had changed. And what that change might mean.

Rachel took pains to look her best, sweeping her hair up, changing into a fresh white apron and splashing cool water on her face. She told herself it was because Mr. Comstock was to be her guest, but she knew better. She wanted to look her best for Mr. Merriday.

The sweltering day had been a long and lonely one. She'd tried to ignore the lonely part, singing to the birds that hopped on the nearby tree branches and even chatting away to the huddle of chickens in the yard. But now she could share her news with Mr. Merriday. What would he have to say?

Finally she heard male voices and forced herself to remain inside until the last moment. She didn't want to betray how eager she was for their company, for his company. So she opened the door to find Brennan and Jacque washing their hands by her door.

Levi waved from behind them. "I washed up at home."

She grinned at this. "I'm glad to have thee join us tonight. This is a sort of celebration. I'm anticipating that Mr. Merriday will have news about thy property and I..." she paused for effect "...have news of my own today."

"What happened to you?" Jacque asked, drying his hands on the hucksack towel.

"All in good time," she teased. "Come in."

She'd prepared fried chicken. Mrs. Brawley, a neighbor, had decided to thin her chickens and had delivered birds already plucked. Since Rachel expected company for supper, she had purchased three.

"Wow! Fried chicken!" Jacque exclaimed and Levi joined in, too.

Soon the four of them sat at her table. She bowed her head for grace and then looked up. "Mr. Comstock, please help yourself."

The blacksmith grinned and took a piece from the platter of crisp, golden chicken. By the time it reached Jacque, only a drumstick remained. She rose and filled the platter again to vocal approval.

"Now, Mr. Merriday, did thee find some land for Mr. Comstock?" she asked as she began to slice her chicken breast.

Brennan chewed and swallowed. "Good chicken, Miss Rachel, and yes, I found two tracts that are near the Whitmores."

"Great," Levi said and then bit into a crispy wing.

"Which one does thee think is best?" she asked.

"The one with its own spring," Brennan said between bites. "In a drought year like this one, springs flow while wells may dry up."

For a moment all four were silent as they contemplated the dry weather and the recent grass wildfire.

"What else?" Levi asked.

"Got a good stand of trees a-course. Creek runs near it, too, and a small meadow where we could build your cabin."

Rachel's heart lifted against her will at this news. She shouldn't care that this sounded as if Brennan would be staying longer, but she couldn't lie to herself.

"Sounds great." Levi continued eating his chicken and cornbread with a smile on his face. "I'll apply for the claim on that land tomorrow."

"Sight unseen?" Brennan asked.

"You were a farmer, weren't you? You know more

about land than I do. I was raised in town to be a black-smith like my dad."

"Is it hard to learn to blacksmith?" Jacque asked.

All three adults turned to the boy.

"'Course you could," Brennan said.

"I think it would be interesting," Jacque said with a shrug. He tried not to look pleased. Then he looked to her. "What's your news, Miss Rachel?"

From her pocket, she retrieved the business card and handed it to Brennan.

He read it aloud and looked at her questioningly.

"Mr. Benson wants to buy my caramels and sponge candy in bulk."

All three males stared at her. Openmouthed.

"Well, what does thee think of that?" she asked.

"What does in bulk mean?" Jacque asked.

"That means they want her to make large batches and they'll sell her candy in their stores in Dubuque," Levi replied. "That's big."

Rachel felt herself turn rosy with pleasure. "I don't know if I can handle that. I mean soon Mr. Merriday plans on moving on—"

"What?" Jacque turned to Brennan. "What? Where we goin'?"

Brennan sent her a dark look. "Nowhere—yet. I had thought of Canada, but I'm not going nowhere anytime soon. It's just I been helping Miss Rachel prove up her homestead and now I'm going to help Levi. No time to get my own land."

Rachel frowned at him. Giving only part of the truth ranked as bad as an outright lie. And getting his own land—that was downright misleading. What about Canada? Had that changed? She wouldn't let herself hope.

He sent her a stern look, forbidding her to contradict him. And he squeezed the boy's shoulder. "Don't be worryin'."

Jacque looked down.

She drew in a deep breath. "Whether or not to sell in bulk is a big decision for me. But a welcome problem."

The meal passed then with the three males talking little and eating every last piece of chicken. She wished Levi were married and Posey had come with him so she would have had someone to chat with, someone to distract her from staring at Mr. Merriday.

Afterward Levi sat with Brennan outside near where Jacque and she washed and dried the dishes. Then Levi thanked her again for a wonderful meal and at Brennan's request let Jacque walk with him toward town.

Rachel guessed why Brennan remained behind and why he didn't want Jacque present. She put the dishes away and came outside. The setting sun was fiery red, predicting another hot day on the morrow. She sat down next to Mr. Merriday. "Thee is planning on scolding me?"

"Why'd you say I was leaving?"

At his unfair question, she starched up. "Because thee has been saying that since the day thee was able to begin talking in June. Thee didn't tell me not to mention it in front of Jacque."

He grumbled, "I know."

He'd poked her and she felt like goading him in return. "If thee plans on reaching Canada before winter, that will interfere with thy plans to help Levi."

"Don't you think I know that?" he snapped and then grimaced. "Sorry, that was not polite."

"Matters have not gone as thee had foreseen," she allowed. *And I'm glad.* Of course she couldn't voice that sentiment.

"I wish that letter would come from Louisiana."

She turned and looked him full in the face. "Does thee really think thee will be able to leave Jacque behind, even if he isn't thy son?"

He glared at her, his brows drawn together almost fiercely. "He's a great little kid. He's had it rough but my keeping him won't do him any favors—whether he's my blood or not."

His statement shocked her. "Whatever does thee mean? Thee is a fine man, Brennan Merriday. Thee has proved that over and over. I'm sorry thy homefolk cast thee out, but the fault did not lie with thee, but with their wicked, hard hearts."

"I don't know why I say things that I know will just fire you up. And I guess after drifting so long and people looking down on me, I just—"

"Then stop thinking that way. Thee is a fine man, Brennan Merriday. No one told me to think that. I know it from thy own actions since thee came to town."

He didn't reply and she let the silence grow between them.

"I read the letter from Posey's father. He understood how it felt when everybody he'd ever known turned against him." The sadness in his voice caught her breath.

She swallowed to clear her throat. "I think thee still believes that the people in thy hometown had a right to turn against thee. They didn't. They were wrong. Thee was right."

He rose, looking as if he were struggling to digest what she'd said. "I thank you for another good meal, Miss Rachel. And I bid you good night."

He walked away with a wave of his hand, leaving her dissatisfied. The man was impossible. Why couldn't he see that he'd done nothing wrong? Why couldn't he let go of the past and live in the present—here in Pepin? Was she foolish to hope in the end he might stay?

On Sunday morning next, Brennan appeared at the door, his hair damp from the river and with Jacque beside him. Brennan was wearing his newer clothing from the Ashfords instead of his work clothes. "We ready to head to church?"

Rachel hid her surprise behind a bland nod. Brennan had never attended church with her or been a part of anything in the community. What did this change mean?

Was this due to his son's presence or Posey's letter? Brennan clearly had not healed from whatever had separated him from his wife and started him wandering. Rachel began praying that God would take control of this morning—more than in general. *God, why does he want to go to church with me and the boy?*

Brennan watched her turn and pick up her Bible from the bedside table and then snag her bonnet from the peg. Brennan accepted her Bible while she tied the pale ribbons under her chin, a pleasant sight.

Brennan tried not to back out now. He'd decided to go sit in the schoolhouse church. But his reasons tangled in the back of his mind. The one that had prompted him clearly was Jacque, what was best for him—whether he turned out to be his blood or not. If the boy had a future here, Brennan didn't want to do anything to harm that. Wanted the boy to fit in. Besides, church was good for a boy—would teach him right from wrong.

As the three of them walked through town, Levi joined them in his Sunday best, too. Levi's happiness over staking a claim and the subsequent granting of permission to court Miss Posey worried Brennan. The grandmother had given her permission, but she seemed an unreasonable kind of woman.

Soon the four of them joined the wagons and people on foot, converging on the log schoolhouse. Noah stood at the door, greeting his congregation. Here was one man Brennan respected. When Noah offered him a hand, Brennan shook it, smiling.

"I'm glad to see you, Mr. Merriday," the preacher said without any reproachful tone in his words.

"Thanks, preacher," Brennan replied.

Inside the door, an older man Brennan had seen around town in a wheelchair held out his hand. "I'm Old Saul, Mr. Merriday. I'm glad to meet you."

Brennan shook the man's gnarled hand, hoping he wouldn't hear any scolding about why he hadn't come sooner.

"I've met your son here before." Old Saul reached over and shook Jacque's hand and Levi's. "We're glad to have you with us this Sunday and in our town."

Brennan doubted that but he mumbled something polite.

The older man appeared frail but he had a look that could pierce a man. Brennan nodded and moved ahead to let others greet Old Saul. He glanced at Rachel.

"I usually sit with my cousin's wife," Miss Rachel murmured.

"Yes, miss," Brennan replied. "I think we'll sit with Levi today."

She nodded and moved forward to the front to sit beside Noah's pretty wife, Sunny.

Then Levi led the two of them to a few pews behind the Ashfords. "This is where I usually sit," the blacksmith murmured. The men sat with the boy between them. "Old Saul used to be the preacher before Noah," Levi said quietly. "He's a good man, always a kind word to everybody."

Nodding, Brennan noted but didn't acknowledge any of the interest his attending church elicited. He didn't want to fit in here. He'd just come because he wanted the boy accepted—that was all.

One tall, elegant lady approached him. "Good day, Mr. Merriday. I am Mrs. Lang, Johann's aunt."

Brennan, Levi and Jacque rose politely.

"I am going to continue as teacher here at least for a few months," she said. "The school board has a teacher coming but the man has met with an accident and so has been delayed. I hope you will be sending your son."

"Of course," Brennan replied without hesitation. "Schooling is good."

Jacque looked undecided about this.

"Johann, I know, is looking forward to the start of school," the woman said, smiling at Jacque and touching his shoulder.

This brightened the boy's face. Mrs. Lang bid them good day and moved to sit with her husband, their baby, Johann and Gunther.

The wall clock read ten and the service started with a hymn, "Just As I Am, Without One Plea," led by an older couple at the front. Brennan stood but didn't sing a note. He was surprised to hear Levi sing with a strong tenor and Jacque piping a boyish soprano.

Levi must have sung louder than usual because people turned to look at him. And then Brennan saw Posey glance behind at Levi and smile. Brennan figured it out. Singing louder was like a bullfrog croaking to attract feminine attention. Brennan wished he could preserve the flash of amusement this brought him.

But soon everyone sat and the singing was done and the preaching began. He wondered what kind of preacher Noah Whitmore would turn out to be. He didn't expect fire and brimstone and pounding the pulpit and he was right. Then Noah read Matthew 10:

Think not that I am come to send peace on earth: I came not to send peace, but a sword.

For I am come to set a man at variance against his father.

And a man's foes shall be they of his own household.

Each word struck Brennan like a hammer blow. The terrible sinking feeling began in the pit of his stomach. He gripped the bench underneath him and willed away images of that dreadful day, the day the state of Mississippi had seceded, the day he'd made his decision known.

He fought free and looked at Levi to see if he'd exposed any of his inner turmoil. Levi wasn't looking at him. He was gazing at the back of Posey's bonnet. Surreptitiously Brennan surveyed the people around him who were blessedly ignoring him also.

He blocked out the rest of Noah's words, forcing himself to stare at the wood floor and go over in his mind what he had to do at Levi's newly staked homestead now that his rib had healed. Surely before fall had passed, he'd receive the letter and have Levi's work done.

At the end of the sermon, Brennan rose with everyone and listened to Noah's benediction. "The Lord bless thee, and keep thee. The Lord make his face shine upon thee, and be gracious unto thee. The Lord lift up his countenance upon thee, and give thee peace."

Brennan felt a touch of that peace. *Must be due to Noah Whitmore, one lucky man.* The three of them turned to find Miss Rachel waiting for them at the rear of the church with—of all people—Mrs. Ashford.

Brennan didn't want to talk to the woman but he had brought Posey's letter. He had meant to slip it to Posey when no one was looking, but when would that be?

"We want to invite the four of you to Sunday dinner," the storekeeper's wife said brightly.

Brennan tried not to look surprised or distressed, as he was both.

"That is a kind invitation," Miss Rachel said, looking to him as if asking him to come up with a good excuse.

His mind was a blank slate.

And that's how they ended upstairs, sitting around the Ashfords' table. Posey's grandmother had not been well enough to walk to church but she sat at the table. Brennan almost felt sorry for her. She had obviously lost flesh everywhere but in her swollen abdomen, another sign it might be heart trouble.

Mr. Ashford said a long and flowery grace and then the meal began—roast beef, mashed potatoes and fresh green beans with bacon. *Almost as good as Miss Rachel's meals.*

Brennan had made up his mind. He would eat and say nothing except thank-you at the end.

Mrs. Ashford started the conversation. "Mr. Merriday, you have certainly improved your situation since coming to Pepin." He swallowed not only his mouthful of food, but also the sharp reply that came to mind. *He didn't want to be judged. Nobody did.*

"You've become quite respectable," the woman continued.

Miss Rachel gasped audibly.

Saying that Mrs. Ashford lacked tact was like saying the Mississippi flowed south to New Orleans. Brennan stared at the woman without a word to say.

"Mr. Merriday was a friend, a comrade in arms with my father," Posey said with quiet dignity. "Mr. Merriday may have come to town sick and in a bad situation, but he has always been respectable."

Levi beamed at her.

"Indeed," Miss Rachel murmured.

"Mr. Comstock," Almeria said, filling the uncomfortable silence, "tell us about your claim."

Brennan was taken aback. He'd never expected this woman to come to his aid.

Chapter Twelve

Levi stepped into the fray, another buffer between Mrs. Ashford and Brennan's temper. "Well, Brennan went out to look at land for me—I've been so busy with work at the forge. And he's a farmer so I thought he'd know how to assess land better than I would."

Grateful to Levi, Rachel felt her tension ease a fraction.

"You didn't go yourself?" the older woman asked sharply.

"I trust Brennan," Levi replied. "And after staking my claim, I went to the land and he chose the right tract. I saw that right away. Has a spring and a creek running near it. We'll not want for water—no matter whether rain comes or not."

The older woman appeared appeased.

Rachel relaxed. Now if Mrs. Ashford would concentrate on Levi, not Brennan—

"Why don't you stake a claim for yourself, Mr. Merriday?" Mrs. Ashford asked.

Steadily chewing his food, Brennan stared at the woman.

Rachel spoke up. "Mr. Merriday never planned to

settle here." Was the woman completely oblivious to the effect of her questions? "He's only here because he was left by that boat captain when he was ill. And he graciously agreed to help me prove up my homestead."

"But why move?" Mrs. Ashford said. "There's land and work for you, Mr. Merriday. Why not settle here?"

Rachel wondered where Mrs. Ashford's change of attitude was coming from.

Brennan continued eating, looking more and more as if he would let loose with something rude at any moment.

Rachel nearly stopped eating but forced herself to go on.

"I'm going to write my parents," Levi said, again diverting attention, "that I'm courting a young lady. I'd like them to come up and meet Posey before—" the man blushed "—before…winter."

Rachel was certain he meant to say *before we become formally engaged* and her heart softened. "I'd like to meet thy family, Mr. Comstock."

"Are you two really gonna get married?" Jacque asked.

The boy's question, which so obviously revealed his opinion that girls were to be devoutly avoided, lightened the mood around the table.

Rachel chuckled.

"Yes, we are," Posey said, smiling at Jacque.

"Children should be seen and not heard," Mrs. Ashford said stringently.

"Sometimes," Brennan began, "adults should be—"

"I've decided to write that Mr. Benson in Dubuque," Rachel interrupted, fearing Mr. Merriday was about to insult their hostess. "I may need to find some local help. Producing in bulk and then shipping the candy while still fresh might force me to find someone to work with me."

"I'd love to help you," Posey said.

"Me, too!" Amanda joined in.

Their responses did not surprise Rachel yet she saw Mrs. Ashford look a bit irritated.

"I will need to discuss terms with Mr. Benson first," Rachel said, "to see if doing business with him would profit me enough that I could compensate anyone."

"Very wise," Mr. Ashford said. "So far, Miss Rachel, you have made very sound business decisions for a woman. Please feel free to discuss Mr. Benson's terms with me."

In spite of the "for a woman" slur, Miss Rachel smiled at him. He had been helpful in ordering her new oven and she liked the man. He and his wife, especially his wife, wanted to be thought important, but they were honest, good people. She tried to catch Brennan's eye to encourage him to show some grace.

He merely sent her a brief scowl.

As soon as he finished his meal, he rose. "I thank you for the good meal, ma'am." And with that he left.

Mrs. Ashford looked surprised. "Well," she said, "well."

Mr. Ashford gazed at her pointedly. "Katharine, Mr. Merriday went through the war and like your sister lost everything because of it. We can afford to be charitable."

While these words appeared to calm the lady of the house, they stirred up a storm in Jacque's eyes.

Everyone but Rachel seemed to have forgotten this boy came from Mississippi.

"The news from the South is disturbing," Posey said. "It's like people still want to fight the war. Hasn't there been enough suffering?" The young woman's tone radiated despair.

"You Yankees took everything!" Jacque stood up, red-faced. He barged from the room and they heard his footsteps thunder down the back staircase.

"Well!" Mrs. Ashford exclaimed once more.

Rachel rested a hand on the lady's. "I think Jacque suffered greatly in the war, too. He lost everyone except his father and I'm sure he witnessed fighting and… killing."

"But we—" Mrs. Ashford began.

"She's right," Almeria spoke up. "You didn't suffer as we did. Your son was in California, a long way from the war and you didn't lose anything to a marauding army or suffer for your support of the Union. There's an old spiritual that starts, 'Nobody knows the trouble I've seen.…'" The older woman shook her head and laid down her fork. "I'm tired, Posey. Please help me to my room."

Levi stood up. "I'll help you, ma'am. If you'll permit me."

Rachel had never seen the older woman smile.

Almeria did now. "Yes, please."

Levi helped her out of her chair, offered her his arm and let her lean against him as he walked her down the short hallway to her room. Posey trailed behind the two.

When Rachel turned, she found Mrs. Ashford dabbing her eyes with a hankie. "I don't know," the woman whispered in a choked voice, "how long we'll have her with us."

Rachel had thought the two strong-minded women would grate on each other's nerves. Yet Mrs. Ashford's sadness appeared completely genuine. Rachel tilted her head and murmured a sympathetic phrase. Mrs. Ashford was a mixture of the maddening and the benign. *Well, aren't we all? Even Brennan Merriday.*

Rachel found Jacque sitting in the shade of her shed where a bit of coolness could be found. Once again she must pour balm upon this young, wounded heart. Where was Brennan? She'd fretted over him all day. But right now dealing with Jacque was all she could handle.

"I ain't gonna apologize to that Yankee," he said, firing up.

"Jacque, I am a Yankee, too, remember?"

He wouldn't let her catch his eye.

She reached down and claimed his hand. "Thee missed a really good apple pie."

He let her take his hand and lead him to the cabin but still kept his eyes lowered.

Inside, she nudged him to sit on the bench at the table and brought out a cookie and handed it to him. "Thee must give up the war, Jacque. The Union was preserved. Slavery is abolished forever. And it's time to let go."

He sent her a disgusted look.

The boy had much to learn and school started tomorrow. She couldn't let him go to a school full of Yankees and continue hating them. The truth would set him free, so she would give him truth. "I'm a Quaker. Thee knows that many Quakers were abolitionists?"

He chewed the cookie slowly, ignoring her.

"Jacque, I understand the war injured thee in many ways, but that does not mean I will tolerate impoliteness. I asked thee a question, please answer it."

"Yeah, I heard of abolitionists and Quakers."

"And the Underground Railroad?"

He looked up at this. "You didn't do that, did you?"

She nodded. "My family hid runaway slaves twice when I was a child."

Jacque looked at her as if she'd just said that a wanted outlaw and she were best friends.

"Slavery was wrong." She sat down across from him.

He folded his arms across his narrow chest and glared at the tabletop.

Her heart ached not only for this boy but for all the suffering slavery had unleashed upon them. God was not mocked. Whatever a man or a nation sowed, that it would reap. "Would thee have wanted to be a slave?"

He glared up at her then. "It's not the same."

"Because thee was born with white skin? Take a moment and think of life if thee had black skin." She fell silent. "Thy mother died, but how would it have felt to have been sold away from thy mother?"

The silence grew and the outdoor noises, the clicking of insects and singing of birds, grew louder.

"My pa…" Jacque corrected himself. "I mean, Mr. Merriday says he went to a slave auction and it was awful." The boy's tone said that he had given this a lot of thought.

"I'm sure it was."

Jacque looked at her then. "He said he saw that they were people. But everybody told me slavery was best for black people. That they weren't smart enough to look after themselves."

The old lie. Rachel rose and lifted one of her books down. "This book was written by a man named Frederick Douglass." She forced Jacque to take the book from her. "He was born a slave, ran away and became an educated man. He is certainly able to look after himself. It is titled *Narrative of the Life of Frederick Douglass, An American Slave*."

Jacque looked at the book as if it were a snake about to strike.

"Tomorrow thee will begin school and will learn how to read and write better. And as soon as thee is able, we will read this, Mr. Douglass's story, together. He knows what it was like to be a slave. After we finish the book, we will discuss slavery."

She realized that she'd just given a promise she might not be able to keep. What if Brennan left, taking this boy with him? Or just left her? Her heart felt crushed by a dreadful weight.

Jacque stared at the book a long while. Then he glanced up. His face had lost its stubborn rebelliousness. "I want to hear what that man's book has to say. You've treated me better than anybody ever has. You feed me good food. You make me new clothes. You talk nice to me."

"Mr. Merriday has done good by you too," she prompted.

He grimaced. "He's okay…for a Yankee."

She let it go at that. They were making some progress here.

He ran his hand up the spine of the book and then handed it back to her. "You think school will be good?"

Rejoicing silently, she accepted the book, returned it to the shelf over her bed and turned to him. "I liked school. That boy, Clayton, will be there but Mrs. Lang will keep him in line at least till the new teacher comes. Make sure thee obeys the teacher and all will work out well."

Jacque nodded. "How come you're so nice to me?"

Rachel let herself stroke the boy's hair and cup his cheek. "I was raised to treat others as I would want to be treated. I suggest thee lives that way, too."

"Even to Clayton?"

She laughed out loud and ruffled his hair. Suddenly it was so hot and she longed to do something she'd done as a child. "Let's go wading in the creek and cool off."

"Miss Rachel! Really?"

Grinning, soon Rachel walked beside Jacque toward the creek, looking forward to taking off her shoes and wading in the cool water. But where had Mr. Merriday gone?

And what would she do when he finished helping to build Mr. Comstock's cabin and left for Canada? Or would he stay? When would that letter from Louisiana come and did she really want it to come? Would this truth set them free or just set them at odds?

After a day of wandering near the river and keeping out of sight, Brennan finally gave in and headed for Miss Rachel's cabin. He didn't want to need her, but he couldn't stay away.

He paused to look through the trees into her clearing. Everything was as usual—neat and tidy, well ordered. Jacque was sitting on the bench by the door, whittling a stick with a small knife. A striped black-and-white stray cat had come from somewhere and was lying at the boy's feet.

Mrs. Ashford's voice came back. *Mr. Merriday, you have certainly improved your situation since coming to Pepin.* Brennan gritted his teeth. That obnoxious woman's words had repeated in his mind all day—no matter what he did. She might be right and he didn't like it. Resisting again, he started to turn away.

Then he glimpsed Miss Rachel come to the open doorway. She scanned the edges of the clearing. Was she looking for him? He didn't like the way his heart lifted at this thought. But it was just a false twinge. He had no heart left. It had been beaten out of him long ago.

Still, he went into the clearing and tried to ignore how her welcoming smile captured him.

"Where you been all day?" the boy demanded.

"That your cat?" Brennan responded, ignoring the question.

"I don't know. She just come this afternoon when we were wading in the creek." Jacque leaned down and the cat let him rub her head with his knuckles.

"You know it's a she?"

"Miss Rachel says she's gonna have kittens soon."

"Yes," the lady spoke up. "I'm hoping she's come to stay. One can always use a good mouser. But, Jacque, remember I said she might have decided merely to visit us. We'll just have to see."

Brennan stared at her. This woman was always taking in strays—this cat, Jacque, him. He stalked to the basin and washed his hands. "I'll go milk the cow."

"I already did that," Jacque said.

Mrs. Ashford intruded again—*You've become quite respectable.*

Brennan's jaw tightened. If only he could have told off the storekeeper's nosey wife, she wouldn't still be digging her spurs into him.

"Come in to supper." Miss Rachel waved him forward. "We're having cornbread and milk."

"And the last of the cookies?" Jacque asked hopefully.

Brennan couldn't help himself. He laughed out loud.

Miss Rachel beamed at him.

He followed her, the boy and the cat inside. Yesterday Miss Rachel had baked a double batch of buttery cornbread, which now disappeared, eaten from bowls of milk drizzled with maple syrup. He savored the salty and sweet and the rich flavors of cornmeal and maple.

The quiet of the cabin and Miss Rachel's good food worked on him, soothing him. Here he felt at home, an unwelcome thought.

Why don't you stake a claim for yourself, Mr. Merriday? Mrs. Ashford had asked.

He put down his spoon and rubbed his forehead. The awful restlessness he'd experienced that evening down by the river goaded him again. He wished he could bid Pepin farewell. He would never feel easy till he put the war behind him and that was impossible here. But some part of him reached for Miss Rachel as if she might make everything right.

"Jacque will be going to school tomorrow," Miss Rachel said. "I will walk with him and thee."

Brennan stared at her. He knew why she said this. She was insisting he act as father to this boy. He nodded, looking her full in the face and then away as her sweetness broke over him afresh. "No trouble. We'll walk over after breakfast and then I'm headin' out to Levi's place. Your cousin is going to help me do some more logging out the clearing. And plowing up rocks for the foundation."

She nodded. "I'm glad to hear that Noah is helping."

"Yeah, the sooner I get Levi set up, the sooner I can head north."

Jacque looked up quickly. "We still gonna leave?"

Brennan didn't like the strain in the boy's voice. And it prompted him to be honest. "I've always planned on going north to Canada."

"But it's terrible cold up there," the boy whined.

Brennan shrugged and Miss Rachel pressed her lips together.

They finished the meal in silence and then Jacque went outside to play with the cat and a bit of string.

Miss Rachel didn't mince words, as usual, but spoke in an undertone. "I don't understand why thee fights settling down and being a father. Why isn't thee happy having a son and friends here? What's stopping thee from staking a homestead claim here?"

He rubbed the back of his neck. "I just can't be free till I leave this country."

"If thee believes that, thee is fooling thyself. Thee will take the war with thee wherever thee tries to settle. The past is a part of us, not a coat one can shed."

He rose abruptly. Words of denial jammed in his throat. "Thanks for the meal," he managed to say. "I'll see you in the morning."

He walked out and told the boy to come to the forge when he finished the dishes for Miss Rachel.

Jacque pouted and Brennan walked away. But with every step, he felt the pull, the unseen bond connecting him and the lady who stood in her doorway watching him leave. She was right, of course, about the past, and that made it all worse.

The first Monday of September the two of them walked Jacque to the schoolyard and Mr. Merriday enrolled him in school. Though the boy was ten, he would work with the first graders but be allowed to sit beside his friend, Johann. Rachel was intensely grateful to Mrs. Lang for her understanding.

Rachel and Mr. Merriday barely reached the main street and he was off, heading toward Levi's homestead. She watched him go. Not for the first time, she wished she could get inside his mind. Or maybe his heart. He'd suffered so and insisted on carrying it forward into the present. Why?

Christ had said, *Let the dead bury their dead.* Why couldn't Brennan bury the past, not let it control him? Slavery had been a bondage to everyone it touched.

But who was she to think she could solve this problem or any other? Shaking her head at her own pride and praying for Brennan, she walked home to set her cinnamon rolls in the oven to bake. She expected boats today and was not disappointed.

Later, as she sold the last of her wares, she watched Mr. Ashford accept the mailbag. For some reason she slowed her steps homeward.

"Miss Rachel!" the storekeeper-postmaster called out. "There is a letter for Mr. Merriday. From Louisiana!"

Suddenly finding it difficult to breathe, Rachel turned and accepted the letter, then slipped it into her pocket. "I'll make sure he gets it. He's working on Levi's homestead today."

Mr. Ashford nodded, but she could tell he was curious about the letter from Louisiana, too.

She trundled the cart homeward, intensely aware of the letter in her pocket. Now she must wait hours for Mr. Merriday to come and open it. She would have to keep very busy so she didn't rip it open herself.

Brennan tried to keep the pace of the work steady enough to reduce the chance for talk. Brennan respected Noah and still owed him for saving his life, but he didn't want any advice. And couldn't preachers always be counted on to give advice?

Noah had brought his horse and plow to turn over the ground where the cabin would be and where a fu-

ture garden would sit. They turned up a fresh crop of
Wisconsin rocks. Brennan had never seen soil like this.
Every furrow was clogged with stones.

Noah had brought over a wheelbarrow the night before. After they had dug out and piled up all the rocks
from the cabin site, the two men filled the wheelbarrow with them. Then they rolled the rocks with strenu-
ous effort to where the two-room cabin would stand.

Then Mrs. Whitmore brought over a fresh pot of
steaming coffee and lunch. She left them with a friendly
wave.

"I'm a lucky man," Noah said when the two of them
were alone again.

Brennan nodded.

"I know you plan on leaving, but have you considered staying at all?"

Brennan concentrated on chewing the sandwich and
damped down his ire at the meddling. "I just want to
get away from the war, from anybody who fought in it."

"I understand. I came to Wisconsin for just that reason."

Brennan looked up. "Then you understand."

"I came to Wisconsin to live but to keep myself separate from the folk here. Sort of live like a hermit."

The idea appealed to Brennan.

"But 'no man is an island,'" Noah quoted. "I found
myself sucked into the community and couldn't keep
apart. I'm glad now because I've been healing. I used
to have nightmares and spells where I'd be back to that
awful waiting time just before a battle. You know what
I mean." Noah shook his head.

Brennan looked at him then. Noah had nightmares,
too? And that dreaded feeling of being dragged back
into the living nightmare of waiting to charge into bat-

tle? "I've had a few spells myself," Brennan admitted, not meeting Noah's gaze. "You still have 'em?"

"Not often anymore. Having my wife and children and living in this fresh new place. I got a new start. And letting God in, not holding Him off. All that is healing me."

Brennan didn't know what to say to this. He and God were not on speaking terms. Noah understood, but he hadn't lost everything, everyone in the war. Noah was a lucky man, luckier than he was.

"I'll say no more." Noah sipped his coffee. "But you could do worse than settle here. You've made friends and…there's Rachel."

Noah's mention of his cousin in connection with Brennan came completely unexpectedly. He ignored it, merely nodded once curtly to acknowledge that he'd heard Noah. But no matter what anybody said, he wasn't settling in Pepin. Miss Rachel would be better off without him.

Dry-mouthed, Brennan stared at the letter on Miss Rachel's mantel. Earlier she'd told him it had come at last, but quietly so that the boy wouldn't hear. Jacque didn't know about the letter and what it might mean for him. Supper had ended and now Jacque played outside with the striped cat, leaving the two of them alone in the cabin.

Brennan reached for the letter. Part of him strained to head out and read it alone. But Miss Rachel had written his letter and he could imagine how much self-control she'd used to keep from tearing it open this morning.

She handed him a clean butter knife and he slit open the envelope.

Saint Joseph's Church
Parish of Alexandria
Alexandria, Louisiana

August 16, 1871

Dear Mr. Merriday,
I write to inform you that Jacque Louis Charpentier Merriday was born on November 13, 1861, son of Lorena Charpentier Merriday and was baptized. You are listed as the father. Lorena's death is recorded on December 24, 1864, and she is buried in the churchyard.

May God bless you and young Jacque.
The Right Reverend August Joseph Martin

Brennan read the brief letter twice and then handed it to Miss Rachel.

"So we have the answer to the question," she murmured. "Jacque is thy son."

He couldn't speak. His face felt frozen.

"What now?"

He stared at her. Finally, he said, "I don't know."

"Jacque must be told."

He rose and shook his head. "Not yet."

She gazed at him a long time. "Soon."

The woman was relentless. "All right."

He left then, memories of his few years with Lorena spinning through his mind. He waved to the boy and the two walked through the dying light to Levi's.

This boy is my son. He repeated the words silently. Some part of him had known that Jacque belonged to him, but he'd resisted it. And it had nothing to do with the boy.

* * *

The evening before, Rachel had watched Brennan walk out of her clearing and then she'd barely slept all night. Now she tried to go through her morning routine, mixing batter for muffins to sell today and waiting for Brennan and Jacque to arrive for breakfast. Had Brennan told Jacque? That didn't seem possible. But he must.

Finally Jacque arrived—alone. "Mornin', Miss Rachel!" The boy stopped and washed his hands outside.

"Where is Mr. Merriday?" she asked, hiding her sharp reaction to his absence.

"He went straight out to Levi's place. I asked him, didn't he want breakfast, and he said Mrs. Whitmore would give him something."

Rachel held in all the aggravation and disappointment and words that wanted to be released. Did the man think avoiding her would let him avoid the truth?

Soon Jacque had eaten and he set off for school. She watched him go and finished her baking. A boat whistled and she hurried into town to sell her muffins.

Then she parked her cart in the shade near the schoolyard and headed up the road. She could not wait till this evening to hear what Mr. Merriday was going to do now.

It was just like him to pull back instead of talking matters over. The man nearly drove her insane and yet she dreaded the day he might act upon what he'd said since the beginning. *I can't bear to have him leave.*

The miles under the relentless sun passed quickly and she was drawn by the sound of someone cutting down a tree. She turned toward the sound and saw Mr. Merriday ahead, working alone. That bothered her, too. A man should never cut tall trees by himself. It was too dangerous.

She waited till the tree trembled and then fell, bouncing and rolling to a halt against the surrounding trees. "Brennan!" she called and then halted abruptly. Why had she called him by his given name?

He turned to her and scowled. "Is something wrong?"

She shook her head at him, disappointed, exasperated. "Surely thee can guess why I have come?"

He motioned for her to come closer while he mopped his forehead with a kerchief. He waved her to sit on a stump and he sat down on one across from her. "The letter."

"Yes, the letter. What does thee plan to do about the fact that Jacque is thy son?"

He covered his face with the kerchief for a moment and then lowered it. "I've decided to ask you to marry me."

His words were so unexpected that she thought she'd imagined them. "What?"

He repeated the proposal or something that might be deemed a proposal. A sorry one.

"Marry? Me?" She stared at him, her heart suddenly bounding with hope. "Has thee fallen in love with me?"

He wrinkled his face. "Love? What's that got to do with us?"

She drew in air so sharply she nearly choked. "Indeed." Her word could have frozen water.

"You're not one of those foolish women," he said with disdain. "You're a good woman and you have good sense." He said the words fiercely, as if someone were arguing with him.

Rachel was not complimented. Her heart began beating in a sluggish kind of funeral rhythm. "And that's why thee wants to marry me?" She mocked him with her words.

He didn't hear her sarcasm or ignored it. "No, of course not. It's the boy. He needs a home and family. And you're right. If I want to shed the past, going to Canada won't help. I'll have to find a way not to remember the war, root it out of my memory—though how that's possible, I don't know."

Being valued for only the services she could provide, not because she was worthy of love. It was happening to her again. "I see."

"It makes sense for you and me to wed. Jacque likes you. You're a good cook and a good woman. I'd do my part. We could be content."

She had told Brennan in all honesty about the previous proposal she had received. Obviously he had forgotten or ignored her. "Content?" she asked icily.

He eyed her. "You're not going to get all fluttery and feminine on me, are you? It could be strictly a business arrangement. If you don't want me to touch you, I won't."

The final insult was too much. She rose—ice gone—molten lava rolling through her. "Brennan Merriday, as a *spinster,* I have been insulted many times in my life. But I don't think anyone—not even the man who needed a mother for his six young children and who asked me to marry him a week after he buried his wife—insulted me quite as thoroughly as thee has done today. Do not darken my door again."

She turned on her heel, ignoring his protestations.

Noah was coming up the trail toward them. She nodded at her cousin and went on without looking back.

Strictly business—the words twisted inside her like red-hot iron. And she knew the hurt was not Brennan's fault. She'd allowed her heart to overrule her head. She'd let herself have feelings for a man, incapable or unwilling to admit he could love or that she was a woman worthy of love.

She would marry no man for *sensible* reasons. Or for *his* convenience. Or to be *content*. Not even Brennan Merriday, the man she loved with all her heart.

Chapter Thirteen

Brennan's stomach growled as he notched a log, preparing to set it in place when Noah arrived at Levi's claim. He'd started a day's work with only a cup of Levi's bad coffee and a scorched egg for breakfast. Levi hadn't questioned why he'd sent Jacque alone again to Miss Rachel's this morning. But he would soon.

Feeling mauled inside, Brennan couldn't face Miss Rachel. He'd clean forgotten she'd already turned down one marriage proposed by a man who wanted only a mother for his children. Of all the people in Pepin he hadn't wanted to hurt, it was Miss Rachel. But the words could not be unspoken.

A phrase from her response to his proposal of marriage repeated over and over in his mind—*Brennan Merriday, I have been insulted many times in my life.*

I should have known better, done better.

Whistling, Noah walked up the trail and hailed him with the smile of a contented man. Soon the two were wrestling a log into the notches Brennan had carved. Brennan concentrated on the work, wishing he and Noah could work faster because as soon as this cabin was up, he would leave Pepin and take Jacque with him.

He couldn't stay after what he'd said to Miss Rachel. He'd ruined everything by thinking of himself, not her. And now Jacque would have to leave the place where he'd just begun to feel at home. It looked like the stray cat had more sense than Brennan did.

It was past time to go. He blocked out Miss Rachel's sweet smile and gentle gray eyes and how they'd revealed the hurt he'd caused her. His leaving was for the best or that's what he tried to make himself believe.

From her doorway, Rachel waved Jacque off to school as naturally as she could. She had never ached so in her life. At the edge of her clearing, Jacque turned back, looking troubled. She tried to smile for him, her lips quivering.

Then he disappeared around the bend and she looked down at herself. Why did she look the same? Feeling this mangled and clawed within, she should have been covered with bruises and bloodstains.

She went inside and sank into her rocker. She must not just sit here, but she could not move. She'd told Brennan not to darken her door again and he hadn't. Jacque had looked confused and troubled at coming alone for breakfast. What had Brennan told him? Jacque had not mentioned the letter so Brennan must not have told him yet.

She pressed a hand to her heart and rubbed at the sharp and insistent pain there. She hadn't been completely aware that Brennan had won a place in her heart—an understatement. But she could have given him no different reply.

The hurt she now felt was beyond anything she had experienced for a very long time, nearly as great as losing her mother when a child.

Rachel realized now that when she'd lost her mother, she felt she'd lost the only person who loved her for herself, not for what she could do. She'd told Brennan about the proposal she'd received and rejected in Pennsylvania. *I thought better of him.* "Oh, Father in heaven, why has this happened?" she whispered, pressing her hand to her throbbing forehead.

"Why did Brennan Merriday come into my life and so misunderstand me that he would say those words?" The offer not to touch her… "I know I'm not pretty," she whispered, tears budding in her eyes, "but…"

She rocked and wept into her hand, wishing she could forget the hurt that offer caused.

"Hello the house!"

Rachel groaned. Company, and it sounded like Amanda Ashford. Rachel's door stood open and she couldn't hide. She rose swiftly, wiping away her tears. She splashed cool water on her face and stood very still for a moment, as if regaining her balance, before walking to the door. This might prove to be the longest day of her life.

"Hello, Amanda. And Posey." She cleared her thick throat. "What can I do for thee?"

"We thought we'd come to help you today," Amanda said cautiously. "Thought you might want to show us how to work with you in case you decide to make a business arrangement with that Mr. Benson."

"A good idea." Rachel couldn't bring up any enthusiasm for work, but having someone with her would be better than sitting alone and crying all day, wouldn't it? "Come in."

Both girls eyed her as if they sensed her distress but thankfully neither asked what had upset her. Soon

Rachel was showing the girls the ingredients for cinnamon rolls.

"But my handful is smaller than your handful," Amanda pointed out.

Rachel considered this, trying to gather her wits. "Let's use a teacup to see the difference." All three of them filled one palm full of flour and then poured it into a tea cup. Indeed the girls' cups were not as full as hers or each other's.

Rachel didn't really have the patience to deal with this, but she worked her way through the problem, showing the girls how the batter was to look and then letting them experiment with how many handfuls it took to make their batter take on the same consistency as hers.

By the time this had been accomplished, she understood the phrase, fit to be tied. She couldn't erase the awful words Brennan Merriday had spoken to her.

Brennan would leave now, taking Jacque with him, and she would live alone here in this cabin and make a living selling her baked goods and sweets. She would be a success and she would be miserable.

Evening came. Jacque arrived for supper but Brennan did not. Jacque looked worried. "What's wrong, Miss Rachel?"

She forced back the tears that had hovered all day. "Did Mr. Merriday read thee the letter from Louisiana?"

"What letter?"

She pressed her lips tightly together to keep from saying something uncomplimentary about the boy's father. "Come in. We will eat our supper and I will make up a plate for thy father. After he eats, thee must ask him to read the letter."

Then Jacque did something he had never done before. He threw his arms around her waist and clung to her. "I don't want to leave you. I want to stay here. I like school and I got my first real friend and you treat me good. Don't let him take me away."

Rachel bent over and hugged the boy to her. Tears fell yet she stifled her sobs for the boy's sake. Finally she commanded herself again and straightened up and wiped her face with her fingertips. "Jacque, I care about thee a great deal and would love to have thee stay here. But that is not my decision, it is Mr. Merriday's."

"Why do I always gotta do what other people say I gotta do? When I'm bigger, I'll do whatever I want."

She brushed his curly black hair back from his forehead. "I am bigger and I don't get to do whatever I want, Jacque." She leaned down and kissed the place between his eyebrows. "I will always be thy friend, Jacque. No matter where thee goes, thee can always come back. My door will always be open for thee. And I hope thee will learn to write and send me letters so I know where thee is."

Jacque nodded, but did not look comforted.

They tried to eat their supper. Then Rachel fixed up a plate for Jacque to take to Mr. Merriday. Downcast, he carried it, covered with a clean dishcloth, out of her clearing.

The stray striped cat wandered into view and walked over to Rachel and then rubbed her ankles, mewing softly.

Rachel bent down and petted the cat. "Hello, Mrs. Cat. Has thee come for scraps? Please come in."

The cat followed her inside and ate the plate of food Rachel had no appetite for now. When Rachel sat outside on her bench, the cat lay at her feet, purring loudly.

Rachel was comforted and she could bear the pain—
not forget it, but bear it. Could God use a stray cat as a
blessing? Why not?

Brennan saw Jacque coming, bearing a covered plate.
The sight brought Miss Rachel to mind and her image
grabbed him in its clutches. His whole body tightened
with the anguish of hurting her. He'd regretted much
in his life but this was the worst.

Jacque handed him the plate with a resentful look.
"Miss Rachel says to read me the letter."

Brennan held the plate but didn't move.

"What does a letter got to do with me? I know you're
fixin' to leave, but I've decided I ain't goin' with you.
You're not my pa. I want to stay with Miss Rachel."

Brennan set down his plate and reached in his back
pocket and withdrew the creased letter. He opened it
and read it to the boy.

Jacque stared at him; Brennan returned the stare.

"That means you're really my pa?"

Brennan nodded, dry-mouthed.

"Why don't you go to Miss Rachel's anymore?"

"I have finished working for her," Brennan said, con-
cealing all the important information. "I'm going to
build Levi a house and then we're heading out."

"I don't want to leave!"

I don't either. How could he tell the boy he'd ruined
everything? "Now we know you're my son and that
means you'll go where I go. And I got to go where I
can get more work. I hear they want men for logging
and building a railroad east of here. We'll go there."

"I thought you wanted to go to Canada," Jacque
pointed out.

"Maybe we will. Maybe we won't. We need money

to get established with a place to live. Both of us will need warm clothes for the winter. You'll need boots and I need new ones. That all costs money."

"Why can't we stay here? You could marry Miss Rachel and we could be a family."

Brennan drew in air. The boy's words pierced him like daggers of ice. "Marrying is a delicate matter. Just because Miss Rachel is nice does not mean she wants to marry someone like me."

Jacque stared at him. "You're not good enough for her?"

"That's right. I'm not good enough for her."

"I know she likes you. She looks at you when you're not looking."

More ice plunged into his heart. If that was so, he'd hurt Miss Rachel even more deeply. He was an idiot lout and no doubt about it. "Go to bed."

Jacque glared at him and turned away, muttering to himself. "I don't want to go..."

Brennan didn't blame the boy. He hated himself for what he'd done. If only the past didn't hang on to him so tightly, if only he hadn't failed Miss Rachel, if only he hadn't insulted her as bad as a man could insult a woman...

Saturday had come and Levi had shut down his forge so he could work on his cabin. In addition to Brennan and Noah, Gordy Osbourne, Kurt Lang and Martin Steward, all near neighbors, had come to help raise Levi's roof and shingle it today. Then the cabin would be ready to furnish.

Brennan didn't like all the company but it would finish the job and his obligation to this friend quicker. Jacque was with Johann playing at the nearby creek.

The September sun rose high yet the day felt as hot as July. The men paused to drink cold water from the spring and mopped their brows.

A wagon creaked into the clearing. Mr. and Mrs. Ashford, with Posey's grandmother between them, sat on the wagon bench. In the rear wagon bed, Amanda, Posey and Miss Rachel clung to the sides as the wagon rocked over the ruts.

Levi hurried forward, beaming. "Miss Posey! Everyone! Welcome."

Brennan hung back toward the rear. Why had Miss Rachel come? He'd avoided her ever since he'd been fool enough to propose to her. But with all these people present they wouldn't have to speak.

Mr. Ashford tied up the reins and helped his wife and Posey's grandmother down. The older woman was breathing with the effort but she smiled. "I wanted…to see…where Posey would be living."

"You'll be living here, too, Grandmother," Posey said and Levi nodded in agreement.

Almeria merely smiled and took a few steps, leaning on Levi's arm. "A good-sized cabin."

"Two rooms with a loft and root cellar," Levi said. "Thanks to Brennan and Noah and everyone else who has helped, it should almost be done today."

Almeria nodded to the men, thanking them breathlessly. "Walk me inside…please, Levi."

Rachel did not like how the woman sounded or looked. She had tried to persuade Almeria to wait to see Levi's place but the grandmother had insisted she view the cabin today. So the Ashfords had left Gunther in charge of the store and set out. Rachel wished there were some medicine to help the woman, but there was so little a doctor could do. And the stress of a trip down to Illinois or to upriver Minneapolis might kill the woman.

Posey had insisted Rachel come, too. Of course the whole town was aware of the breach between Mr. Merriday and herself. Did Posey hope to bring them close enough to begin speaking again? But he'd said nothing and neither had she. She saw how Brennan avoided her. They would just be polite to each other and not incite further gossip.

Inside the cabin, Posey's grandmother looked around, wiping her eyes with a hanky. Rachel moved farther into the cabin and looked out through a square hole where a window would soon be.

"I need to sit down," the grandmother said, holding on to Levi's arm tightly.

Noah hurried outside and he and Mr. Ashford brought in a bench the men had used. Soon Almeria sat on the bench leaning against the wall. The men moved outside and the women gathered around Almeria.

Rachel began to worry. This short jaunt might have taxed the older woman too severely. She was gasping for air and her face was beet-red.

"Perhaps we should take you home now, cousin," Mrs. Ashford said.

"I…am going…to die…today."

"No!" Posey exclaimed. "Grandmother, don't say that."

Rachel looked through the window at the men gathered there. "Someone please fetch the lady some cold water."

Martin leaped to obey. Brennan and Gordy stood at the window; Noah and Levi remained, hovering close to the door.

"Levi," the older woman gasped, "come here."

He ducked inside, doffing his hat.

"I am glad…you have…provided Posey with…land. I wanted…to see…it…before…"

Martin Steward came in and handed the mug of water to Posey.

Posey held it for her grandmother, who sipped slowly, feebly.

When she'd drunk enough, she said, "I…wish… I could…live to see…you wed."

Levi looked to Posey who was weeping, clutching the cup. "Ma'am, I love Posey with all my heart. I'd marry her today if I could."

Posey nodded her agreement.

Sadness swept through Rachel. Posey's grandmother shouldn't be denied the joy of witnessing Posey's wedding. "You can," Rachel said, an idea coming swiftly to her. "Noah, could you help these two? Can't they recite their vows here in their home for her grandmother's sake?"

Noah stepped over the threshold. "I can see no objection. Both are free to marry and of honest character. I could perform the ceremony here before these witnesses."

"But we're sewing her wedding dress," Mrs. Ashford objected.

"There's no reason they couldn't have a formal ceremony later," Rachel said.

"Yes," Almeria gasped. "I…" The woman couldn't go on.

Mrs. Ashford sat beside her on the bench and put her arm around her, trying not to weep.

Noah cleared his throat. "Levi, Posey, do you wish this?"

Posey looked at Levi. Each asked the other this question without words. In reply they joined hands in front of Almeria.

Rachel shifted and saw through the open window Brennan outside, also frozen and watching.

Noah bowed his head and prayed for God's blessing. Then he began the ceremony. "Will you, Levi, have this woman as your wedded wife, to love her, comfort her, honor and keep her in sickness and in health and, forsaking all others, keep ye only unto her, so long as you both shall live?"

Levi cleared his throat and answered, "I will."

Rachel could not tear her gaze from Brennan's. The two of them were riveted by these words.

"Will you, Posey…" Noah continued.

Rachel felt almost as if she were taking the same vow as the young woman holding Levi's big hand—to Brennan who stared back at her.

"I will," Posey whispered, her voice muffled by tears.

Then Noah led the two through their vows.

"I, Posey, take you, Levi, to be my wedded husband, to have and to hold, from this day forward, for better, for worse, for richer, for poorer, in sickness and in health…"

Rachel felt her heart wrung. How she longed to make the same promises to Brennan. But he wanted her only as a mother to Jacque. Or that was all he would admit.

Noah finished, "Those whom God hath joined together, let no man put asunder."

Rachel realized she was weeping and wiped her face with her handkerchief. When she looked up, Brennan had vanished from the window. Of course he had.

Posey knelt in front of her grandmother, as did Levi.

"Now… I can…be easy," the older woman managed to say. "Take care…of…my girl."

"I will, ma'am. I'll make sure Posey never has reason to regret this day," Levi said with an evident frog in his throat.

The older woman patted his hand and then Levi carried her out to the wagon and set her on the bench. Mrs. Ashford clambered up beside her and Almeria leaned heavily against her. Mrs. Ashford was openly weeping.

Rachel glanced once more around the clearing for Brennan but he had vanished. She climbed onto the rear of the wagon and watched Levi kiss Posey goodbye till the evening.

"We'll finish up the roof, dearest," Levi said. "I'll come as soon as I wash up tonight."

"Yes," Mr. Ashford turned to say. "You're family now, Levi. You'll eat meals with us till you two move into your cabin." Then he urged the team to make a wide circle and head back to town. Rachel wrapped an arm around Posey's waist and held the girl close, letting her weep on her shoulder—while Rachel wept unseen for the vows she would never say.

Brennan rose early the next morning and roused the boy. Levi had paid him last night and now made him a breakfast by the river.

"I wish you wouldn't go," Levi said again. "You could work steady here."

"We're going," Brennan said with as much force as he could.

Jacque said nothing, just looked dejected.

Soon they finished the eggs Levi had scorched for them and drank the bad coffee and set out, heading eastward. The day was a windy one. Brennan traveled at a spanking pace, wanting to be away from the settlement before people began streaming toward the school for Sunday worship.

The plan worked. Soon they were far east down an Indian trail and then onto an old military road that would take them toward Green Bay. Birds flew high overhead in large groups. Brennan and the boy had days of walking ahead. His heart weighed as heavy as lead and his feet did not want to carry him away from this place, from Miss Rachel.

But he'd wounded a fine woman. He'd carry this latest guilt the rest of his life. He'd been run out of his own town by his own people like Cain in the Bible. And he would wander like Cain the rest of his life.

All that day Brennan and Jacque walked east away from the lowering sun on the old military road—really a track of wagon wheels through the forest—to Green Bay.

Something was making Brennan uneasy. The farther they walked eastward, the more he glimpsed glimmers of fire far away in the trees. Once in a while smoke lifted above the forest.

Everything was tinder dry and each footstep sent up a plume of dust around their feet. Jacque did not speak and neither did Brennan, but he kept watch on the flickers of fire far back in the trees.

Ahead was a clearing and a small cabin. The owner must have heard them coming because he was standing at the end of the trail to his home. "Hello. Where you come from and where you going?"

Brennan still did not feel like talking but he took pity on the man who so obviously wanted some news from outside the forest. "Hey. We're from Pepin on our way to Green Bay area. I hear there's work there for loggers."

"You got a ways to go then."

Brennan nodded and decided to ask the question that

had been bothering him. "I've been wondering about the flame I see sometimes back in the trees—just a flicker here and there."

"Oh, hunters leave campfires burning when they set out in the morning. Some Indian. Some whites. It's been so dry they should throw some dirt on them, but…" The man shrugged.

The hunters' carelessness troubled Brennan but he let the subject drop.

"This your boy?" the man asked affably.

Brennan had to swallow down the sudden thickness in his throat. "Yes, this is my boy." *My blood, my only kin.*

"I got a good spring here. Need water or anything?"

"Yes, thank you." Brennan smiled at the man. After drinking deeply at the spring, they started walking.

"Good luck!" the man called after them and within moments he was no longer in sight when Brennan glanced over his shoulder.

The two trudged onward, Brennan surveying the thick forest on both sides of the faint old road. Rachel's face kept coming to mind. He kept pushing it away. The solitude of the trail was not what he wanted or needed right now.

He picked up his pace, trying to think ahead for him and the boy. He hoped he'd find some school in Green Bay for Jacque but his mind didn't seem to be able to concentrate. He would deal with that when he got there. Working with a group of loggers would keep his mind busy and tire him out so that he'd sleep better than he had since he'd insulted a lady who didn't deserve such.

Rachel had wanted to stay home and lick her wounds, but she'd forced herself to go to worship at the school and had accepted Noah's invitation to spend Sunday at his house. Now she sat beside him on the Whitmores' wagon. He was taking her home.

"I'm sorry Mr. Merriday left," Noah said.

"I am, too." Each word was torn from Rachel.

"I know you had feelings for him."

She nodded, not bothering to deny the obvious, still aching with such suffering. It was beyond words.

"It's too bad he didn't let God begin healing him from the war. I'd hoped being around you, Levi and then his son would begin to help."

"Sometimes the pain becomes part of a person and he can't let it go."

Noah exhaled in a sign of dejection. "Rachel, I know you say you never intend to marry, but I hope you know that any man would be fortunate to win you."

She turned to look at him, her mouth open.

"You and I lost our mothers too young. That hurt runs deep. But you are worthy of love, Rachel Woolsey."

Rachel remained speechless. What had caused her cousin to say such things?

They rounded the bend into town. Many people had gathered on the porch of Ashford's General Store. Noah pulled back on the reins, stopping the pony.

"Glad you're here, preacher," a man Rachel didn't know said. "Mrs. Ashford's mother is dying."

Noah turned to her. "I'll drive you home and come back."

"No, I'll stay. I might be of help." *And I might as well be miserable here among the mourning instead of miserable alone.* Rachel shook off this self-pity. These were her neighbors and they needed her as much as she needed them.

Chapter Fourteen

When Jacque nearly stumbled, Brennan realized the hour had come to set up camp for the night. He'd been distracted, watching the gleamings of fire that still appeared, scattered in the distance. He'd also been aware of a large stream nearby, hearing it run over the rocks. He wanted, needed to be near water.

Gripping the boy's shoulder, he stopped to listen for the subtle sound. "This way, son," he said, leading the boy through the thick evergreens and scarlet maples.

About a quarter of a mile from the military road, Brennan and Jacque arrived at the creek. Its creekbed was unusually deep, but after the dry summer the water ran low. While Jacque gathered dried twigs and branches, Brennan quickly gathered rocks, lining a small hollow for their campfire.

Soon Brennan had started a small fire and was brewing coffee in his battered kettle. With a knife, he opened two cans of beans and set them to warm on rocks edging the fire.

"How much farther we got to walk?" Jacque complained.

"I don't know. I guess we'll get there when we get

there," Brennan said, still scanning the surrounding forest, fear simmering in the pit of his stomach. "Why don't we cool off in the creek while the beans warm?"

Jacque sent the two cans of beans a sour look.

Brennan didn't blame him. Both of them had become accustomed to Miss Rachel's fine fare. At the thought of leaving her, Brennan's heart squeezed so tightly, he almost gasped. "Into the creek, boy. We'll wash the day's dust off."

The dip in the creek did refresh them and they sat down and ate their beans and coffee. Then Jacque dug into his knapsack and pulled out a wax paper bag. He opened it and offered it to Brennan. "Want one?"

The sweet fragrance of caramel hit Brennan full in the heart. Miss Rachel's caramels. The scent caused his mouth to water and his knees to soften. Why had he hurt her? "No, thanks." He looked down.

"I'm going to make them last," the boy confided. He unrolled just one from wax paper and popped it into his mouth, then he sat, not chewing, just letting the caramel melt on his tongue.

Brennan didn't blame the boy. Miss Rachel's caramels should be savored. He banished her face from his mind. Or attempted to.

The wind began to blow harder. Brennan glanced up, watching the tops of the trees sway. He stacked more rocks on the windward side of the campfire to keep it from being spread or blown out.

He didn't have to tell the boy to go to bed. Jacque rolled himself into his blanket and fell sound asleep within minutes.

Brennan sipped the last of his bitter coffee, feeling the rushing wind strong on his face. He'd walked all day; he would sleep tonight. He added wood to the fire, then rolled into his blanket and closed his eyes.

Sleep came, but also dreams. He woke with a start. "Rachel…" The darkness was relieved by scant moonlight. He heard the trees around him swaying with the wind. He rolled onto his back and stared at the blackness, listening to the trees creaking, and felt leaves falling onto his face, covering his eyes wet with regret. *Rachel…*

Dawn had come. Rachel tried to eat breakfast and ended up giving it to the cat. She then had punched down the dough that had risen overnight in her cool root cellar. She rolled out the dough and formed the cinnamon rolls and set them to rise a second time. When she went out to preheat her oven, the wind stirred up swirls of dry leaves, whispering around her ankles.

She looked up. The birds were having trouble flying. The wind drove at them and they beat their wings, fighting to keep from being blown away. Her robin managed to get back into her nest in the deep crook on the leeward side of the wide oak trunk. Rachel hadn't felt strong wind like this here in Wisconsin. A sense of foreboding tried to wrap itself around her. She resisted it and went on with her tasks.

The ache over losing Brennan and Jacque had not lifted. As she headed back to her kitchen, sudden tears splashed down her cheeks. She pressed a hand over her mouth, suppressing a sob. How long would this wrenching loss torment her? A week, a month, a year, the rest of her life?

Brennan rose with the sun. All around the wind gusted and birds squawked and flew in bunches like waves overhead. He set coffee to brew and stared at the fire, listening to the bubbling, boiling water. The sound mimicked his inner unease.

Dreams of Rachel had interrupted his sleep over and over last night, rendering him less able to face what the day might bring. He rubbed his eyes and watched the boy still sleeping.

The fir trees around them shuddered with the force of the wind. The flames under the kettle danced with the stiff draft in spite of the ledge of rocks he'd stacked to protect it. Brennan tried to keep his balance mentally, not let fear get a toehold. Everything within him shouted, *Go back!* But he couldn't. He couldn't face her.

He shook Jacque awake and they ate a breakfast of hardtack and hot coffee. Jacque's dislike of the hard, tasteless bread and unsugared coffee blazed on his face. He looked at Brennan with accusation in his eyes. Or was Brennan just imagining it since he felt so guilty for obliging them to leave Miss Rachel?

The wind bumped up another notch and then another. The trees around them swayed lower. Squirrels and chipmunks and other small creatures raced past as if fleeing the wind.

After finishing the coffee, Brennan scooped up wet sand from the creek bank and threw it onto the fire. The flames sizzled and died. He caved the rocks into the fire site. He looked around. In vain he wished this hard wind would blow out the flames in the forest he'd seen yesterday.

Rachel heard no boat whistle but when the cinnamon rolls had baked, cooled and been frosted, she started to roll her cart toward town. If she couldn't sell them, she'd give them away. Food must never go to waste.

The wind gusted against her, trying to lift the hem of her skirt immodestly high. She turned back and found a length of string and tied it loosely but securely just below her knees to keep her skirt from flying. Then she gripped the cart handles and headed for town, walking like a hobbled horse.

The birds that often flew with her and chattered to her must have all taken cover. *An ominous sign.* She glanced high and saw how the treetops of the high pines swayed above her. When she reached town, she did hear a boat whistle.

But before she reached the dock, the boat was already pulling away. The one passenger that had been let off held on to his hat and bent into the wind. He paused to pull his hat brim politely to her and then headed toward the land agent's office.

Rachel realized as she watched why the boat had left so quickly. It fought against the west wind as it wended its way out into the current away from the shore. Did the captain fear it might have been battered against the eastern shore?

A gust hit Rachel and nearly knocked her from her feet. She saved herself by holding on to the cart handles. She rolled the cart toward the Ashfords' store and parked it in back. Dust swirled up into her face and she shut her eyes and mouth till it passed.

Then Rachel lifted the first of two trays of rolls from the cart and carried them up the back stairs to the Ashfords' living quarters. The wind wanted to grab the tray from her and fling it into the trees. She hurried up the last few steps and kicked the door hard, asking for entrance.

Posey opened the door.

Rachel handed her the tray and stepped inside, grabbing the door as it tried to bang against the side of the building. She dragged it back and secured it. "The wind is wild today."

Posey looked crestfallen.

Rachel suddenly hoped she hadn't blundered into a scene of mourning. "Thy grandmother?"

"She lingers, sleeping but restless," Posey said.

Rachel reclaimed the tray from her and carried it to the large dining room table and set it down. "I'm so sorry. Is there anything I can do?"

Posey shook her head tearfully.

Mrs. Ashford stepped into the hall and saw her. "Miss Rachel."

"I brought rolls," Rachel said lamely.

Mrs. Ashford hurried forward and grasped both Rachel's hands. "Thank you for your thoughtfulness. I'm so distracted I don't think I did more than make coffee this morning."

"I have another tray I'm going to give Mr. Ashford. I'll take them to him now."

"Then please come back," Posey implored.

Rachel did not want to come back to this house that no doubt would soon be plunged into mourning, but staying alone would be worse.

"I'll put on some tea," Mrs. Ashford invited.

"I'll be right back." Rachel hurried to deliver the rolls to Mr. Ashford, telling him to give them away to anyone who wanted them. Then she gripped the railing outside and climbed back up to the Ashfords' door. She heard a bump. Looking down, she saw that her cart had been blown over and it hit the side of the log store.

She ducked inside. She began to think of her root cellar at home. She would stay for a while and then go home and prepare for whatever this storm brought. Her fear billowed like the wind. Where were Brennan and Jacque? Had they found shelter?

The wind knocked Jacque off his feet. The orange sun had risen higher and the gusts had become harder to resist. Brennan stopped and helped the boy up. Jacque clung to him, his arms around Brennan's waist. The boy looked up, fear plain on his face. Far in the sky high above the treetops, an eerie red glow flickered.

"We'd better..." Brennan said, the wind snatching at his words, "find a low spot...and wait this storm out." He gripped the boy's hand and led him back into the woods toward the creek they had been near all day.

In a sudden gust, the trees bent nearly double. Brennan dropped to his knees, shoving the boy under him. He resisted the wind, huddling to the ground. When the gust ended, he hurried the boy between the swaying trees and flying twigs and branches.

They found the creek again and Brennan, bent protectively over the boy, guided him to an area of rock, carved out by higher water, a shallow cave. He pushed the boy back under the ledge. Just a few feet from them, even the creek's low water leaped in whitecaps.

"What's happening? A tornado?" Jacque cried out.

In the din, Brennan crawled under the ledge and pulled the boy near, speaking into his ear, "I don't think so. There's no rain. Just a windstorm." Turning his back to the wind, he wrapped his arms around the boy, grateful for the narrow outcropping and its protection. What was coming? Had this hit Pepin? Was Rachel safe or hurt?

Unable to maneuver it in the wind, Rachel left her cart wedged between the Ashfords' store and their shed. The wind tore away the string and whipped up her skirts. Holding them down, she stumbled, head bent, to her cabin. When she arrived, she found Mrs. Cat huddled by her door, mewing. She let the cat in.

And then she hurried around her place, moving her cow and shooing her frantic chickens into the small barn—the coop seemed a dangerous shelter for them in the high wind. After carrying water and feed to the barn, she shut the door and tested the latch and found it secure. The water bucket banged against her side so she carried it into her cabin with her.

As the wind tried to snatch them from her, she shut and latched her shutters. Then she bolted the door after herself and said a prayer for the safety of her animals, her birds. Mrs. Cat rubbed against her ankles. In the dim light, Rachel scanned the stout, full-log walls around her. Would they stand against this storm?

"Don't worry, Mrs. Cat. We'll be safe inside." Her heart thumped at the perilous wind, loudly buffeting the walls around her. But what of Brennan and Jacque? Had they found shelter? Or were they on the open road without stout log walls and a root cellar for protection? *Oh, Father, protect them in this storm.*

The wind gusted harder, harder, and then flames blew past them. Brennan had been looking east but now he saw another burning branch fly by. He gasped and pulled Jacque more tightly to him. The wind wasn't extinguishing the fire that had shimmered in the distance; it was fanning it to leap higher. Higher into the trees, into a vast forest as dry as tinder.

A thought occurred to him. He tried to let go of Jacque, but the boy clung to him.

He put his mouth next to the boy's ear. "I need to

wet a blanket to put over us. There's fire in the air."
He'd seen this in the war, in the midst of cannon bar-
rages in battle.

"Fire?" Jacque tore from him and tried to bolt.

Brennan gripped him. "Don't run! We're safe here
by the water! Under cover!" *As safe as we can be.* The
wind kept snatching away his words. "I'm going to soak
a blanket in the water."

Jacque looked wild-eyed, but he nodded.

"Stay in the cave, son." Brennan shoved the boy as far
back as he could into the shallow protection. Then he tore
a blanket from his backpack and waded into the creek,
pushing the blanket under the water. The wind knocked
him to his knees. He was able to grab a protruding rock
with one hand, fighting against the wind and current.

The howling and whistling of the wind deafened him.
He crawled out of the creek, dragging the wet blanket
behind him. He saw Jacque's mouth open as if he were
crying out, but the word was carried away.

He slid close to the boy and wrapped the blanket
around them loosely. But the wind dragged at it—even
heavy with water—and he found he had to sit on the
edge of it and tuck it around Jacque.

More burning branches, many large enough to knock
a man out, blew past them. The shallow cave below
ground level wasn't much but it was enough to keep
them from the worst. He hoped. A noise assaulted his
ears and he realized it was the crackling of the fire.

It surged into a roaring. He craned his neck and
in the distance saw the fire begin to devour the forest—flames leaping from treetop to treetop, racing toward them. Yanking the sopping blanket overhead, he
wrapped himself around the boy. *Dear God, help. Save
us. Rachel.*

* * *

The wind buffeted the cabin without cease. Rachel rocked in her chair. She'd been forced to move away from the chimney because strong gusts of air blasted down it and into the room, flaring ash and bringing the smell of soot. To escape, she had moved to the far wall near the end of her bed.

Mrs. Cat had—for the first time—leaped up onto her lap and sat huddled there. Rachel was grateful for the cat's company. She stroked the soft fur and murmured comforting words that soothed the cat and herself. Her pulse raced with the wind.

She prayed silently. She imagined everyone at worship in the town school and went through the rows, naming those she knew and praying for those she didn't by description. But the faces of Brennan and Jacque lay like a transparent photograph over all the other faces. The thought of them out in this… She blanched and prayed more fervently. *Save them, God—even if I never see them again. Save them.*

Something large slammed the side of the cabin. She cried out and the cat jumped and raced under the bed. Rachel sat, shaking, hearing something like a locomotive outside. She reached under the bed, grabbed the cat by her scruff and was down in the root cellar within moments.

She clung to the cat who yodeled with fear. Her heart pounded. "Oh, Lord, do not forget thy servant here! And keep Jacque and Brennan safe and oh, Lord, bring them back—alive!"

"Rachel! Rachel!"
She roused in her bed and rolled out and blinked in the sunshine seeping in around the shuttered win-

dows. She had not undressed the night before, fearing her cabin might break under the wind's assault and she would be forced to flee. Early in the morning when the wind had finally ebbed, she'd crawled out of the cramped, hard-dirt root cellar and fallen into bed.

"Rachel!"

For a moment her mind tried to transform it into Brennan's voice. But it was Noah's.

She ran to the door and unbolted it. "Cousin!" She ran and threw her arms around him, gratitude flooding her.

He held her close. "Thank God. You're safe. I couldn't come until the wind died and the sun came out."

Then Sunny ran over, carrying their little son. "Rachel! Oh, thank God!"

The three of them drew together with little Dawn squeezing in their midst, clinging to their knees. The embrace released Rachel's tears. She couldn't hold back her fear. "I'm so worried about Brennan and Jacque."

Noah and Sunny stepped back. "We are, too." Noah claimed her hand. "But there is no way of knowing where they are."

"We'll just have to trust God," Sunny said, jiggling her son on her hip, but looking somber.

Dear Sunny. Dear Noah. Rachel gazed at them, knowing there was no other recourse. Then she scanned her familiar clearing. Leaves, pinecones and downed branches littered her yard. Part of a tree had slammed her west wall. "What was it? A tornado?"

"We never got any rain," Noah said. "It was some terrible cyclone is all I can figure."

"Did you look outside last night?" Sunny asked.

"No, why?"

"The sky to the far east was red," Noah said grimly.

"Fire?" she whispered.

Noah nodded, looking sickened. "I'm afraid so. The forest was so dry…"

To the east—the direction Brennan and Jacque had gone. Fire vast enough to turn the sky red. Her throat constricted. She turned to look east, but saw only the fresh dawn.

"I'm driving around, checking on my flock," Noah said. "So far no one has been seriously hurt. But many will need repairs to their roofs."

"Rachel, if you're up to it," Sunny said, "Posey wanted you to come to town. Her grandmother passed away last night."

Rachel felt a twinge of sadness, then gratitude that God had provided Levi for Posey. But where was Brennan? Would she ever hear from him? Know what had happened to him? To Jacque? *Please.*

"Has thee had breakfast?" Rachel asked.

The cow bellowed from the barn, reminding her she'd not been milked last night. The sound prompted her stomach to growl with hunger.

"Yes, we've eaten and we need to get going. We have many more settlers up this road to check on," Noah said, shepherding his wife and daughter toward the wagon. "When we're done, we'll stop at the Ashfords' before we go home."

"I'll do my chores and go there as soon as I can," Rachel said, yet remained outside and waving to them until they disappeared around the bend.

Mrs. Cat sat at her feet, licking her paws. Then she mewed plaintively as if saying breakfast was an excellent idea.

A robin warbled from above.

Rachel looked up with joy. "Her" robin had made it through the storm. She answered the bird who then flew away to find her breakfast also.

Rachel's mind brought up the words from Matthew: *Are not two sparrows sold for a farthing? And one of them shall not fall on the ground without your Father.* Brennan and Jacque were precious not only to her but also to God. Tears trembled from her eyes. "I will trust thee, Father."

She walked to the barn, allowing tears of sorrow and thanksgiving to fall freely. She milked the cow then let it and the chickens out and then went in to make herself and Mrs. Cat breakfast.

She would take time to bake a cake for the Ashfords. People would be coming and a cake would be welcome. She would not give in to despair. God's eye was on Brennan and Jacque. But how she wanted to see them for herself.

Chapter Fifteen

❧

Four days had passed since the storm. Each day added another millstone around Rachel's neck. Images of Brennan and Jacque in a fiery forest streamed through her mind—memories by day and dreams at night, horrible dreams that burned with bright orange flames.

She moved through her days trying to appear normal. She was failing, of course. Even Mrs. Ashford spoke in a gentler voice to her. Did everyone guess that she walked around feeling half dead? And why?

In spite of her unrelenting anguish, Rachel had baked all morning. The town was holding two memorial services today. Almeria and Old Saul had expired hunkered down during the terrible storm, perhaps their hearts could not survive the stress, no one knew for sure. Noah had asked everyone to attend to honor and bid farewell to the dead and to give thanks that no one nearby had been injured or killed by the terrible storm that had raged over them. After the funeral would be a meal to spend time together, sharing memories and comforting the mourning.

Boats had brought the news of a terrible fire in Chicago that had killed thousands and destroyed much of that city. And then came the news yesterday that in eastern Wisconsin near Green Bay two villages, Peshtigo and Sugar Bush, had been destroyed—literally. The combination of the forest fires and the cyclonic winds had whipped many small wildfires into a deadly maelstrom. Over a thousand had died and vast acres of forest had been reduced to ash.

Rachel felt sick every time she thought of it. She'd turned away when the boatmen began sharing tales of whole families being caught by the flames in their cabins and dying. She'd been taught as a child that she lived in a fallen, cursed world but she had never felt anything this disastrous so close to her, not even the war.

Feeling as if she were a windup toy, now she loaded her wagon with the cakes she'd baked. Before leaving she returned to her cabin to make sure everything was as it should be and checked on her animals to make sure she hadn't forgotten their care. Yesterday she'd burned rolls. Only their smoke roused her to the fact that she had been lost in thought, sitting on the bench, awake but in a daze.

Her robin called to her and she looked up, but she couldn't reply to it. Her voice had become rusty. She smiled feebly and then gripped the handles of her cart and started for town, leaving Mrs. Cat sleeping in the shade of the barn.

Father, I need to know. Please let me know whether they are alive or dead. The word *dead* shook her to her core. Despair wrapped itself around her lungs, but she pressed on.

She was glad of the people milling about the schoolhouse. Posey hurried up to her and hugged her. Posey tried to speak but her tears clogged her throat. Rachel hugged her close.

Levi stood behind his bride, his hat in his hand. Rachel read his concern for Brennan and the boy. When he looked at her, his expression of general sadness deepened. She held out her hand and he gripped it. "Miss Rachel," he murmured.

He then nudged her from the cart and rolled it toward the tables of food under the shade trees. He returned. "Let me escort you both into the schoolhouse." He offered her and Posey each an arm.

Rachel was touched by the tender and gallant gesture of kindness. She tried to smile at him but her lips trembled too much. "Thank thee," she whispered.

Inside the church, Levi led her to Sunny and then he and Posey moved to sit with the Ashfords. Sunny kissed Rachel's cheek and held her hand. Their little boy slept on Sunny's lap and Dawn sat beside her. Noah already stood at the front of the schoolhouse. A few more people entered.

And then Noah cleared his throat. "Heavenly Father, our small village has suffered little compared to many. We thank you for your protection and ask you to comfort those who mourn and those who have suffered this week."

Noah's words were honey to her heart, but the deep ache remained.

"This week we lost one who was our shepherd…" Noah audibly struggled with his own grief. "And we lost a dear sister in Christ whom we had just started to know. We know they are with you, Father. In Christ's name. Amen."

Everyone looked up.

Then Noah's expression startled Rachel. He looked as if he were staring at a ghost.

She swung around to find out what had shocked him so.

At the rear a disheveled and grimy man and boy stood in the open doorway. Rachel cried out, "Brennan! Jacque!" She leaped up and raced to them, heedless of everyone else.

When she reached him, Brennan stopped her from embracing him by grabbing both her hands together. "Rachel," he said in a raspy voice. "You're safe."

She burst into tears. These were the words she had almost uttered.

Rachel looked more beautiful than Brennan had remembered. And she shone with her special joy and even better—appeared happy to see him.

She looked down. "Jacque, thee is safe."

Heedless of his grime, Jacque wrapped his arms around her waist. "We come home, Miss Rachel, for good."

She burst into tears.

The sound wrenched Brennan's heart and he dropped to one knee. "Yes, we've come home, Miss Rachel. If you'll have us. I was a fool. But now I see it doesn't matter if I'm not worthy of you. I love you. Will you be my wife?"

Rachel heard "I love you." And then she heard applause around her. The sound startled her back to herself. She glanced around and mortification seized her. She broke free and ran outside.

Brennan raced after her and caught her just as she entered the cover of the trees. "Rachel, stop!" Then he coughed and couldn't speak for a moment.

She halted. "What's wrong? Is thee ill?"

He bent over, gasping, and then managed to say, "I did breathe in some smoke. It makes me cough some."

She grasped his shoulders. "Thee was in the fire?"

"Not the worst of it, but bad enough. God kept us

safe. We're a little singed and smoky but alive." His expression turned grim. "Many died."

"God kept you safe?" she repeated. "When has thee ever spoke of God?"

He claimed her hands. "I don't want to talk about that now. I just want to know if you'll marry me or not."

She gaped at him. "Thee is in earnest? Thee loves me?"

"Miss Rachel, I was a fool, but God opened my eyes. You're the best thing that ever came into my life. I love you with all of my sorry heart. Will you marry me and make me the happiest man on earth?"

She couldn't help it. After all the strain, she laughed, feeling the fear that had bound her release. And then she threw her arms around him. "Of course I will marry thee, Brennan Merriday. Thee is the only man I have ever loved and will ever love."

And then Brennan did what he'd longed to do for the past five days—and longer if the truth be told—he drew her into a full embrace and bent his head. He claimed her sweet lips and kissed her as if he didn't, he'd die.

And Rachel kissed him back with all the love she'd saved for one special man, this man, her brave Brennan.

"You two gettin' married then?" Jacque's hopeful voice came from behind her. "And I don't ever got to leave Miss Rachel and Pepin ever again?"

She laughed again and turned, but did not step out of Brennan's embrace. "Yes, Jacque, we are getting married and thee will be my son and we will stay here together."

Jacque ran to them and they included him in their embrace, their joy.

Finally, Jacque pulled free. "I'm hungry. There's food on those tables."

Again Rachel chuckled with a joy she could not hide. "Come, I have brought two cakes and several dozen cookies. Thee can eat some cookies."

She recalled then today's solemn occasion and her joy receded and she became serious then. "We must go into the schoolhouse quietly. Old Saul and Posey's grandmother have passed. Noah is holding their memorial services."

Both Brennan and Jacque accepted a handful of cookies to nibble and drank from the school pump, then the three of them entered the school as quietly as they could.

Noah finished his sentence about Posey's grandmother witnessing the small wedding in Levi's barely finished cabin and then looked toward the three of them. "Brennan, I take it from your singed clothing that you were in the fire."

"Not the worst. The boy and me were fortunate to just be on the far edge of it. God protected us."

Noah waved them forward. "Please come and tell us what you experienced. We've heard there was a great conflagration and many died."

While Rachel and Jacque sat down beside Sunny, Brennan walked forward. Noah shook his hand and sat with his wife, too.

Brennan turned to face the people he thought he'd never live to see again and his heart softened toward them. They weren't perfect and they had misjudged him, but he'd kept his truth hidden so it wasn't their fault.

"My son and me walked down the Indian trail to the old military road to go to Green Bay. I could see fires in the forest. It made me wary. Then that wind come up. God provided a creek beside a sort of cave. It was just a ledge of rock and a crevice where the water, when it was higher, had carved out a place. We hid in there and fire broke over us."

Not a sound was heard inside the schoolhouse.

"I wet a blanket and threw it over us. The fire raged around us, but I kept wetting the blanket. That and the cave preserved our lives."

A murmuring flew through the congregation.

Brennan decided now was the time to let it all out. "I've been mad at God a long time. Too much bad. Too much loss. Too many years. It made me a bitter man." Brennan shook his head, pausing to cough. "But that was all the war and that was due to men's wickedness and hate. This fire was bigger, greater than anything man can do."

He paused to swallow. "I had forgotten how big God is, how powerful." He looked up. "A lot of people died and I grieve for them. But God's ways are higher than I can understand. Who am I to judge God? I'm just a mortal and I'll live my life as best I can, do what I can for others."

He steadied himself against his fatigue. "That's all I got to say." He felt a smile break over his face. "Except that Miss Rachel has accepted my proposal and will be my wife."

"Oh! Wonderful!" Mrs. Ashford exclaimed, leaping to her feet. "Oh, I'm so happy."

Brennan laughed. Today even Mrs. Ashford blessed him.

Noah went to the front. "How close did you get to the big fire?"

"Jacque and I walked toward it to see if we could help, but the desolation was so great that we turned back and headed home." Brennan paused to look at Rachel. *Rachel, you are my home.*

"We couldn't do much," Brennan went on. "But on the way here, a courier passed us and he said he was spreading the word that our governor's wife has called for Wisconsin people to send whatever they can to the Peshtigo and Sugar Bush survivors. They are sending boxcars of supplies from Madison—"

"Couldn't we get a wagonload and drive it to Madison to be sent on?" Levi had risen and now looked embarrassed to have spoken up in the meeting.

Noah nodded. "I think that's an excellent idea."

"I would be glad to drive the wagon," Brennan offered. "I wanted to do more but the suffering was heavier than I could help. I had nothing but a knapsack."

Noah requested contributions of charity and within minutes the relief effort had been organized. On the morrow people would bring what they could spare— food, clothing, medicine—and Brennan would drive the wagon down to Madison.

Noah urged Brennan to take his seat. He held up his hands and everyone turned to him. "This has been a momentous day. We have honored Almeria Brown and Old Saul, one a newcomer and the other known well and much beloved by us all. We've announced the marriage of Levi and Posey Comstock and witnessed the return of two we thought we might have lost forever. And—" Noah grinned "—saw Brennan get smart enough to propose to my cousin."

General amusement greeted this statement. "Let us rise and thank God for His mercy. Our village could have been devastated by this fire. We were spared but we will stretch out our hands to those who were not. We cannot understand why this happened.

"As Isaiah the prophet said, 'For my thoughts are not your thoughts, neither are your ways my ways, saith the Lord. For as the heavens are higher than the earth, so are my ways higher than your ways, and my thoughts than your thoughts.' We will accept God's will in this and do what we can."

Then Noah blessed the food for the meal. And everyone went out into the quiet sunshine.

Brennan held Rachel's hand and would not let it go. He and Rachel sat with Levi and Posey at one of the tables. No one appeared to fault them for not helping set up the potluck picnic. Indeed everyone smiled and teased them.

Rachel felt as if a great weight had been lifted from everyone. She leaned her head against Brennan's shoulder. She smelled the smoke in his clothing and shuddered to think of him and Jacque under a wet blanket in a shallow cave, while flames raged around them. Without any self-consciousness she leaned over and kissed him. He kissed her back.

Johann Lang came over. "Can Jacque come and play?"

Rachel beamed at him. "Of course."

"I'm glad you and Brennan will marry," Johann said. "It is good to marry."

Brennan listened to the boy's words and his own laughter bubbled up. "Remember that when you get older."

"I will!" Johann shouted and then he and Jacque were running to the other children gathered around the swings.

"I'm so happy," Posey said, though wiping her tears with her hanky. "I was so afraid you wouldn't return and Miss Rachel's heart might never heal."

"I'll admit it," Brennan said ruefully. "I was a fool. Levi was the smart one." Brennan winked at his friend. "He had enough sense to find a girl and stick to her."

Mrs. Ashford bustled over. "Ned and I planned on having a party to celebrate Posey's wedding a week from next Sunday. So why don't we add your wedding to the party? I talked to Sunny about it, Rachel, and she said you get your dress ready and we'll do the rest. I love weddings!"

Rachel smiled and nodded. "Yes, Mrs. Ashford."

The stranger who'd come to town the day of the storm and who'd been staying at the land agent's office came up behind Mrs. Ashford. "I thought I wouldn't be seeing you. I was going to leave tomorrow. Remember me? I'm Jake Summers, I sit in the state legislature."

Brennan looked at the man. "You talked to me… earlier this year." Brennan decided to leave out the fact that they'd talked in the saloon.

"Yes, I came back to ask you once again to run for county sheriff. I have just enough time to get your name on the ballot."

"I'm not leaving Pepin," Brennan began.

"You don't need to. If you win, you just need to make regular rounds after you meet the mayors of the towns and villages. We don't have much crime. And your reputation from running off those river rats this June has spread. You can win in November."

Brennan began to shake his head.

"I think thee should let him put thy name on the ballot," Rachel spoke up. "If thee is to be sheriff, then the people will vote for thee. If not, then we will accept that. Thee would make an excellent sheriff."

Brennan stared at her, then chuckled. "You heard the

lady who is going to be my wife. Go ahead then. We'll let the people decide."

"Oh!" Mrs. Ashford exclaimed. "The county sheriff from our own town!"

Brennan watched the storekeeper's wife hurry off to spread the news.

The state legislator shook Brennan's hand and said he'd ride with him on the wagon to Madison so they could talk more.

Rachel leaned her head on Brennan's shoulder again, sighing with obvious contentment.

The sound ignited such joy within Brennan, he felt fairly lifted off his seat. *Thank you, God, for this precious woman and her love. And my son. And now perhaps a new career. I have more than I ever expected.*

Epilogue

Rachel had not thought it necessary to have a special dress for her wedding, but Mrs. Ashford had insisted. Rachel was not marrying just anybody. She might be marrying the next county sheriff!

Rachel had allowed herself to be outvoted. Posey had brought out a royal-blue dress her late mother had saved for good occasions and with some alterations and new embellishments, Rachel's wedding dress had been prepared.

When Brennan returned, he found that a ready-made black suit had been presented to him by the town. After all, if he won the election, he'd need a good suit to wear to his swearing in.

Brennan was inclined to refuse but when he looked at the Ashfords' happy, expectant faces, he relented. The old anger that had simmered just under the surface had drained out of him. He was a happy man.

Now he stood between Noah and Levi, his best man, at the front of the schoolhouse. He looked over all the smiling faces.

Within a few months, he'd changed from an abandoned tramp, a reviled Reb, to a man with a son and a groom who was marrying the sweetest woman in town. If his chest expanded any farther, his buttons might go flying off around the room. Jacque sat in new clothing beside Sunny, beaming.

The door at the rear opened. Posey, Rachel's matron of honor, stepped inside, carrying a bouquet of fall flowers, rich in gold and deep red. Then he saw Rachel in the doorway. Sunshine glowed around her as if God's light came from her. Well, it did. If others couldn't see it, he could.

Everyone rose for the bride as Posey led Rachel down the aisle to his side.

Brennan found his mouth had gone dry. Rachel's subtle beauty was radiant today in the rich blue that reminded him of a clear, untroubled sky.

Noah began, "It is odd for me to ask, Who gives this woman to marry this man? because of course, as her cousin standing in for her father who couldn't be here, I do. And I must say that I am very happy to see that Rachel has found a man who truly values her. I give Rachel to Brennan unreservedly."

Noah continued the wedding ceremony. Rachel handed her bouquet to Posey and took Brennan's hand.

She smiled at her groom, her lips trembling with tears of joy. She had come to Wisconsin to begin a new life and God had given her a rich one. The emptiness in her heart had been filled with love. She'd always had God's love but now she'd been gifted with a good man's love. It was a treasure more dear because she had thought it would never be.

"Brennan, you may kiss your bride," Noah said finally, beaming at them.

Brennan bent and she rose up on her toes and their lips met—briefly but completely.

Then they turned, hand in hand.

Noah lifted their clasped hands. "Ladies and gentlemen, I give you our newest couple, Mr. and Mrs. Brennan Merriday."

The congregation rose and applauded.

Brennan pulled Rachel under his arm. He'd been driven out of his hometown once and here he was applauded and welcomed. He had found home, family and love at last. *Praise God from whom all blessings flow.*

* * * * *

Allie Pleiter, an award-winning author and RITA® Award finalist, writes both fiction and nonfiction. Her passion for knitting shows up in many of her books and all over her life. Entirely too fond of French macarons and lemon meringue pie, Allie spends her days writing books and avoiding housework. Allie grew up in Connecticut, holds a BS in speech from Northwestern University and lives near Chicago, Illinois.

Books by Allie Pleiter

Love Inspired

Wander Canyon

Their Wander Canyon Wish
Winning Back Her Heart
His Christmas Wish

Matrimony Valley

His Surprise Son
Snowbound with the Best Man
Wander Canyon Courtship

Blue Thorn Ranch

The Texas Rancher's Return
Coming Home to Texas
The Texan's Second Chance
The Bull Rider's Homecoming
The Texas Rancher's New Family

Visit the Author Profile page
at Harlequin.com for more titles.

HOMEFRONT HERO

Allie Pleiter

Have I not commanded you?
Be strong and courageous. Do not be afraid;
do not be discouraged, for the Lord your God
will be with you wherever you go."
—*Joshua* 1:9

To Suzanne,
a brave hero and a warrior in her own right

Acknowledgments

A wise writer brings lots of good counsel
with her into a historical manuscript. In addition to
John M. Barry's invaluable book *The Great Influenza*,
I owe thanks to many other good people who served
as sources: Paula Benson, Dr. John Boyd of the
81st Regional Support Command, Susan Craft,
Kristina Dunn Johnson at the South Carolina
Confederate Relic Room and Military Museum,
Mary Jo Fairchild at the South Carolina Historical
Society, Mary J. Manning (and the entire outstanding
museum) at the Cantigny First Division Foundation,
Nichole Riley at Moncrief Army Community
Hospital, Stephanie Sapp at Jackson Army Base
U.S. Army Basic Combat Training Museum,
Christina Shedlock at the Charleston County Public
Library and Elizabeth Cassidy West and the other
dedicated librarians at the South Caroliniana Library
at the University of South Carolina at Columbia. Any
factual errors should be laid at my feet, not at the
excellent information these people provided me.

Chapter One

Camp Jackson Army Base
Columbia, South Carolina
September 1918

"I still can't believe it." Leanne Sample gazed around at the busy activity of Camp Jackson. Even with all she'd heard and seen while studying nursing at nearby University of South Carolina, the encampment stunned her. This immense property had only recently been mere sand, pine and brush. Now nearly a thousand buildings created a self-contained city. She was part of that city. Part of the monumental military machine poised to train and treat the boys going to and coming from "over there." She was a staff nurse at the base army hospital. "We're really here."

"Unless I'm seein' things, we most definitely are here." Ida Landway, Leanne's fellow nurse and room-mate at the Red Cross House where they and other newer nurses were housed, elbowed her. "I've seen it with my own eyes, but I still can barely believe this place wasn't even here two years ago." Together they stared at the layout of the orderly, efficient streets and structures, rows upon rows of new buildings standing in formation like their soldier occupants. "It's a grand, impressive thing, Camp Jackson. Makes me proud."

Leanne had known Ida briefly during their study program at the university, but now that they were officially installed at the camp, Leanne already knew her prayers for a good friend in the nursing corps had been answered. Different as night and day, Leanne still had found Ida a fast and delightful companion. Ida's sense of humor was often the perfect antidote to the stresses of military base life. As such, their settling in at the Red Cross House and on the hospital staff had whooshed by her in a matter of days, and been much easier than she'd expected.

Still, "on-staff" nursing life was tiring. "There was so much to do," Leanne said to Ida as she tilted her face to the early fall sunshine as they chatted with other nurses on the hillside out in front of the Red Cross House. "Too many things are far more complicated in real service then I ever found them in class."

"A free afternoon. I was wondering if we'd ever get one. Gracious, I remember thinking our class schedules were hard." Ida rolled her shoulders. "Hard has a whole new meaning to me now." This afternoon had been their first stretch of free time, and they'd decided to spend an hour doing absolutely nothing before taking the trolley into Columbia to attend a war rally on the USC campus that evening.

"However are you going to have time to do this?" Ida pointed to a notice of base hospital events pinned to a post outside the Red Cross House. "I feel like I've barely time to breathe, and you're already lined up to teach knitting classes."

"I've managed to find the time to teach you," Leanne reminded her newest student.

"Don't I know it. I tell you, my mama's jaw would drop if she saw I've already learned to knit. I guess you've found right where you fit in the scheme of things around here."

Ida was right; Leanne had found her place on base almost instantly. As if God had known just where to slot her in, placing an opening for a teacher in the Red Cross sock knitting campaign. If there was anything Leanne knew for certain she could do, it was to knit socks for soldiers. She'd run classes for her schoolmates at the university; it seemed easy as pie to do the same thing here. And it would help her make friends so quickly—hadn't she already? In only a matter of days the vastness of the base seemed just a wide-open ocean of possibilities.

Of course, there were others who were less thrilled at the opportunities ahead of Leanne—namely, her parents. Mama and Papa had come to see her settled in, and they hadn't left yet. They'd already stayed on in Columbia two days longer than planned. Papa attributed it to "necessary business contacts" here in the state capital, but Leanne knew better. Mama wasn't at all calm about the prospect of her daughter being an army nurse. Leanne had agreed to meet her parents for a last luncheon before they caught their train, a final goodbye off base before tonight's rally. In truth Leanne worried that despite already-packed bags, Mama would invent some other reason to delay their return to Charleston.

Ida must have read her expression. "Oh, stop fretting about your mama and papa, will you? Don't give them reason to stay one more minute. You're in for a ten-hankie bout of tears no matter what, so best just to get it over with. Don't you give them one inch of reason to stay off that train."

Leanne couldn't argue. She'd declared to herself that even Mama's fits of worry would not be permitted to dampen the eager wonder she felt to finally be in service. Leanne squared her shoulders and straightened her spine. "I am a United States Army nurse. I am an educated woman—" she shot a sideways glance at Ida as she adjusted the colored cape that designated her as a leader of the newly graduated nursing class "—and I am a force to be reckoned with."

"I'll say an amen to that!" Ida flashed her generous smile that widened further as she pointed to a large new bill posted in a spot all its own. "Speaking of forces to be reckoned with, I reckon our evening will be highly entertaining." She peered closer at an announcement for the "rousing patriotic speech" to be given by "a true wartime hero." "'Hear the daring exploits of Army Captain John Gallows,'" Ida read aloud. "'Thrill to the tale of how he saved lives at the risk of his own.' Well, where I come from a gallows is something to be feared."

Leanne could only laugh. Some days Ida sounded as if West Virginia were the wild, wild West. "Oh, that might still be true here. The Gallowses are a very formidable Charleston family."

"Have you met them?"

"I've not had the pleasure, but I believe our fathers know each other back in Charleston. A fine family going back for generations."

Ida leaned back and crossed her arms while eyeing the dashing photograph of Captain Gallows that illustrated the announcement. "Fine indeed. He's certainly handsome enough." She adjusted her stiff white apron as if primping for the photograph's admiration. Ida did like to be admired, especially by gallant army officers. "I can't think of a better way to spend our first free evening off base. Perhaps he'll let me sketch him."

"Why is it you want to sketch every handsome man you meet?" Leanne teased. Already she could see it might prove hard to keep her artistically inclined roommate focused on her duties. Ida was a free spirit if ever there was one, and while she took her nursing very seriously, her adventurous nature already pulled her too often away from her tasks.

"I'd be delighted to sit for you," came a deep voice behind them. "Especially if you are so partial to handsome war heroes."

Ida and Leanne spun on their heels to find the very man depicted in the photograph. Complete with the dashing smile. Even out of his dress uniform—for he wore a coat, but not one as fancy or full of medals as the one in the photograph—he was every bit the U.S. Army poster-boy hero. His dark hair just barely contained itself in its slick comb-back underneath his cap. He carried himself with unmistakably military command—Leanne suspected she'd have known he was an officer even in civilian clothes. He certainly was very sure of himself—a long moment passed before Leanne even noticed he leaned jauntily on a cane.

Ida planted one hand on her hip. "Well—" her voice grew silky "—no one can fault you for an excess of modesty. Still, my daddy always said a healthy ego was a heroic trait, so I suppose I can let it slide, Captain Gallows." She drew out the pronunciation of his name with a relish that made Leanne flush.

Captain Gallows was evidently all-too-accustomed to such attentions, for he merely widened his dashing smile and gave a short bow to each of them. "How do you do?" He pointed to the sign. "Say you'll attend to-night's event, and my fears of facing an audience full of dull-faced students and soldiers will be put to rest."

"Are you one of the Four Minute Men, then?" Leanne asked. Her father had been asked to serve on the nationally launched volunteer speakers board, called "Four Minute Men" for the prescribed length of their speeches, but Papa had declined. Still, from the super-latives on his bill, Captain Gallows could go on for four hours and still hold his audience captive.

"The best. They give me as long as I want. They tell me I'm enthralling."

"I have no doubt they do. I'm Ida Lee Landway, and this is my friend Leanne Sample. We've just joined the nursing staff at the base hospital."

The captain tipped his hat. "How fortunate for our boys in the wards. Miss Landway, Miss Sample, I'm delighted to meet you. Tell me what I can say to con-vince you to come to the rally."

"Oh, it won't take *much*," Ida cooed.

"We were just on our way over to town early and al-ready planning to attend," Leanne corrected. "No per-suasion will be required." He certainly seemed a cocky sort, this Captain Gallows.

"I'm not so sure," he replied with a disarming grin. "I was on campus this morning and one of the students told me she would come, but she would bring her knit-ting. Not the kind of response I'm used to, I must say. I'm trying to see it as a patriotic act, not an expectation of my inability to fascinate."

Definitely a cocky sort. "Don't take that as an af-front at all, Captain Gallows. I'm meeting my parents for luncheon and I have my knitting with me right now."

"Well, I can't say I haven't longed for a sharp pointy stick in several conversations with my own father."

Leanne didn't find that especially funny. "The Red Cross encourages us to knit everywhere we can, Captain Gallows." She tried not to glare as she pointed to the bag currently slung over her shoulder. "I assure you, I knit even in church, so the presence of anyone's yarn and needles need be no dent to your confidence. Our boys need socks as much as the army needs our boys."

Gallows tucked a hand in his pocket. "Duly noted, ma'am." He turned to Ida. "Does the Red Cross know what a fine champion they have in nurse Leanne Sample?"

"They ought to," Ida boasted. "She's been here a week and already she's teaching two knitting classes at the hospital."

"Impressive," Gallows replied. "I'm sure the fellows here at the hospital have told you there are days when a pair of warm, dry socks are the highlight of the week. I suppose if I just remember that while you all are staring down at your needles instead of up at me, I'll be just fine."

The man enjoyed being the center of attention—that much was clear. "You needn't worry. Most of us can stitch without even looking. I've knit so many pairs of socks I think I could probably knit in my sleep by now."

"Not me," Ida said. "Leanne's a good teacher, but I fear for the feet that'll have to put up with my socks. I'll have to stare down a fair amount—" she paused and batted her long auburn eyelashes "—but not the *whole* time."

"Well, then." Gallows rocked back on his boot heels. "I have my orders. I'm to be enthralling but not distracting. Have I got it right?"

"I have no doubt you do such a job very well," Leanne replied, not wanting to give Ida another chance at that one. "Good day, Captain. We've a trolley to catch, but we'll also catch your enthralling-but-not-distracting presentation this evening."

Gallows tipped his hat. "You do your bit, I'll do mine."

Chapter Two

Captain John Gallows planted his feet—or rather one good foot, one bad foot and the tip of his cane—on the porch of the Camp Jackson officers' hall. He'd envisioned his homecoming so very differently.

Still, he was in South Carolina, if not yet in Charleston. And home, in the form of his formidable and sharp-pointy-stick-worthy father, had come running to him.

"John." His father pulled open the door before John even set hand to the knob. He gave John a stiff clap on the back. The force made John put more weight on his bad leg than he would have liked. "Our boy, our hero, home for a bit from the grand tour of rousting up recruits, hmm?"

His father undoubtedly considered talking up war a poor substitute for winning one, but John shook off those thoughts as he shook his father's hand. "You know me," he said, applying his most charming smile, "ready to open my big mouth for a good cause."

"Welcome home, dear," John's mother cooed as she emerged from the hall behind his father. "Oh, look at that medal." She smoothed out the front of his uniform and the medal for bravery that continually hung there now. "My son. Decorated for valor." The pride in her voice was warm and sugary.

John had saved six lives, but only really in his efforts to keep his own. That didn't feel like bravery. He wasn't even supposed to be on that navy dirigible except for a favor he was granting to his commander's buddy. Still, John could spin a rousing tale and history had thrown him into a dramatic scenario. As such, John had been healed up quickly and delivered to several American cities to give speeches. He was eager to return to fighting, but hoped this recruitment tour would better his chances at being admitted to pilot training. Pilots, now those were the real heroes. If doing his best to stir up the patriotic spirit wherever and whenever asked got him closer to that kind of glory, he'd gladly comply.

"How handsome you look," Mama went on. "How much older than twenty-two. You walk differently, even."

John winked. "That would be the cane, ma'am," he joked, swinging it the way Charlie Chaplin did in the movies. He tipped the corner of his hat for effect.

Father made some sort of a gruff sound, but she laughed. "No, that would be the *man,* son. I'm not talking about your gait, but the way you carry yourself. With wisdom. Authority."

"Flattery. Don't you think you're just a little bit biased?" he teased her.

"Of course I am," she said, reaching up to lay a hand on each of his shoulders. "Oh, I am just so glad to have you home!" She hugged him tight. "And for so long a leave! Why, I wouldn't be surprised if they had this nasty business sewn up before y'all even had a chance to get back over there."

"Now, Deborah," John's father replied in his "let's

be sensible" voice, which had the desirable effect of re-moving Mama's hands from John's shoulders, "I hardly think they'd want Johnny back here making all those speeches if the end is near." His father's gaze flicked down momentarily to the black cane. "Besides, you're here to get the best of care while that leg heals."

"How is it?" Mama asked, following Father's gaze.

It hurt. All the time. But John had figured out early on that truth wasn't always the desired answer. "I'll be fine," he said, employing his now-stock reply to all such questions. Most days, it was the truth. Yet every moment since the train had pulled into Columbia, he'd felt odd…as if his body suddenly found his home state a foreign land.

Mama tucked her hand in John's free arm. "To think of my boy, dangling up there over the water, saving lives at the risk of his very own." Her voice trailed off and she leaned her head against his shoulder.

Saving lives at the risk of his very own. The words came directly from the press wire he'd seen. From the paper they'd read when they'd pinned the medal on him. From the leaflet that papered the cities where he spoke. Funny, all that bravery sounded like it belonged to someone else, even though John had vivid memories to prove otherwise. No man forgets hanging upside down from the stay wires of a dirigible a mile up and a mile out to sea. An army captain, in the *air* and out to *sea*. A fluke of circumstance that turned into a near-death disaster. He'd take the memory of nothing but air between himself and his death to his grave, even if he never spoke of it again. He *wished* he could never speak of it again, never again hear himself be lauded for an act that had no selfless heroism to it at all. It wasn't admirable to go to drastic lengths to save an airship when the alternative was crashing into the ocean with it.

"A heroic tale, surely," Papa boasted. "I imagine the ladies think even more highly of you now."

Father was right in that respect. The only thing ladies liked more than a man in uniform was a decorated hero in uniform. And John—like every member of the well-bred Gallows family—was a social success even before he slipped into uniform. He'd not lacked for company for one minute of his hospital stay, the voyage home, or his multi-city speaking circuit. "Well, now," he quipped, "hard to say. The nurses are supposed to be attentive. It's their job."

"I have the feeling 'above and beyond the call of duty' has a new meaning." Oscar Gallows laughed. He'd been a dashing soldier in his own day, Mama always said. "Seems to me y'all won't hurt for company one bit."

"Do you have to stay at the camp?" Mama asked… again. "Why can't you come home to Charleston? You'd be so much more comfortable at home with us."

"The hospital reconstruction therapists are here, Mother. And I am still on active duty. I've got to go where they send me."

Mama pouted. "Tell them to send you home to your mama's good care."

"That's no way for a Gallows to serve, Deborah. John has duties to perform even while he heals. You wouldn't want him to finish up the war as a mere spokesman, would you?"

Oscar Gallows began strutting toward the general's house where they had a luncheon engagement before John's big speech tonight. His father walked quickly, giving no quarter to John's injured leg.

John wasn't surprised. A Gallows gave no quarter to anyone, least of all himself.

"It's so *dry* here." Leanne watched her mama mop her brow and frown over her glass of tea. "And dreadfully hot without any kind of breeze. I don't know how you don't just shrivel up."

In truth, Columbia was a lovely town. It held the University of South Carolina and the state capitol—both as fine cultural centers for the region as any of which Charleston could boast. While it lacked the sea breeze, it also lacked the rain-soaked humidity that sent Charlestonians running out of their city to their beach houses. "I'm half a day to the coast, Mama. And no, I won't shrivel up. For goodness' sakes, I'm a nurse… I imagine I've learned how to care for myself in the process."

"That place is just massive," Mama moaned, casting her glance across town in the direction of Camp Jackson. Mama had made it clear, over and over and despite Leanne's many statements to the contrary, that she had fully expected Leanne to return to Charleston after completing her courses at the university, not join the service as she had done. "And so drab." Mama put a dramatic hand to her chest. "What if they decide to send you overseas?"

"They won't send me overseas, Mama. I'm needed here. Can't you see what an opportunity this is?"

Papa, who had been rather quiet the entire trip, put a hand on Mama's shoulder. "She needs to do her part, and far better here than over there. She'll learn a great deal." Leanne had the distinct impression he was half lecturing himself. "Honestly, Maureen, Columbia is not that far from Charleston."

"Not far at all, Papa," Leanne assured him. "And

I'll be able to feel so much more useful here." She'd learned a great many things already, and was about to learn a great deal more. The world was changing so fast for women these days—there was talk of voting and owning property and pursuing careers in literature and painting, serving overseas, all kinds of things. Awful as it was, the war gave women the chance to do things they'd never done before. The lines of tradition were bending in new and exciting ways, and if they would only bend for this time, she couldn't bear to miss exploring all she could in a town that was right at the heart of it all.

Leanne yearned to know she'd made a difference—in lives and in the healing of souls and bodies. She felt as if she would make too small a contribution in Charleston now that the university had shown her how far a life's reach could be. Leanne wanted God to cast her life's reach far and wide.

As they finished their luncheon and walked reluctantly to the train station, Mama smoothed out Leanne's collar one last time.

"I'll be fine, Mama, really. I'm excited. Don't be sad."

Mama's hand touched Leanne's cheek. "I'll pray for you every day, darlin'. Every single day."

Leanne took her mother's hand in hers. Mama's promise to cover her in prayer ignited the tiny spark of fear—the anxiety of God's great big reach stretching her too far—that she'd swallowed all day. Her assignment in the reconstruction ward of the camp hospital, helping soldiers recover from their wounds, was so important, but a bit frightening at the same time. She swallowed her nerves for the thousandth time, willing them not to show one little bit. "I'd like that," she said with all the confidence she could muster. "But I'll be home for Thanksgiving before you know it. And I'll write. I'm sure the Charleston Red Cross will keep you so busy you'll barely have time to miss me."

"I miss you already." Mama's voice broke, and Leanne gave a pleading look to her father. The Great Goodbye—as she'd called it in her mind all this week—had already taken an hour longer than she'd expected.

"We've lingered long enough, Maureen." Papa took Mama's hands from Leanne's and tugged her mother's resistant body toward the station platform. Leanne thought that if he waited even five more minutes, Mama might affix herself to a Columbia streetlamp and refuse to let go. "It's high time we let our little girl do what she came to do." He leaned in and kissed Leanne soundly on the cheek. "Be good, work hard." It was the same goodbye he'd said every single morning of her school years. It helped to calm the tiny fearful spark, as if this was just another phase of her education instead of a life-altering adventure.

"I will." Leanne blew a kiss to her mother, afraid that if she gave in to the impulse to run and hug Mama, Papa would have to peel them tearfully off each other.

"Write!" Mama called, the sniffles already starting as Papa guided her down the platform toward the waiting train. Leanne nodded, her own throat choking up at the sound of Mama's impending tears. Papa had joked that he'd brought eleven handkerchiefs for the trip home and warned the county of the ensuing flood.

Leanne clutched the hanky he'd given her as she stood smiling and waving. As sad as she was to see them go, she couldn't help but feel that this was a rite of passage, a necessary step in becoming her own woman. Childhood was over—she was a nurse now. Part of the

Great War. Part of the great cause of the Red Cross and a new generation of women doing things women had never done before.

It is, she told herself as she turned toward the university auditorium where she'd promised to meet Ida, *a very good sort of terrifying.*

Chapter Three

It could have been any of the dozens of halls, churches, auditoriums and ballrooms John had been in over the past month. He paced the tiny cluttered backstage and tried to walk off the nerves and pain. He tried, as well, to walk off the boyish hope that his father had stayed for the presentation. Foolishness, for not one of these maladies—physical or mental—would ease with steps. He knew that, but it was better than sitting as he waited impatiently for his speech to start.

If only he could run. It would feel wonderful to run, the way he used to run for exercise and sheer pleasure. More foolishness to think of that, for it would be torture to run now. John's uncooperative leg ignored his persistent craving to go fast. The fact that he went nowhere fast these days proved a continual frustration to his lifelong love of speed. He'd been aiming to drive those new race cars when the war broke out, and he'd heard some of the race-car drivers were trying to form a battalion of pilots. Airplanes, now there was the future—not just of warfare but of everything. Nothing went faster than those. When the army had hinted he'd have a chance at the Air Corps, he'd signed up as fast as he could.

And he did end up in the air.

On the slowest airship ever created.

John's only chance at air travel came in the form of a diplomatic mission on a huge, sluggish navy dirigible—the furthest thing from what he'd had in mind. Still, as he was now about to tell in the most enthralling way possible, even that fluke of history had managed to catapult him into notoriety.

Pulling the thick red velvet curtain to the side, John couldn't stop himself from scanning the sea of uniforms for the one he would not see: Colonel Oscar Gallows. Mother had surely pleaded, but even as a retired colonel Father wasn't the kind of man who had time to watch his son "stump" for Uncle Sam. How often had the colonel scowled at John's oratory skills, calling his son "a man of too many words"? *And not enough action*—Father had never actually said it, but the message came through loud and clear.

John consoled himself by scanning the audience for the scattered pockets of female students and army base nurses. Nearly all, as Nurse Sample had predicted, were knitting. He tried to seek her out, looking for that stunning gold hair and amber eyes that nearly scowled at his swagger. It was clear her friend Ida was taken with him—women often were, so that was no novelty. Leanne Sample, however, fascinated him by being indifferent, perhaps even unimpressed. He scanned the audience again, hoping to locate her seat so he could direct a part of his speech especially to her. Her kind were everywhere, a sea of women with clicking needles working the same drab trio of official colors—black, beige and that particularly tiresome shade of U.S. Army olive-green.

There she was. My, but she was pretty. Her thick fringe of blond lashes shielded her eyes as she bent over her work. She seemed delicate with all that light hair and pale skin, but the way she held her shoulders spoke of a wisp of defiance. He made it a personal goal to enthrall her to distraction. To draw those hazel eyes up off those drab colors and onto him.

In full dress, John knew he'd draw eyes, and easily stand out in this crowd. And if there was anything he did well, it was to stand out. Gallows men were supposed to stand out, after all. To distinguish themselves by courageous ambition. Ha! Even the colonel seemed to realize that John's path to notoriety had only really been achieved by climbing up and falling down on a ship he should never have been on in the first place. This from a man who'd spent his life trying to stand out and go fast. His life had been turned on its ear in any number of ways since this whole messy business began.

The university president tapped John on the shoulder. "Are you ready, Captain Gallows?" John could hear the school band begin a rousing tune on the other side of the curtain.

He did what he always did: he dismissed the pain, shook off his nerves and applied the smile that had charmed hearts and reeled in recruits in ten American cities. "By all means, sir." He left his cane leaning up against the backstage wall, tilted his hat just so and walked out into the myth of glory.

Proud.

Did Captain John Gallows earn such arrogance?

Yes, he was heroic, but the man's self-importance

seemed to know no bounds. As he told the harrowing tale of his brush with death, dangling from airship stay wires to effect a life-saving repair while the crew lay wounded and helpless, Leanne could feel the entire room swell with admiration. Women wanted to be near him, men wanted to be him. His eyes were such an astounding dark blue—rendered even more astounding against the crisp collar of his uniform—that one hardly even noticed his limp. He didn't use his cane on stage, but Leanne reasoned that they'd arranged the stage in such a way as to afford him the shortest walk possible to the podium. The way he told the story, however, it was a wonder the audience didn't break into applause at his very ability to walk upright. While his entanglement in the dirigible's stay wires had saved his life, it had also shredded his right leg to near uselessness. He never said that outright, but Leanne could read between the lines of his crafted narrative. She guessed, just by how he phrased his descriptions and avoided certain words, that his leg still pained him significantly—both physically and emotionally. He did not seem a man to brook limitations of any kind.

"Now is the time to finish the job we've started," he said, casting his keen eyes out across the audience. "Our enemy is close to defeated. Our cause is the most important one you will ever know." Captain Gallows pointed out into the audience, and Leanne had no doubt every soul in the building felt as if he were pointing straight at them—she knew she did. "When you look your sons and daughters in the eye decades from now, as they enjoy a world of peace and prosperity, will you be able to say you did your part? Can you say you answered duty's sacred call?"

Cheers began to swell up from the audience. The

young students off to her left began to stand and clap. Next to her, Ida brandished her newly employed knitting needles as if she were Joan of Arc charging her troops into battle. Despite her resistance to Gallows, Leanne felt the echo of a "yes!" surge up in her own heart. Her work as a nurse, her aid to the troops and even her leisure hours spent knitting dozens of socks for soldiers answered her call. Homefront nurses were as essential to the cause as those serving overseas. She understood the need for combat, but wanted no part of it. Leanne longed to be part of the healing. And beyond her nursing, she was using her knitting, as well. She'd taught hospital staff how to knit the government-issued sock pattern, and she'd teach her first class of patients later this week. When those classes were off and stitching, she would teach more. For there was so very much to be done.

When someone behind her started up a chorus of last year's popular war song "Over There," Leanne stopped knitting and joined in. It felt important, gravely important, to be part of something so large and daunting. To be here, on her own, both serving and learning. The whole world was changing, and God had planted her on the crest of the incoming wave. While her grandmother had moaned that the war was "the worst time to be alive," Leanne couldn't help but feel that Nana was wrong. Despite all the hardship, this was indeed the best time to be young and alive.

If Captain Gallows wished to stir the crowd to the heights of patriotic frenzy, he had certainly succeeded. More than half the students in the room were now on their feet, cheering. Even Leanne had to admit Gallows was a compelling, charismatic spokesman for the cause. Perhaps she could be more gracious toward his very healthy ego than she had been earlier that day.

Captain Gallows made his way off the stage as the university chorus came onstage to lead in another song. She could see him "offstage" because of her vantage point far to the left, but he must have thought he was out of view for his limp became pronounced and he sank into a nearby chair. As the singing continued, she watched him, transfixed by the change in his stature. He picked his cane up from where it lay against the backstage wall. Instead of rising, as she expected him to do, he sat there, eventually leaning over the cane with his head resting on top of his hands. He looked as if he were in great pain. From the looks of it, his leg must have been agonizing him the entire speech. And surely no one would have thought one lick less of him had he used the cane.

Leanne watched him for a moment, surprised at the surge of sympathy she felt for this man she hardly knew and hadn't much liked at first, until the dean of students approached Captain Gallows. Instantly his demeanor returned to the dashing hero, shooting upright as if he hadn't a pain or care in the world. That was more in line with the behavior she expected of him. So which was the real John Gallows—the arrogant, larger-than-life hero—or the proud, wounded, struggling man she'd caught a glimpse of the moment before? There was no way for her to tell now. The captain and the dean walked off together, and Leanne remembered there was a reception of sorts for him afterward. As one of the Red Cross knitting teachers, she'd been invited. She hadn't planned on going at first, for she hadn't a taste for such things and it would be awkward since Ida hadn't been asked. She'd go, now, if just to help make up her mind as to what kind of man he truly was.

"You know, I think I will go to that reception after all," she said as casually as she could to Ida as they packed up their things to exit the hall.

"Well, now, who wouldn't?" Ida didn't seem the least bit slighted by her lack of an invitation. Some days Leanne wished for Ida's confidence and, as Papa put it, "thick skin." Instead of sulking, Ida only offered her an oversize wink. "Tell the good captain he can recruit me any day," she whispered, visibly pleased at Leanne's startled reaction.

"It's a good thing I won't and he can't," she replied, hoping no one else heard the scandalous remark.

"Says you." Ida laughed, and sauntered away.

Yes, he was a hero. Yes, he was vital to the cause. Still, Leanne couldn't see how even the most rousing of Gallows's speeches could overcome her distaste for the man's monumental air of self-importance.

Chapter Four

Leanne was just barely ten minutes into the reception, not yet even to the punch bowl, when Gallows swooped up behind her and took her by the elbow.

"Save me," he whispered as he nodded to the library shelf to their left. "Pull a book off the shelf this very minute and save me from Professor Mosling, I implore you." She couldn't help but comply, for Leanne knew that calling Professor Mosling long-winded was an understatement. Mosling thought very highly of himself and his opinions, and shared them freely with unsuspecting victims. At great length and with considerable detail. Last month she'd been cornered for three quarters of an hour by the man as he shared his views on the use of domestic wool for socks. Mosling raised an arm with an all-too-hearty "There you are, Gallows!" Leanne snatched the largest book within reach and angled her shoulders away from the man.

"Really, Captain Gallows, there is much to be said for—" she realized in her haste she'd neglected to even scan the massive volume's title "—*Atlantic Shipping Records of the Cooper River*. I find it a most fascinating subject," she improvised, finding herself stumped.

"As do I," replied Captain Gallows, his eyes filled with surprise and a healthy dose of amusement even though his voice was earnest. "Please, do go on."

Go on? How on earth could she "go on"? "As I'm sure you know, the Cooper River runs right through Charleston, providing a major seaport thoroughfare…" It felt absurd; she was stringing together important-sounding words with almost no sense of their content. Still, Gallows's eyes encouraged her, looking as if she was imparting the most vital knowledge imaginable.

"Do forgive me," Gallows said to the professor, "but I simply cannot tear myself away from Miss Sample's *fascinating* explanation."

The ruse worked, for Mosling huffed a little, straightened his jacket and then seemed to find another suitable target within seconds. "Oh, yes, well, another time then."

"Indeed," said Captain Gallows, actually managing to sound sorry for the loss despite the relief she could see in his eyes. "Very soon."

As soon as Mosling had left, Gallows took the huge text from her and began to laugh. "*Atlantic Shipping Records?* A most unfortunate choice. I could probably better explain these to you than the other way around."

Leanne raised an eyebrow, not particularly pleased to be roped into such a scheme. "I was rather in a hurry and quite unprepared."

"Perhaps I should have asked you to teach me knitting." He looked as if he'd rather read *Atlantic Shipping Records* from cover to cover than take up the craft— as if he found it a frilly pastime better suited to grandmothers in rocking chairs.

"Many men have, you know. There was a time, centuries ago, when knitting was purely a man's craft. And you can't argue that every hand is needed. Perhaps we can arrange a lesson for you yet." She couldn't for the life of her say where such boldness had come from. Perhaps Ida was rubbing off on her.

"If anyone could…" The fact that he didn't finish the sentence made it all the more daunting.

Leanne chose to shift the subject. "You gave a stunning presentation, Captain. The boys were on their feet cheering by the end of things."

He leaned against the bookcase, and while she had the urge to ask him if he'd like to sit down, she had the notion that he wouldn't take to such a consideration of his injury. "You stopped knitting there for a moment. I saw you."

He made it sound as if her pause revealed secrets. "I was inspired. It is a harrowing tale."

A flicker of a shadow came over his eye at her use of the word. Only for a sliver of a second, however, and it was so instantly replaced by a cavalier expression that it made her wonder if it had been there at all. "Ah, but so heroic and inspiring."

"It makes it unfair that your leg pains you so much." She hadn't planned on making such a remark, but somehow it jumped out of her.

She expected him to give some dashing dismissal of the judgment, but he paused. He looked at her as if she were the first person ever to say such a thing, which couldn't possibly be true. "Why?" He had the oddest tone of expression.

"I…" she fumbled, not knowing the answer herself. "I should think it a terrible shame. It seems a very brave thing you've done, and I would like to think God rewards bravery, not punishes it."

"God? Rewarding me for being caught on a failing airship?" He laughed, but far too sharply. "The very thought." He took the book from her, snapping it shut before replacing it on the shelf between them. "You have a very odd way of thinking, Nurse Sample."

What did the captain think of his "fate"? Or his Creator? Did he even acknowledge Him? Unsure what to make of Gallows, Leanne pressed her point. "Odd? By thinking God is just or by thinking you brave?"

That got a hearty laugh from him. He spun his cane in his hand, almost like a showman, and stared at her a long, puzzling moment before he said, "Both."

She wasn't going to let him go at a clever dodge like that. "How so?"

Gallows's face told her the conversation had ventured into difficult territory. "Are you always so pointed in your conversations?"

"Would you prefer we return to *Atlantic Shipping Records*? Or I could get the good professor to rejoin us…"

"No," he cut in. He pulled a hand over his chin, groping for his answer while she patiently waited. Leanne found herself genuinely curious—and surprisingly so— as to what this man truly thought of himself when no one else was watching. "Wars need heroes," he said eventually, "and those of us in the wrong place at the wrong time find ourselves drafted into that need. I've been too busy staying alive and playing hero to worry about who did the drafting or why. I don't ponder whether I limp from justice or bravery, Nurse Sample. I just try to walk."

His smile had a dark edge to it as he turned and walked away. With an odd little catch under her chest, Leanne noted that while he hid it extremely well, he still limped.

Ashton Barnes was a big, barrel-chested man who barked orders with the intensity of cannon-fire. He'd been one of Colonel Gallows's protégés, rising fast and far to head up a logistical marvel like Camp Jackson even though he was barely pushing fifty. The general's balding head stubbornly held on to what was left of his white-blond hair, the rounded pate in stark contrast to the rectangular metal glasses he wore. Fond of cigars, hunting and blueberry pie, Barnes was the kind of larger-than-life commander a bursting enterprise like Camp Jackson required.

Every soldier knew Barnes as firm but fair, and even though one might consider Barnes "a friend of the family," John knew better than to think his last name bought him any leverage with the general. His talents earned him the man's eye, not his pedigree, and John had seen Barnes at the rally, sizing up his performance from the back corner. He'd known the job they'd given him to do yesterday, and he'd done it well, so John wasn't surprised to receive a summons to the general's office this morning.

While he also prided himself on good soldiering, drama and attention were John's strongest weapons to wield. He'd known within the first ten minutes how to draw this particular audience into the cause. Really, what young man doesn't want a chance at heroism? Doesn't yearn to know he's stepped into the destiny life handed him? The kindling was dry—it was only his job to strike the match and set it aflame. In his more whimsical moments, John sometimes wondered if his father was at all amused that John's "gift for instigation," as Mama always put it, had been put to such a virtuous use.

No sense pondering that. Father was undoubtedly back in Charleston and it was General Barnes's approval that mattered at the moment. When John walked into the general's office and stood at attention, Barnes gave him a broad smile. "Outstanding speech. I could have piled all the 'Four Minute Men' into one uniform and not done as well. We had two dozen new recruits before lunchtime today, and while I haven't talked to the navy I suspect they did just as well." He gestured toward the chair that fronted his desk. "At ease, son, get off that leg of yours."

John settled into the chair. "I'm glad to see you pleased, sir." He'd always liked Ashton Barnes, but he was smart enough to be a little afraid of the man and the power he wielded.

"I am. I am indeed. I knew you were the man for the job." Usually a straight shooter, John didn't like the way the general watched the way he laid his cane against the chair. Why did people always stare at the cane? Why never the leg? Or just at him? The general at least did him the courtesy of acknowledging the injury. That reaction was always easier to bear than those who did a poor job of pretending to ignore it, like his father. Barnes nodded toward John's outstretched right leg. "How *is* the leg getting on?"

John stared down at the stiff limb. It never bent easily anymore so he'd stopped trying in cases where there was enough room. "Fine, sir. I'm better than most."

"I suspect you are." Barnes took off his glasses and pinched the bridge of his nose. "I don't like to see our boys coming home in pieces like this. Victory can't come soon enough, in my book."

The general had handed him the perfect opening, and John was going to take it. "I mean to go back, sir. As soon as I can."

"So your father tells me."

So Father *had* spoken with Barnes. John had suspected it—expected it, actually, given the colonel's clear-but-unspoken distaste for his current assignment. It struck John as ironic that Oscar Gallows's long, deep shadow lent John half the "marquee value" his current speeches produced. The Gallows family name got him this job as much as his silver tongue. After all, Gallowses were pillars of Charleston society long before John had been lauded as a hero.

While it goaded John that his father had lobbied the general behind his back, anything that sped up his return to combat was a welcome development. "I don't think it'll take more than three or four weeks here for me to finish healing up. Maybe two if that brute of a therapist has me doing any more exercises. I'm grateful for the chance to toot the army's horn, but with all due respect, I'd rather be back in France."

The general steepled his hands. "Much as I'd like to appease your father, or you, your doctors haven't cleared you for duty."

He didn't say "yet." John didn't like the omission one bit. Father probably caught that one as well, which may have been why he'd skipped the rally. Wounded out of the service wouldn't play well with Oscar Gallows.

It didn't play well with him, either. He'd throw the cane away tomorrow and grit his teeth until they fell out before he'd listen to any doctor tell him he couldn't go back up and finish what he'd started. He had no intention of being left behind among the wounded, even if others thought him a hero. His heroism was unfinished business, as far as John was concerned. He needed to be back in the fight, not sitting over here spouting rousing tales while his battalion earned a victory. "They will soon enough. Sooner on your recommendation, sir."

"I won't say you haven't been valuable overseas, but you're of no value at all if that leg fails you when you need it most. I admire your eager spirit, John—" Barnes knew what he was doing when he intentionally used his given name like a friend of the family would— "but don't let your impatience get you killed. You'll go back when you're ready, and I'm of no mind to send you off a minute before."

It was the closest thing to a promise he'd had yet; John wasn't going to let this "friend of the family" go at a mere hint. "But you'll send me? When I'm ready?" He was ready *now*.

"I imagine I will, yes." He spoke like a true commander—leaving himself the tiniest of escapes just in case.

He may never get another chance like this. The colonel had obviously asked for it. *He'd* asked for it. He'd just given the army several weeks of record-breaking recruitment speeches. John stood, without his cane. He extended his hand. "I'd like your word on it, sir. I'll give speeches until I'm blue in the face, I'll rouse up recruits out of the sand, but I want to know you'll send me back when I'm ready."

Barnes hesitated for a moment, John's message of "I will hold you to this" coming through loud and clear. "Very well," he said after an insufferable pause. They shook on it. John had his guarantee. He wouldn't end the war as a campaign poster. He'd go back where he belonged and make a name for himself on the battlefield, where it really mattered. "Thank you, sir."

"I'd say you're welcome, Captain, but I'm not so sure."

John allowed himself the luxury of picking his cane back up, even though it shot pain like a bolt of lightning through his hip to bend over so far. "I'm sure enough for the both of us," he said when he was upright again, making sure none of the strain showed in his voice.

"You should know it would help, Gallows, if I could have your cooperation on a—shall we say an unconventional little campaign of ours."

Now it came out. Give and get, push and pull. Why was he surprised the general had a trick up his striped sleeve? "Anything you need, sir."

"Don't be so agreeable, son, until you've heard what it is the Red Cross has in mind."

John sat back down again, the ache in his leg now matched by a lump in his throat.

Chapter Five

A few days after the rally, Leanne sat in the hospital meeting room helping an older nurse struggle through her first cumbersome knitting stitches. "Yes—" she smiled at the confused grimaces given by many of the women around her "—it does feel funny at first. Give it a few days, and you'll be amazed how quickly you take to it."

Another nurse held up the yarn Leanne had distributed at the beginning of class. "It's drab stuff, don't you think? I'd rather go to war in red socks. Or blue."

"As long as they're warm and dry, we don't much care what color they are," came a voice from behind Leanne's shoulder. She turned to find Captain Gallows poking his head into the room.

"Captain Gallows, have you decided to take up knitting?"

"Well, since my job is to encourage, I thought I shouldn't stop at soldiers." He stepped into the room and leaned against the doorway. Leanne suspected he was well aware of the fine figure he cut standing in such a cavalier manner. Around her, stitching ground to a halt. The young woman Leanne was currently sitting next to actually sighed and dropped her knitting to her lap. "Knit as if our lives depended upon it, ladies," Gallows said with a gallant flair, "for I dare say they do. An army fights on its feet, you know."

"Y'all sound like the Red Cross poster," a hospital cook to Leanne's left remarked, holding up the very beginning of a sock.

"Good for me." He grinned. "That means I've gotten it right. It seems I *am* your poster boy. Or will be, next week."

"How very fortunate." Ida, who had stopped into the class to have Leanne correct a mistake on her current pair of socks, nearly purred her approval. "How so?"

Gallows sat down, and for the first time Leanne noticed how a shred of annoyance clipped his words. "I'm your new student." There was the tiniest edge to the way he bit off the *t* in the last word.

"You?"

"Under orders, it seems." He looked at the yarn as though it would infect him on contact.

Leanne dropped a stitch—something she never did. "Am I to understand that you've been *ordered* to learn how to knit?" She tried not to laugh, but the very thought of gallant Captain Gallows struggling with the turn of a sock heel was just too amusing an image, especially after the way he'd acted earlier. He may have long, elegant fingers, but they'd tangle mercilessly under so fine a task. Not only had he been dismissive, but Leanne was sure the captain hadn't nearly the patience for it. He'd make a ghastly student.

Her assessment must have shown on her face, for his look darkened. Even though this was very obviously not his idea, he didn't take to being doubted or dismissed. Oh, others might be fooled by his very good show, but

Leanne could tell he wasn't the least bit happy at the prospect of…whatever it was he'd been ordered to do. Which, actually, she wasn't quite sure of yet. "You're to knit Red Cross socks?"

"More precisely, I'm to be photographed learning how to knit Red Cross socks. I suppose as long as the rascals get the shot they want, whether or not I actually master the thing is beside the point."

"Not to me," Leanne countered. No set of cameras was going to turn her beloved craft and service into a three-ring circus. No, sir, not with this soldier.

"Leanne's never failed yet—every student she's had has managed at least one pair of socks," said the woman to Leanne's right with an enormous grin.

"If not dozens," Ida added, her grin even wider. "I doubt she'll let you be her first failure. Especially not on—did you say camera? Photographs?"

It was starting to make sense. Although many people had taken up the cause, the Red Cross was still woefully short of knitters. They'd been trying to convince more males to take up the needles in support of soldiers, and hadn't had much luck. Capturing photos of someone with Captain Gallows's reputation learning to knit would go a long way toward convincing other men to do likewise. They'd never find a more convincing spokesman. But goodness knows what they'd done to secure his cooperation, for she was sure he wasn't pleased at the prospect by any means.

"I'm evidently the man to convince America's men to knit. Or at least America's boys."

"Our dashing hero put to the needles." Ida giggled. "Why, it's a fine idea when you think of it. I know I can't wait to see your first sock, Captain. I expect you could auction it off to the highest bidder and raise loads of funds for the Red Cross."

"I declare, Ida, you're brilliant." Leanne jumped on the idea. If nothing else, it'd force the captain to see the project through, not just sit long enough to knit on film, but to actually learn the thing. And that was a most entertaining prospect. "I think you've hit on the perfect plan."

"You're joking." Gallows balked. "It'll be a hideous thing unfit for service to any soldier's foot."

"All the more reason that it should serve in some other way, then." Leanne couldn't suppress a wide smile. "We could set up a booth to auction it off at the Charleston Red Cross Christmas Banquet in November. My mama's on the committee. I think a deadline would be a grand motivation for your progress, don't you?"

Gallows stared at her, half amused, half daunted. "I don't think the general knows who he's dealing with. That's downright mischievous, Miss Sample."

"Oh, no," said another of the women. "I think it's the best idea ever. I wouldn't be surprised if Leanne's class size doubled the moment folks found out."

"And you do your best work with an audience, Captain Gallows. You told me yourself."

"Did I?" He had the look of a man who knew he was cornered. Leanne couldn't hide the delightful spark of amusement and conquest she felt at turning the captain's monstrous ego to a useful purpose. The woman was right—her classes would swell with new students once word got out that the dashing Captain Gallows was a fellow knitter. And with an audience to watch his triumphs and failures, he'd simply have to succeed. Perhaps even excel. And wouldn't that be something to see?

"I am undone," he said, throwing up his hands.

"Overthrown. When you keep your appointment with the general this afternoon, I hope you won't throw me to the wolves. Or is it the sheep in this case?"

"The general?"

"You're to see General Barnes at two o'clock. He wants to explain his idea to you, but I have the most peculiar feeling it is you who'll be doing all the explaining. The man ought to be warned."

Leanne blushed. "You overstate my influence, Captain Gallows."

"No," he countered, giving her the most unsettling look, "I don't think I do." He got up—with a grimace of pain Leanne doubted anyone else noticed—and saluted the group. "Press on, ladies. Next week I join the forces. Until then."

He made his way out the door, but Leanne was not done with this conversation. She told the group to continue knitting and caught up with the captain a ways down the hall.

"You're serious?" she said as he turned, suddenly wondering if the whole thing had been one of Ida's pranks.

"I assure you," he replied, "I'd hardly make something like this up. I'm not at all sure my dignity will survive the day."

So he had been cornered into it. By what? She motioned for them to continue walking. "If you don't mind my asking, what on earth could make you agree to something like this?"

He gave out a slight sigh. "Let's just say the general has something I want, and like most good commanders, he's wielding it to his advantage." He chuckled and leaned back against the wall. He made it look cavalier, but Leanne suspected by the way he cocked his right hip that he was very good at finding obscure ways to take the weight off his leg. "Blackmailed into needlework. I'll never live it down."

"What, exactly, is the general proposing?"

"I'm sure he'll tell you at two o'clock."

"I'm sure you'll understand that I'd rather know *now*."

Gallows took off his hat and sighed. "It seems a hoard of photographers from *Era* magazine will be invited to take pictures of you teaching me to knit. They'll write an article saying how easy it is, and how much everyone's help is needed, probably even publish a copy of the Red Cross pattern or whatever it is you call the directions. I'll go on and on in dashing terms about how important it is, and how every boy should step up to the plate and do his bit. You'll be famous for a spell and I'll hold up my end of the bargain—which evidently now will involve producing an actual sock, thanks to your quick-witted friend back there. I should think it all is rather obvious."

Leanne crossed her arms over her chest, not caring for his tone. "I should think it all rather obvious that I ought to have been *asked*. I don't much care for being made a spectacle of, Captain, even if it is your favorite pastime."

"No one asked me, either. I'm following orders."

"And you strike me so much like a man who always does what he's told." Leanne turned to head back to her classroom.

"I'm not!" he shot back. "Not unless it gets me what I want."

Leanne merely huffed. No one seemed to give one whit about her opinion in all of this. She marched off to her classroom without a single look back.

Chapter Six

❧

Captain Gallows sat entirely too close. Leanne shifted her chair farther away from him as they sat in the Red Cross House parlor. Then she set her knitting bag on a small table and pulled it between them for good measure. Their first photo session was in three days, but he'd pestered her nonstop until she'd agreed to give him an off-camera lesson first.

"I still don't know about this," she said. They were two minutes into the lesson and she was already regretting giving in to his persistent demands. "You're supposed to be photographed learning how to knit."

"And I will." While Gallows's smile was worthy of a matinee idol, it was a genuine one—or at least, it seemed to be. He had another manufactured smile—she'd seen him employ it during the reception after his first appearance. That smile was just as cinema-dashing, but it never reached his eyes with the same intensity. It stopped somehow at the edges of his mouth.

She could see the distinction between his "public" and his "private" smiles as clear as day, but others didn't seem to. It bothered her—and she suspected it bothered him—that she could tell the difference. It felt like too much information to know, like walking into a room that ought to have been locked. Why did she, of all people, see through his facade? Worse yet, he knew she recognized her effect on him. And it bothered her that he knew she knew. The whole business felt like an emotional house of mirrors—awareness reflecting back onto confusion upon discomfort. Knitting was supposed to be calming.

Leanne picked up the set of needles she'd selected for him. They were slightly larger than the usual sock needles, but Captain Gallows needed something substantial that wouldn't get lost in those large hands. "Some would say learning ahead of the photographs that are supposed to *show* you learning would be cheating." Where was the nerve to talk to him like that coming from? One simply didn't tease a war hero as if he were a little brother. Certainly not this war hero. Still, the spark he would get in his eyes when she did was an irresistible lure.

He raised an eyebrow, the gleam emanating full force. "I'm not cheating. I'm *rehearsing.*"

"Really?" She gave him an expression she hoped showed her dislike for the way he wrangled semantics to his advantage.

"Remember, it's my job to make this look easy."

It bothered her that he actually had a point. The Red Cross cause would only be served by his mastery. "This, of course, places no small amount of pressure on my teaching skills."

His eyes sparkled. "Let's not dwell on how much is at stake."

Leanne handed him the yarn and needles, and despite the fact that they had looked so enormous in her own grasp, they looked nearly small in his. He turned the objects over in his hands, peering at them as if with the right look they'd give up secrets. He shifted his eyes from the dull green yarn to look at her. They were an exquisite indigo, his eyes. A deep-sea blue, like mussel shells or the last hour of a summer's evening. "Wait a minute, there are four needles here. My mother knits with only two. You're not pulling one over on me or anything, are you? It *is* easy?"

So his mother knitted. She tried to imagine little Johnny Gallows sitting at his mother's feet while she knitted him a Christmas sweater and couldn't bring up the image. The man in front of her looked like he'd never been small—or innocent—a day in his life.

He certainly looked far from childlike now. It was as if his personality only intensified the closer one stood. And he was so fond of standing close. She moved her chair back an inch. "Oh, some take to it naturally." She made her voice sound more casual than she felt. If he'd noticed her retreat, he didn't show it. "Minnie Havers," she went on, "why, she had her first sock done almost within the week. Took to it like a fish to water. Others, well, I'd say it's more of a struggle. And no, Captain, I quite assure you all socks are knitted with four needles like these. Surely a man of your aptitude should master it in no time."

John held up the needles. "No time, hmm?"

"Most do. Well, most *women,* that is. I haven't taught my first class of soldiers yet. Those start next week."

"I am your first male student?" He enjoyed that far too much.

Leanne cleared her throat rather than answer. "I find it's a matter of dexterity. Do you have a great deal of dexterity, Captain Gallows?"

She regretted the question the moment she asked it. "I've been told I have the hands of a surgeon." He said it in a way that made Leanne sure she didn't want him to elaborate.

"Let's get started." Leanne had never actually taught a man to knit before. Normally it involved a lot of her holding the yarn and needles together with the student, repositioning fingers, adjusting the tension of the yarn. Touching. She'd never given it a moment's thought before, but now it meant touching a *man's* hands. *This* man's hands. The air between them was charged enough as it was. It seemed foolish, but Leanne was afraid to touch him. It would cross some kind of line she hadn't even realized was there.

She attempted, in response, to teach him without touching his hands. This resulted in nothing short of disaster. His frustration built on her tension, tangling their composure tighter than the yarn in their fingers.

"It feels like wrestling a porcupine," Captain Gallows grunted when a needle slipped through the stitches and fell to the carpet at his feet. "The annoying little sticks won't stay put." She knew it would pain him to reach over and fetch the needle, so she bent and picked it up as quickly as she could. The look on his face—reflecting the limitation she knew he would never speak of—almost made her shudder. Captain Gallows was obviously used to mastery of anything he attempted, and the effort required to do what he clearly deemed a simple task simmered dark behind his eyes.

"It's much more difficult for larger fingers." While she'd meant the remark to soothe his feelings, it did just the opposite. He looked as if he'd snarl at the yarn within minutes. A shameful corner of her heart enjoyed watching the arrogant captain meet his match, but the part of her that could see through his bravado winced at causing him further pain. No one likes to have their weaknesses displayed. "You know," she confessed in the hopes of easing his nerves, "you were right to keep this first lesson between us." Under any other circumstances the phrase "between us" would have been harmless. When "between us" meant between her and Captain John Gallows, however, the words darted between them like an electrical charge.

He grunted again. "Ease up, Captain. Hold that yarn any tighter and you'll lose circulation in your fingers."

He dropped the knitting to his lap and closed his eyes. "If I'm going to make a complete fool of myself in front of you, we might as well drop the formalities. Let's just watch *John* Gallows fail at knitting for the moment, rather than the spectacle of *Captain Gallows* botching needlecraft, shall we?"

Leanne wasn't sure what drove her to lead his hands back down to the needles, and gently position them in the correct way. It wasn't a wise choice. They were tanned, strong hands; large and well-groomed. It was the warmth of them that struck her most of all. She wasn't sure why that surprised her. Perhaps because it served as a reminder that he was human, flesh and blood with fears and feelings like any other man. She'd forgotten that he'd been dragged into this bargain as much as she. He shifted his weight in a way that told her his leg was starting to ache, but anyone could see he wasn't giving in until he'd done a respectable stretch of successful stitches. He was making a genuine effort.

She tried again to reposition his fingers. Some odd little shudder went through his hands when she touched him. Or was it her hands that shuddered? Or had she merely felt a tremble but not seen it? She forced a casualness to her touch as she showed him again how to wrap the yarn around his right index finger—the one with the long scar down the side. "You don't need to strangle it, Captain, just let this finger do the work."

"John," he corrected as he fumbled his way through a stitch—labored but correctly done. "At least off camera."

"Well, John." The familiarity felt more daring than she liked, even though she worked to hide it from her voice. "It feels odd to *everyone* at first, not just war heroes." John rolled his shoulders and scowled as he produced a second stitch—also correct but less forced. "See? There's no need to mount a battle here." She leaned over to adjust his far hand again, catching a whiff of his aftershave. He smelled exotic and sophisticated.

"This must get easier." She couldn't tell if it was a question or a demand.

"Yes." She felt the first smile of the afternoon sneak across her lips. "It does."

He looked up at her for the first time. Were she knitting at the moment, she would have surely dropped a stitch. He would have enjoyed that. "It must. I've seen young boys do this."

"That is the idea, isn't it?" And it was. It wasn't just some general's folly to decide to convince America's boys to knit. The clicking needles of American women and girls simply weren't enough. The Red Cross was so desperate for woolen socks that this "farfetched scheme" to recruit boys was, in fact, important to brave men risking their lives across the ocean.

"And you'll teach injured soldiers to do this?" he asked. "To pass the time in the hospital as well as meet the need for socks?" What he hadn't realized was that five tidy stitches had worked their way onto his needle while he spoke. While many might accuse John Gallows of great arrogance, his only knitting sin was the universal fault of trying too hard.

"Yes, that's the idea. It's been done successfully in some other hospitals, so I am eager to try it here."

"Done successfully, you say? Well, then, I simply can't allow this to elude me, can I? My own grandmother," he went on, "who can barely see well enough to know which Gallows is who, can do this." Three more stitches.

"Your grandmother knits?" *Keep him talking*, Leanne urged herself, realizing that talking was the key to keeping him from overthinking the simple stitches.

"Constantly. I have several holiday sweaters in the most atrocious patterns you can imagine. And a few scarves that could scare away the enemy." He looked down, a little stunned to realize he'd made it all the way to the end of the double-pointed needle. "Now what?"

She didn't have to force herself to take his hands and show him how to switch to the next needle. And while she didn't dare look up at him while she touched those hands, she could feel his smile behind her. "See, just like that. All lined up like soldiers, they are. Well done."

He said nothing until the silence forced her to look up at him. When she did, Leanne felt it burrow its way under her ribs and steal her breath. "Well taught, Nurse Sample."

"Leanne," she heard herself say, but it was as if Ida's daring nature had inhabited her voice. "Off camera."

Chapter Seven

❧

"**O**ne more inch…just one inch farther…*ugh!*" John growled in exasperation at the joints that would not bend to his will. It was as if the plaster cast on his leg had never come off—the stubborn limb refused to regain the needed flexibility. He gripped the bench harder and set his teeth against the pain, leaning into another push. It was probably no accident that the "reconstruction clinic," the gymnasium on base that housed the staff and equipment designed to rehabilitate wounded soldiers, was olive-green rather than hospital white. To John, the gymnasium was no less a battlefield than the front line. It reminded him that he was a soldier—and that a soldier belonged on the front lines, where he intended to return as soon as possible, even if he had to thrash his leg into submission every step of the way.

"Whoa there, stallion. You're not going to get what you want out of that leg by beating it up." Dr. Charles Madison pushed John's leg back down. John hated how easily the small doctor could do it, too. The weakness in his leg made him crazy, and Madison had a gift for showcasing just how much strength John had lost.

"It doesn't bend a single inch farther this week."

Complaining felt childish, but John's frustration stole his composure as easily as the dirigible stay lines had shredded his leg. Patience was not a virtue Gallows men either possessed or cherished. John pulled himself upright with something just short of a snarl.

"This isn't the kind of thing that goes in a straight line." Dr. Madison, his Bostonian accent sounding entirely too fatherly, sat down on the bench next to John. He set his clipboard down with a weariness that spoke *do we have to go over this again?* without words. "It's going to be back-and-forth. And if you push it too far too fast, I promise you it will be more back than forth. Flex your foot."

John shot him a look but obeyed. The doctor could make "flex your foot" sound like "go sit in the corner."

"You've got more rotation than you did last week. You tore nearly every tendon from your hip down. It's a wonder you've still got use of the leg at all, Gallows. Those tether lines could have ripped the whole thing off."

"Yes, yes, I'm so *fabulously fortunate.*" John launched himself up off the bench and hobbled to the bars on the wall nearby. Did Madison think he didn't know that? And if those lines—those horrid steel lines that felt like they were slicing his leg off from the inside out while he dangled—had severed his leg, where would he have been? Falling thousands of feet out of the sky to drown in the ocean. If he lived through the fall. The mere thought of that terrifying, helpless hanging sensation, those minutes of absolute dread that felt like hours of twisting over what he was certain would be the site of his death, sent that icy sensation through his chest again. He hated this sniper-fire fear of that memory which could attack him without warning. A wrong comment or even the slightest hint of falling—and he slipped all the time these days—would catapult him back to those moments in the sky. Somehow he knew that if he ever had to hang upside down again for any reason—some exercise or calisthenic someone dreamed up to rehabilitate him—he'd stop breathing altogether. Die of remembered fright on the spot. Just the kind of way every war hero ought to behave.

"For a talented spokesman, I wonder sometimes if I ought to punch you for the thoughtless things you say." Madison cornered him against the wall and pinned him with severe eyes. "Look around you, son. Wake up and see just how fortunate you are. That imperfect leg you so despise is at least *still there*. You've your wits about you and the admiration of many. Take a walk with me over to another hall of the hospital—the one with no visitors—and see some of the ghosts we can barely call men. Complain to them as they sit in chairs mumbling because not only their arm but their mind is gone."

John was in no mood to be smothered by the silver lining of his own survival. Madison didn't get like this often, and it bothered John to no end when the doctor lectured him on his advantages. He needed no reminding. "I know I ought to be glad I'm alive," he mumbled with reluctance. That was, in fact, part of the problem. Part of the thing niggling at the back of his mind, taunting him on the edges of sleep. He was alive. He was fortunate. More than that, he was lauded and admired. He just never felt like he earned it. And that wasn't the sort of thing one mentioned to anyone. Humility was one thing—and another one of those virtues not especially prized by Gallows men. Feeling like a fraud? That was another. "I let my frustration get the better of my mouth."

John had been down that particular hospital hallway. He knew soldiers who, once maimed, wanted nothing more than to get back out on the front lines so they could be shot down and end their misery. They wouldn't put their families through the shame of suicide, yet they couldn't face the prospect of a lifetime without a limb or an eye or whatever. Those men clamored back to the battlefield with a dangerous "death wish."

He wasn't one of those. John wanted back in the battle so he could prove to himself he was the hero everyone seemed to think he was. Whatever he did— and honestly, he didn't even clearly remember most of it—up there to those dirigible lines was sheer, terrorized survival, not heroism. Grab this or fall. Secure that or risk it ripping off and taking him with it. He climbed out onto that airship not because he wanted to be brave, but because it was try something or die. He was working only to save himself, and that other lives would benefit from his actions was the last thing on his mind. That wasn't the kind of thing one ought to get a medal for. The fellows who had risked their lives to pull in wounded mates, who went back out into gunfire to drag their captain to safety? Those were the men who should be making speeches and wearing medals. He wasn't here stirring up patriotism because he was brave. He was here because his name was Gallows, he had a silver tongue, took a good photograph and had somehow managed not to die.

Ida tossed her nurse's hat down on her bureau. "You know, I thought I was an admirer of the male physiology."

Leanne looked up from the outline of reconstructive exercises she'd been studying. "You're not?"

"I think how God put us together is one of the most amazing things ever. Y'all would think there's no way to make it tedious." Ida leaned back in her chair and looked up at the ceiling, her long auburn mane tumbling down behind her. She had a gift for striking dramatic poses.

They sat in their shared bedroom at the Red Cross House. It was comfortably furnished by army standards, with a pair of beds, bureaus and desks much like the dormitory rooms she'd had at the university. It had color and comfort, two things the bland army housing clearly lacked. She found she couldn't fully approve of the way the U.S. Army piled soldiers into barracks that looked more like hospital wards than homes. The standardized, militarized buildings utterly lacked the pleasant feel of the Red Cross House. Not that the Red Cross House was perfect, but Leanne had come to appreciate privacy for the dear commodity it was in military life. It made her grateful she enjoyed Ida's company so much. "I take it you're not fond of your current rotation?"

"I have babysat my five-year-old cousins and heard less complaining. And I declare, I could be tending a ship of pirates and hear more civilized conversation. To think I thought being surrounded by soldiers would be a good thing!" She flung out one hand as if addressing the universe. "I had to smack one private's hand three times for attempting to get…too private."

Leanne laughed at Ida's pun. "Your sense of humor serves you well." Ida's vibrancy made her a grand friend to have in trying times. "I imagine you're just the kind of care some of those boys need. Have you drawn any of them yet?" Ida was an immensely talented artist. She'd tacked a few of her better sketches up on the wall of their room and Leanne thought they rivaled some of the things she'd seen framed on the best walls in Charleston.

Ida opened one eye from her dramatic recline and shot Leanne a look. "I have not. They don't merit my talents. Truly, I'm not askin' for chivalry. Just a little civility would be fine with me. Goodness knows, with the work I put into seeing them healed and healthy, it's the least they could do. A man's broad shoulder is one of the finest things God has ever made, but I had to muck out the gouges in one today that rivaled a Tennessee swamp. By rights, he should owe me nothing less than a fine dinner for my troubles."

"Have you been to Tennessee, Ida?"

Ida groaned. "I feel like I have now. At least that one had the decency to pass out eventually. At the start, he was fighting me like I was the enemy." She pulled herself upright. "And speaking of pain and chivalry, how was your knitting lesson with Captain Gallows?"

Leanne winced. She'd hoped to avoid this conversation with Ida, who was quick to insert a romantic intention into just about any male-female interaction. Leanne hadn't really decided what to make of John Gallows, and she didn't want Ida jumping to all kinds of conclusions. "Well—" she planted her eyes on the outline "—I did change my mind about it being unnecessary. As it turns out, Captain Gallows did most certainly need a dress rehearsal."

Ida raised an eyebrow.

"Really, I'm not sure he had any more trouble than any other first-time student, but it did seem to fluster him more than he liked." She remembered the look on his face, amazed how it still surprised her for reasons she couldn't quite work out.

"Fluster?" She leaned on her desk, planting her elbows in a "tell me all about it" pose.

Leanne looked down to see she'd written "John?" above an illustration of leg exercises. She quickly crossed it out and turned the page. The last thing she needed to do was to refer to Captain Gallows by his given name in front of someone with Ida's imagination. "I believe the captain is used to mastering things quickly, that's all. He'd thought it would be easier—I did, too, actually—but even with larger needles his big hands make it difficult. It took longer than either of us thought it would."

"But you succeeded in teaching our brave hero?"

Leanne wasn't sure she succeeded at anything except bringing herself into a further state of confusion. Still, she was relatively certain Gallows would look more in command of his stitches at the first photo shoot tomorrow. He'd actually been right. Had they just taken photos, it would have been clear to her or any other knitter that he wasn't really knitting. It was painfully obvious to her when people pretended to knit in paintings or photos—their needles were always pointed upward, waggling about in a way that couldn't possibly produce stitches. John had wanted to make sure he was knitting so that it looked real in the photographs. While she'd first chalked that up to vanity, she'd realized it was a sort of integrity. An honor she hadn't really attributed to the man with the gleaming cinema-star smile. "Yes," she said feeling a regrettable hint of color come over her cheeks. "We made it work and I think tomorrow will be a success."

"You'll be famous. Have you thought of that?"

Leanne sincerely doubted anyone even noticed her

in the same room with someone like Captain Gallows. "Not really."

"I heard the quartermaster talking about the supplies he needed to get for all those *Era* magazine people. They're talking about putting Captain Gallows on the cover." She nodded at Leanne. "If he's on, *you're* on. We're gonna have to get your hair done up right and everything. Have you even given a moment's thought to that?"

Leanne had actually thought about what she wanted to wear. Not because of the cameras, but because of something John had said. Something about sky-blue being his favorite color. She had a blouse the color of the sky. Mama had said the color suited her especially well. The sleeves had a delicate ruffle at her wrists, which she supposed would be the only part of her to make it into a photo of any kind.

Yesterday, her planned obscurity didn't bother her at all. As a matter of fact, General Barnes had said something to the effect that she'd "hardly be noticed" and she'd been almost relieved at the assurance. Today, after the supreme teaching effort required to get Gallows to any kind of competency, she found herself miffed. No one had ever asked what she thought of this campaign. Of course she agreed with the need to get more people knitting for the soldiers. And it was dreadfully difficult to convince boys to pick up the yarn and needles with images of their doting grandmothers clouding their vision. But it all seemed so…so…contrived. As if both she and John had been tricked into something far beyond their original intentions by people who didn't really care about the true purpose.

John seemed to actually care. He covered it up well, but she could see it in the way he chose his words, the way he would try over and over to get the stitches right. But she had the niggling sense that his ego wouldn't allow anyone to know he cared. Would he let go of all that bravado if they knew each other better? Did she want to know John Gallows better?

Would he even take the time if given the chance? Leanne found she couldn't be sure he took this as seriously as she. She took this very seriously, and it bothered her that no one else seemed to. Certainly not the general nor any of the *Era* staff. They'd made no effort to get in touch with her directly, and learn more about the knitting program. Clearly the publicity angle involving the captain was all that interested them. It was probably just another way to sell magazines. And could she really be sure of John's motives? John Gallows was known in Charleston as a charmer who collected—and then dismissed—female admirers. What if he'd been behind it from the beginning, picked her out for what he hoped was a compliant spirit? Yet another damsel who would merely swoon under his spell? She felt her annoyance rise just picturing those magazine people angling lights and asking for wider smiles. Sky-blue? Suddenly Leanne wanted to wear bright red. To stand out. To stand up.

"Leanne!" Ida was off her chair, facing Leanne, waving her hands as if flagging down a battleship. "Where'd you go, honey? Y'all are frowning like we're at a funeral. It's just hair."

Leanne slapped her notebook shut. "Yes, I want you to do my hair up nice. And would you lend me that bright yellow dress you have? The one with the buttons on the cuffs?"

Ida swung back on one hip, eyes wide. "Not fading into the background tomorrow, are we?"

"Absolutely not. The method might be a bit…unorthodox, but the cause is important. No one's going to push me and all the other dedicated knitters out of the picture tomorrow. Not while I'm around. There's more to what we're doing than Captain John Gallows, and the American people need to know that."

Ida stood up, saluted and winked. "Yes, ma'am!"

Chapter Eight

✦

John's leg was screaming at him from inside perfectly pressed trousers. His shirt collar tightened around his neck like a starchy, menacing hand. At least in war, no one gave a fig what a man looked like or how he stood, as long as he got where he needed to be. Here, he was waging a battle with the barbed wire under his skin while smirking and making small talk with a dozen people who had no idea what torture it was to bend his right leg at a natural angle. And hold it for the endless seconds it took to get the right image. They'd been at it for hours, and already he was coming to hate the funny accordion-faced camera as much as he loathed the pointed metal knitting needles. People said the camera loved him, but he did not return the affection.

"You were right," Leanne remarked after the first handful of photos. "It would have been dreadfully hard to learn under these conditions." A man in a plaid vest had repositioned her hands dozens of times, and even John could hear the frustration in Leanne's words. Obviously the wonder born of buzzing activity and bright lights had died down quickly for her, made worse by the tactless positioning of photographers who made it very clear they weren't too worried about getting her in the shot.

Which was a waste, for she looked beautiful today. John could tell she'd taken extra care with her hair and dress. "You should wear that color more often," he ventured when one assistant all but pushed her out of the way. The bright yellow made the peach of her skin fairly glow. He yanked his hat back from some apple-cheeked boy charged with brushing nonexistent lint from it. "Clark, I want Miss Sample in the next shot."

Clark Summers looked up from his camera with a dubiously raised eyebrow. "Do you now?" His tone implied that what Captain Gallows wanted didn't much matter at the moment.

Someone fired off one of those flash contraptions, making Leanne jump. The photographer rolled his eyes as if he considered working with such innocents penance for some earlier photographic sin.

"I do," John replied. He poured so much Gallows command into those two words that the hat boy sat down in deference. "Surely you don't plan to slap me on some magazine cover without a pretty girl by my side. I'm supposed to recruit young lads to the cause, aren't I? You don't expect me to do that without a lovely lady on hand to admire my efforts?"

John regretted those last words the minute he'd said them, but his leg was making it hard to think well. Miss Sample's spine shot straight and the needles dropped to her lap. Worse yet, her foot began tapping. Nothing good ever came out of a lady tapping her foot, ever. The fire he had suspected was lurking under all that peaches-and-cream was sneaking out under all this scrutiny. He liked that, although John was convinced

that amusement could well be the death of him. If his
leg didn't kill him first.

He made up his mind, then and there, to ensure he
saw Leanne Sample someplace much closer to his own
territory. Someplace where he held most of the cards.
He smiled as it came to him just where that was.

The captain had nerve, she'd give him that much.

It wasn't that she minded being pulled out of the standard nurse's rotation—those shifts could be dreary, indeed—it was that she hadn't been given a choice at all.
The smug grin on John Gallows's face as she signed
the clipboard admitting her to the reconstruction gymnasium pressed down on her, glossy and manipulative.
Clearly he thought he'd done her some kind of favor.
While other nurses might fawn over the chance to work
so closely with such "a hero," Gallows's manipulative
nature canceled out any gratitude Leanne could muster.

She walked straight toward him, hoping her annoyance showed as she held his gaze. "You press your advantage with entirely too much ease, Captain Gallows."

He sat lengthwise on a bench, slowly hoisting a small
weighted bag on his ankle. He was pretending it took
no effort. "Not at all. We're allowed to request specific
attendants. I requested you."

Leanne stood over him crossing her arms over her
chest. "I fear I'm not sufficiently qualified to supervise
your exercises." She stopped short of saying "given the
extent of your injuries" because she knew that would
bother him. Then again, perhaps he deserved to be bothered after the way he'd behaved at their photographic
session yesterday.

John leaned back on the bench, the white of his exercise shirt stretching across his chest. "Nonsense. You'd

only be taking temperatures and walking lads out on the lawn anyway. I know you like a challenge." It really was a crime what white did for the man's eyes.

"You do not know me at all, Captain. If you did, you would know I'm not one to play favorites. Or be played as one." She wouldn't give him one inch of the satisfaction of thinking that she'd been even the smallest bit flattered by his special request of her—she was rather ashamed of it herself. She wasn't blind to the way women looked at John Gallows, how they flocked around him like gulls to a fish boat, circling and diving for scraps of regard. There was something regretfully pleasing in being singled out, even by him. But her mission here was so much more important than any small boon to her vanity, and she was aggravated with herself for forgetting that—and aggravated with him as well, for making her forget.

She watched his eyes narrow the slightest bit as the orderly pulled his leg farther up, noticed the teeth grit inside his constant smile. "Would it help you to know I had a practical reason for requesting you?"

She raised an inquiring eyebrow.

The leg started its descent and she could see his grip on the bench loosen. "They're going to stuff my leg into horrid packs of ice this afternoon, and I'll have to sit there like a landed fish at market." He nodded at the large orderly currently removing the weighted bag from his ankle. "No offense to Nelson here, but I'm going to need more distraction that he can provide. And it might prove a good time to practice my—" he hesitated a fraction of a second "—new skill."

"Your *knitting?*" She emphasized the word. The public spectacle of his knitting had been his doing, after all. She was going to see that he owned up to it. Nelson looked down, hiding his smile in the business of taking weights out of the bag.

"You enjoyed shouting that." There was too much tease in his voice for it to be an accusation.

"I did not shout. And you're enjoying the way you've shanghaied me."

"Nurse Sample, there you are. I see you've met your new assignment." Dr. Madison came up behind her. "Well, of course you've already met, that's the thing of it, isn't it?" He looked over the top of his round glasses at Leanne. "You've your work cut out for you, but I suspect you already know that."

This was how Papa's horses must feel at market. "Tell me, Doctor, will I ever have the pleasure of being *consulted* before pressed into service regarding our esteemed captain?"

Dr. Madison blinked. Evidently it had never occurred to him that giving personal attention to a celebrity rather than clocking time in the hospital wards might not thrill her. Surely it would never occur to Gallows. Madison looked at her for a second, flicked his gaze to the captain, who shrugged. "Yes, well, there it is." He made some kind of notation on his chart and went on as if he'd never heard her. "You're to take three laps around the track, Gallows, followed by the ice for thirty minutes, then a rubdown."

Leanne's eyes went wide. "Not by *you* of course," Captain Gallows assured her. "Whatever else I may be accused of, I am always a gentleman. Nelson over here, however, is a brute. It's more of a pound-down, I promise you."

Dr. Madison handed her the clipboard. "Three laps, one slow, followed by one quick, then the final slow. Long strides, no cane."

Captain Gallows grinned as he pulled his khaki shirt back on. "I'll have to lean on *something,* Doc."

Dr. Madison smiled and turned toward the next bench. "Oh, I'm sure you'll improvise."

Nelson gathered up his things, scurrying out of the way of the captain's grand plan. Leanne felt neatly cornered. Part of her was irritated at his manipulation. A large part. Then again, she remembered Ida's groans about the unpleasant lot she'd been assigned in the wards. Perhaps it was best to look at this with gratitude. Thirty minutes in an ice bath sounded rather painful; could she really blame Captain Gallows for seeking the most distraction possible? And if he actually was planning on knitting, well then she could take satisfaction that her classes for soldiers recognized knitting's ability to distract a man from tedium or pain. And Gallows was in pain, even if he worked hard to hide it from the world. She could see his pain. Maybe she *alone* could see it, and he knew that. Perhaps he felt he could drop the bravado, let his guard down a bit with her. She was here to learn to help soldiers heal, after all—why not this particular soldier?

Why not? The shameless grin on his face as he held his elbow out to her was why not. "Shall we promenade, Nurse Sample?" One would think from his tone that *he* was escorting *her* around the walking track, not the other way around. Honestly, the man's showmanship knew no bounds.

She slipped one arm into his elbow, holding the clipboard with the other. "What shall we talk of while you *exercise,* Captain?" She felt the hitch in his step, the flinch in his arm when he put unaided weight on his leg. He made sure it wasn't visible to an observer, but it was impossible to hide with her arm in his. She suspected he hadn't counted on that. She suspected he also didn't intend for her to hear the soft curse he muttered under his breath—but hear it she did.

"Anything you choose," he said aloud.

Finally, something in *her* control. "Let's start our discussion, then, on why it is inappropriate to take the Lord's name in vain as you just did."

He made a small groan. "I asked for distraction and you offer a lesson on manners?"

"Courtesy is a most engaging subject, Captain. Take, for example, the fact that most people of faith do not take kindly to a casual use of God's name. I'll ask you to refrain from such language in my presence," she couldn't help adding, "as any true gentleman would."

"Well, I am nothing if not a gentleman." They turned the first corner. He clearly hated being forced to go so slow; impatience and frustration radiated out of his body. "I'll admit, however, to a…" He paused, selecting careful words. "…a respectful indifference to spiritual matters."

"Truly? I was told there were no atheists in foxholes."

"I've done precious little time in foxholes, thank… thank *goodness,*" he corrected himself with a nod toward her. "And I'm not an atheist. I believe God exists, but I don't bother Him with my petty schemes. Your Lord and I? Well, we're not on close terms." He clipped off the end of his last word, cutting his step short. They were only halfway around the lap.

Wordlessly, Leanne shifted their arms so that she held his elbow. He didn't allow himself to lean on her at first, but as they walked on, she felt him sink in slightly to the hold she had on him. It cost him something to do that, and his concession dissolved what was left of her annoyance. "I believe God yearns to be bothered with all our 'petty schemes,' as you call them," she said gently. "Every last one of them."

"He'd never have time to save the world if we bogged Him down with all that. God has a war to win out there. He's on our side, don't you know?"

In hospital rounds she'd had already, Leanne had seen enough meek and wounded soldiers to disagree. They were pale, shallow shadows, echoes of the men they must have once been. "God is in favor of justice, but I can't believe war does not grieve Him. Not as such costs to His children. Not when men...when *boys* come home like this."

"And what do you believe about the other side's boys? Are the enemy boys God's children, too?" He nodded to a slim young man grimacing through each step on a new prosthetic leg. John held the soldier's glare—for it was just that. Gripping two bars as a pair of burly orderlies coaxed him into awkward, painful steps, the look he gave John was sour. As if John had no right to parade his good fortune in front of such a pitiful existence. Leanne felt the air chill, felt John stiffen even as she did herself. "Did God's children do that to him? Why would God make His children wound each other in such horrible ways?"

The patient took one more dark look at John before allowing himself to be turned back the other way, and Leanne found herself grateful to have ended the exchange. It surprised her to realize not everybody admired Captain Gallows. As a matter of fact, based on the incident that just transpired, she was quite sure some men hated him. His golden achievements must seem to them like salt in their wounds. "God did not wound that man. A fallen world's ugly war did that. Hate and greed bring war, evil brings war." She tipped her chin in the direction of the amputee as they turned another corner. "God takes no pleasure in any man's pain and death. I believe God loves the enemy who did that as much as the patriot who endures it."

John was slowing, his gait growing more and more uneven as they went. "But one side is right and the other side is wrong. God cannot be on both sides. It wouldn't square."

She stopped and turned to face him, both to make her point and allow him rest. The effort of the smooth walk he'd just now manufactured had sweat dripping from his temples. His cavalier expression was only a neat mask over the pain in his eyes. "God is God, Captain Gallows. He's not required to 'square' with anything we think or do. I'm not convinced that we don't annoy Him so endlessly with our demands that He take sides."

John took a step away from her, pointing with new vigor. "Ah, so you *do* agree we annoy the Almighty?" He pivoted, as if to stride away in victory, momentarily forgetting his weak leg. The movement tripped him up, so that she had to catch his arm as he tipped against the wall of the gymnasium or he might have tumbled to the ground then and there. For a moment the cool mask was gone, replaced by a frustrated rage that stiffened him all over. For a split second he was hard and dark and dangerous, the kind of man who would smash something or put his fist through a wall. She almost let go of him, the glimpse frightened her so. Then, as if she'd imagined it all, he rearranged his body so that his leaning looked cavalier, lazy even, crossing his bad foot over the one now supporting his weight as if he hadn't a care in the world. "And here I thought courtesy would prove no distraction. Nurse Sample, you outdo yourself."

The way he said *distraction* had a steely knife's edge

to it. A defensive blade brandished at her under a slick grin. Leanne didn't know what to do with that. Despite his gift at annoying her, she had found herself actually looking forward to having a serious conversation with the captain. Her boldness in broaching the subject of her faith surprised even her as they walked. Normally, Leanne shied away from spiritual discussions, preferring her passions to rise only around her knitting needles. Where had this eagerness to challenge John Gallows's faith—or lack of it—come from?

Even more surprising was that the captain allowed it—at least for a moment or two. Then matters went too deep, and he had yanked the conversation back under his control.

His statement was no compliment at all. "I…" No reply came to her.

She waited, expecting him to gloss over the moment with another of his smooth comments, but he did not speak, either. His look just now as he stood there with what she suspected others would find a cocky grin, only warned her never to trip him up like that again. As if she'd intentionally gone past his facade, as if it were her fault her beliefs wouldn't "square" with how he saw the world. As if the moment of weakness she'd just seen was an unforgivable sin—on his part and on hers.

Which it wasn't. A man of his influence—even a hardened soldier—wouldn't shy from showing true anger or appropriate fear. Yet, John Gallows kept his mask of dashing mastery up everywhere but with her. She seemed to see underneath the mask with far too much ease. Why was that?

Clearly he was wondering the same thing, if the hint of a glare behind his eyes said anything. And that was hardly fair. She'd not sought to deliberately expose the chinks in his armor. He had no right to blame her when she hadn't even asked for this assignment.

"If I am to walk you, Captain," she said as coolly as she could manage given the firestorm in his eyes, "you'll have to come off that wall." To her great shock, she then offered him her elbow and her best Charleston hospitality smile. "Shall we?"

Chapter Nine

John hadn't slept well. Leanne's narrowed eyes, strong to the point of defiance, kept appearing behind his closed lids. He'd read her wrong, thought of her as an appealing, even engaging amusement while he worked to be well enough to return. He hadn't planned on her being such a challenge. His good looks and silver tongue never rendered women much of a trial, and while he was never so much of a cad as to abuse these gifts, he wasn't above leveraging them to his advantage. The fact that he didn't seem to have much of an advantage over Leanne Sample, that she pushed back on his ideas with challenging ideas of her own that stole his sleep, was making him prickly and irritable. It was the creamy quality of her voice that clouded his thinking, he decided as he made his way to the gymnasium the next day for his morning therapy.

Usually some form of weight-bearing torture came first, a half an hour or so of pain and sweat under the merciless hands of Nelson. Oh, he'd laugh and joke his way through it, but the truth of it was that the session hurt—a great deal—and the prospect of gentler therapy with the lovely Nurse Sample was the only enticement to keep his temper in check. Enduring laps around the track with her hurt just as much as Nelson's "ministrations," but they came with a far better view.

Resigned to yet another round of "useful pain" as Dr. Madison liked to call it, John pushed open the doors of the reconstruction room to find Leanne waiting for him. She wore a broad smile—no, a triumphant grin. She stood in front of an arrangement of horizontal bars, the banisters used to aid soldiers in walking therapies, grouped together to form a small square. Nelson was standing by with an equally mischievous grin—something that looked out of place on his brute features— and a phonograph.

"What have we here?"

"I've invented a way to make this morning's exercise much more pleasant."

John started to say something about her very presence accomplishing that already, but swallowed the remark as too flirtatious. That didn't stop him from thinking it. Being grateful for it. He managed a nondescript "Really?" as he took off his cap and coat, hanging it on the rack. At least the presence of a lady meant he'd not be required to work up a sweat in his undershirt, which seemed to be Nelson's methodology of choice.

"You mentioned yesterday how difficult it is for you to shift weight, particularly stepping from side to side."

All he'd told her during their endless final lap was that he no longer danced as well as he did before. "I don't recall putting it in such clinical terms." Suddenly the phonograph made a disturbing sort of sense. "You don't mean…?"

"I do indeed. Today—with the approval of Dr. Madison, of course—your therapy is the waltz. Suitably adapted, I daresay, for your particular condition." She ducked under the front banister to stand in the center of the small square, raising her hands in a presentational gesture that made him laugh. "Captain Gallows, may I have the honor of this dance?"

Intriguing didn't come close to covering what he felt about today's therapy. "You know, *I'm* the one who's supposed to do the asking."

"And when did you ever subscribe to convention?" She gestured him inside.

Laying down his cane, John ignored the pain that shot through his side as he ducked himself inside the tidy square of banisters. He'd have managed it even if it hurt ten times more than it did. "I take it Nelson and the phonograph serve as our dance band?"

"You catch on quickly." Hoping the smile on his face didn't match the shameless grin he felt, John raised his arms to assume the standard ballroom dance position. She dodged out of his reach. "We'll be going a bit more slowly than that at first. Arms on the railings, please."

"Well, that's hardly fun." He couldn't help himself. Genuine amusement hadn't buoyed him up like this in months.

"Oh, this is not about fun."

"Says *you*."

"Concentration will be required." She had her teacher voice on, the one she used in the Red Cross knitting classes, as she resolutely placed her hands on the railings to each side.

John cleared his voice in mock seriousness, calculating how close he could position his hands to hers and still keep his balance. Yesterday he'd hated these bars. Today he rather liked them. "Of course."

"Just side to side at first, please."

"But you said I was to *waltz*." It was childish to tease her like that, but she seemed to bring that out in him.

She shot him a look that all-too-clearly said *Would you like to return to pain with Nelson?* Then she nodded her head toward one side of the box. "To your right." She stepped to slide her foot and her body toward the bar on one side of the box. He did the same, despite the spike of pain it sent through his thigh. "Very good. Now your left." He did as she asked, grateful that side produced much less pain. "Again." They went through the clunky, side-to-side maneuver three more times until he could manage it with a bit of ease despite the pain. It took far longer than he would have liked.

"Whose idea was this, in any case?" he said as they began the fourth repetition.

"You may not like the answer to that question, Captain." They swayed together to the left.

"Surely you're not going to tell me Dr. Madison or Nelson hatched this scheme?" *Right.*

Left. "I asked God to send me an idea for some inventive way to help you other than those dull laps. The thought came to me in the middle of the night last night, and I was delighted when Dr. Madison found the idea—how did he put it?—'ideally suited to our good captain.'"

She'd prayed on his behalf. Or on her behalf toward the goal of helping him—and had kept him in her thoughts even in the middle of the night, no less. The idea of it worked its way under his skin like an itch. "I'm dancing on orders from the Almighty?" *Right.*

"I told you, you wouldn't like the answer." *Left.*

His leg was burning but wild horses would not stop him now. "On the contrary, I believe God has just gone up a notch in my admiration." A bolt of pain hobbled his right step and sent him lurching against the bar, wiping away whatever spark the moment held.

"Would you like to rest?" she asked quietly.

"I would like to *waltz*," he replied in the most commanding voice he possessed. *With you, not with a fence.*

Leanne should have thought this through more carefully. So taken was she with the novelty of the idea that she completely forgot the necessity of touching while dancing. Truly she hadn't thought Captain Gallows would get much beyond swaying back and forth, given the extent of his injuries. She knew how much the motion pained him, how the repetition only made it worse. The phonograph next to them was really no more than an enticement—a carrot on a stick to help him get through the first difficult session.

And it had worked. Entirely too well. For now the square of railings fairly well boxed her in, fenced her in close quarters with John and his obvious determination. The man had been shown his target, and hurtled toward it at all costs. How ironic that she knew she could not distract him from her creative distraction. There was nothing for it, she supposed. This session must end in a waltz, so it would be best to ensure it was contrived, awkward and exceedingly short. "And waltz you shall," she pronounced in her best *this is exactly how I planned it* voice. "But not yet to music. I fear we'll need a slower tempo." Somehow the innocent accommodation sounded all too daring—most likely due to the triumphant look in John's eye.

"Only at first. I'm sure it will come back to me."

Hopeful, Leanne placed her hands elegantly on the banisters.

She might have known it wouldn't work. John shook

his head, the gleam still in his gaze. He had her, and they both knew it. "Nurse Sample, may I have the honor of this dance?" He raised his left hand, palm up, nearly commanding her to place her hand in his. She did so, inwardly cursing how close the railings boxed them in, startled at how neatly her hand rested in his palm. Startled still more at the warmth of his right hand behind her shoulder blade. Of course he would have been an excellent dancer, preceding the injury—men of his social prominence always were.

Before she could count out the tempo, John chose to set it himself. "One…two…three. One…two…three," giving himself almost two full seconds to execute every shift of his weight without the support of the railings. She picked up the counting for him when it became clear the exertion clipped his words, eventually falling into a ponderously slow humming of the *Blue Danube*. She knew his leg must hurt him terribly, and yet she also understood his need for this victory. However slow, however painful, John could not leave this room halfway to a waltz. His spirit simply didn't allow for compromise—it was the best and the worst thing about him. Here, haltingly sliding his feet to a beat more suited to a funeral march than a Viennese waltz, he still possessed a commanding dignity. Before she could stop it, her mind conjured up the daydream of what it would have been like to be spun around the ballroom by the John Gallows of before his injury. He'd have been dashingly elegant, strong and smooth in his steps. It took her a moment to realize she'd stopped humming, and he'd most definitely noticed.

"Yes," he said, smiling even though she noticed a bead of sweat streaming down his temple, "I do think our song is over. For now, at least. And you're right,

Nurse Sample, this is infinitely more enjoyable than laps around the gymnasium." His smile doubled as he pulled a handkerchief from his pocket—monogrammed, she noticed—and wiped his brow. "Do thank that God of yours for His excellent initiative."

"I'd prefer you thank Him yourself."

"He and I aren't on speaking terms at the moment." She took a breath to argue, but he held out a silencing palm. "But you can add this item to your list of good and worthy deeds, my dear—you've made a chink in the wall."

Chapter Ten

Leave it to me, John thought as he hobbled toward the hospital meeting room where Leanne held her knitting classes, *to be given the task of heroic knitting.* Bombing half of Germany would have been easier. Keeping the upper hand with Leanne Sample was hard enough without the complications of physical pain and ridiculous needlework. He'd made a whole two inches of progress on his sock—two inches in probably twice as many hours of work! This masquerade would have ended two minutes after the first photo shoot if Nurse Sample hadn't gleefully roped him into actually finishing the sock. As if any of that was nearly as important as his job recruiting soldiers. As burning as his need to get back *over there*.

No, there was nothing for this but to produce one stellar sock for auction and be done with it. "Behold, ladies," he declared as he pushed open the door to the classroom with his cane, "someday this will coddle the bravest calves in Europe."

John let fall the two inches of sock ribbing he'd been holding aloft and came to a dead halt. Expecting his attentive audience of Red Cross knitting nurses and their eager applause, John instead came face-to-face with Leanne and the wounded private from the other day's gymnasium session. Sitting in his wheelchair, grinning, with a ball of yarn and Leanne's full attention.

"If all my students had your enthusiasm, Captain, we'll have every brave calf coddled in no time," Leanne said, without looking up from her task, guiding the other man's hands on the knitting needles. The private made no effort to hide satisfaction at his current "teacher's favorite" status. "Private Carson, I believe you know Captain Gallows? My classes with soldiers don't start until next week, but the private was kind enough to join the nurses as my test male student."

Wasn't *he* her test male student? Carson merely nodded a cordial greeting, and John wondered why he felt outmaneuvered every time he was with Leanne Sample. "I've missed a stitch," he said, even though he promised himself never to point out the imperfections in his work, "I'll need you to help me fix it before it shows up in the photographs tomorrow." Leanne was supposed to be *his* teacher. Some other nurse could tend to the private and his newfound interest. Private Carson wasn't about to have his profile splashed all over the country's newsstands in the name of patriotic pride. Yes, the whole idea was to get boys to buy into the Red Cross campaign, but Leanne Sample was *not* supposed to achieve his job before he did.

Then again, Carson would give the wagging tongues in the barracks someone else to target with the teasing John endured for his "new hobby." Why hadn't *he* thought to drag another soldier in here with him? How hard would it be to get a bored soldier to sit in a roomful of pretty nurses? Most of them would sit through making hair ribbons for that kind of company, much less the kinds of incentives General Barnes had put at his disposal. But then, if John had the choosing of a soldier to share his work, he'd have picked one who smiled a bit less—especially at Nurse Sample.

"Of course, Captain," Leanne replied, although he didn't care one bit for the sparkle that lit up her eyes. "You are indeed my first priority. Mistakes happen even to the best of us. It's how we fix them that matters."

John was sure he'd just been lectured, but couldn't exactly say how. He shifted his gaze to the private, who despite his pale hair and bony face, looked sheepishly triumphant if a bit confused. "I'm sure, Private Carson, you can spare the good teacher?"

"Actually, I was just about to hand the private over to Ida's attention. She's mastered ribbing faster than anyone, and Private Carson is a quick learner."

Ida looked up from her socks. "Why thank you, Leanne." Her expression was pleased, but dubious. As though she, like John, hadn't quite figured out who had the upper hand. "My, but I am warming to the idea of coed knitting classes."

John tapped the canvas rucksack slung over his shoulder—the most masculine container he could find to hold his yarn and needles—and pointed out the door with his cane. With a wide smile, Leanne swept her knitting into the large basket at her feet and rose to follow him out the door. He hobbled halfway down the hall, not bothering to keep a slower, steadier gait, and then turned toward her. "What was that all about?"

She blinked at him. "I should think it's obvious. I asked Private Carson to join the class. You remember him from—"

"Yes, of course I know who he is," John cut in, the

unpleasant memory of the man's glare pulling a knot up from the pit of his stomach.

"I do tend to other patients, Captain. Carson was on my shift yesterday afternoon, and I felt it a nice gesture given the…tensions…of the other day."

"And he said yes?" What a fool thing to say. Of course he said yes; he was sitting in the room, wasn't he?

"I would think you'd be pleased. The magazine hasn't even printed and already you've had results."

John sank into a bench at the end of the hallway, strain and fatigue getting the better of him. His leg was always failing him at the most inopportune moments. He tried—without much success—to remind himself that Carson's legs failed him continually. He should feel pity for the young man, and sympathy—nothing more. He had nothing to fear from the private. Fear? What exactly did he think Carson could take from him? Nurse Sample's attentions were hers to grant anywhere she pleased; he had no justification for his sudden envy. "Why on earth did you ask *him?*"

She sat down next to him. "He seemed so dreadfully sad and empty. So envious of you. I didn't really think about it, to be honest. I suppose I thought about how I knit when I'm sad. I'm rather stumped as to why it couldn't wait until the soldier classes start next week, but I believe that's how the Holy Spirit works."

John looked at her. "Holy Spirit or bad idea, he'll get a fair ribbing for it. Pun intended. I have, and he doesn't look to have a thick enough skin for it. I'm afraid it's not a popular idea. Soldiers aren't supposed to knit. They're supposed to fight in the war."

"Stanley Carson is not at war anymore. He has a new battle to fight now, even you can see that." She set her basket down at her feet. "And I'll remind you, my dear courageous Captain Gallows, that not all battles are fought with guns and ships."

She believed so strongly in what she was doing. He had to respect that, as ludicrous as he found the not-yet-a-sock in his canvas bag. "If you tell me you fight yours with yarn and needles," he said as he leaned his cane against the wall, "I shall have to moan. Really, save the slogan for the posters."

She pulled away from him on the bench, crossing her arms like a scolding schoolmarm. "Private Carson had nice things to say about you today. Whereas I suspect he would have called you all sorts of names had I left things as they were in the gymnasium."

"*I* can take it. And oh, I'm quite sure you saw to his appreciation." He regretted the jealous outburst the moment it left his mouth.

"*You* were late. Private Carson was not only on time, he was early." Her words were sharp, but her smile stole his annoyance.

"I had important appointments. I do have more pressing concerns that socks, you know." He wasn't about to let her know how miffed he'd grown at the press relations assistant who'd kept him twenty minutes over. Leanne Sample would not know that she had become the high point of his day. Not when she was so adept at stealing his upper hand.

"Speaking of which, I believe you said you needed my assistance? Mistakes to be fixed?" She held out her hand as if she'd find his errors endlessly entertaining.

He hoisted the bag over to her feeling like a pouting schoolboy turning in poor work. "Save me from this madness, for G—"

She raised her eyebrow, the sack still midair, her silent reproach stopping him in his tracks.

"I declare," he said in a sugary tone, feeling the prissy language trip on his tongue, "but you are a challenge."

"Thank you." She reached into the bag. "I'm sure our Heavenly Father appreciates your efforts." She scowled at the short span of ribbing he'd so proudly displayed earlier. "Whatever did you do here?"

"Knit."

"Well, yes, I know it's *supposed* to be knitting, but it's rather a tangle." She peered closer at his yarn, and he leaned in as well, trying to see whatever it was that she saw. It brought their heads close. She smelled of lemon and something rather rosy. He didn't like the idea of Edward Carson getting a whiff of lemon and roses one bit, didn't want her bending over any man's hands but his. He parked his elbow on the bench back, his arm resting just inches from her shoulder. He watched while she poked at stitches and pulled at loops, her tongue peeking out over one rosy lip while she analyzed. When she turned to look at him, they were entirely too close, although she minded it much more than he. "You forgot to move the yarn from front to back." She flushed, and he felt the color in her cheeks ripple through a warm spot in his chest. "It has to go in between the needles like I showed you. You'll have to undo these two rows here or you'll end up with far too many stitches."

"Undo? We've got another photograph tomorrow." He applied his most persuasive smile. "Can't you just fix them for me so we can move on?"

"Captain Gallows, are you asking me to cheat?" Even her eyes were smiling, wide as they were.

"Can one even cheat at knitting? I'm merely drawing on your expertise. Your assistance. I've obviously made of muddle of it on my own. Please, or we'll have no real progress to show tomorrow. Can't disappoint the boys now, can we? Think of Private Carson." Actually, he didn't want her thinking of Private Carson at all.

She paused, her gaze flicking to his sock-in-progress and back. He was genuinely disturbed by how much he wanted her cooperation. He enjoyed getting his way, to be sure, but this was something altogether different. "I shall fix the first row for you." He felt himself smile. "But the second one will be yours to fix. I will stay and supervise if you find it necessary."

Normally John wasn't much for compromise. He'd make an exception in this case. Especially if it meant keeping her on this bench next to him. She began to undo the stitches, her small fingers working the yarn with an expertise he had to admire. "So tell me," he pressed, feeling victorious, "did you really ask Carson out of genuine concern for his welfare? Or just because you knew it would annoy me?"

"I had no way of knowing it would annoy you." That was true, technically, but he could tell that she suspected he'd be bothered, all the same. He could see the smile even with her face turned toward his sock. "I did think it might serve to cheer him up. He seemed so lost, sitting there as if there were no use left for him. God just popped the idea into my head and I knew it was the right thing to do."

"The Lord Almighty just pops things into your head, does He?" Faith seemed so simple, so effortless to her. As if it was like breathing. As if anyone could master it. And yet the idea of arranging for her to be his therapeutic assistant had just popped into his head with what might be called supernatural force. The notion that these thoughts might be connected made him decidedly uncomfortable.

She spared a glance up from the needlework. "My best ideas are always from Him." She paused, her eyes doing something he couldn't quite identify, before adding, "You were."

Chapter Eleven

John stifled an impulse to gulp. "Me? Are you saying I am from God or that I was your best idea?"

John was glad this brought a hearty laugh from her. Things had taken on a strange tension in the past few moments. "I suppose I should say both. You must know I believe each man is God's creation. I'd have thought that would be clear enough, especially given that I am in nursing."

So she did feel it a calling. That didn't surprise him at all. She went so carefully, so completely about her work and she'd seen so much humanity in the private he'd so readily dismissed. He couldn't remember the last time anyone other than his father had made him feel even the slightest hint of shame. Most found his ego, his driven nature, a valuable commodity. But this woman reminded him that his responsibilities—as an officer, and as a man—meant showing consideration for others, something he was far too prone to forget. "And me?"

She held up the sock, the row she'd fixed now neatly rounding the needles in orderly ribbing. "Well, I suppose the merit of that idea might have to wait until your sock is finished. But it is a grand start, I must say. And you've been a good sport."

He effected a general-worthy huff. "An average man might break under such pressure."

Her laugh died down to a soft, fluffy sound he liked very much. "And we all know that you, Captain Gallows, are decidedly exceptional." They stared at each other, time as soft and gentle as her laugh. He realized, with a start, that he felt physically different around her. Pliable and light instead of heavy and rigid. He very nearly forgot his pain. She handed the sock back to him, and he shamelessly made sure their hands touched as he took it. She had the most exquisite hands—porcelain pale yet strong as could be. He dropped his first stitch as he tried to picture those creamy digits laced between the calloused thickness of his own fingers, quickly replacing the stitch while she pretended not to notice. They worked in companionable silence for a minute or two. He thought about asking her why she hadn't requested they return to class, but decided he didn't want to suggest any return whatsoever. Instead he stopped his poor stitching and pulled out a slip of newspaper from his coat. Dr. Madison had given this to him yesterday, and its delivery was the real reason he came to class today. He'd hoped for a personal delivery—more private than the full class, and most certainly more cozy than the company of Private Carson. As such, now seemed the perfect time. "I have something for you."

She looked up, surprised. Good. He enjoyed surprising her.

"It's a poem from a Boston paper, from the War Between the States. Of course, those Yankees use a different name, but we won't hold that against them in this instance."

She smiled. "How very gracious of you." When he unfolded the paper and cleared his throat, her eyebrows arched further. "A recitation? Goodness, I am honored."

He started to say she was also beautiful, but stopped himself. She was the kind of woman more moved by poetry than easy compliments. And he could barely believe he was about to recite poetry for her. His father would cuff him and tell him he was soft, but his father was not staring into those stunning hazel eyes. He noticed, to his great pleasure, that she stopped knitting and gave him her full attention.

"Faith and hope give strength to her sight,
She sees a red dawn after the night.
Oh, soldiers brave, will it brighten the day,
And shorten the march on the weary way,
To know that at home the loving and true
Are knitting and hoping and praying for you."

Normally John would have said it was foolishly poetic to call a lady's eyes "glistening," but there was no other word for how she looked at him when he finished. A very tightly held piece of him flew out of his grasp as she did. He thought, at that moment, that he would do twenty painful laps around that horrid gymnasium if it meant she would look at him that way again. Or a while longer. He felt the curve of her smile deep in his chest, warm and disarming.

"You are a most amazing man, Captain Gallows." She said it with something he dearly hoped was awe.

"John," he blurted out, not caring that they were in a very public hallway where anyone could walk by.

"John," she said quietly. Her eyes flicked down, and

the delicacy of the gesture affected him just as surely as if her eyelashes had brushed his cheek.

She looked up at him twice after that, and they both pretended to go back to their work. By her third intake of breath he gently pushed the hand holding her needles down to still on her lap. "Go ahead."

"Pardon?"

"You're trying not to ask me something. Even someone with my alarming lack of subtlety could see that. Leanne." He used her name, not wanting to lose the closeness of the moment. "Ask me anything."

She hesitated again, carefully choosing words, tentative as a doe. "How did it change you? Your accident. You speak so gallantly of it, and yet I can't help but think it was a harrowing experience."

He saw the question hiding in so many eyes after his speeches. *What's it like, to almost die?* Some were genuinely interested, others grotesquely fascinated. "How did it change me?" He discarded his stock answer of having been a better dancer before, knowing she deserved the truest answer he had. Trouble was, he wasn't sure what that answer was. "I suppose," he started, no idea where he was going, "that not much frightens me now. Except, perhaps, the idea of not being worthy of the second chance I've been given."

He needn't have worried she would find such words foolish, for the comment only doubled the warmth in her eyes. "I think that a very worthy thing to fear. Far too many soldiers have come home ready to squander their lives, as if they've suddenly inherited some grand fortune and must spend it immediately." She began stitching again, her fingers working without any attention or even a glance downward. Why was he so enthralled by Leanne's delicate hands? "Then there are those like Private Carson," she went on. "I think he fears he hasn't come home worth anything at all. I think it's good you recognize the gift you've been given." A small laugh ruffled around the edges of her words. "Even if you are dreadfully cheeky about it."

"I prefer to think I'm wonderfully cheeky about it." Her laugh was full and musical, as warm as her eyes and as clear as sunlight.

"Oh, I've no doubt. Pity the poor soul who can see through your bravado, my good captain."

Had she realized what she just said? "Can you?" Her laugh stilled, and even John was stunned by how dark his words had become without his realizing it. "What do you see?"

He watched her falter, then find her courage. He would wait. He wanted—needed—to hear her answer to this question. She finally looked straight at him, steady and honest. "I think that charming as you are, you are in more pain than you let on to anyone. I think what happened up there in the sky changed you even more than you know, and you are wise enough to be frightened of that fact. I think I amuse you, that you are used to getting your way far too much and…" she flushed, the needles in her hands finally stopping their movement "…that you have a very regrettable habit of making me say too much."

John ought to have had a clever comeback for a sermon like that, but his wit failed him. After far too long a pause, he resorted to the only superiority he could manage. "Well, now, you've given me no choice."

"I've misspoken. I'm sorry."

"On the contrary, I can't see how I can respond to that with anything but an invitation to the officers' ball Friday evening. You do in fact—" although he didn't really like her choice of words "—*amuse* me, far more than perhaps is good for either of us. And you're absolutely right, I always get my way so don't bother to decline. You do say far too much, but that should come greatly in handy at a ball, seeing as now I can't dance and I haven't any more poetry. And we've already seen you are a master of distraction."

"An officers' ball?"

"The *USS Charleston* crew is having a grand event thrown for them in New York. The ship earned its liberty flag."

"Surely you're not asking me to go to New York!"

John laughed to think she thought him capable of such celebrity. "Not at all. The general's throwing a much smaller ball here, though, as a twin celebration. I can't promise you the splendor of the Astor Hotel, but I suspect it will be a grand evening just the same. Besides, after our last session, I would think you'd find it in my medical interest. It was you who suggested I waltz, after all. To deny me is to deny my continued recovery."

She liked the idea. How could she not, when she herself had come up with the idea of a waltz to improve his movement? And truly, what woman can resist a ball? Yet she was trying. "I'm sure I'm not allowed to go."

"Anyone may come as a guest of an officer. And even if you weren't allowed, hasn't it yet become clear to you that I'm not much for rules? Aside from your therapeutic assistance, you and I constitute a community service. Barnes is giving the ball, he makes the rules—and he'll allow it if I ask him. I know that man. He will just see it as an extension of the publicity campaign—which it *isn't*," he added quickly. "This is purely a social request."

She completed a stitch and eyed him. "Oh, no, it isn't. You've something up your sleeve."

"I'm crushed you would think so." She was right, of course; he did. "Have you peered into my soul and found me so deeply lacking?"

"It does not take much observation to know John Gallows is fond of schemes." She put down the stitching. "May I suggest a novel approach? Why don't you tell me the *real* reason why we're going, and I might surprise you by consenting. It will save us both time and considerable energy."

She meant it. That struck him as both disturbing and irresistible. At first he held back, hiding in a few botched stitches and clamping his mouth shut so hard his teeth nearly clacked.

"I would like to take you to the ball," he said, hoping the half-truth would suffice but rather sure it wouldn't. He looked up, expecting her to gloat, but found the most extraordinary expression on her face. Not victory, not amusement but genuine pleasure.

She waited. Glory, but that woman knew how to wield her silences. "And why," she said eventually, "would you like to take me to the ball?"

It had somehow become a game, a match of wits rather than some battle he must win. "There's no mystery there—men like to take women to balls. The dancing is so dreadfully dull if there are no women present."

"Ah, the *dancing*." Her eyes lit up. "You want to dance at the ball, is it? Jumping the gun a bit, aren't we?"

"Why? We danced the other day."

"It's just that you don't strike me as the kind of man to do things he doesn't do exceptionally well."

"I dance exceptionally well for a man of my...experiences." He started to say "limitations," which wasn't like him at all. A Gallows never bowed to limitations. "And yes, I want to be seen dancing."

Her eyes widened in understanding. "You want General Barnes to see you dancing, don't you? You want to show him how well your leg is so that he'll send you back."

He thought about denying it, but there really wasn't any use. "Partly."

"Entirely." She pushed out a sigh. "Why deceive him like that? You've made great strides, but your leg is not healed by any means. Certainly not enough to do what you're asking."

"I can accomplish one waltz, for goodness' sake. That is, if you help me."

"I'm sure you could find any number of women willing to aid you in this deception. As you said, men ask women to balls all the time."

He leaned in. "I need *you*." She knew how to let him lean on her, how to offer support in ways that weren't obvious. Any other woman would make him look— and feel—like an invalid. He had to look like the most capable man in the room. "Please do this for me." He'd sworn he wouldn't plead.

"I can't."

He gave her his best Gallows command. "You can. Just help me through one dance in front of Barnes. I shall be a model patient after that."

"You will not ever be a model patient. It will hurt, John."

"It hurts *now*. I'm no stranger to pain for a worthy goal."

She paused for an unbearable gap of silence until John was sure he'd burst. Then she began twirling the yarn around her finger the way she did when she worked out a problem, and he knew he'd prevailed. "I've nothing to wear."

A "thank-you" swelled in his heart, and for a frightening moment he wasn't sure if the gratitude was directed at her or Heaven. "I'll buy you a dress myself if I must call that bluff." He knew he would stop at nothing to get her acceptance—but if her arguments were on such trivial matters now, then victory was surely close at hand.

"Here is my proposition—if you get as far as the gusset on your sock, I'll waltz with you at the ball." She pointed to the bottom of her sock's cuff, the part where he imagined the heel began.

"That far? By Friday? You're mad."

"I could say the same of you, trying to make a show-place out of an officers' ball."

She had him. And he had her. He hadn't enjoyed anything this much since France. "Please ask God to stop popping ideas into your head. I fear I won't survive the next one."

Chapter Twelve

Leanne turned slightly, watching how the fringe of the delicate champagne underskirt swished elegantly. It made the most delightful sound as it moved beneath the smooth rose overskirt. She was nearly ready for the officers' ball.

She'd owned the rose-and-white cameo for years, but it sat at her neck with a new regal air. Ida had loaned her some pearl ear bobs and pulled up Leanne's hair in a way that set them off beautifully. "I know Captain Gallows is a handsome fellow, but who knew it went deeper than that?" Ida said as she tucked a cream rose into Leanne's hair.

"Why do you say that?"

"Well, I'm no expert on such matters, but I do know it takes far more than a handsome face to catch your fancy. There must be a fair amount behind those gorgeous eyes."

It was unnerving to have someone else recognize the tumult going on inside her. "Pardon?"

Ida sat back on one hip. "You really think I didn't know? Honey, it's all over your face every time that man walks in the room. I know you try to hide it—he does, too—but neither of you are having much success. And tonight, why, you're fairly glowing."

Leanne felt her face flush. "I…"

Ida set down the hairbrush. "Relax. There's no shame in enjoying the attentions of a handsome man. Half of Columbia would line up to be in your place. I've never thought we had much choice in where our hearts landed, anyways."

Leanne turned to her friend. "My heart? He would not be the one my heart would choose. And yet, in the past few days I've seen…compelling things in his nature. It's as if I can't help it—I see too deeply into his character. And he into mine. But, Ida, why on earth would I have such a response to a man without faith? I can't have a future with such a man."

"How do you know he's got no faith?" When Leanne raised a dubious eyebrow, Ida continued, "Well, yes, I know he acts like a rollicking fellow on the outside, but if you say he goes deeper than that, why not straight-out ask him?"

Standing and straightening her skirts, Leanne eyed herself in the mirror. Her dress was stunning, her hair lovely, the evening air was perfect but none of these things explained why Leanne could not squelch the thrill she felt this evening. Like a princess. A princess with entirely the wrong prince. "I don't have to." She sighed, fingering the cameo. "We've spoken of it directly. I believe he admires my faith, that much is true, but he surely does not share it."

"Gracious, Leanne, it's a ball, not a marriage proposal. You said he asked for your help in something—" for Leanne would not break John's confidence about the waltz "—and you're helping. What would he learn about God if you turned him down?" Ida helped Leanne into her shawl, sighing her approval as she cast her gaze from head to foot. "Perfection." She handed Leanne her evening bag. "Maybe it isn't the faith he *has* that's important here, but the faith he *could* have." Ida chuckled a bit. "Why, could you imagine what God could do with a fellow like that once He got through to him?"

She'd had the same thought dozens of times since meeting John Gallows, and it hadn't rendered her attraction any less dangerous.

It was the oddest thing to watch John turn as she entered the parlor. His entire countenance changed, as if someone had just sent an electric current through him. Most unnerving of all was the knowledge that the "current" had been the sight of her. She could understand the shock, however, for no less than twice the voltage seemed to shoot through her at the sight of him.

John was in the same dashing dress uniform he had worn for his presentation—hung with medals and strung with gold cords so that he looked every inch the hero—but it seemed to have double the effect on her this time. Maybe because now she knew more about the man under all those very fine trappings. He had his hat tucked under his elbow, so that the glossy curves of his hair picked up the flicker of the lights behind him. He looked at her stunned as if they'd never met, and yet smiling as though greeting a long-lost friend. She was sure she had the same expression on her own face, for John looked like the John Gallows she knew, and then again like the most handsome hero God ever created. Ida sighed a swooning "My, my, my!" behind her. Some small part of her was glad they were friends, glad she'd been privy to his weaknesses, for had she met him in all his glory like this she would surely have been starstruck.

"I'd never have thought I'd be so happy to reach a gusset," he said, reaching into his pocket to show the nine inches of ribbing she'd required of him. In her fluster over the party, she'd completely forgotten the bargain she'd struck. John Gallows was very good at dissolving her sensibilities. "I'd have hated to miss this." He walked toward her, the cane making him look like some grand English lord. "You look absolutely lovely."

He truly meant it, she could see it in his eyes, but he paid the compliment with such oversize gallantry that Leanne was sure she was more pink than her dress. After the long moment it took to find her voice, she managed a "Thank you."

"Tonight will be a new experience for me," he began as he laid the sock on the hall table, donned his cap and extended his arm. "I'm not accustomed to everyone's eyes being on someone else. I find I can't decide if you've foiled my plan or helped it immensely."

She slipped her hand into the crook of his arm, feeing for all the world like Cinderella. "Captain Gallows, you overestimate my appeal."

"Oh, no," he said with a look that made Leanne's insides flutter in ten directions, "I don't believe I do." Ida opened the hall doors for them, grinning entirely too widely as she ushered them into the golden stillness of the fall evening. The weather was perfect beyond measure, and while they both paused at the top of the Red Cross House stairs to take in the glory of the evening, his gaze came to rest unapologetically on her. "I talked Nelson out of calisthenics today," he said as he gripped the railing to work his way carefully down the stairs. "I told him I'd shift my weight all afternoon and that you and I would walk to the Assembly Hall. In dress boots at that, so it ought to count for six laps if not seven."

He looked steeled for battle, so determined to reach the goal he'd set for himself that she felt guilty for her own doubts. It was a perfect evening for walking, but wouldn't that run the risk of taxing his leg in advance of the ball? "Are you sure you want to walk?"

"If you had any plans to push me in one of those horrid wheelchairs, I think I'd sooner crawl." He was trying to make a joke, but the edge of disdain in his words gave him away. He loathed this weakness. In many ways, John had no more made peace with his injuries than troubled Private Carson had. "Besides, why on earth would I want to lessen the time I get to spend alone with you?"

They'd reached the bottom of the stairs, and he rearranged his stance with a dramatic flair, as if they were stepping off into a parade. She half expected him to wave to a crowd she could not see. "Captain Gallows, do you ever come offstage?"

"Not if it can be helped." He twirled his cane before launching them forward. "And you will call me John for this entire lovely walk or we'll turn back right here. And don't get all worrisome about my stamina. I've already planned to stop and rest at least twice."

"A wise choice."

"Actually I'm telling myself it's simply because the sunset is so grand. I expect you to play along." He puffed up his decorated chest and did a spot-on imitation of Dr. Madison's Bostonian accent. "No use resisting. It's for my medical benefit and I am a hero you know."

"Does everyone always do your bidding?"

"Well—" his smile turned from the manufactured one to a grin of genuine warmth "—I am *knitting,* so what does that tell you?"

She laughed, once again enjoying the thought that she may have been among the first to best John Gallows at his own game. "That God is mighty indeed."

He did not offer one of his clever comebacks. They walked in companionable silence for a minute or so, and the glorious washes of amber painting the sky did indeed remind her of God's own glory. *"The Heavens declare the glory of God."* She sighed without thinking.

His own sigh held much less reverence. "Do you attribute everything to the Almighty?"

"I suppose I do. Does that bother you?" She watched in admiration as the breeze played with the fringe of her skirt. Finer ladies would have balked at the prospect of traveling to the party on foot, but she was glad for the chance. Walking—even their slow, laborious laps— had become part of their relationship. She believed they had their best conversations when walking or knitting. Truth or difficult subjects were always best conversed when there was some activity to focus one's attention.

"It baffles me, more like it." He looked at her with narrowed eyes.

She thought of Ida's comment about what feats God could accomplish if he ever got through to a man like John Gallows. Even if it were true, it was a precarious hook on which to hang her hope's affections. "I'm not likely to stop, even for you."

"It's not just preaching—you really see Him in everything, don't you?" *Baffled* truly did capture his expression.

"Even in you." She wanted to grab the words out of the air and shoo them away the minute they popped out of her mouth. Ida's fool notions had run away with her composure. Leanne stared down at her slippers, mortified, until John reached out and tilted her chin up to face him. It was far too private a gesture for such a public place, and her face tingled with heat.

Worst of all was the look on his face; the notion pleased him. Immensely, from the look of it. "I suspect that's why I find you so delightfully annoying. You do always look as if you've just unearthed some new virtue out of me. Have you any idea how disconcerting that is?"

Disconcerting was an apt description. John was disconcerting beyond measure. She began to wonder if tonight had been a mistake. With the fancy dress and the dashing hero in his dress uniform, she'd started to feel too much like Cinderella…and there was no happy ending to be had in this fairy tale. If John succeeded in this show of strength he planned in front of the general—and Leanne was fairly certain he would, since she knew him well enough now to know that John Gallows would reach his goals or die trying—then he might soon find himself sent back overseas as he'd planned. The brief interlude between them would be over and forgotten.

Guard yourself and your heart, she told herself. *You aren't going to the ball to be wooed, or dazzled or swept off your feet. You are here as his friend—and his nurse—to help him because you said you would. That was all—all there was, and all there could be.*

They walked on for another block—the second of six, for the base was a large complex—and she could feel his gait stiffening. Pointing to a bench just ahead, she manufactured a wince and said, "Oh, bother, I've got a pebble in my slipper. Could we sit down over there?"

John stopped, speared by the transparency of what she was doing. "Don't do that!" he snapped at her.

"What?"

Did she actually think he couldn't see through her ruse? Didn't she know that he was absolutely sick to death of people trying to pamper him with weaknesses invented to nullify his?

"Don't coddle me." He barked it out far sharper than he would have liked; her eyes widened in a remorse he felt twisting under his ribs. "You've no more got a pebble in your shoe than I have a third leg." His wounded dignity wouldn't allow him to completely soften his words, but he tried. "I don't want that, most especially from you."

"I am sorry." She looked down, and he wanted desperately to put his hand to her chin and tip her gaze back up to him again. Her kindness was a welcome sting.

"I'd like to sit down, Leanne, but I'd like to sit because *I* need it, not because you've decided I should." Her honesty had become a precious commodity to him, refreshing in his posturing world of military hierarchies. "Will you grant me that? Grant me the honesty I like so much about you?" He gestured toward the bench, glad to have that over with.

"I suppose I could have just asked you if you were ready to sit down," she offered as she arranged herself on the bench.

"Better still, just don't concern yourself with it. I promise you, I'll tell you when I need to stop."

She gave him a sideways glance as her two rose slippers peeked out of her fringed skirt. Had she arranged them so evenly on purpose, or was she just that elegant in how she sat? "That's not what you do in the gymnasium."

"In the gymnasium, I'm under Madison's harsh thumb. Tonight is purely in my realm." Certainly she never dressed like this for the gymnasium. And while he thought she looked lovely even in her nurse's uniform, he couldn't help but be charmed by how transparently pleased she clearly was with how she looked in that dusty-rose color. A little smile would light on the corners of her face when she played with the lace at her sleeves. She reminded him of one of his little cousins, twirling in some new party frock. That had been part of his aim tonight, to spend time with her in his realm instead of under doctor's orders or the tyranny of Red Cross knitting. "I can't let you have the upper hand on every occasion, and you've no idea how skilled I am at punchbowl warfare."

"Oh, I can easily guess. I've no doubt the army has the right man for the job." She looked at him, one eye narrowed as if assessing a student's progress. "Actually, for both jobs. I have to say I found the knitting photographs a cockeyed scheme at first, but I've come to see the brilliance in it."

John wasn't quite sure he'd come to that level of endorsement yet. "So you're telling me it's worth the endless ribbing I take from the soldiers back in camp?" He'd heard every version of a knitting joke, many of which could never be repeated in polite company. No doubt Carson had heard even worse if he dared to knit in the barracks.

"The Red Cross officials tell me they're in dire straits. If you can convince young men to take up this cause and not feel like a—what was the word?—*sissy* about it, then you will have impacted the lives of thousands of brave soldiers. I watched those boys in the audience. They admire you. They want to be like you. Your gifts suit this challenge. God's placed you in just the right place at just the right time."

He laughed. "You make my sock sound like a noble crusade."

"It is."

Leanne was so straightforward, so refreshingly uncomplicated. Her socks really were a noble crusade to her. *Socks.* Who'd have ever thought he'd spend so much time thinking about socks? He angled himself to face her on the bench, not caring that it sent a pang through his hip. "Does the Red Cross realize what they've got in you?" When he'd first asked her that, he'd found her commitment—her passion—misdirected. Now he was coming to see why she dedicated herself the way she did.

"Oh, I suppose no more than the army realizes the secret weapon they have in you."

He settled for rising off the bench and extending his hand. "Let's go further convince them, shall we?"

"You're ready to go forward, then?" She placed her hand in his.

John helped her to her feet, tucking the hand into the crook of his elbow and liking very much how it felt as it nestled there. "Oh, my dear Leanne, I was born ready."

Chapter Thirteen

Liberty bond sales were essential to the war effort, and General Barnes capitalized on anything crucial to the war. It may not have rivaled the Carolina Hall or anything at the State House across town, but the general had staged a respectable event. He'd been smart enough to invite several state capitol dignitaries and a few of Columbia's finest families as well. Barnes knew strategic allies on the home front were as necessary as those overseas.

Transformed from its daily duties as an assembly hall, the space sported bunting and flags, a serviceable army orchestra and as festive a selection of food and drink as could be had during wartime. Despite the affair being well underway—for it had taken a good deal of time to finish their journey here—most of the room turned to look at John and Leanne when they entered. John was clearly used to being at the center of attention. He seemed as at home in the spotlight as she was foreign to it.

"They're staring at you," he whispered as they circled around the reception.

"They're staring at *you*," she replied, wondering if

the flush would ever leave her cheeks this evening. A waiter with a tray of punch cups appeared, and John selected one for her without taking one for himself. Of course, she realized, he needed one hand on his cane while the other leaned ever-so-slightly on her. She sipped it quietly as she watched John's eyes scan the room for General Barnes.

"He's not here."

"No, he won't appear for another half an hour or so. Probably holed up in some library with cigars and senators." When she raised an eyebrow, he added, "The man never throws a party just to throw a party. I'll know how many items he's ticked off his agenda just by the way he stands." When she finished her cup of punch, he offered, "Shall we mingle?"

The mayor of Columbia greeted her warmly, remarking on how the addition of Camp Jackson had invigorated the state capital.

"She's heading up several classes for the Red Cross knitting campaign, too," John offered, when the conversation turned to Leanne's activities as a nurse. "I'm her newest student, you know."

"So I hear, young man, so I hear," cooed the mayor's wife. "Well, if anyone can get our boys onto yarn and needles, I suspect it's you." The woman turned to Leanne. "You know, our ladies' guild might be able to supply you with more yarn, if that would help."

"It would indeed, thank you," Leanne replied. By the time they'd circled the room, John had maneuvered assorted conversations to no less than six offers of help for the Red Cross classes. He seemed to be able to draw assistance from people with uncanny ease. "You've not asked a single person for their help," she whispered with amusement, "and yet I find myself with half a dozen offers of much-needed assistance."

"I thought all good Charleston girls were taught the art of social commerce."

"Not in the way you employ it. I'm afraid I don't go about it with quite so much…" As she searched for the words, John's demeanor shifted dramatically. She did not need to see the general to know he had entered the room; John stared at him with an intensity that prickled her skin. Surely it was dangerous to place so much importance on one dance—she couldn't help thinking tonight would end very badly. John was already leaning heavily on her arm just to walk around. It didn't seem possible that his scheme could be achieved. Then again, hadn't he just achieved more than she'd ever bargained for in a handful of "innocent" conversations?

"He'll work his way over to that side of the room," John said, pointing to a series of windows that faced west. "We should do the same."

This would work. He'd convince the general of his leg's health without his even being aware of it. That's why this was so brilliant—anything so obvious as a physical test or exam would heighten the commander's awareness whereas this would sneak the idea in under his consciousness. Leanne had declared it "propaganda" in jest, but she wasn't that far off. Of course she didn't know he'd paid the band leader to ensure a slow waltz two numbers after General Barnes entered the room. When it arrived, John took a deep breath, laid his cane up against the chair railing and extended his hand as if this were the easiest thing in the world. She caught his eye with such an expression of encouragement that it felt as if ten pounds lifted off his frame.

She was delightful to hold. To truly hold, the way he used to hold a dancing partner. Leanne was light and airy on her feet, yet keenly aware of where and when he needed to lean on her. The sessions they'd had with the bars told her just which steps were most difficult for him.

One, two, three…it was the slight twist at the end of the third step that pained him, but not too badly at first.

One, two, three…they circled within yards of the general. Out of the corner of his eye before turning, John caught Dr. Madison pointing him out to the Barnes. Never mind the scowl on that pessimist Dr. Madison's face, he'd made it halfway around the room and he wasn't even sweating yet.

"Smile, my dear," John said as he caught Leanne peering around his shoulder to check if the general was watching. "This isn't supposed to be so serious. I'm charming, rememb—" A wrong twist sent a spark of pain through his hip and he almost missed a step. He'd aggravated something, for the pain stayed throughout the steps now instead of waxing and waning. No matter; he could endure it.

"Are you all right?" She applied the smile he'd requested, but worry darkened her eyes.

"Delightful." He leaned on her a little harder as they made the difficult turn.

"You most certainly are not. Shall we stop? I could feign a turned ankle."

"I told you not to do such things. I'm fine." He cursed the traitorous rivulet of sweat he felt stealing down his temple. "Halfway around the room again so we pass in front of him."

"John, you're in pain. Stop this before you hurt yourself."

"Just let me put my weight on you on that third step

and we'll be fine. And land sakes, try to look enthralled. I'm to be sweeping you off your feet, remember?"

"It is getting you off your feet that I'm most concerned with at the moment."

John's leg was on fire now, but he'd pass out before he'd pass up the chance to waltz past the general one more time. He tightened his grip on Leanne's shoulder and stared into the welcome distraction of her eyes. "Stay with me. Just a few measures more." He discovered he was gritting his teeth.

"John…"

The final measures of the waltz placed them right in front of the general, and John turned Leanne just enough to face her toward Barnes as they stood still at the song's conclusion and applauded the orchestra. He leaned in to catch her ear above the noise. "What's he doing?" he whispered, more breathless than he would have liked.

"He's talking to Dr. Madison."

"Laughing?"

"It looks rather more like a frown, I'm sorry to say."

"And Madison?" He needed just a few seconds more before he could turn and face Barnes convincingly.

"Scowling like a bear."

"Excellent. Now, I'll turn to face him, and if you'd be so kind, duck over to the side of the room and fetch my cane. It'd be lovely if you could be rather insistent that I use it, for I plan to refuse a time or two."

Leanne narrowed her eyes. "Really? This has become an exercise in playacting."

"You're my secret weapon, Leanne. Just a minute or two longer and then I shall be yours to command. I'll knit baby booties if it comes to that."

"Honestly." Her words were harsh, but the amusement hiding behind her glare did her no favors in making her seem stern. She turned in the direction of his cane, but not before he brought her hand to his lips and placed a lingering kiss there. She smelled of roses, and her eyes made the fire in his leg fade to embers.

A long hour later, Leanne raised an eyebrow as John turned to the car that had brought them back to the Red Cross House and barked at the driver not to wait. She said nothing as the car rumbled off down the street, just as John had said next to nothing as they'd driven home. She'd caught him looking at her a dozen times on the short trip, silent, a quizzical smile on his face.

"Did things turn out the way you wanted?"

"I'm not at all sure."

She didn't know how to respond to that. "What were you expecting?"

"I wasn't expecting anything. The point was to hand him an impression without him realizing it."

"I thought you did marvelously. I have no doubt you were a superb dancer in your day." She regretted the backhanded compliment the moment it left her lips. They'd never discussed his full prognosis, whether Dr. Madison expected him to regain full use of the leg. John certainly seemed to brook no doubts on the issue. "You *are* a superb dancer now."

The correction was useless. He looked at her, and for the first time she saw the doubts he tried so very hard to kill. "I needed your help." He whispered it like a confession.

"You were smart enough to ask for it. I was glad to give it." She smiled at the memory of all the eyes upon her and John. "We were a very convincing pair, weren't we?"

John took a step closer, his hand on the house railing. "We were. I was the envy of every man there."

"Oh, I doubt that." He was the center of the attention, so handsome and charming people flocked around them when they left the dance floor. If anyone was an object of envy, it was her. She had little doubt that every single woman in the ballroom coveted her position on the captain's arm.

"I didn't dance with anyone else now, did I?" The way he said it let her know John was aware of how she'd noticed the attentions of other ladies at the ball.

She crossed her arms over her chest. "You couldn't have. No one else knew our system."

John stepped in again. "Our *secret*. But even if they did, I wouldn't have danced with anyone else." He'd downed several glasses of champagne after they'd danced, saying he needed it to dull the pain, and she suspected that was the reason his words took on such a dramatic flair. She also knew John used dramatic flair to get what he wanted.

His eyes were intense, as dark blue as the night sky behind him. It was becoming clear he wanted to be closer to her. Clearer yet was that she was beginning to want it, too, despite a hundred reasons to resist. He leaned in, and while she took a breath to stop him, no sound would come out of her mouth. He ran one finger down the length of her hand. The sensation made her head spin. "I can't dance with anyone else. Just you. Another of the Almighty's impressive ideas, I suppose."

Leanne was thankful he'd managed to say the one thing that would shake her senses back into place. "John."

"We're an excellent pair. Socks come in pairs." He let his finger feather against her wrist.

She removed her hand. "We are a mismatched pair."

He looked into her eyes, his voice silken. "I don't see it that way."

"You are looking for the conquest you did not gain tonight. And you have had too much champagne."

"It kills the pain."

"It kills the *senses,*" she corrected. "We are a pair of friends, and that is how it must stay."

He stepped entirely too close. "Are you sure?"

Leanne pulled in a deep breath. "Not at all, but as Dr. Madison would say, 'there it is.' Good night, John."

John took her hand and kissed it dramatically. It was a showy kiss, not the delicate kind he'd placed on her hand at the end of their waltz at the ball. "Good night, my dear friend Nurse Sample."

Leanne was grateful she could almost laugh. "Do you even know how to be friends with a woman?"

"You'll find I can be the epitome of paternal civility."

Now she could laugh. "Don't you mean 'platonic'?"

He tipped his hat. "Perhaps I should not have downed that last glass. But it is a lovely thing not to have one's leg on fire every moment. So perhaps your friendship will allow you to forgive my indulgence."

"We are all in need of forgiveness." She stepped up onto the short flight of stairs that led into the house.

"Not you." He looked up at her with an unchecked, wide-eyed admiration. "You're perfect."

She fought the urge to lean down and kiss his cheek. Never in her life had she been so tempted to cross such a line—but it would do neither of them any good. She was his friend. She was his nurse. That was all she could ever be. "I most of all, Captain Gallows. Good night."

He put his hand on his heart, a theatrical wounding, before turning off to spin his cane as he disappeared into the night.

Chapter Fourteen

Leanne was reconsidering her agreement to meet John today. Yes, they needed to prepare for Monday's photograph session, but she wasn't at all sure time alone with John was a good idea. Before the ball, they'd decided it would be smart to have John's sock heel nearly completed in the photographs. It would show off well, and most knitters knew turning a first sock heel was a significant accomplishment for the novice knitter. She wanted John's sense of victory to show up in the photographs, hoping to convince the intended young boys to see how challenging knitting could be. Still, it was a complicated lesson, requiring much more interaction and—regretfully—much more touching than she would have liked given how things had transpired after the ball. To cancel, however, felt like too much of an admission, and she needed to return the sock he'd left at the Red Cross House last night. She suspected John saw right through her insistence that they meet outside "for the good sunlight." The way he looked at her now, Leanne had little hopes of hiding how she fretted over the prospect of being in close quarters with him.

"I half worried you wouldn't show," he teased when

she arrived at the bench they'd designated. Leanne felt like a walking battle—the conflict of "just fine" and "horrid" tumbling in her chest—whereas John looked as if nothing had transpired between them.

"You can't go forward without this," she ventured without too much cheer as she produced the unfinished sock, which only served as an unneeded reminder of the previous evening. "And I could never miss the great Captain Gallows turning his first sock heel." Leanne steeled her determination to get past this awkwardness and focus on the work to be done. She changed the subject by asking "Does your leg pain you much today?"

"It hurts twelve ways to Sunday this morning. You'd think I'd set the thing on fire last night for the way it's acting up. Not to mention my head. I hardly slept."

Leanne hadn't slept much, either, but for entirely different reasons. "I'm sorry."

"Dr. Madison seemed to take no end of pleasure in torturing me this morning. Lectured me like some rascal schoolboy about how I had no right 'gallivanting around like a circus pony' last night." John shifted uncomfortably on the bench. "A circus pony. The man's a monster who feeds on other men's pain."

She sat down cautiously next to him. One the one hand, John did strike her as a petulant child, sulking and thrashing about. On the other hand, it was clear Captain Gallows nearly always got his way and suffered obstacles with little grace indeed. "He is trying to keep your best interest at heart."

"My *best interest*," John barked back, "is waiting for me back in France, if Barnes would stop listening to overcautious coddlers and just sign the orders."

"It's good we have such an engaging project to distract you. Sock heels are challenging."

John stretched out his stiff leg. "You're alone in your enthusiasm. I've been called 'a heel' so often in the barracks this morning, it's losing its appeal."

"Don't listen to them. A sock heel is a great personal victory. Just the sort of stuff warriors thrive upon." Now she was letting her nerves make her hopelessly wordy. Perhaps friendship with John Gallows wasn't possible after all.

Not with the way he stopped her hand when she pulled her knitting from her bag. "Leanne." It was unfair how the sound of his voice danced over her name.

"Yes?" It came out a tight, girlish gulp.

"I do know how to be friends with you. I'll be a perfect gentleman."

To know her discomfort lay so transparent to him just made things worse. His words were perfectly aimed at the very thing that troubled her most; John Gallows very rarely bothered to be a perfect gentleman. She'd heard the stories, she'd seen his full-blown charm unleashed. It would be so much easier to hate him, to dismiss him as a cad, if he behaved badly. If he pressed his cause, or even if he discarded her for some other, more permissive female, she could dismiss him as the overblown, cinema-worthy hero with secret feet of clay. To her dismay, he did not. In fact, today John seemed more natural, more "offstage" than she'd ever seen him. The effect only heightened her attraction. His efforts to be "friends"—and the knowledge those efforts were exclusively on her behalf—well, that was distracting beyond measure.

Leanne fled for the safety of the stitchwork. She pointed to his sock, determined to keep her hands from his for as long as possible. "Start across here, stopping three stitches from the end."

"Yes, ma'am."

He'd never "yes ma'am-ed" her in any of their previous sessions. How on earth did he manage the paradox of such a respectful twinkle in his eye? To keep going with this was risky indeed, playing with fire. Were this any other task, she would simply write down the directions and leave him to his own devices. Turning a sock heel, however, really was something that needed teaching face-to-face.

"Will you look at that?" John said when the heel began to cup, to take on the distinct curvature that turned a tube into a sock. At first she thought he was joking, but he was genuinely impressed. With himself, of course, but with the technique as well. He held it up, turning the work this way and that. "I'll never dismiss a sock as ordinary ever again."

What red-blooded American knitter could dismiss a man's respect for a well-turned heel? "It is extraordinary, isn't it?"

"Extraordinary," he said all-too-smoothly, dropping the knitting to look directly at her.

Leanne raised an eyebrow and applied a "please behave" expression to hide her inner smile.

"In the most platonic of ways, of course," he declared, not bothering to hide his grin one bit as he continued the required stitching. "You're right, this is going to be far more difficult than I thought." When she looked at him, he added, "The knitting, I mean. Tricky stuff, this."

Leanne began to wonder if her resolve would last an entire sock.

"Turn a little to your left, please, and hold the thing up a little higher." The photographer assistant's voice grated like a rusty hinge as the afternoon heat increased the friction. Leanne was trying hard to be pleasant, but the stiff starch of her nursing uniform—they'd asked her to come in uniform today—grated like Mr. Palmer's voice.

John had stopped trying to be nice twenty minutes ago. "It's called a *sock,* Palmer," he snapped at the young assistant. "I know it doesn't look much like one now, but that's the whole point of this, isn't it?"

"It is a rather fine ankle and gusset. It will photograph wonderfully, don't you think, Mr. Palmer?"

"Just *grand,* Miss Sample." Mr. Palmer droned as if rather be doing just about anything else.

John bristled. "You wouldn't take that tone if you'd just put your feet into a warm, dry sock after four days in the trenches."

Leanne hadn't the nerve to ask John how his morning session with Dr. Madison went, but it didn't take a cross examination to see John wasn't pleased. It made her grateful she'd had her first soldiers' class this morning and hadn't been in the gymnasium. John stalked through the photography session like a uniformed grizzly bear, smiling when called upon but otherwise dark and surly.

The photographer peered around his large camera. "Slide a little farther over on the chair, Captain Gallows. We don't need that much of Nurse Sample in the shot." Evidently photographers had little need to master social graces for he seemed to have no idea how dismissive his command sounded; as if she were a vase to be moved or a lamp casting an unwanted shadow.

John nearly growled. "Nurse Sample is in the shot or you'll have no captain to shoot. Do I make myself clear?"

The photographer's remark did sting a bit, but Leanne had no wish to become the center of a photographic squabble. "I assure you, Captain Gallows, it's not necessary that I be featured."

"These young boys aren't interested in learning knitting from their grandmothers. They want to know pretty young ladies like Nurse Sample will spend time with them if they sign up. They won't *know* that if you don't *show* it, now will they?"

The photographer's words may have been "Yes, of course," but his tone was much closer to *you stick to your job and I'll stick to mine.* By the end of the session, Leanne couldn't imagine how any of the images would do the Red Cross much good. *I don't know much about "red,"* she thought with a sour humor as she pulled her knitting from the prop basket they'd given her to use at these sessions and returned it to her usual canvas bag, *but "cross" certainly applied today.* John looked as if he would throw his cane across the room at the next person to ask him to smile. He dumped his sock on a table at the back of the room and hobbled out into the hallway at the first opportunity. She'd never seen anyone slam down a piece of knitting before.

She caught him in the hallway. "John…"

"I need to stop all this parading and get back to France. *Now.*"

Leanne touched his elbow gently. "You have things to finish here, John."

He turned to her. "I've nothing to…" He caught himself, running one hand down his face while the other gripped his cane with white knuckles. "It's not that what you do isn't important. You wouldn't understand, I'm afraid."

"Perhaps you should try to explain it to me." She

started to tell him to sit down, but remembered how poorly he took such orders. "Would you care to rest your leg on that bench over there?" she said in a deliberate tone meant to highlight it as a request, not a command or manipulation.

John didn't answer; he simply set off toward a bench in irritable, limping silence.

Leanne let him arrange himself to his comfort on the bench, then sat next to him, her knitting bag on her lap. He brooded wordlessly for a minute or two, clearly not ready for conversation. Deciding it was better to wait him out than try to draw him out, Leanne reached into her bag and began the process of stitching up the toe of the sock she'd used in the photographs. *If he needs to speak about it,* she prayed, genuinely stumped as to how to help the captain out of his bitter gloom, *let him do so to me. You know best what he needs—likely better than he knows himself.* The prayer calmed her, and she stitched on at peace with his prickly silence, trusting God knew when and where to start the conversation. She would show patience, even if he had none.

Chapter Fifteen

❧

"**I** am first and foremost a soldier," John opened up after they sat there awhile. "Not a spokesman. I wonder some days if the army sees me as anything more than a mouthpiece, a hired verbal gun."

He'd said as much other days. She started to remind him that his speaking was a true gift, but stopped herself. He was blind to that gift, at least for today. Instead she tried a different tactic. "It can't be a bad thing to respect your body's need to heal. What possible purpose could be served by going back before you're fully capable?"

John gave a bitter grunt. "Capable? Who's ever truly capable of facing battle? All men go to war with wounds, whether they are physical or otherwise. You think these boys, these young fellows funneled straight out of school onto ships, are *capable?*"

No, she didn't. Some of these boys looked so young and glory-hungry it made her heart break to know some of them would return with Private Carson's hollow shadows in their eyes. "You're an impatient man."

"You bet the…" She watched John swallow a curse.

"Yes, I am, but even a patient man would be tested by Barnes's dawdling."

She watched the way John's leg relaxed and regained a bit of its flexibility. Did he realize how much his temper tangled his healing? It made her wonder if the skewed importance he'd placed on that waltz hadn't been half the reason for his failure. He'd waltzed smoothly in the gymnasium. His gait always evened out when she got him talking. His pain seemed to disappear onstage. "I believe you will go back, John. Does that help?" It was true, but only half the truth. She believed he would go back whether it was wise for him to go or not. She was coming to realize that, wise or not, spiritually sound or not, a small part of her would leave with him when he left.

He turned to look at her, and Leanne feared that part of her would not remain small for long. The blue in those eyes conquered her reason all too easily. "I must go back. I don't know that I can explain it any more clearly than that. Honor comes close, I suppose, but I don't know that I could explain that to you, either."

She could see that. Despite the fact that all the scheming and persuasion might lead one to think otherwise, John Gallows was a warrior, a man driven by pride and honor. "Yes, I suppose honor comes close."

"Honor takes different shapes for different men. Don't you see? That's what makes a man into a soldier or a sailor, not the outcome of some physical test. Tomorrow is a foolish exercise in things that don't matter."

Tomorrow. John had an exam with Dr. Madison the next day to assess his physical progress, one he'd hoped to circumnavigate with his waltz in front of General Barnes. Dr. Madison had told her it was a straightforward enough exercise—timed completion of tasks, measurements of flexibility ranges, such things.

Such things as could not be manipulated. Facts even the cunning John Gallows could not bend to his liking, could not wield to serve his notion of honor.

She nearly gasped, so striking was her insight: John's body was at war with his honor. That's what drove him to try anything—even a waltz—to sidestep his physical assessments. She instantly understood the basic struggle that drove him to do what he did. It had been there all the time in the steel edge in his eyes, the defiant way he brandished his cane, the cocky nature he hid behind: his honor would never, ever surrender to his body. The fact that he'd suffered a serious injury would never override his warrior nature—in fact, she was quite sure it would only feed the man's need to prove himself.

John hated when she looked at him like that. All too often in conversation with him her eyes would widen, her lips part in the most unsettling way and her face would alter as if hit by a ray of sunshine. It always gave him the nerve-racking sense that she was receiving some sort of divine revelation—usually about him, which made it all the worse. He would have much preferred God left him alone. "I think I understand," she said as though that was the last thing she expected.

It certainly was the last thing he'd expected. "Really? I rather thought I'd botched the explanation, myself." He waited for some speech of chastisement from her, the "be sensible," "you've suffered a serious injury" or worst of all "don't be such a selfish, ungrateful cad" sort he'd been expecting her to launch into any moment. Especially after the way he'd just behaved in that insuf-

ferable photographic session. He'd deserve every word
of it if she did decide to scold.

She didn't. She just stared at him for a long moment, as if reading some startling new information in
his face, and then resumed her knitting. With the most
confounding smile on her face. She understood. How,
he'd never guess, for he knew the thought was foreign
to her. She was a creature of peace and comfort, he of
pride and battle. He mostly just let her knit in silence
because he was truly stumped at how to respond. Land
sakes, when was the last time a woman stumped him?

A few minutes later she came to a decision of sorts,
for she put down her knitting, sat upright and turned
to looked him in the eye. "John, I should like to ask
you something."

Did she have any idea how beautiful she looked when
she got like that? Warm and effervescent as if she held
the secret of life in her hands? "Anything."

"Well, actually, I would like to ask you to let me do
something."

He couldn't help himself. "Why yes, *of course* you
may kiss me." The resulting flame in her cheeks was
entirely too irresistible, and he laughed until she did
as well.

She covered her face in her hands like a schoolgirl.
"You are incorrigible. Really. I am trying to be serious."

He'd known that, knew it would mortify her and had
been helpless to rein in his impulses. Only half of him
regretted it, which was a dubious sign indeed. "My apol-
ogies," he said, truly meaning it. "I made a promise to
be a gentleman the other night, and I mean to keep it.
Very well then, let us be serious. What is your request?"

She could not raise her eyes. "I cannot ask now.
You've dashed my courage." He felt her words like a

thorn, knowing he deserved the prick. She pushed her
knitting back into the bag and went to rise.

John caught her elbow. He could not, would not let
it go after she'd been so forgiving of his misbehavior
after the ball. "Please," he pleaded, tugging her back
toward the bench. "I am sorry. Truly. Please, Leanne,
ask me anything you like. I can't imagine denying any
request you have to make."

Leanne let her eyes fall closed for a second, muster-
ing her nerve. What could possibly be so difficult for
her to ask? "I should like to ask…if you would allow…
I should like to pray for your leg. I don't see any other
way for you to pass the exam as quickly as you feel
you must save with God's help. If not for your peace of
mind then for mine."

John didn't know what he'd expected, but this surely
wasn't it. "You want to pray for my leg? For the test?"

She looked embarrassed by the thought. "Yes."

He blinked. It had been a long time since someone
surprised him so. "For *your* peace of mind?"

"What you want seems terribly foolish and a waste
of many of your gifts. And yet, somehow, I can see
why you want to be there even when you are so needed
here. I don't know which is right, so how can I do anything but leave it to God to decide? I cannot go on having no peace about it. And, quite frankly, neither can
you. When you are angry and frustrated your leg is
only worse."

"Your prayers are yours to make, by all means."

Her face reddened further, and he felt heat prickle
his own palms. "I meant here. Now. With you."

John's discomfort with the notion was nearly physical, and yet he found himself completely unable to
launch any refusal. She was genuinely trying to help,

and it clearly meant a great deal to her. "He's bound to know I don't...subscribe. Why assist someone who shows Him no regard?"

"Because we are all His children, and He delights in granting our requests—if they are for our good, of course."

Now it made sense to him. "So if you pray for my success and I achieve it, then you can be assured God considers it for my own good? And should I fail tomorrow's test, the same assurance holds?"

"That is rather putting it oddly, but I suppose, yes."

"Doesn't speak much for my role in the achievement, does it?" He shifted in his seat. "I suppose I should feel rather insignificant now that you put it that way."

She smiled. "I don't think you are capable of feeling insignificant."

He coughed, rattled beyond words. This was going to be awkward. He could already feel a sweat breaking out above his collar. The photographic crew had left, and they were essentially alone, but they were still in a *hallway*. In the middle of a *building*. Ought such things happen rather in churches, in private or on ancient mountaintops? Here seemed so—ordinary. Yet try as he might, he could not find it in his heart to deny Leanne this request. "I'm not at all sure how one goes about such things." He sighed, trying not to sound put out. "Closing of the eyes and folding of hands, isn't it?"

A warm amusement replaced the flush on her features. "Nothing is required of you. You may close your eyes if you like—I always do—but you need not pray with me, only allow me to pray for you." A sparkle lit her eyes. "It won't hurt. I suspect you won't even feel a thing."

I doubt that, John thought, although he didn't know

what on earth he'd do if he *did* feel something other than the acute uneasiness he currently suffered. God did not simply show up on army benches at the request of insistent young ladies. John realized he did not especially want God showing up in any of the everyday parts of his life, did not welcome the idea of the Almighty following close behind his ordinary undertakings, even at Leanne's insistence. He watched her fold her hands, fighting the urge to take a deep breath as she closed her eyes. He'd dived off high cliffs into unknown waters with less trepidation.

"Holy Father," she began in a tender voice, "I come to You on behalf of my friend John and his desire to serve." John shut his eyes, finding the moment too intimate to keep them open. "Cast Your hand over all that happens tomorrow. Let Your will be accomplished. If it is through the strength of his leg and the regard of General Barnes, then let it be so. Your will is to be trusted, so help us both to trust that tomorrow's outcome is as You wish. I thank You for the many who serve, for the comfort of all those who have lost—lost abilities, loved ones, dreams and health." John found her voice so peaceful and so full of grace, he had to open his eyes to confirm they had not amazingly transported to some sacred space. She was so changed when she prayed, and yet it came from her as easily as any common words she spoke. "All lives are precious to You, and I thank You for the price You paid for our lives in the sacrifice of Your Son, Jesus. May You guide my path and John's both tomorrow and always, in Jesus's name, amen."

After a second's hesitation, Leanne opened one eye to his startled gaze and whispered, "It is customary to say 'amen,' if you agree with the prayer."

John didn't know if he agreed with either the prayer itself or the woman who prayed it, but the "Amen" sounded full and satisfying as it slipped from his mouth.

Chapter Sixteen

John had grown to hate the gymnasium. Without Leanne, it loomed as a drab battlefield on which he waged his personal war against the leg that had become his enemy.

"Gallows. Ready to show me what you can do?" Dr. Madison walked over with the clipboard and pen John had come to loathe almost more than his leg. The doctor was sly, always adjusting the paper so that John could not read whatever notes were being taken. To make matters worse, Madison had a habit of becoming disturbingly cheerful when a benchmark approached. The doctor's upbeat manner made John feel like a child about to take a school test. Some days he half expected to walk out of a session with a letter grade marked on his forehead. Today was the ultimate "pass" or "fail."

The exam consisted of several exercises to show his flexibility, two tests of strength and the dastardly test of stamina. "How far, how fast" haunted him every lap of this place, especially when Leanne was not by his side. And she was not by his side today—by his choice, not hers. The distraction of her presence was a risk he could not take. Today was John against pain, pure and simple. John would prevail, pure and simple.

"Weights first, shall we?" Dr. Madison's smile broadcast confidence as they walked over to the groupings of free weights, pulleys and dumbbells that occupied the north corner of the room. Some considerate soul had placed these benches next to the windows, so that soldiers had a view of a lovely patch of green as they endured therapy. "You worked eighty pounds easily on your left leg last week. If you can get to forty-five degrees with sixty pounds on your right leg, I think you'll have shown grand progress."

It was the angle that always posed the problem. Any brute could hoist a pile of iron. It was bending like a pretzel while one did it that always eluded him. "And we all know I'm nothing if not grand." John smiled as he removed his tan day uniform shirt and hung it on the series of pegs by the wall. He settled himself on the bench, breathing deeply while Nelson loaded the weights.

Breathe in. Brace. Extend. Bend. The healthy left leg complied with ease. Nelson removed half the weights so that John's right leg hoisted forty pounds. Some pain, but nothing to faze the likes of him. Fifty pounds hurt enough to silence his chatter, but still he managed it with the appearance of ease. Fifty-five stung. Nelson loaded the final five-pound weight and John focused every ounce of his being on the muscles in his right leg. The last six inches of the extension were nasty, but he made it not once but twice. Nelson smiled.

"And the flex next, please." Dr. Madison merely raised one eyebrow in appreciation as he made some mark on his paper. John rolled over as if in the comfiest of beds. The flex was much easier.

Three more exercises met the requirements John knew Dr. Madison placed on his return orders. "Range of motion, your specialty," the doctor joked as they moved to a wall marked with a large collection of arcs and lines.

"Where are my cameras?" John casually wiped the sweat from his brow with a rough towel.

"Ever the comedian. To the right, if you will." John held the bar bolted to the wall and swung his left leg to the right. While it was hard to hold his full weight on his bad leg, the move wasn't that challenging. It's opposite—moving his right leg to the left—produced some pain. It was the next exercise—side steps with his body weight involved, precisely the move Leanne was attempting to improve with her waltzing scheme— that proved difficult. He closed his eyes, imagining his careful twirls around the room with Leanne, grafting her image into his memories of easy dances and care-free parties before the war. His leg cramped up a bit with the second try, but he was able to meet the black mark on the wall he knew to be his goal. How irritating to have one's future hanging on a smudge of paint two inches out of reach.

"Nurse Sample's ingenuity agrees with you," Dr. Madison remarked with amusement. "Two inches greater range. Perhaps we should enlist more violinists."

"I'd prefer if you enlisted better cooks," John said as he turned to stand with his back against the wall, bending to the far left as instructed. "I've lost weight in the time I've been here. How is it the army managed better rations in France than on its own…" He caught a sight out of the corner of his eye that stole the end of his thought. Through one corner of one window, perhaps where she thought he could not see her, John saw

Leanne. She was seated on a small bench by the corner of the yard outside the gymnasium—one of the many chairs set out for reconstruction patients to sit and take in the sun.

"Captain?" Dr. Madison pushed his clipboard into John's vision. "On its own what?"

"…soil," John finished, fishing the thought back up from the depths of his brain where the sight of Leanne had banished it. He'd asked Leanne not to attend today's examination, and yet there she was, sitting on the hill facing the gymnasium. "Soil," he repeated, fighting the urge to blink and shake his head as he performed the "touch your toes" movement he knew came next. "How is it the army can't cook on its own soil?"

"I expect it is the sheer number of mouths to feed now." It was true: Camp Jackson had swollen beyond capacity weeks ago, with men and facilities tucked into every conceivable corner. Dr. Madison peered down to see how close John's hands got to his boots. John pressed the extra two inches to brush the top of his laces, pretending the lightning bolt of pain currently shooting up his right leg wasn't really there. He returned to upright, half expecting to find Leanne gone, the image of her under the tree a figment of his imagination.

"Again, please." Dr. Madison's tone was dry, rather less impressed than John would have liked.

He started to say "Why?" but replaced it with "Certainly," making it sound as if reaching for his boots was the highlight of his dressing routine rather than one of the most painful parts of every morning. When he returned upright for the second time, he fixed his eyes on Leanne to block out his leg's complaint. Why would she come here when he'd asked her not to? The answer hit him when he recognized the particular fold of her hands. Why must he continually experience the sight and sound of Leanne Sample praying for him? That's what she was doing, he could tell. Hang her, she had to pick the one thing he'd find even more distracting than her presence! She had no way of knowing he'd catch sight of her, probably thought she was hidden, and if Dr. Madison had not asked him to bend to the left in this particular spot, he most likely would have missed her. Which begged the even more disturbing question of how "fate"—for it was much easier to consider it fate than Who he knew Leanne would credit for the coincidence—had lined up this glimpse at this particular moment. *She's praying for you. Right now. Your name is leaving her lips, flung toward the vault of Heaven to do something she doesn't even think is wise.*

"Gallows? Captain Gallows!"

John managed to wrench his attention back from Leanne's folded hands. "Pardon?"

"Are you finding your exam so dull as to daydream out the window?"

"It's so dreary without the pain," he lied, enjoying the disbelieving *"hrmph"* the remark drew from the doctor. "I'm all healed, thanks to you."

Dr. Madison gave him the look of weary toleration he gave all John's "I'm healed!" lies and pointed toward the track painted on the gymnasium floor. "You're much improved, I'll grant you that. Laps, please."

Laps, as they had always been, were the true test. John could gut through any measure of pain for the handful of seconds it took to produce a pose, but laps were his ultimate enemy. No matter what mental fortitude he possessed, he could not will his knee not to buckle. He could not persuade his tendons to unfreeze, could not fool his way through a final lap without the help of his cane. John could sway the muses of speech and appearance, but time and distance were two masters he could not best. He'd grown to hate the incessant tick of Dr. Madison's stopwatch and the battlefield of those cold green ovals with their merciless white borders.

"One mile, eighteen minutes?" John tried to make it sound as if he were selecting between steak or lobster entrees.

"Twenty will suffice."

In truth, John's best time at the mile had been twenty-three minutes, and they both knew it. In fact, they never talked as if any of this were ever half as painful and difficult as it truly was. That was the game they played. "Well, as I'll not be stalling for time with the lovely Nurse Sample on my arm, I expect that should pose no problem." With a wink and a salute, John set off.

She shouldn't be here. He'd told her not to come and she'd argued against it, until he'd told her she would prove too much of a distraction. Part of her told herself he was a soldier who needed to focus on the vital task at hand, but another, more rebellious part of her latched onto the look in his eyes when he'd asked her to stay "where that pretty face can't undermine the mission."

"I'm not blind." She'd sighed to Ida the evening before as they'd each sat on their beds after supper. She'd just related how she'd dared to pray over John's leg, and the dozen emotions of that encounter washed over her with new vigor. "I know my heart is beginning to wander toward him."

"He's mighty wander-able." Ida's West Virginia drawl languished over the words and she braided her hair into the thick plait she did every evening. "I can't blame you at all, but you'd best keep the eyes of your soul wide open, as my daddy would say."

"John has so many good qualities…" She'd told herself that over and over.

"But there are so many…considerations in his case."

"Considerably!" she joked. "He maneuvers people and situations to suit his own ends far too easily. He is a charmer in the best and worst sense of the word—a silver-tongued man if there ever was one." Leanne curled her toes up under her skirts and let her head fall back against the bedroom wall. "And he couldn't be further from any kind of faith. He's an unsuitable prospect on any number of levels."

"Were you picking a horse, I might agree. Matters of the heart don't come quite so clear-cut, I find. Even in horses, though, it's the yearling that makes the least sense on paper that just may well take the race by storm."

Leanne managed a chuckle. Ida often had the strangest way of looking at things, and yet they made their own kind of wise sense. "Are you calling Captain Gallows a long shot?"

"I'm just saying the finish line is a long ways off, and you'd best take this race one turn at a time." Ida tied her braid up in a silk ribbon—one of the few luxuries still within wartime reach. "You've put tomorrow in God's hands. How about you leave it there?"

Leanne had gone to sleep meaning to do just what Ida said, but couldn't now that the day was here. She'd made too many errors during her rounds this morning, to the point where the doctor had sent her home an hour early and told her to rest. Rest? How could she rest not being allowed to watch John's test? Unable to stay completely away, Leanne had hid herself on the hill where she could see just into the gymnasium but not in a spot where she'd see him in particular. From here she could watch over *where he was* without watching over him, and John would never catch sight of her.

She had brought her Bible, hoping to find comfort in the words, but found herself lost in fervent prayer instead. *I fear his leaving, Lord. I fear he means too much to me. I fear he'll never know You and that means we must never be together.* Thoughts and surges of concern washed up over her, disjointed as they were heartfelt. *Guard his leg from pain. Send strength to those wounded muscles. Send him calm, Lord. You know his fear won't serve him well today.* The prayer that barely formed itself into words, the one that covered all the others, was simply, *Do what's best for him. Save him from going if he ought to stay. Send him if he needs to go. He can't yet see what You want for him—spare his life until he sees You at work in it. Spare him. Spare me this storm I've tried so hard not let into my heart.*

Leanne hadn't even realized how much time had gone by—she'd been watching the lights in the tiny corner of the gymnasium she could see, foolishly thinking they'd shut off when John was finished. A tap on the bench back startled her, and she jumped in fright only to see the tip of John's cane resting on the seat beside her.

Chapter Seventeen

❧

"You'd make a poor spy."

John, on the other hand, would make a very good spy, for while his voice sounded tired, nothing of the day's outcome showed on his face. There was no hope of hiding what she was doing, and she found she didn't really want to keep her concern a secret. "How was the testing?"

He eased himself down beside her, slowly, the way he did when his leg pained him most. "I don't know," he said. "I really don't know. It could go either way, I suppose. I met some of the standards, came close enough in three more that Madison could sign the orders today— if he chose to."

"That's good, isn't it?" She noticed his fist was clenched around the arm of the bench.

"I would rather have left him no room to choose."

That was John, always needing the world to turn on his own terms. No wonder his brush with mortality had rattled him so. "How do you feel about the results?"

"You mean other than the wrenching pain and the frustration?" He attempted a smile—the false one he applied to make light of his pain—and tapped his cane against the boot of his good leg. "I think Madison will send me off."

He said it so easily, as if he'd been asked to take the hallway on the left instead of the right. The part of her that tried to trust God with today's outcome fell prey to a surge of panic. He might really go back. "You do?" She nearly gulped it.

"Mostly because I told him I'd make his life a living nightmare if he kept me. It isn't wise to cross a Gallows, you know." The momentary dark flash in his eyes showed John for the warrior he was. It was probably a very dangerous thing indeed to wake the ire of such a man. Just as quickly, the darkness receded and he raised an amused eyebrow. "And you know I asked you not to come here."

"You asked me not to attend your testing and I did not. And, well, I thought I'd placed myself where you couldn't see me."

John looked as pleased to hear this as she was embarrassed to admit she couldn't stay away. "Had Dr. Madison not asked me to bend to the left, I wouldn't have. As it was, I happened to look up at just the right moment to see where you were…and what you were doing."

He knew! Leanne felt as if she were glass, her emotions laid plain to his insistent eyes.

"Isn't God everywhere? Still you had to be here, watching over me in the gymnasium?" His eyes fairly glowed. It wasn't fair that he was so handsome at this moment when she felt so vulnerable.

She wouldn't answer his question. He wasn't really seeking an answer in any case. Leanne knew exactly what he was doing, peeling away her excuses for needing to be here, forcing her to admit what they both already knew. What they'd brushed up against the night of the ball.

John moved one hand to touch her arm. "I was angry at first. You're a terrible distraction, and I did miss one lift simply because you threw my concentration."

She looked down, but John ducked his head to catch her eyes and return her gaze to him. "Then during the laps, those horrid, endless laps when my leg was screaming and I needed to walk faster, I thought of you. Out here, doing…what I knew you were doing. And…"

She could see he was deciding how far to step out, what to believe about the test he'd just endured. Had God shown His face to John in those laps? Could it be that simple? "And what?"

"And I gritted my teeth and walked faster than I've ever walked before for longer than I thought possible. Because I felt…pulled along. By you. Or by…well, I don't know just yet, but I suspect you have several theories."

It was the closest thing to a consideration of faith she might ever get from him. A smile bubbled up from the part of her heart she'd tried so hard to ignore. "No, only one. I prayed exactly that. I prayed that God would pull you mightily toward the outcome He had planned, even if it wasn't what you or I wanted."

John stared at her, deeply, his eyes a mighty pull of their own. "What is it you or I want?"

"Captain Gallows, you've never drawn a single breath not knowing exactly what you wanted." She'd meant it as a snappy retort, a way to stave off the warmth in his steady gaze, but they were the wrong words. He'd turn them on her, most certainly.

He did. "You're right. I do know exactly what I

want." He reached for her hand. "If you didn't want it, you'd have been able to stay away from here."

What would be the point of denying it? It was so clear, so strong, resonating between them even now. She ought to pull her hand away, to resume her insistence that they couldn't be together. She couldn't draw the breath to do it. The heat of his hand on hers, the way his thumb followed the shape of her wrist dashed every sensible thought from her grasp. When he feathered one finger down the side of her cheek, Leanne felt as if she'd dissolved into thin air, mere breath and yearning. When he took her face in his hand and gazed at her as if the whole world were found in her eyes, everything else fell from existence. "You've undone me, Leanne. I don't know how, I don't know when, I don't even know what to do about it, except this."

His kiss was careful, reverent, unlike anything she'd expect from the dashing Captain Gallows. It wasn't Captain Gallows's kiss, she realized; it was John's kiss. A kiss filled with one young man's wonder, as though it were the first honest thing this hero had ever done. She'd read novels where men "claimed" their women with powerful kisses, but this wasn't anything like that. He'd surrendered to her in this kiss, surrendered to the pull between them neither of them seemed able to stop or control. He inhaled as though the scent of her could heal his pain, clung to her as though her touch flooded him with peace. It was as if the whole world shimmered, as if the war itself paused at the sudden gush of grace.

Every inch of John's body, every corner of his being burst out of some dull fog he'd not even realized was there. Leanne was the opposite of everything he sought in a woman and yet, that was just the point—he *hadn't* sought her. He hadn't set out to win her; rather, they'd been pulled steadily toward each other since that first day.

"Did you know," he said as he let his forehead fall against hers—a hopelessly romantic gesture he'd vowed never to do—"how easily I picked you out of the audience that day? Oh, I cast my eyes over the full crowd because that's what I've been trained to do, but it was as if all I could do was crave the sight of your wide eyes."

She made a little gasp that wrapped itself around his heart. "Then it wasn't just me? You really *were* staring right at me? I thought it just a trick of presentation, the acclaimed Gallows oratory technique."

It felt important—poetic, even—that their eyes had so locked in a crowd of hundreds of people. It lit a glow in his chest to know his gaze had affected her so strongly. "So you felt it, as well?"

She cast her eyes up to the tree limbs that shaded the bench. "Oh, I must admit it made you terribly intimidating. Had I not seen you bend over in the stage wings, I might never have thought you a mere mortal."

John liked to think no one caught him with his guard down. Not especially at an event like that. "You saw me in the wings?"

"Don't be upset. It was my first glimpse of the person you really were. I think that's when I first began to…"

She couldn't even bring herself to finish that sentence. Were her feelings that strong? Or was she that much of an innocent? "I can't even tell you when or how I first 'began to.' Like I said, you snuck up on me." He kissed her forehead, finding the flutter of her lashes against his chin a most exquisite sensation. He moved to kiss her mouth again, wanting to cover her in a dozen tender touches.

Leanne pulled away slightly. "You are too persuasive, John."

He moved back in, grinning with a pure happiness he hadn't expected. "It is one of my many gifts."

She pulled farther away. "No, truly, John, I must ask you not to take advantage of how I feel. I'm... I'm not used to such strong attentions. In fact, I should never have let you kiss me."

She had an analytical look in her eyes, as if solving a thorny problem. Certainly not like any woman he'd just kissed so soundly ought to look. "I'm rather glad you did. I'd like to think you were glad I did, as well."

"That's just it. I can't think clearly with you so close, looking at me like that."

"It is a classic symptom, you know. I'm having a bit of trouble thinking myself."

She took a deep breath. "John, please. There are so many complications. How am I to deal with the truth that we ought not to be together? Not now. Not when... you're...leaving, perhaps."

How like Leanne to look straight at the thing he was trying to deny. "But it is not also truth that I'm here, now, and feel what you feel?"

"Life is more than 'here, now,' John, even in wartime. And while it is true that I...feel what you feel, there's another truth. You don't share my faith, and even what I feel can't change what I believe about the match of hearts and souls. How can it be right to consider a future when we don't share the God who holds that future?"

He placed his hand over hers, and while she tried to pull it away, he wouldn't let her. "I don't believe that has to come between us."

"I do."

Her voice wavered. She turned to look at him, and
he saw how he'd unraveled her resistance. The honorable part of him admired her all the more for clinging
to her convictions, while a darker part of him wanted
to pull them down one dishonorable kiss at a time. It
stung the conscience he wasn't sure he still had. Where
was the grace and mercy Leanne attributed to God in
a tangle like this?

"You feel something for me, and I for you. If God
creates us, then He surely creates what we feel. He must
have known this would happen. He must know what
you feel, what I felt when I kissed you."

"John, the choice is neither yours nor mine. I am
under orders, just as you are. I am no more free to ignore God's instructions simply because I wish differently than you are to ignore the general's."

"But you *do* wish differently. That must matter for
something."

"It makes little difference. Faith means I surrender
to God's will in my life, trusting He knows better than
my foolish heart."

Her sad smile was a torturous enticement. She was
velvet and porcelain and tenderness, and she was stealing his heart even now by refusing it. He couldn't recall
wanting a woman more ever in his life. "What if I don't
want to surrender you?"

She stood up, putting distance between them. "Please
don't press me beyond my strength, John. If you do care
for me, grant me that."

He hated the idea of her thinking of him like some
advancing foe, something God must protect her from,
something she must flee. Still, Leanne was right; he
never stopped pushing until he got what he wanted, and
now that he'd realized what—*who*—he wanted, he knew

his own nature. Dark as it was to admit, John knew himself perfectly capable of charming her beyond her resistance, unforgivable as it was. "I can't not be near you. You can do no better, today's already proven that."

Leanne covered her face in her hands. "Perhaps it is God's wise kindness, then, that you do leave."

She'd done it. She'd found the one way to cause him greater pain than any of his wounds.

Chapter Eighteen

"What on earth happened to you?"

Leanne had barely made it through the door of her bedroom before she sank to the bed and gave in to the tears. Everything was so mixed up inside, crying seemed like the only response she could manage.

Ida sat down beside her, putting an arm around Leanne's heaving shoulders. "John failed the exam?"

"No."

"He passed?"

"We don't know anything yet." Leanne let her head fall onto Ida's shoulder. She was so weary all of a sudden.

"Y'all do not look like someone who doesn't know anything. Y'all look like someone who knows too much. What is going on?"

"Oh, Ida, I do know too much. I've gone and lost my heart to John Gallows. It's awful. It's wonderful and terrible all at the same time." She took the handkerchief Ida produced from a pocket and sighed as more tears came. "He's the wrong kind of man and the timing couldn't be worse. Still, when he kissed me it felt like I'd fallen off the end of the earth. I can't think when he's around, and yet I can see some things so very clearly. He cannot be the one for me, I know that, but…"

"Hold on there, he kissed you?"

Leanne felt her cheeks burn at the memory of the way John had touched her face, the things she saw in those eyes before his tender kiss. "He did." New tears stole down her cheeks. "Why did it have to be so wonderful, Ida? Why couldn't it have been awful and easy to refuse instead of leaving me with the horrid way I feel right now?"

Ida's smile was nearer a smirk. "You've not been in love before, have you?"

"No." Leanne dabbed at her nose. "But I am not in love."

Ida chuckled. "I don't have loads of experience in this department, but once is enough to let you know it feels like…well, just like you're feeling now. And he kissed you, did he?"

"Wonderfully." Leanne fell back against the coverlet. "It made it so much worse."

"So we can assume the captain feels the same way about you?" Ida leaned back on one elbow.

"He said as much, and more. He said the dearest things to me, I thought my heart would pound right out of my chest." Leanne rolled to her side to face Ida. "I almost couldn't do it. I nearly couldn't tell him not to kiss me again. My thoughts were so tumbled, when he said the timing and our faith didn't need to come between us, an enormous part of me wanted to believe him. It still does." She covered her eyes with her hands, frustration mixed with her still-pounding pulse. "I know better than this, Ida. I know he's most likely leaving—I've known that from the first. And I know what I believe. Why must he test it so?"

Ida pulled her feet up to hug her knees. "Let me see. Two people who don't belong together but can't keep their hearts from locking on to each other. I ought to sketch you right now—you could illustrate two hundred novels. This story is as old as time."

Leanne moaned. Sometimes Ida's humor was a blessed light. Other times her wit was too sharp not to sting.

"I'm not making light of you how feel. A breaking heart is the worst pain there is. My mama told me love is the most awful wonderfulness a person can feel. Loving the wrong man—especially one that loves you back—is just about the most pain a soul can bear. But it begs the question—are you sure he's the wrong man?"

Leanne did not care to tangle the matter further. "What do you mean? Look at where we are, who he is. How could he not be the wrong man?"

"Well, what if he is the right man at the wrong time?"

"Ida, I don't…"

Ida put up a silencing hand. "I'm not saying you should deny your convictions—I don't think the Good Lord ever wants one of His daughters to do that for a man—but here and now can't be the whole story, can it?"

"That's just it. We've no future together, not unless lots of things change. It already hurts just to be near him. I cannot endure more of it on such a thin hope. I've asked God over and over to show Himself to John, to do something about this whole muddle. I prayed so hard over his test and how he strives beyond what's wise, but I don't see anything coming of it at all." She let out an enormous breath, feeling as if she could sleep a week and not lose this weariness pressing down on her. "In fact, it's all only gotten worse." Leanne looked up at Ida.

"I want to wish he'd never kissed me. I *ought* to wish he'd never kissed me, but..." She knew no matter how much it hurt, she'd never regret John's kiss. It's what made it so "awfully wonderful" as Ida said.

"That, my dear friend, is a most hopeless cause. When will you know if he is shipping out?"

"Tomorrow, I suppose." Leanne pulled herself upright. "I can't imagine he'll let Dr. Madison and the general rest until they give him their decision."

"Well, then, our task is to get you through tomorrow. We'll deal with the outcome when we know what it is."

Leanne managed a weak smile. "Remind me—over and over—that God already knows what it is, will you?"

"Absolutely." Ida pulled her into a hug. "Over and over."

One of the great truths of military life was that morning came quickly—whether it was welcome or feared. John dressed for his 0900 meeting with General Barnes with a weary anxiety. There had been nothing to do after Leanne's declaration except walk away. He almost turned when he heard a small sound from her—a cry?—but did not trust himself to behave with any restraint if he went back to her at that moment. Still, he felt certain she'd slept no more last night than he had. Had his leg not been so sore, he might have gotten up in the middle of the night and walked over to the Red Cross House just to see if there was a light on in her window. More like some love-struck schoolboy than the decorated war hero who was about to win his return to the front.

John deliberately left his cane in the outer room and walked into the general's office unaided. It hurt, but he absolutely refused to submit to any limp whatsoever. His dramatic entrance was lost, for Dr. Madison and General Barnes were standing over a large piece of paper on the general's desk. John executed the customary salutes, after which Barnes held up the paper. It was a sample cover of *Era* magazine with John and Leanne in their first knitting photographs. "Outstanding work, Captain. You hit the newsstands in two weeks."

A month ago, John would have been thrilled to grace the cover of *Era,* even for something as ridiculous as the Red Cross knitting campaign.

This morning as he looked at the photograph, he didn't see his impending glory. All he could see were Leanne's and his eyes. Hadn't the photographer made some remark about "photographic chemistry"? Now with the clarity of hindsight, John recognized it as the first sparks of the flame that had been lit yesterday afternoon. A flame that singed far more than it warmed this morning. "Well, sir, it's mission accomplished, then." He'd have preferred to relish the victory more.

"The director of the Red Cross called me this morning. They're over the moon with the article, calling you their new 'Homefront Hero.'"

"Leave it to Captain Gallows to be declared a hero on two continents in as many months," said Dr. Madison.

"That's our Gallows." The general nodded, signaling John and the doctor to sit down. "No challenge too great, no job too hard."

"I did have a bit of help, sir. Had Nurse Sample been unable to teach a lug like me, I doubt the Red Cross would be so pleased."

"Nonsense. We know who we've got in you. You've got a star quality we need at the moment. Our battles at home are as big as the ones over there." John didn't like what Barnes was implying. It wasn't in his plans to be too valuable over here—it's why he'd resisted both the speeches and the photographs at first. He'd worked hard to turn both into leverage he could use to get back to France.

John pulled himself upright in his chair. "With all respect, sir, it's time for me to get back over to those battles. In two weeks I'll have finished all I can do for you here. I have big plans."

"The captain has too many big plans in my opinion," Dr. Madison interjected. "He works himself too hard. Encourage that, and he'll not heal that leg as he should."

"You have your results from yesterday?"

Madison handed Barnes a file, but the doctor's face was a frustrating blank. John felt his leg turn to knots as the rest of his body tensed with anxiety. He'd wanted to ace the exam, to give Madison no choice but to pass him through; the tiny window of doubt he'd left with those last two exercises was driving him mad. Leanne's prayers that God would grant the wisest outcome despite John's wishes was driving him madder still.

General Barnes opened the file and donned his glasses. John looked at Dr. Madison, but the man would not return his stare. Was that good or bad? Why were these men drawing this out so when they knew all that was hanging on their decision for him? *Please,* the silent groan echoed up from somewhere so deep inside John he was startled to think it might actually have been a prayer. Out of nowhere, he remembered the story Leanne told him on one of their insufferable laps about a Roman captain who asked Christ to heal his daughter. Out of respect for the Almighty's authority, the soldier didn't require a visit, just a command. *Fine then, I respect Your authority. Please, Sir, if You're all Leanne says, You know how much I need this.*

"A remarkably fast recovery," Barnes said without looking up.

"An alarmingly fast recovery," added Madison, and John glowered at him.

The general removed his glasses. "Madison here says that you do, in fact, meet the physical qualifications for being returned to active service. However, he's recommending against it."

"It's simply not wise to rush this." Dr. Madison pinched the bridge of his nose.

"Gallows, you've been working hard. I reward hard work when I see it. Even when someone else doesn't see it my way." Barnes smiled. "I'm overriding the doctor's recommendation and sending you back."

John shot up out of his chair, all pain forgotten. "Thank you, sir. Thank you!"

Barnes motioned him back down. "Don't thank me until you've heard it all. We still need your particular gifts on the home front. The truth is you're not done here yet."

How very like the army to offer something with one hand and snatch it back with the other. "Meaning?"

"John, I've got places you need to be." He pulled a slip of paper out of his coat pocket and handed it to John. "Those higher up like what you've done here. I've been asked to ship you to Chicago in a week. They heard our recruitment rate has doubled since your presentation and they need you to do what you did here."

"Chicago, sir?" Fully aware of the general's rank, John was still ready to argue. *"Chicago?"*

"Only for a week of speeches at Fort Sheridan. Oh, you'll thank me for this—it's the president's baby, that base, all big and fancy and they plan to give you quite the send-off before you ship out to air corps."

"Air corps? Pilot training?"

Barnes smile widened. "You didn't think we'd keep you on the ground after all that airborne heroism, did you?"

Pilot training. It was better than he'd hoped. He'd have a chance at the real future on a ship of speed. On battle aircraft. "Yes, sir, thank you, sir. You'll absolutely not regret this." He dared a look at Dr. Madison. "*Either* of you."

"I regret it already." Dr. Madison sighed.

John shook the general's hand. Pointing at the magazine cover mock-up, he said, "May I, sir?"

"By all means. I'll make sure a dozen of them go to your family when they hit the stands."

"Thank you again." John shook Madison's hand for good measure, even though the doctor looked sourly outranked. He saluted, snapping his heels together for emphasis even though it shot flames up his leg, and turned to go.

"Your cane, Gallows," the general called, the hint of a laugh in his voice showing how pleased he knew he'd just made John.

John turned with a smile wider than the commander's. "Left it outside, sir. Not needed."

Madison frowned even further, Barnes grinned and John ignored the fire in his leg as he nearly sauntered from the room.

Chapter Nineteen

John stood outside the general's office, smelling victory in the fall air. The camp hummed with activity; new soldiers seemed to be pouring in daily. The overcrowding had bothered him before—every man was well aware things had gone far beyond capacity and even the officers were feeling crammed in like sardines—but not today. Today the bustle was music. He was going back. John spun his cane like Charlie Chaplin, whistling. There was far too much energy shooting through his body to be bothered with anything mortal like pain. They would send him back. His final chapter in the Great War would not be in the role of poster boy, but of soldier. He was leaving.

He was leaving Leanne.

It was for the best, he saw that. They were too different to share a lifetime, and war split even the truest of matches. He looked at the *Era* cover image Barnes had given him. Even in the stark black-and-white, her eyes pulled him in. Was it just his imagination, or was that spark already present between them back when this was taken? Had his annoyed amusement been something more all along? Did it matter now?

She could not hear about his leaving from anyone other than him. He knew that, but dreaded the conversation. They'd need to be together at least once more in order to finish the photographic sessions. He ran his hand over the paper and wondered what would show in their eyes on that final image. Would fate allow him a farewell kiss? Would Leanne? John thought of the single sock, nearly finished yet never to see a mate, and thought it would make a fitting parting gift. There would be nothing gained by waiting to deliver the news. It'd be best to tackle the task now, while he was still feeling the thrill of achievement.

The house matron no longer asked his name, merely gave him a pleasant-but-supervisory smile as she went up to Leanne's hallway on the second floor. The creak of the stairs cast his mind back to the dance, when she'd come down those same stairs, an absolute vision in rustling rose satin. That was the first time he'd wanted to kiss her—but that time was more about a man and a pretty girl than the far deeper stirrings of the previous day. Yesterday had told him he could love Leanne Sample, perhaps already did, but could not have her. John nearly laughed at his sorry lot. He knew her weaknesses, knew how to overthrow them, but was bowing to her request that he stand down. Nobility proved dismal company.

She knew the minute she saw him. He'd spent the past few minutes searching for the kindest words, only to realize they weren't needed.

"Captain." In a single, sad word, Leanne robbed his victory of satisfaction.

He took a careful step toward her, noticing the way her hand tightened on the banister as he approached. How her hands fascinated him. He'd see them for years when he closed his eyes at night—those hands, and the color of her eyes. "I'm not leaving for two weeks, but I am leaving." He did not want to have this conversation in a Red Cross House parlor. "Walk with me, please?"

Her grip tightened. "What more is there to say?"

"A great deal." He wasn't sure he could ever make her fully understand why he was going, but it was better to try than to spend this remaining time in such tension. "Please, Leanne, I beg of you." He'd never used that phrase with anyone, ever.

"I'll get my wrap." He hated the thin, fragile tone of her voice, hated knowing it was he who hurt her so. Leanne turned to go back up the stairs, only to meet Ida bringing a wrap down to her. Ida shot John a "don't you hurt her more" look and handed Leanne a handkerchief, as well.

They walked in silence. John led them purposely to the bench where she'd prayed over his leg. It felt a kindness to remind her that she'd prayed over the outcome of this test, prayed that God would allow the result best for all, not just the desire of either of their hearts. This was best for all concerned.

"I'll regret leaving you," he began, knowing it was a poor start. "Can you understand why I must go back? Why I can't leave it at dangling over the ocean? Only a fool with a piece of ribbon considers that bravery, not I."

"Is that how you see your honor?" Her words were sharp for the first time. He'd finally caused her enough pain to overpower her infinite grace.

"Yes," he replied. He never spoke of this to anyone, but he would not leave her without the truth. "I can paint the most valiant picture of my daring escapade when it's called for, you already know that version. It's nearly all fiction, Leanne. Yes, I saved lives, but do you know what that stunt up in the dirigible truly was? Pure fear of dying. Not bravery, nor honor, just fear. I didn't climb out onto those stay wires to save the crew or the mission, I went out because it was the only thing I could think of to do to keep from dying."

"You sought to keep everyone from dying."

"No, that's only how it looked. I gave no thought to anyone else on that ship, only to my own skin. There was no heroism in it, no nobility. And as for daring? Well, let us just say you'd be surprised at the lengths a man will go to stay alive." He looked out over the lawn, not wanting to see her reaction, feeling sharp and raw as if he'd just ripped the bloody bandage off a wound. "And you'd be surprised the lengths other men will go to make it look like something it never was, just for the sake of gaining a poster boy to acclaim."

Her silence drew his eyes back to her despite his own resistance. It was unfair, what her face could do to him. Even hurt and angry, the morning sun set sparkles in her eyes and spun a halo of light through her hair. She seemed as weary as he, yet the stillness made her seem ethereal.

"You lie even to yourself, John." Her sigh was so delicate, so full of regret that he felt her emotion ripple down his own spine. "God spared your life and you tell yourself you must throw it away in order to deserve what He's granted? He places you here and you run back to harm? Why must you thrash your life about like a battle-sword?"

She said every question except one, so he said it for her. "Why must I leave you?"

Leanne did not reply.

"Leanne, I've always had to leave you. We are at war. It has only been a matter of 'when,' never of 'if.'

It's a wonder we met at all. Consider that God granted us the gift of some time together. Not much time, but some. We should make the most of it. I don't want to spend my final days here keeping clear of you when I would much rather spend them *with* you."

"I cannot stand pain as well as you can."

She couldn't have made her decision more clear. He'd promised to be a gentleman—he'd abide by her wishes. John stood, gathered his cane and pulled the magazine cover from his pocket. "I hope it is not too painful to have this." He handed it to her. "It's the eyes I like most. We'll do fabulously. General Barnes tells me the Red Cross is thrilled."

Leanne took it, running a delicate finger over the "Knit Your Bit" slogan that splashed across the top of the image in large red letters. She managed a shadow of a smile as she looked up at him.

"I'm not sorry for any of it, Leanne. Not one bit of it. You're…" He didn't even know what he wanted to say to her. There wasn't a word for what she was to him, so he chose the closest one he could find. "You're a gift."

The final photo session was to show John stitching up the toe of the sock. John mastered the grafting stitch with ease, even though Leanne often found it the hardest skill to teach. She'd chosen to do this final step without rehearsal, not because it didn't need preparation, but because she couldn't endure any more time alone with John. He'd made it easy for her, sending word he was too busy with Chicago preparations to do anything but manage the photograph.

Things were indeed chaotic at the camp—soldiers were coming in at twice the rate they had been over the summer and an outbreak of a common flulike soldier ailment called "the grip" had taxed all the nursing shifts. Still, Leanne saw easily through John's ruse. He was avoiding her, plain and simple, and she was glad for it.

All of her prayers for peace and contentment dissolved at the sight of him in full uniform again. She'd thought it impossible for him to grow any more handsome in her eyes, and yet achievement of his goal lent him an even more commanding presence. Even the sock he displayed made things worse. The cuff spoke of their first lessons, their verbal sparring and his oversize persona. The ribbing of how they'd grown to know each other, the gusset of the waltzes that had opened her heart to him and now the toe would speak of the end. Complete and yet incomplete, for a single sock is insufficient unto itself.

"It's a pity there'll be no pair," he said as they sat down in front of the lights. Had he seen the same symbolism in what they'd done together?

"You know the skills now. I can send you with the yarn and needles to finish the job." She'd tried to make it sound like the banter of their earlier lessons, but it fell hopelessly short.

"It isn't to be," he'd replied. She couldn't understand how his eyes could hold such regret and satisfaction in the same gaze. Perhaps it was by God's design of male and female, how men could go to war and how women could wait at home. But there was no waiting here, just as there was no second sock.

"Come on, you two, you've no energy today," the photographer complained. "I need to see victory in those eyes, Captain Gallows. Show me victory!"

After a handful of exposures, the photographer came out from behind the camera. "Thank you for your tireless service," he said in poorly hidden frustration, looking directly at Leanne. "We'll only need the captain for these final shots." John balked, but Leanne was glad to stop trying to be something she wasn't under those hot lights. There was no hope of recapturing the spark of that first photograph. Not here, not today.

Dismissed as she was, Leanne still couldn't bring herself to leave the session. She watched from the back of the room as they shot the last exposures of John. His eyes found hers between shots, kept looking at her even though she could not always meet his gaze. Then the photographer would call for him to pose, and somehow John could instantly transform, could pull the charismatic presence up from some well she didn't possess. He was every inch the hero, tall and dashing. Every boy would want to be him.

"Should bring a pretty penny at the auction, Captain," the photographer's assistant admired when the final flash had gone off. "Carolina's most famous sock."

She'd forgotten about that. Somewhere in the letting go, she'd convinced herself he'd give the sock to her. That when all this was over, she'd have that one memento, the fitting but painful symbol of their time together.

"Not much else a single sadly knit sock can do, is there?" John replied. "It had better fetch a fortune—I doubt it's good for anything else."

It had better fetch a fortune indeed. That single sock had cost Leanne her heart.

Chapter Twenty

❧

"**B**ut you told me to do that other stitch here." The soldier from Atlanta had every right to look annoyed. Leanne had given him completely wrong instructions. She'd been useless in today's knitting class. She'd been useless in most of her duties, her mind dangerously preoccupied with the one student she no longer taught.

"I'm sorry, soldier, you're absolutely right—the pattern does say to knit that row." No amount of prayer had banished John from her mind, no Psalm had replaced the loss with contentment or trust that God knew what He was doing. Her mind knew what was right but her heart refused to comply—and the tug between them had overthrown her concentration. Leanne looked around the classroom to realize she was missing a student. "Where is Private Carson?"

"I was wondering the same thing," Ida said. Whether Ida had come to the soldiers' class for moral support or for the view, Leanne was glad to have her. "He was going to turn his heel today, wasn't he? I'm surprised he isn't here."

Just the thought of turning a heel brought back John's delightful admiration of the process. Why must everything remind her of him? She knew he most likely stayed away from the base hospital now, but Leanne found herself looking for him around every corner anyway. Was she searching for him, or watching out to make sure she didn't see him? She could not decide.

"Maybe he's got the grip," another soldier offered. "Poor fella, if he does."

"I do hope that's not the case. I'll check up on Private Carson this afternoon."

After class Leanne pointed herself in the direction of the barracks housing recuperating soldiers. Everyone at the base seemed to know the location of every soldier, so it shouldn't be too hard to find Private Carson and arrange for a makeup class if he chose. He was still so physically weak in many respects, and the grip was a nasty business even for the healthiest of soldiers. *Don't let that be what kept him from class, Father,* she prayed as she walked.

"A nurse!" One soldier standing near the barracks saluted with a wry smile. "They're sending you *to* us now? I hadn't realized it got so bad."

"I beg your pardon?"

"Those two barracks got dozens of men down with the grip. If you ain't here to help, you'd best keep your distance."

"Do you know if Stanley Carson's come down with it?"

The soldier took off his cap and gave her the strangest look. "Stanley Carson from Georgia? The one missing a leg?"

"Why yes, that's him. I'm worried that he didn't show up for a class I teach." The man's expression grew alarmingly grim. "Has something happened to him?"

"You teach that sock class, don't you? I think Stan

liked that. He talked about it a lot. When he talked, which wasn't much." The man offered his hand. "Roberts. Pleased to meet you, ma'am." He looked anything but pleased. As a matter of fact, he looked as if he'd have rather been anywhere but talking to her at the moment.

"Can you tell me where to find Private Carson? I've a training session in an hour and just wanted to check up on him."

Roberts motioned to a bench a few feet away. "Why don't you sit for a minute, Miss…"

Leanne reluctantly took a seat. "Sample. Leanne Sample." Roberts wrung his cap in his hands. "Mr. Roberts, what is it?"

Roberts sat on the edge of the bench. "I sure am sorry to be the one to tell you this, but he…well, they found him yesterday afternoon. He's gone, ma'am. Passed."

He'd never looked well, always so gray and sad. Still, the shock of it was one more blow to her frail composure. "I'm so sorry to hear that. I hadn't realized his injuries still posed such a threat."

Roberts gulped audibly. "Stan didn't die of his wounds, Miss Sample. You know how sad he was. Carson…well, ma'am…he done ended things on his own, if you understand my meaning. I really am sorry you had to hear it from me, but seeing as you seemed to know him and all, I thought you ought to know."

Leanne's throat went dry. "Private Carson…took his own life?" It seemed too horrible to think. She'd thought her class a bit of hope for him, had been so proud of the tiny spark she could occasionally light in his eyes. To think it hadn't been enough, to think she'd been so busy with John, never taken the time to talk to the man about her faith, turned her throat from dry to burning with tears. She hadn't done enough.

"It happens. Sadder than anything it is, but Carson, well, he never could seem to find his place around here. He was proud of that sock, though. You ought to know that. The only joke he ever made was about how he'd only need one sock at a time."

One sock. Complete yet incomplete. And here Leanne thought her heart couldn't break further.

Chapter Twenty-One

Something was wrong at the general's office.

John was used to the chaos behind the calm—he'd been involved in enough military promotional junkets to know that the appearance of control required frantic backstage maneuvers—but this was something altogether different. It had been brewing for days, now that he thought about it. Clerks buzzing about offices with frowns, higher-ups huddled in secretive meetings and a general undercurrent of alarm. Either the war had taken a turn no one wanted to publicize, or something else had reared its ugly head.

"Captain Gallows, you'll need to wait. I'm afraid the general is behind schedule." The clerk at the reception desk looked as if he'd been up all night. John felt the hairs on the back of his neck stand up. Barnes watched the clock with an obsessive punctuality—if he was behind schedule, something was most definitely amiss.

Feeling his leg respond to his body's tension, John chose a chair that offered him views into several offices. A group of officers, sleeves rolled up and ties loosened, bent over a table of documents. All three of the office's telegraph machines clacked without interruption, each telegram quickly scanned, ripped off the machine and rushed off to other offices. Whatever it was, it went well beyond Camp Jackson.

John caught the words *hundreds* and *Devens* as a pair of men in doctor's coats came out of the general's office. They halted conversation immediately upon exit. A minute later the door opened again, a weary General Barnes leaning out. "Taylor, get me a meeting with the mayor and the university president before three." He wiped his hands down his face. "And find more coffee and some sandwiches."

"Yes, sir."

Behind the general, John saw a handful of nervous men pacing in front of a United States map covered in lines, pins and numbers. This was no overseas crisis. Whatever was happening had pins placed up and down the Eastern Seaboard, with more than a few heading into the Midwest. Were they mobilizing troops? Preparing for the possibility of an air strike? Most of the push was to send men overseas right now—it was why the camp was teeming with bodies, all funneling in from elsewhere to board ships to the front. Soon enough he'd be one of those walking up the gangplank of a transport ship to walk down onto French soil. If they were gearing up to go faster, that'd be all the same to John, maybe save him this detour to Chicago, as well.

"Gallows." Barnes pointed at John, nodding back toward his office. Without further invitation, the general turned and walked back in, leaving the door open for John to make his own way inside.

John felt like he'd stepped inside a beehive. In the outer office, there was at least an effort to appear calm. Not in here. A doctor pushed past John without so much as a word, barking orders to two clerks about bed partitions. John heard the word *quarantine* twice in as many seconds. "Sir?"

"Influenza's run mad down the coast. Ships are coming in on skeleton crews with heaps of bodies. Philadelphia's a mess, Boston's a disaster. I want you on the train to Chicago tonight, but you're not to go to Fort Sheridan. You'll be met in Chicago and taken to an office downtown. It's time to keep everyone calm and we'll need your silver tongue to help do that. The *Era* cover couldn't be hitting at a better time—you'll have enough celebrity from that to get the attention we need." He stuffed a pile of papers in John's hand. "These'll get you off camp and anywhere you need to go."

"I need papers to get off camp?"

"This isn't an ordinary influenza. We're about to lock down in quarantine, Gallows. At least until we can figure out what's going on. As far as the public is concerned, this is just a bad case of the grip, understood? Under control and nothing to worry about."

"And what the public doesn't know is…?"

"We just heard from Devens, sir." A clerk walked in without even looking up from the telegraph he was reading. "Four hundred dead and still climbing as of 0900 hours this morning." Barnes growled and the poor lad looked up. "Oh. Sorry, sir." He handed the paper to one of the men standing in front of the board, and the sets of numbers pinned up all over took on a grisly importance.

John knew Devens was an army camp outside of Boston—Dr. Madison had talked about his time there. Half of Camp Jackson's new soldiers had just poured in from Philadelphia. America's military was evidently at war with a new enemy. And if the general had just asked to meet with the mayor and the university president, this wouldn't stop with men in uniforms. John's gut turned to ice while his leg began to burn.

With the gravest expression John had ever seen on the man, Barnes pointed to an envelope marked "Gallows" and a handful of gauze masks. "Whatever it is, it's killing soldiers and it's on its way here, if it's not here already. So pack your bags and wear these. Wire me from Chicago. Dismissed."

Private Carson was dead. John was leaving. The wondrous new world awaiting her at Camp Jackson seemed nothing more than heartache upon heartache as Leanne made her way back home. She hadn't realized that she'd expected her knitting to save Carson, to draw him back from his personal darkness, but she found herself devastated that it had not. *I know a pair of needles cannot mend a soul,* she cried out to God as she walked, *but couldn't it have made this one bit of difference? I can't understand why You placed a burden in my heart for the poor man when it did no good at all.*

The lament seemed to apply to more than just poor Private Carson.

Leanne couldn't fathom going to some training class. She couldn't eat or sleep, she could not talk to John—although she yearned to—and it seemed unfair to cry on Ida's shoulder yet another time. Leanne did the one thing she always did when at the end of her rope: she knit. Grateful she'd brought her knitting bag to sit with Private Carson should he wish it, Leanne found a quiet spot in the sunshine and began stitching. Around and around, stitch after stitch, Leanne let the craft soothe her soul.

Her prayers could always find their way up out of the yarn when she knit in solitude, but peace eluded her today. Tired of her own complaints, Leanne tried to pray for the soldier who would receive the pair of socks she was working on, but it was no use. Her thoughts refused to focus. Instead of picturing some wet and tired soldier, her imagination only conjured up images of Carson alone and afraid, hopeless in the dark. Worse, her thoughts turned to John. She saw him clenching his teeth as he tried to run on his bad leg. Falling while scrambling over battlefields. John crawling in search of safety as gunfire pounded around him. John lying wounded on some foreign shore.

Leanne looked down at the sloppy stitches and sighed. Had it come to this, that she could not even knit? It seemed like every solace had been taken from her. She gathered her things and began walking toward home when she noticed a young man slumped on a nearby bench, bent over in a violent cough. She looked around for the man's companions but found no one. She hurried up to the poor lad and put a hand to his shoulder. He was shaking. Another grip case, to be sure. "You need help, soldier."

"No, I'll be all right. I was fine this morning…" A violent cough prevented further words.

The young man looked up, forcing Leanne to swallow a gasp. His color was dreadful. She hadn't hid her reaction well, and fear crept into his glassy eyes. "Well—" Leanne put on her calmest nursing voice "—you've obviously caught whatever they told me is going around the camp. We'd best get you back to the infirmary."

"I'm supposed to be on duty in fifteen minutes."

"I don't think that's going to happen. What's your name?" It was one of the first points of bedside manner; learn the patient's name and use it frequently.

"Harper. It hurts." He sounded painfully young, like a child moaning to his mama.

"I expect it does. You'll not make it in far that condition. The hospital's right around the corner, we'll head straight there. Can you stand, Mr. Harper?" He managed a tottering rise, hanging on to her for balance. She noticed small spots of red on the soldier's handkerchief. "Where are you from?"

"Boston. Shipped out—" another cough, this one worse than the last "—a week ago."

"The way boys are pouring in, I suppose it's unavoidable lots of you come down with something." She forced a conversational quality into her voice as they limped along, but inside she was wondering if he had the stamina to make even the short walk to the hospital.

Thankfully it wasn't long before more soldiers happened by and with their help, Leanne managed Harper through the hospital doors to discover the ordinary outbreak of grip on camp had turned into something far larger. Two dozen or so young men lay on beds in varying states of a similar illness. A nurse Leanne didn't recognize, looking like a white specter in her uniform and a surgical mask, thrust a mask at Leanne and her soldier companions. "Go wash," she barked as another nurse gathered a collapsing Harper from Leanne's grasp.

"What's happened?"

The nurse's eyes—the only real part of her face Leanne could see—darted anxiously. "Some sort of virus."

"Not the grip?"

"Does this look like the grip to you?"

Leanne hadn't seen enough of the malady to answer. Still, it was true: these boys looked far worse than those she'd seen earlier. There had been stories in the paper of "the Spanish sickness" hitting some of the forces in

Europe. It was powerful enough to slow the German offensive, so perhaps some soldiers had brought back this new strain. She'd been taught influenza was highly treatable. Even the worst cases required not much more than a quarantine for a handful of ships as they docked. Her nursing teachers had spoken of it as an expected outcome of global combat, something to be managed with a clinical calm. The sort of thing a wartime nurse must expect to encounter.

There was no clinical calm here.

"Why are you hesitating?" Artie Shippens, John's only bunkmate at Camp Jackson before three more officers had moved in last night, tossed down the cloth he'd been using to polish his boots. "You've been itching to get out of here since your arrival. Barnes just handed you a golden ticket out of town. You should be running to catch that train."

"They're not even shipping me to Sheridan anymore, which tells me Sheridan's in worse shape than whatever's starting here. No matter where I go, I'll end up in the thick of it, if I'm not already. Besides, my family is here. What if this thing, whatever it is, gets into Charleston?"

"You act as if a soldier's never come down with the grip before. This bursts through a camp for a few weeks and then everyone gets better. That's all this is."

John put down the stack of masks Barnes had given him. "I know what I heard, Artie. That is not all this is. They're panicking up there at the headquarters, even if no one will tell you that. Telegrams are coming in with death tolls. Not men ill, men *dead*." He eased himself onto his cot, his leg throbbing. "There's a huge outbreak in Philadelphia, and we docked a ship from there just three days ago."

"I played cards with them the other night. Took 'em to the cleaners, those boys from Philly. They said there had been a load of sick boats, but the grip don't kill nobody. Pack your bags and hit the road."

John chose not to argue. He ought to be doing just what Artie said, but somehow he couldn't get himself moving.

Artie stood over John. "Aw, no, don't tell me. Do *not* tell me you've got second thoughts about leaving that knitting nurse. Shoot your own career in the foot on behalf of a woman? She's not worth it. Not with all you've got to gain."

"It's not that." She'd told him to leave. Leaving was best for all concerned. It couldn't be that, he was just stunned by the fact that he'd been handed an escape from the disaster evidently about to strike the camp. John looked at Artie, calculating how many of his card victims from the other night had already fallen ill. For all John knew, Artie might already be infected, and himself from sleeping four feet from the man. The trio that had arrived last night had done their fair share of coughing, too.

Artie snapped the tin of polish shut and tucked it into his locker. "If you tell me it's because you need to finish that confounded Sock Brigade of yours, I'll have to consider shooting you." Artie had taken to calling John's Red Cross photo campaign "The Sock Brigade" the day John brought the yarn back to camp and hadn't let up yet. Artie would have a field day once the issue of *Era* found its way to newsstands.

"We finished the final photographs. I'm sure it's the only reason the general is able to ship me out so quickly.

When I'm gone, you'd best take those winnings and bid sky high for my sock at the Red Cross auction."

"Off to Chicago while they lock us down tight back here. There are twenty men if not fifty who'd line up to be in your shoes." Artie started to laugh, but finished it with a small cough.

John sat up. "You're all right? Feeling okay? You said you were playing cards with Philly boys."

"Fit as a fiddle. Honestly, John, this kind of panic doesn't suit you."

He was done trying to talk himself out of it. "I need to see Leanne before I go."

"Don't do it, John." Artie's eyes were serious. "You know it'll just make things worse."

John put his jacket on. It would only take him minutes to pack, anyhow. "I can't not say goodbye."

"You can, and you ought to. Chicago, John, put your mind on that big shiny city. Hey, maybe they'll snap you stitching with a movie starlet." Artie leaned against his locker, waved his polishing cloth like a lady's hankie. "Oh, Captain Gallows," he crooned in a high-pitched voice, "what fine, fine stitching you do." His poor imitation was cut short by another cough, causing John to freeze in the middle of his buttons.

"I'm fine, Gallows, stop it. Go make your mistakes with your knitting teacher and stop mothering me."

Chapter Twenty-Two

Leanne washed her hands again as she went off her shift for a lunch break and tried not to think about the hollow fear in Mr. Harper's eyes. She'd seen plenty of sick men in her short time here. Some of the expressions worn by men in the reconstruction gymnasium could chill her blood. Private Carson often looked worn to the bone. Still, there was something deathly in Harper's gaze that simply would not leave her.

"I sure am sorry to hear about Private Carson," Ida said. Every nurse on camp had been scheduled into double shifts as sick boys kept pouring into the hospital. "Seems an awful shame, even as sad as he was. I was certain he was turning a corner as surely as he turned his sock heel."

"It's heartbreaking, Ida. He was someone's son. Someone's brother, perhaps. No one should feel that alone, no matter what their injuries. God rest his tortured soul."

"No one will feel alone now. We're packed in like sardines, and now they're talking about quarantine?" They'd announced it to the hospital staff not twenty minutes ago. Ida rolled her shoulders with a weary yawn. "The whole base? It can't be that bad, can it? It's just influenza."

"The head of medical department was rushed over to the capitol building a few hours ago. Perhaps that 'Spanish Flu' they talked about in the papers is worse than our usual influenza."

"I heard they're starting to get cases over at the university. Someone said they'd be asking some of us who took classes there to go over and help if things got troublesome."

Leanne thought getting away from Camp Jackson and John Gallows might be the best thing for her right now. "I'd go. Would you?"

"We always made a great team. I'll tell the head nurse when I go back on shift." Ida sighed, following Leanne's gaze out the window in the direction of the officers' quarters. "I'm sure he's fine."

"How can I know? What if he's already one of those sick?"

"You just saw him yesterday."

"That doesn't mean anything. Mr. Harper said he was fine in the morning, and he could hardly walk by the time I found him. No one knows how these things get transmitted. John spends lots of his time in crowds, with strangers from everywhere."

Ida's hand came on her shoulder. "You're not helping yourself thinking like this. He'd have been brought in here if he was sick, you know that. John would find a way to get word to you if something else had happened."

Leanne turned away from the window. "He might not. I told him not to come find me before he left. I didn't think I could stand to be around him, but I find it's even worse not knowing if he's all right." Leanne held her forehead, willing away the headache she could feel coming on.

"When's the last time you had something to eat?" Ida asked.

"I can't remember. Breakfast, I think." It was already well past two.

"Well, there's half your troubles right there. We're supposed to be on a meal break, let's go get some food before they stop giving us breaks altogether."

"I do feel rather peaked from all this."

"Mama always said the world looks worse on an empty stomach." Ida held out her elbow to "escort" Leanne down to the dining hall.

She and Ida found a seat by the windows in the far end of the near-empty hall and shared a tuna fish sandwich, a peach and a pot of tea. The tuna didn't sit especially well in Leanne's stomach, but the tea felt wonderfully warm and comforting.

"A veritable high tea. Feel better?"

"You're a good friend to have in a tight spot, Ida."

Ida raised an eyebrow and hoisted her teacup. "Y'all remember that when that magazine cover comes out and you're famous."

The thought of being seen everywhere with John, now that they would never see each other again—or at least, not for a very long time—made Leanne put down her cup.

Ida sat back in the metal chair. "That will be hard, won't it? Having that picture all over the place, seeing his face paired right up with yours? I don't think anyone else will see it, but I sure see what went on between you in that photograph. Y'all only have eyes for each other."

Leanne rested her head in her hand, tired now that

she'd eaten. "I was supposed to look at him with admiration."

"Oh, you're admiring him, that's for certain. He's admiring you, too, but nothing in that look has anything to do with knitting." Leanne squeezed her eyes shut, feeling physically, emotionally and now even photographically vulnerable. "Relax, no one who doesn't know can see it. To everyone else it'll just be grand publicity."

Grand publicity felt like the last thing Leanne wanted. Her stomach gave a sour little flip, and she let her gaze wander over the scattered chairs and tables, wondering when John had eaten last and if he had any good friends in a tight spot.

"Leanne!"

It was funny how she thought she heard his voice. Then she did see John. He was striding across the dining hall, ducking and dodging chairs and tables at a pace far too brisk for his comfort. He never limped if it could be helped, and he was visibly hobbling in his rush. She pushed back her chair and went straight to him.

He had her by the shoulders before she could even say hello. "Are you all right?"

"Yes, of course I'm fine."

"We're locking down in quarantine. Within hours if not already."

"They just told us. Is it really that bad?"

John kept his hands on her. "I had to see if you were all right."

"*Told* you," Ida said with a wry smile. "How about I just head on back upstairs and leave you two to talk?"

"Someone said you were at barracks fifteen today." John pulled her down to sit at a table. "Why on earth did you go there?"

"I went over there to see if Private Carson was all

right. He didn't come to his knitting class. It's terrible, John. Stanley Carson is dead."

"Lots of men are dying. And not just here. Army and navy camps are reporting death tolls in the hundreds."

Rumors often exaggerated. "People don't die like that from influenza. And, John, Private Carson wasn't sick. He took his own life yesterday. I can't believe it. We were so sure he was gaining hope, so sure we'd managed to lift his spirits a bit."

"I'm sorry about Carson, but do you hear what I'm saying, Leanne? Men are dying from whatever this is, and quickly. If they haven't yet here, they will."

John fought down the surge of fear in his stomach that had continued to grow since his visit to Barnes's office. It was very likely he had been exposed. He'd wrestled with that, surprised that his primary reaction to this threat was one of regret. Not the regret of perhaps not making it back to the front—for that would have sent him on the next train to Chicago. No, his initial, gut-level response was that he regretted not fighting for Leanne. If he were to meet his end in one of those hospital beds, he did not want to leave things with Leanne the way he had. The only doubt in his coming here was that he might expose her somehow, but what kind of foolish thinking was that? She was a nurse in a hospital about to be locked down in quarantine. She was in more danger of exposure than he.

The moment he'd walked into that hospital cafeteria and seen her again, he knew. Not in a monumental, defiant kind of way, but the quiet certainty of truth: he would not be on that train tonight. He would not leave her to face this alone, nor did he want to face whatever was coming his way without her beside him. The last time God had dangled him above death his thoughts had been only for himself, and he was finding that truth very hard to live with. If God were to dangle him above death again, he would seize this second opportunity and be worthy of the medal he wore. He would not leave. Hang Barnes and his schemes; this captain was going to stand and fight.

John allowed himself the luxury of running a hand down her cheek, glowing at how her eyes fluttered as he did so. "You're not feeling ill—not at all?" She felt a bit warm to him.

"I'm upset and haven't eaten well, but not much more is wrong with me than that. John, please tell me what you know and why you're looking at me like that. Are you well? Surely you've been around some of the men who've fallen ill."

"Have they given you masks to wear?"

"Of course they have."

"Wear them. I managed to wring some facts out of one of the general's clerks, and what he said made my skin crawl. Leanne, influenza doesn't kill men off like this. Not by the hundreds as they say is happening. In bases up and down the seaboard. This is no ordinary virus, Leanne." He took her hand. "I heard one of the doctors use the word *epidemic*. I doubt they'll use that publicly, but I can tell you the word is being bandied about behind closed doors."

John stared into Leanne's eyes, struck by the sudden strong urge to kiss her, right there in the dining hall, no matter what she'd asked of him earlier. She could be lying in a bed fighting for breath before the sun set tomorrow, so could he for that matter, and here he was just holding her hand. She'd done something to him, something he both hated and craved at the same time, but something he needed to be near if the world was truly falling apart the way he believed it was. If they came after him in a few days to drag him to Chicago, he'd fight that battle then. For now he must do all he could to ensure Leanne's safety. He brought his hand up to her cheek again, pleased when she did not resist. "Do all you can to stay safe."

"And you, as well. I'll worry about you when you go. I'm going to pray for your safety every day."

"I'm not going."

"What?"

"Change of orders in all this chaos. I'm not going anywhere." He didn't like lying to her, but now wasn't the time to go into everything. "Don't ask me to stay away, Leanne. I can't. Not now."

The tender look in her eyes told him before her words consented. "I won't." He would have fought, worn her down until she consented for her own good, but was doubly pleased she'd agreed without persuasion.

He'd been defenseless against her prayers, now he found he could almost welcome them. "Would God laugh at my prayers for your safety?"

Now it was her hand that found his cheek, and the sensation was like a homecoming. "Never," she said softly. "He would welcome them with more joy than you imagine."

John placed his hand over hers, wanting to do so much more. Had they been anywhere but where they were, John was sure he would have dared to kiss her. Instead Ida's voice came up behind them to break the spell.

"We're to go over to the university. It's starting over there, and they're turning one of the dormitories into a makeshift hospital. There's a truck leaving in ten minutes."

"More sick?" Leanne asked. "Students?"

"As bad as here, if not worse."

It took John two seconds to decide. He was already packed, after all. "I'm coming with you." Leanne offered no argument, only tucked her hand into his elbow as they set out.

As the truck bearing them and a handful of others pulled up to the university dormitory, all conversation stopped. A dozen campus medical staff streamed frantically in and out of the building like white ants. Around them a more gruesome parade of fifty or so students—mostly men in various states of illness—streamed into the building from all directions. Coughing filled the fall air. One man to their left was being carried on a chair by two companions, a bloody handkerchief clutched to his mouth. Two white ambulances, their red crosses standing out like warning beacons, were backed up to the dormitory. Maintenance men, also in masks and looking as if they'd rather be anywhere else, hauled dormitory beds into the medical building at the direction of several more masked nurses. John felt Leanne's hand tighten against his arm, and for a split second the urge to pull her away gripped him. Fear's instinctual desire to flee, to take his train ticket and somehow parlay it into an escape for the both of them, wrapped around his throat like a noose.

Dear God, save us.

He meant every word of this first prayer, and prayed it wouldn't be his last.

Chapter Twenty-Three

Mere hours later Leanne slumped against the wall and wiped her forehead with one hand. It had become clear no one really knew what to do. They began by placing patients in neat rows separated by canvas screens to prevent transmission of the virus, but the number of patients exceeded the number of beds within two hours. Workers scrubbed down dormitory floors as fast as they could, but still could not keep up with the stream of new patients.

The sheer numbers of ill made Leanne's mind reel. The constant wave of moans, ebbing and flowing from rows upon rows of beds, was like a sea of misery. At first patients would be alarmed by the pain; influenza wasn't supposed to hurt like this. They'd panic, thrashing about or crying for relief no one knew how to bring. Then, as the illness wore them down, their panic would fade into the most miserable fatigue. Leanne had to lift more than one head for a patient as another nurse struggled to get drops of medicine down his throat. All within hours of her arrival on campus.

Sweat tainted the air, and the sharp scent of disinfectant often cut through the mixture of odors Leanne associated with any sickroom: blood, urine, vomit, sweat, all in volumes that gave the ward an air of disaster. It smelled like a battlefield. It *was* a battlefield, with bloody wounds born of no weapons the doctors had ever seen. It was the color that frightened most of all. Those sick would begin to take on a ghastly blue-gray tone, starting with a vague pallor at first and progressing to ghoulish blotches that spread as the disease progressed. No one knew stages or symptoms, new information would be passed from doctor to nurse as it arrived, but all of it felt futile in the face of the onslaught that kept coming.

They began laying patients on the floors between other patients, forcing Leanne and the other nurses to literally step over groaning men and women to move through the ward. At one point Leanne was darting back and forth between no less than eighteen people, struggling to stay abreast of the soiled sheets, cries of pain and doses of medicines that seemed to do no good. And the blood. The blood was worst of all, for it seemed to be everywhere, unstoppable, staining and spilling and casting its sign of catastrophe over anything left clean and white. Every hour less and less was left clean and white.

Near the end of her shift Leanne found a Charleston family friend, an agriculture student she'd known last year. She barely recognized Charles Holling as he moaned the most dreadful request she could imagine: Holling was begging to die. He was in the far corners of the first room, a horrid shadow of the handsome boy she'd known back home. His words sent a chill down Leanne's aching spine, and she sank to his bedside to wrap one purple-blotched and swollen hand in a cool cloth and hold it tight. It was a wonder she recognized him at all, for his blue color and sunken face made him look barely human.

"Charles, it's Leanne Sample." The man's glassy eyes found her in their roaming and she glimpsed the soul still fighting inside. "Do you remember me? Your brother took me to the St. Cecilia's Ball." She pulled down her mask for one second, allowing him to see her familiar face before replacing it as he gave way to another round of blood-spattering coughs. Holling dissolved into pitiful tears when from somewhere in his incoherence he finally recognized her. "Let me die," he moaned. "It hurts too much."

"No, no, you must recover. You must fight and live." She mopped his discolored forehead.

"I want to die," he demanded loudly, as angrily as his racked body would allow. His howl changed the atmosphere of the room as if he'd thrown a shroud over the lot of them, inviting death to hover and prevail.

Leanne did the only thing she could do in the face of such horror. "May I pray for you?" What else to do or say in the face of such suffering? What other comfort could she give? He gave a whimpering nod despite his hopeless eyes, and Leanne began to pray aloud. It only served to calm his cries to wordless moans, but she was grateful for even that small relief. She mopped his brow again, spooned a bit of water into his foul-smelling mouth and begged God for the worst to be over. *If he was among the first to fall, Lord, then let him be the first to recover. Heal his...*

"Nurse!" A young woman gasped as she lay curled and retching two cots over. Holling rolled to his side, lost again to the fog of his now-quieter moaning. Leanne forced her weary body to rise, grab the last two sets of clean sheets left in the room and tend to her next patient.

Mr. Holling got his wish. Leanne returned to him not twenty minutes later to find his moans had been stilled not by the blessed escape of sleep but the arrival of death. Her first day of classes Leanne had learned to take hold of a wrist to find a pulse. She felt hollow and frail as her fingers told her no pulse was there to find. The room swayed slightly around her as she took the stained sheet and pulled it over the young, lifeless face.

She knew his family. She knew his name. She wrote it in slow, careful letters onto the tag she affixed to his foot to declare Charles Dayton Holling the first official influenza death on the University of South Carolina campus.

As he stared at the dormitory, watching the patients stream in and knowing Leanne was inside, John battled a wave of helplessness. He preferred his destiny be in no one's hands but his own. And yet as he watched the chaos swirl around him, John couldn't help feeling as though he'd been swept up in something far larger than his own will. Really, it was the only explanation. What had he hoped to accomplish by coming to the campus in the first place? Self-determined men didn't do nonsensical things like disobey orders and throw themselves directly in harm's way for sentimental reasons. Were Barnes to find him right now and demand to know the motives behind his actions, John wasn't sure he could give any explanation at all.

"You there!"

John turned to find a burly-looking man pulling several boxes on a wheeled cart. "Yes?"

"We need help here. Can y'all lend a hand?"

Pointing to his leg with his cane, John was forced

to concede, "Bad leg. Afraid I'm not much for pulling and pushing."

"All I need's a man who can cut open a box with a knife. Reckon you can do that?"

John needed something to do, and the prospect of something with his hands, something physical, fit the bill. "I can."

"Mighty grateful. We're as shorthanded as they come today. Head on over here.

"Dan Colton, of the Chattanooga Coltons," he said with a wry grin after giving John's elegant cane a once-over. He set John up with a small knife and what seemed like an endless stack of bandage boxes in need of opening.

"Nothing to it. Cut this open, put the bandages in this here cart and Travers—" he pointed to another skinny lad "—will wheel it into the building." He nodded back to the set of delivery doors behind him. "Better to do it out here than in there with all them sick folk."

The pace required didn't offer much chance for conversation, and John and the two men settled into a quiet, efficient rhythm until the first cart had been unloaded. It was a frantic but simple business, the sort of hard labor John had known back in his father's textile mill, the kind that cleared a man's head for thinking. He found himself grateful for the activity, for the chance to feel as if he were contributing in some way other than making pretty speeches. The chaos lent him anonymity; when he took off his captain's jacket, he was just a willing pair of hands like any other.

When Colton returned with another cart, his expression had darkened. "It's getting worse by the hour. Mercy, but I never seen anything like what's going on in there. No wonder they done locked the campus up tight. Ain't nobody coming or leaving till this thing is done, whatever it is."

"The university is under quarantine?" John shouldn't have been so surprised, not with Camp Jackson already under lockdown.

"Well, sure." Colton wiped his face with a grimy handkerchief. "I figured it was the only reason you were still here and not back with all the other soldiers at camp."

John let the gravity of his circumstance sink in for a moment. The university was quarantined. There was no going back on his decision now. Quarantine meant no help in, no release out. He was here, and he was going to stay "till this thing is done." Somewhere in the back of his mind, John had known the irrevocability of his choice all along. He'd known he was throwing away his one chance of escape when he walked onto campus, electing to see Leanne safe rather than board that train. He waited for the panic to hit him, the consequence of his decision to rise up and frighten him.

It didn't.

Instead John couldn't shake the feeling that as frightening as things were, he was *meant* to be here. Not just here cutting boxes, but here at the center of this "plague"—and the word was being used all around him now—and with Leanne. There wasn't any other reason for the inexplicable stillness at the center of his very real fear. He'd never felt such surety giving speeches, even if Leanne thought it a fine use of his "gifts." He was a cool head on the battlefield, but this was a different sort of focus. Any man with half a bit of sense would have taken the golden ticket General Barnes had given him and escaped all this, but he hadn't, and he knew he *ought not to have*.

This, he realized, must be what valor feels like. This brand of courage was the way the man everyone thought he was would have felt up on that airship. The man who deserved that medal wouldn't have been scrambling for his life, desperate and terrified, but solid and centered the way John felt right now. Surely there was no less danger—in fact, John would have wagered he stood less chance of getting out of the university alive than he did of surviving that airship's crash. He knew he could not leave Leanne to face this alone, and whether he succumbed to the virus or not was…

John stopped his own thinking, realizing he was about to finish his thought with the words, "…in God's hands." The surprising realization froze him for a moment, knife midair. He didn't really believe that, did he?

"You okay?" Travers was staring at him. "You sick?"

"No," John said, "I'm well. Just—" he fished for a word "—startled."

Travers wiped his sweating forehead with his sleeve. "Ain't we all?"

Was he calm about being here because he was where God wanted him? It seemed a foreign thought—one Leanne might have, but not him. Still, the words had a ring of truth to them. He would not have been able to leave the base with the other medical personnel if he didn't possess those travel orders General Barnes had given him. He would not have those travel orders if he hadn't passed the physical exam. And somewhere inside John knew, disconcerting as it was, that he would not have accomplished those laps had he not spied Leanne sitting on the hill praying for him. The fact that he'd seen her at all—and at the precise moment he most needed to see her—seemed too much of a coincidence to put down to luck, for he'd expressly asked her to stay away and Leanne was not the sort of woman to defy a specific request like that. His mind seemed pulled inextricably back to her prayer that afternoon on the bench, the one where she'd prayed over his leg to "Let Your will be accomplished."

As he cut open the next box, John found himself entertaining the impossible notion that God's will had, in fact, been done. In him.

He was here with Leanne.

He was in peril but alive.

And he was amazingly content with all of it.

Chapter Twenty-Four

Leanne had never seen a man die before. The waste of it all, the sheer mass of life draining out of bodies in that building seemed to crush the air from her lungs. Or worse, as if she were breathing in death itself, as if the flimsy, suffocating mask were not keeping the virus out but forcing it down her throat. She stumbled out of the ward, feeling she'd spent three days in there instead of three hours. Despite orders, she pulled off her mask to gulp in fresh air. How alive the world looked, with sunlight and green grass. How thankful she was to leave behind that desperate place of stark white, bloodred and deathly gray.

How thankful she was to see John waiting for her.

She had no strength to draw lines of faith or sense, she merely fell into his open arms and let him hold her up. How many times had she been his support? Today he was the strong one, and she was glad of it to her weary bones. "It's awful in there. Ghastly. There are so many of them, all so sick. We haven't enough of anything."

He didn't say anything. What was there to say? He had no words for such a calamity any more than she.

She clung to his shoulder, letting the soothing rhythm of his healthy breath and the steadiness of his heartbeat return her to the outside world. "Let's get you inside," he suggested after a moment or two.

"No, please, not yet. I need to be outside for just a little while, to feel the breeze and see the sun." Today felt a hundred years long, and although the sun was low in the sky, she needed every last scrap of it she could find. "There's a garden over behind that building. I used to go there when I was a student."

"Of course," he said, following her.

His limp was pronounced as they set off, and Leanne was glad it wasn't far. "It hurts, doesn't it?" She ached everywhere; she could hardly imagine how John's leg must pain him after a day like today.

"Hardly seems to matter in all this, does it?" He assessed her face as they walked. "You are all right? Not feeling ill?"

"I can't feel anything. And yet I feel too much of everything. Charles Holling, someone I knew back in Charleston, he died. Practically right in front of me. He begged for death, he was in so much pain. I couldn't…"

John tightened his grip on her arm. "Don't. Try not to dwell on it, try to be here, now, not back there."

"How? How do I do that?"

John's shrug reminded her that he had been in battle, had seen landscapes strewn with bodies worse than what she had just seen. "You force your mind to stay where you need it to be. You tell yourself over and over you're here and alive. Over and over until you start to believe it."

"I can't."

He stopped and turned to her, taking each of her shoulders in his grasp so that she felt the cool of his cane press up against one arm. "You can. You must. Look into my eyes and say it—'I'm here, I'm alive.'"

"I'm here, I'm alive." Her words had no strength.

"We're here, we're alive," he repeated, eyes locked on hers.

"We're here, we're alive. Thank God, we're here, we're alive." She brought her hands up to clutch his arms, craving the feel of his strength.

"I do, you know," John said softly. "I don't know how to begin to explain what had happened to me this afternoon, but I do thank God we're here and alive. I realize God kept you safe and kept me with you."

"John." She exhaled. Was he saying what she thought he was saying? "You shouldn't be here. You could have saved yourself from all this. You're too important."

John's hand came up to cup her chin. "I couldn't leave you. I needed to be here. I ought to be here."

Her breath caught as he ran his thumb across the curve of her cheek. "You ought to be safe." She fought the surge of feelings his words sent over her. "They'll need you back at Jackson. You ought to leave." She was trying hard to mean it.

"I cannot. You know the quarantine order, no one can come or go until it is lifted." He said it with a complete lack of panic, when Leanne thought he ought to be feeling as though he'd hung himself by his own choice.

"No." She turned her head away. "Now you're trapped here because of me."

"Everything has lined up to such order. Don't you see it all fits only one way? You prayed for me, prayed that the outcome would be not what either of us wanted, but God's will. This is. I see that now."

Astonishment filled her heart to overflowing. "John?"

"You've done the inconceivable, Leanne." He almost laughed, his astonishment evidently no less than her own. "You've saved the last soul on earth I would have ever thought possible."

Her eyes welled up, and John smiled as he wiped the single tear that stole down her cheek. To know such joy, now, seemed impossible. "Surely you don't think yourself so unworthy?"

Leanne placed a hand on John's chest and felt his heartbeat pounding under her palm. Alive. Here. Now. The darkness that had always lurked in the corners of his eyes had vanished, an unlikely, irrational peace of in its place. "To be frank, I don't know what I think." He pulled her closer. She did not resist. "I'm quite sure, however, what I feel."

Leanne could scarcely draw breath. The world had unhinged itself in a single day, coming apart at the very seams, and yet here was this wonder unfolding at the very same time. It seemed unthinkable that God's will had been done, and yet John could believe that answer to her prayer more swiftly than she. To think that he had walked knowingly into danger, for her. It was a heroism too great to bear. "I've no words..."

None were needed. He bent his head and kissed her softly, and she felt life blooming back into her. Then his kiss was not so soft, and she found herself returning the urgency in his kiss with a vitality she thought all but gone. His embrace pushed back the despair, blocked out the sick ward's horrors. When John pulled back to look at her, his eyes burned fiercely with the sense of "here now and alive" she desperately needed.

What a splendid strength John had; how grateful she was for his presence. The wonder of his fresh faith offered deep encouragement—had she really been so weary just moments before? John pulled her tightly to him, and she marveled how perfectly her shoulders tucked under his, how her head fell naturally against his shoulder. "I've still no words," she said against the warmth of his chest.

"Rendered you speechless, have I?" His tone was almost a laugh, and she felt herself smile. To smile, in the face of all this. What a gift that was.

She looked out at the fading daylight, thinking today's tragedies would only double with the coming darkness. It seemed as if dawn could only bring worse news. "Whatever is to become of us?"

John's chest expanded with a sigh as large as her own. "God only knows," he said. Kissing the top of her head, he added, "And goodness, I actually mean that when I say it now. It's going to take me a little while to get used to all this."

He did not say what she knew they both were thinking: a little while might be all they had.

The next day became a surreal, catastrophic struggle of life and death. John continued his work with the supply effort while Leanne and the other medical staff fought for life inside. He caught glimpses of her as they worked through the day, but rarely had time to say much more than a few words. Now, grateful for the dusk that marked the end of a long day, John and Leanne found half an hour to sit on the steps of a nearby building and share what meager food either could roust up for dinner.

John had coaxed some priceless meat—a pair of sausages—out of the cook in an effort to restore Leanne's appetite. He'd planned to let her eat both of them if he could, despite the fact that they smelled wonderful enough to set his own mouth watering. All of his world had the most awful smells these days, but he would gladly forsake the savory meat if he thought he could convince her to eat it. Leanne's color gave him pause. "Eat, my dear." Her shy smile, the one that always appeared now when he used the term "my dear," tickled him. He put the tin plate on her lap and stretched out his leg.

His confounded leg. He'd overused it in the worst way today. The thing ached to the point of distraction now, but all his pain medicine was still back at Jackson and anything they had here must be saved for patients. "This long day's end is only the beginning." He pointed to the plate. "You must eat more."

Her gaze was on the horizon, the purple dusk now barely visible through the trees. "Is this what war is like, John?"

He'd had the same thought dozens of times today—that this was a war. "Yes." He found himself hard-pressed to elaborate on such a drastic declaration, but her silence worried him. "This morning I couldn't help thinking I didn't need to go back to the battlefield because the battlefield has been brought to me."

When she still offered no reply, he took her hand. "You'd think that would be an awful thought, but it's not. I know I ought to be here. I've had my eyes opened in so many ways. I'm seeing God's hand in places I always put down to luck and self-importance." He put his arm around her shoulder, drawing her to him. She felt too thin, too void of the vitality that had charmed him back before the world fell apart. "That's you. That's you in my life and I wouldn't trade that for twelve shiny medals."

Leanne softened against his shoulder. The structure's thick wooden front columns, still warm from the strong fall sun, baked his aching back. The soreness in his leg eased up the smallest bit. He offered up a word of thanks for the moment's peace in a day of struggle, and the prayer came as easy as his breath.

He felt her sigh against his ribs. "I fought so hard to resist you. I suppose you know that."

Her admission made him chuckle. Was she unaware how hard he'd fought to resist *her?* "Well, I have often heard how irresistible I am. And here I am bearing sausages. It took six compliments to lure these out of the kitchen, so we're feasting thanks to my legendary charm." He tipped her chin toward him. "But you are not eating nearly as well as you should. I am worried about you. Let me care for you, Leanne." John swallowed, realizing he was dancing around what he really wanted to say. "For I do care for you. A great deal." He kissed her forehead and thanked God again, grateful to be granted this time with Leanne. "We must be the only two people in the world to have any reason to be thankful for this."

"And hate it at the same time. John, I feel too much all at once. I'm so happy, and yet so tired and so sad. And frightened. And worried. How can I feel hungry on top of all that?"

"Every soldier knows a body needs to eat, hungry or not. Your strength is important." He broke off a bit of sausage and held it in front of her as one would a small child, tucking it inside with a smile when she relented and opened her mouth. She consumed the luxury dutifully, without enjoyment, but she ate two more bites besides.

They sat without conversing. Around them the sound of hammers pierced the gathering dusk alongside birds and crickets. Mere months ago the constant hammers at

Jackson had meant building—barracks and structures that sprang up in astonishing speed as Camp Jackson burst into being. Now the hammers were building only one thing: coffins. Twenty in the past four hours alone. Eventually, Leanne looked up at him. "I do wonder if we are at the end of the world."

He could hardly blame her. He'd had the thought himself walking past the outbuilding they'd set up as a morgue two hours ago. Still, it bothered him to see her optimism failing, so he attempted a jest. "Are you saying my faith is a sign of the apocalypse? I had no idea I was so influential."

She didn't laugh, merely pulled a telegraph paper from her pocket. "Dr. Madison dropped this off earlier."

"Madison's here?"

"He was on campus lecturing an orthopedics class when the quarantine order came. He chose to stay and help however he could."

John found his presence oddly comforting—a small piece of his past that had traveled with him to this surreal present.

"John, he told me one hundred and thirty men have died at Jackson. How many will die here?"

John cast his eyes down to the yellow half sheet Leanne held out. It was a wire statement from Army Surgeon General Victor Vaughan. While John might conclude it was Vaughan's job to size up threats in the worst possible light, this exceeded the staunchest pessimism. "If the epidemic continues its mathematical rate of acceleration," the smudged type declared, "civilization could easily disappear from the face of the earth within a few weeks."

It wasn't that hard to believe. Death felt as if it lurked around every corner, hid in every sunken set of eyes.

According to the velvet box back somewhere in the bottom of his rucksack, John had faced death down, had "saved lives at the risk of his own." Still, John could not escape the truth that he'd felt terror at that episode and mostly peace here. Is that what faith did? Gave one peace in what might be the end of the world?

"I'll admit to very little knowledge of God, but I cannot think He would grant me you and then not give me the world to enjoy with you. Does it look like the end of the world? I've seen battlefields that show nothing but devastation, so yes, I suppose it does. But it does not feel like the end of the world, at least not to me. It feels like war." He gazed into Leanne's eyes, willing her his battle nerves. "I know war, Leanne. I know what to do in war. In the one out there and the one right here. Victory isn't out of reach. You hold on to that thought. I've far too many things I want to show you to consider anything else. I plan to take you up in a plane and show you the sky from God's point of view. Would you like that?"

She smiled for the first time this evening, and popped another bite of sausage into her mouth. "It sounds wonderful."

Chapter Twenty-Five

❦

"I ought to have you shot!"

John pulled his head away from the phone receiver and Barnes's tinny bellow. It was funny; he'd endowed the general with so much power over his life before, and now his anger didn't faze John at all. "It was very foolish, I agree. Still, I'd do it again given the chance."

The general's sigh was closer to a growl. "Your father will have my head for not getting you out of here."

Ah, so it was true. John had long suspected it was the Gallows name, rather than his silver tongue, that earned him a spot on that train. Father's leverage was still as powerful, his connections still strong if his father knew of the epidemic as fast as Barnes. "Father knows me well enough to know I'm not much for orders. One doesn't get the medals for being a good boy, but rather a brave soldier. Amazing how often that involves ignoring wise advice, isn't it?"

John could almost hear Barnes pinch the bridge of his nose. "Son, what good are you to anyone if you die over there?"

"Begging your pardon, General, but I could have died just as easily in Chicago and I'm tremendously useful over here." John had raised the recruitment rates in three states, had driven auditoriums of young men to their feet in cheers but had never felt more useful than he had in the past twenty-four hours. "I'm a soldier, and I don't have to tell you, this is war." Whatever it was he was seeking in his return to the front, he had already found it. The stand he'd taken here, holding the line against this deadly enemy, had settled his soul in more ways than one.

"Captain Gallows," Travers called from the hallway, "we got four less boxes than we thought. What do we do now?" Late last night someone had recognized him, and his anonymity was gone, but it hadn't mattered. Influenza had little respect for rank or status.

"What's going on?" Barnes asked through the line.

"Five minutes," John called to Travers, then returned to the receiver. "Enough of the staff has fallen ill that I've been drafted into figuring out how to make five loaves and two fishes feed the five thousand." Leanne had drawn the Biblical comparison, saying they'd need one of Jesus's miracles to make the meager supplies meet the herculean need. She'd also kissed him and told him she thought no one short of Christ more suitable to attempt the feat. He'd grinned; evidently his spiritual awakening had yet to squelch the legendary Gallows ego.

"What?" Barnes sounded duly baffled.

"Instead of getting me out, sir, can you wield that leverage to get supplies in?" They'd created a self-contained "no contact zone" around the dormitory and two adjacent halls—a quarantine within a quarantine—and John had worked out a non-contact drop system in the dormitory's west door. He found it no coincidence that the idea sprang from a cloister of French nuns whom he'd frequented for excellent chocolates. "We're in dire straits for bandages, medical alcohol and chloroform."

The general made a gruff sound. "You and half the Eastern Seaboard."

Travers shifted in the doorway. "Captain Gallows, sir?"

"You do what you can from out there, I'll do what I must from in here," he said to the general.

"Bandages, medical alcohol and chloroform?"

"That's what they tell me. At least today. Tomorrow is anyone's guess." If anyone could throw his weight around in Columbia, it was General Barnes. As fearful as the general's wrath might be once this was over, it was better to have the man as an ally for the present battle.

"Anything else?"

John couldn't resist. "A good steak might help. And some yarn."

Leanne mopped another puddle of drying blood from the floor. Every square inch of the room was occupied by moaning bodies. Doctors darted between catastrophes, barking orders at nurses, all so tired themselves that civility had been abandoned.

A young woman to Leanne's left gave out a raspy cry, clawing at her chest. She'd torn open her blouse, for the supply of hospital gowns had disappeared along with the civility and clean linens. "There now—" Leanne grabbed the woman's hand and laid it back down on the cot "—they'll bring more medicine soon." It seemed the kindest of lies, for in truth Leanne had no idea how long supplies would hold out. "Try to rest." She redid the young woman's buttons, and wiped her brow. There were no sheets to tuck her under. Leanne smoothed her tangled hair, for there were no pillows to place beneath her head. Kindness was the only treatment she had to offer.

The woman quieted some, and Leanne rose to arch her back against the growing ache. She needed to leave the din of moans and cries, just for a minute or two to catch her breath. She found Ida in the ladies' washroom, catching her weary glance as they ducked over the line of sinks. "I'm worn to the bone and then some," Ida said, splashing water on her face and then leaning back against the wall. Towels had disappeared from the washroom, if they were ever there at all.

"I hurt everywhere," Leanne replied, using a wet hand to wipe the grime from her neck. The suffocating smells spun her senses and tumbled her stomach if she moved too fast. Her tongue dragged inside a parched, pasty mouth for the sheer mass of bodies had baked the room to a suffocating heat.

"Did you hear that doctor when he came in yesterday?" Ida asked, flexing one wrist in slow circles. "Took two steps in the door and pronounced it 'the very cradle of death.' As if we'd all somehow benefit from the description."

Leanne didn't find it much of an overstatement. "That's the worst part, isn't it? How hard they're trying to hide that they don't know what to do?"

Ida's sour laugh echoed against the tile, bloodstained even in here. "Do we do any less? Telling patients medicine is on the way, that relief is coming?"

Leanne looked at the blood caking her fingernails, unable to recall the last time those fingers had touched yarn and needles. "It's a horrid false kindness, isn't it?" She scraped her hands against the slivers of soap left by the sink and washed again, the cracks in her knuckles stinging from the harsh lye. "Still," she said as she rinsed, "it calms most of them, and that's help enough." She cupped her hands and drank, the bitter trace of soap sending her into a fit of coughing. Even a decent drink of water had become a luxury in the ward. She coughed again, shut her eyes against the ache that doubled in her chest and wiped her hands on her skirts for lack of any hand towels.

Ida stared.

"Nasty soap." Leanne had tried not to give in to complaints, but she felt too battered to keep this one in. "I'm fine." She cleared her throat again, feeling as if she'd swallowed gauze bandages instead of poor water.

Ida made no reply, but stood there with dull shock written all over her face as Leanne grabbed the counter with one hand while the other went to her throat. Coughing again, Leanne followed Ida's gaze to her own skirts, damp from her hands.

Two bright red smudges.

Leanne looked at her hands and saw not the dried brownish-red smears of the ward's endless blood, but lines of fresh red in the creases of her palms. She fought the urge to cough again as she forced herself to look in the dingy mirror above the sink.

Red spots, bright as alarms, spattered one cheek. The edges of the room began to spin out of her vision, and she clutched the edge of the sink as another cough tore up out of her chest to shower tiny red drops across her clenched fist.

I'm to die, then, Leanne thought as she slumped against the wall, the tile cool and soothing against her flushed cheek. She heard Ida's cry for help and the squeaky bang of the washroom door as if it were a thousand miles away. She closed her eyes, feeling something in her core begin to unwind, like a snagged thread unraveling a sweater's knitting. *I've come undone.*

John was standing over a telegraph machine someone had brought in from the university's administrative offices, working with a clerk to wire calls for favors to every family member or family friend he could list. If the Gallows name held any weight, now was surely the time to wield it. Still, even a pedigree like his couldn't produce linens out of thin air, nor medicine when no one knew what drugs worked. Travers had begun to wear a bag of camphor pellets around his neck and brought one for John to use, but he declined. He suspected the smelly folk-remedy held about as much credence as the Gallows moniker against their invisible foe. Still, he sent out the next telegraph to a textile mill down the river from his family estate, asking for any help they could give.

Thanks to his new curative, John smelled Travers before he saw him. "Hank," John called, not looking up from the buzzing metal box, "I'd always thought the term 'I can smell you from a mile away' to be an exaggeration, but in your case…"

The look in Travers's eyes stopped him midsentence. The man clearly bore bad news. John wasn't sure he could stomach another shortage of anything, given how dire circumstances already were. He straightened up slowly, feeling sparks shoot down his leg as he reached for his cane. "What isn't coming now?"

Hank looked down, twisting his cap in one hand. John hated how the masks made everyone's face so difficult to read. Hank shifted his weight. "It's Miss Sample, sir. They told me to come fetch you."

John grabbed the back of a nearby chair. The words

came slowly, thickly out of his mouth. "What about Miss Sample, Hank?"

Hank said nothing. Which said everything.

"Where is she?" He whacked the chair away with his cane, betrayal rising in his throat like bile. *"Where is she?"*

"Down in the second building with some of the other nurses that done got sick this afternoon."

John pushed past him into the hallway, his cane banging over and over on the wooden floor as he tumbled into something close to a run. Leanne could not fall ill. It was as simple as that. God would not give him her heart for two meager days and then tear it away. Everything else could fall to pieces, he could lose everything else but he could not, *would* not lose her. Not this way.

"Leanne!" he called as he rounded the corner to the ward Travers had indicated. He'd pulled his mask down, not caring what lay in the air he swallowed with each stinging breath. The burning in his leg had already lodged in his lungs and his heart, what was a mask to him now? John wanted to hit something, to punch through a wall or bellow curses into the wind, but he skidded to a stop in the doorway where Ida stood with apologetic eyes.

Panting from his dash, his leg absolutely screaming, John locked his gaze onto Leanne's face. She lay in the third of four cots, curled on her side and clutching her stomach, eyes narrowed in pain above a mask smattered in the bloody droplets that announced her fate. "Leanne." It was almost a cry, a howl rather than her name. "No."

He lurched toward her, but Ida caught his shoulder, pointing silently to the mask hanging around his neck. He couldn't care less about that useless square of cloth now, but Leanne managed a "John, please," that only served to send her into a wave of gurgling coughs. Her skin was the pale gray he'd come to hate, her brow beaded from fever so that damp curls of hair framed her face. It was agony to sink down beside her, the burning in his leg still no match for the shot-through sensation in his chest. He'd fallen from heights and not felt the wind so knocked out of him as when he clutched her hand. It was cold, dry and clenched tight with suffering.

"I'm not so bad," she lied with hopeless eyes.

"Leanne," he said, any other words beyond him. "My dear."

No shy smile greeted his endearment. "John."

"You're in pain." He grabbed the towel from its basin on the floor beside her and mopped her brow. Even though he was no stranger to pain, the thought of her suffering made him crazy. She was too sweet, too fragile to be wracked in the fever's agony.

Her eyes fluttered shut as he cooled her forehead. "Not much yet."

That was the worst of it; she knew what was coming. They both did. He returned the cloth to its place and took her hand. It felt wrong; it was too cool and stiff, rigid but without life. The hideous purple spots had already begun to form on her wrist, and a cold coil of helplessness began to wind its way around his spine. "You won't die." The words were foolish. Nurses had begun affixing postmortem identification toe tags to patients upon arrival, not having time to wait until they'd passed. No one had yet recovered. No one. "You'll be spared, you'll see."

"Wouldn't that be lovely." Her head rolled listlessly to one side.

John hated the surrender in her voice. He had no intention of surrendering Leanne to this evil beast. Had it been a visible foe, he would have run straight at it, roaring with his bayonet lunging. But there was nothing to plunge his bayonet into, no target to shoot. He could not blow up the bridge to the next life before she crossed it. He couldn't do anything, and that was worse than any pain.

"I'm so very hot," she whispered, and John brought the cloth to her brow again. He folded it across her forehead, and she sighed. Any tiny bit of comfort felt better than the resignation clawing at his heels. She shifted, wincing as she did, and he rearranged the thin scraggly pillow beneath her head. She was lucky in that; despite the university laundry running nonstop, pillows and clean linen were becoming more scarce every day. And he was thankful she wasn't in that sea of near-corpses on the first floor, but here with a small number of nurses who had fallen ill. She stood half a chance that way, he told himself. "I'll sleep," she said, her eyes finding him again. "It's better when I sleep."

John ran a lock of her hair through his fingers. "You need your rest. You need it because you're going to live. Those students? Those socks? They need you."

Her eyes fell closed, but she smiled.

"I need you." His voice broke with the power of that truth. Self-sufficient, self-important, self-absorbed John Gallows needed. Perhaps it really was the end of the world.

"But you've finished your first sock," she said, speaking with such a thin calm that he wondered if she was still awake. "You'll be surprised. The second one is so much easier."

"I still need you." He wasn't talking about socks at all.

Chapter Twenty-Six

It burned. Parts of her burned, then cooled, then burned again. The air had grown thick and hard to breathe, hot and liquid against her throat. The scents around her were familiar, yet some part of her knew they were cause for alarm. There were times—hours? days?—when her stomach would feel hollow and still. All of her felt hollow and still, like a water glass emptied out. Then there were the insufferable spaces where time twisted over on itself in pain, where every breath felt like it took hours and filled nothing. Voices and faces would ebb in and out of her awareness. Sometimes she conversed with them, knowing they were friends and yet not being able to place them in her life outside the heat and pain. Other times they were only noises she could not understand.

Days were hard. The bright sunshine hurt her eyes, made the sights and sounds too sharp. For a little while each day, however, the storm would subside and she could be in the world. Feel the cool gauze on her forehead, taste the salty broth someone held to her lips. She was very sick, she knew that, although she wasn't sure how. Every once in a while, especially when light returned to the room, Leanne would feel something tell her not to fight, not to strive. An inner voice assuring her that whatever this was, it was out of her hands.

She was sure the voice came in the growing light because the dark was so awful. Sleep and wakefulness wove together without clear lines, so that she never knew if her eyes would open to dark or light. In the light there were shapes and movement, but the dark held only sound and space. Once she thought Charles Holling came to her in the darkness, as pale and hollow as she felt. He didn't plead to die like she remembered, only asked very politely as if he were a gentleman asking a lady to dance. She would tell him she didn't want to dance, or to die, that John was here somewhere, and then she would turn and look for John in the darkness. She would push her hands out of the fog draped over her, and find the solid warmth of his hand. It was as if she floated, wandered, but his hand would anchor her back whenever she touched it. She'd call his name into the fog, and often his answer would come back like a lighthouse beacon. He held her to this place, to this time, even to this pain. It made her think of John's accident, hanging over the sea by the dirigible stay wires that both tore him and saved him at the same time. How did she know that? Had she been there to see it? She couldn't remember. Nothing made sense.

Nothing except God. God made the only sense there was. He was here. She heard His voice, only not in true words. God spoke to her thoughts and breaths, in colors and sensations. All her senses seemed to weave together—sometimes tight and coarse, other times loose and billowy. When the world was tight and coarse, she would feel God beside her, holding, protecting. When the world was loose and billowy, she would feel Him underneath her like the wind under a seagull. The Lord of Time whirled her in and out of time's grip, the Author of Life pushed and pulled at her breath, the Lamb of God cradled her in her suffering. One set of words kept coming to her, over and over. She knew it to be truth, but couldn't remember where she'd learned it. *In life or in death I belong to Christ.*

Chapter Twenty-Seven

John startled awake to a hand on his shoulder, every joint of his body reminding him of the hard floor that had been his bed for two nights. His head turned quickly toward the cot beside him where Leanne lay with her back to him. Was she all right? Had someone woken him to deliver bad news?

The hand squeezed his shoulder in assurance, and John squinted in the sunlight to see Dr. Madison pulling up a metal chair. He looked as tired as John felt.

"She's still with us," he whispered, handing John a tin mug of mercilessly strong coffee. "I just checked and her pulse is weak, but steady."

Hearing their voices Leanne gave a soft moan and shifted a bit, but did not wake. "Even in her sleep," John said, looking at the too-sharp angle of her shoulder, "she's in too much pain. She's barely woken in two days."

"And you've barely slept in two days." Madison nodded to him over his own cup. "She'll have my hide if I don't keep you well enough to celebrate her recovery." He winced as he swallowed. "This is dreadful. I'm trying to be grateful it's hot."

"Thank you." John gulped down the hot brew with gratitude. Leanne sighed softly. "It's hard to be grateful for her prolonged pain, but I'm glad she's still with us."

"Pain is an odd companion, but try to think of it as the body's way of fighting to stay alive. They say you never feel a mortal wound, only the one that won't kill you."

It was funny how Madison, who had once been the only thing standing in his way, the enemy to be conquered, had become a friend. Unable to sleep, John had talked for an hour to Leanne's sleeping form in the middle of the night last night about this strange world they now occupied. "You wouldn't recognize it," John had said as he wiped Leanne's hands—still paler by moonlight than their ashen color by day. "Our Dr. Madison, my chief inflictor of therapeutic pain, has become a source of comfort. A friend, if you can believe it."

He liked talking to her when the room was dark. Sleep eluded him anyway, and he hoped his monologue kept Leanne anchored to this world where he needed her to stay. "I hardly know what to do with this topsy-turvy exchange of blessings and curses. They seem to turn my world upside down and set it to rights all at the same time. If this is the world with your faith, I almost think I'd rather have something more constant and predictable." He'd fallen asleep fingering the gold cross they'd taken from her neck, now his constant companion in his pocket. It was still in his hand now as he stared bleary-eyed at Madison.

"I have news, John." Madison had never called him John in all their time together. "Boston has reported a survivor."

John sat up straight, for this was news indeed. There had been no reports of anything but fatalities from any of the camps. John had stopped watching patients being brought into the hospital, unable to stomach the fear in their eyes. Every person believed the trip through those doors ran only one way. The only variable so far was the rate of death—some died shockingly fast, others lingered cruelly for days. "Someone has lived?"

Madison took off his glasses and pinched his nose. "It is perhaps more accurate to say someone has not died. A single soldier. His fever has resolved. It's not much, but it's more than we've had to go on before."

Someone had not died. It was far more than anything they had before. John let his head fall back against the wall, glad to grasp even a thin hope of relief. "Thank God above."

"I thought you'd want to know." He managed a weary smile. "I thought it might convince you to actually sleep. I am still your doctor, you know." Madison drained the tin mug with a groan of displeasure. "I'll sit with her if you like."

"You'll do no such thing from the looks of both of you," came Ida's voice from the doorway. "I've a mind to ship the both of you off to some pantry and lock the door." She crossed her arms like a scolding school-marm. "When's the last time either of you ate?"

"I think I just chewed this coffee." John surprised himself with his first joke in ages. Someone hadn't died. The hourglass could be turned.

"I thought as much. Besides, I'm going to give Le-anne a bit of a bath so you're to be gentlemen and flee the room. Off with the pair of you."

"Bacon and eggs," Madison wished aloud as he rose slowly from his chair. "Four of them, with hash browns and fresh strawberries." He extended a hand to John, who was still propped up against the wall on the floor.

"Eggs Benedict," John managed through gritted teeth as his leg—and the rest of him—loudly protested the night's sleeping quarters. "With perfect toast—" a wince cut through his words "—and orange marmalade. And ham. And real coffee, not whatever *that* was." John fetched his cane but left the cup of murky black liquid on the floor. He looked at Ida's barely amused face. "They've a survivor up in Boston, you know. Madison just told me."

"It's all over campus already."

John leaned over Leanne's discolored face, saddened to see her eyes seemed to have sunk farther into their hollows overnight. She was thinner still, ashen where she wasn't the harrowing purple that marked this disease. She had quieted overnight—he preferred to think of it that way, simply as a quieting, rather than entertain the notion she was weakening. Still, her brow wrinkled in discomfort, and her body lacked the peaceful ease of true sleep. He smoothed a damp lock of hair off her forehead, saddened to find it still warmer than it should be. "There's a survivor up in Boston, my dear. Someone can survive. Someone *has* survived. Stay right here with us where you belong." He kissed her cheek before pulling his mask back up, then nodded to Ida. "Find her some yarn. She'll want it for when she wakes up."

After a breakfast that rivaled any half-edible gruel John had endured in the battle trenches, he ignored the rock settling in his stomach and settled down for a stretch of real sleep. An hour in an actual bed, horizontal, on something that wasn't a floor, felt like a luxury. After that he was up, shaven and back at work in the small room in one of the adjacent inner quarantine buildings he'd commandeered as his "office."

Colton walked in halfway through the morning. John

hadn't seen the man in almost a full day, since Travers had fallen ill shortly after Leanne. To see such a hard-working young man laid low was bad enough, but it served to make Colton and John doubly anxious about the state of the contagion.

Colton looked calm enough, so John ventured, "How's Hank?"

The big man shook his head. "Not good. Fella's just a whip of a thing, so it's hit him hard. They got him in the 'big room.'"

The "big room," as Colton called it, was a sea of misery on the first floor of the "hospital" dormitory, a vast ward of bodies in various states of the disease. Every time John walked by it he offered up a prayer of thanks that Leanne was tucked away in a ward on the upper floors. He wouldn't state it now, but to him the "big room" seemed like it smothered its occupants in a sheer mass of death.

"Hank's a tough fellow," John offered.

"And your Miss Sample?" The romance between John and Leanne had become common knowledge. It was hard to have any privacy in such close quarters, and the urgency of their world right now wouldn't allow for much subtlety. John took a novel pride in claiming her as "his," through a look, a quick touch of her hand in public places, the use of endearments. It was an odd thing: John used to pride himself on his ability to woo the most desirable lady in any crowd, often seeking her out for the mere challenge of besting other gentlemen. Now, as his mother would have put it, he "only had eyes for one."

"She's still with us," he quoted Dr. Madison with a deep gratitude. "With plans to stay that way. Boston is reporting a survivor, did you hear?"

Colton smiled. "I did. Camp Devens has just one so far?"

"That's all I've heard, but that's all I need to hear." John had shared the news with every ear that would listen, but he knew Colton held Travers as a friend. "Madison's sent word for more information from the doctors at Devens, but nothing's come through yet."

"Maybe there ain't nothing to tell. Some things just *is,* you know." John wasn't sure if Colton was offering encouragement or kindly caution. The big man didn't elaborate, just looked at the pile of pipes and mattresses at John's feet and raised an eyebrow. "What have you got going here?"

Fortified by food, sleep and hopeful news, John was attempting something that felt no less miraculous than Christ's loaves and fishes. "I'm attempting to see if one bed can somehow be reassembled into two. Or even two into three."

He pulled apart the mattress he'd unstitched into two layers of batting. "Maybe we can just put these on boards nailed to a pair of desks." The dormitory mattresses were thin to begin with, but no one was seeking luxury here. "I think we can split the wire mesh up into two, but I'm not sure it will hold."

"Won't hold me." Colton chuckled. "Then again, you could fit some of them boys in each of my pant legs, they's coming in here so thin."

John could only agree. Each day the incoming patients looked more ill—and more frightened than the last. "Philadelphia was fool enough to hold a liberty bond parade and they ended up with hundreds of cases. Here, hold this," he said, pointing to wire mesh he'd just unwoven from a disassembled bed.

"Locking us up tight was the smart thing to do then.

Only it don't feel so smart from the inside, does it? My heart jumps through my mouth every time I cough even just a little."

John, Colton and every healthy person inside "the line," as it had come to be called, lived in the same state of watch: Have I caught it? Is this the first sign? The constant vigil had worn John's mind down to a near numbness, but in sleep, his imagination roused again, in the worst of ways. "I dreamed of being chased by a huge tiger, nipping at my heels while I ran through a jungle." He began threading a screw through a hole in a pipe.

"A tiger?" Waters chuckled. "Not a little bird?"

News wires reported a day ago that as alarm had been raised in the general public, children had begun jumping rope to a macabre little rhyme:

I had a little bird
Her name was Enza
I opened the window
And In-Flu-Enza

It was amusing and horribly sad at the same time.

"No, a big snarly tiger. You'd think I'd enjoy a dream of running, the way I hobble around."

Colton picked up one corner of John's new invention, inspecting the thing. "Did you outrun the tiger in your dream?"

"Woke up in a cold sweat before I could find out." While the sensation of running should have felt wonderful, John would have gladly passed it over to skip bolting upright out of the nap with his heart pounding.

"Well, then, how's about we say you outran that nasty tiger and saved your pretty girl, too? Sounds like a mighty fine dream to me when you put it that way."

John had to smile. "I thought you said some things 'just is'?"

"Well," said Colton as he handed the wrench to John to tighten the bolt, "I didn't say 'all things.' Well, now, looky here. This just might work." John showed him how the two salvaged sides came together to hold a mattress. "You are pretty smart for a war hero, Captain Gallows."

John smiled at his contraption. "If you can't outrun the tiger, you'd best outsmart him."

Chapter Twenty-Eight

Once he'd devised the frame of the bed, John took a mattress down to send off to a ward of Red Cross volunteers to see if the ticking could be easily halved. Beds—even poor ones—were a commodity. Ill patients were actually placed on the floor beside near-dying ones to wait for the bed. John had made two attempts before coming up with a successful design, mostly because he couldn't stomach the thought of finding himself on a floor waiting for someone above him to breathe their last.

He went to see if Leanne was awake, hoping to share all his good news. What he found stole every ounce of optimism.

She'd lapsed into delirium again, weakly thrashing and succumbing to coughs that sounded as if her body was attempting to turn itself inside out.

"Been like that about an hour," Ida said, not bothering to hide the concern in her voice. "A bit more and I was going to send for you. She calms to your voice, and I'm afraid she's going to hurt herself."

"How's her fever?"

She winced as she answered. "Worse."

"How?" It was a foolish question—the disease seemed to take a unique course with every victim. Madison regularly bemoaned the sheer vacuum of protocol at every doctor's disposal. No one knew why one patient died within hours while others hung on for days, why one showed symptoms another did not. "She was improving. She ate something. I watched her."

"Perhaps it's just a minor setback." Ida's eyes betrayed the thin lacquer of optimism she'd applied.

"Surely." Liars, the pair of them. John peered at Leanne's too-gray face, willing himself to find some new source of color though he knew he would not. "She'll improve again, and keep improving." The ominous black hole in his gut grew deeper as he noticed one of the room's six beds was now empty. John looked up at Ida, who turned away to some pretended detail. Death had visited the room during the night.

The ghoul would not be allowed to stay. "I'll stay with her tonight." He spoke with all the command he could muster, brooking no refusal. If Leanne was going to leave him, he would not miss the goodbye for all the world.

Ida took a breath to argue, but simply shut her mouth again. "She'll be glad of the company, I'm sure." She gave the unreadable smile he'd come to call her "nursing mask," the one he'd heard Leanne describe as a way to keep what she called "unkind news" from worried patients.

A feathery touch on his arm drew his attention, and he turned to see Leanne's gaze wander in disjointed alarm around the room. "My dear," he said softly, angling himself down to her level despite the pain it caused him. Ida was right; the sound of his voice seemed to anchor her. Leanne's gaze found his and held it, if weakly.

She licked her dry, crackled lips, and he held a wet cloth to them for her to drink a few drops. "You should drink." She obeyed, wincing as she swallowed—many of the patients complained of throats so sore they seemed as if they were on fire. "I know it hurts, but you must." Dr. Madison had warned him that the most feared enemy was dehydration, even if it did feel like asking patients to swallow knives when they drank. He put the wet cloth to her brow, smoothing back her hair, noticing with horror that strands of Leanne's beautiful yellow hair fell out easily at his touch.

"John?" His name was not much more than a gasp of breath, and yet it was everything.

"Yes."

"John?" she said again, soft but less weak.

"Right here." He took her hand as it seemed to hover off the bed in search of his. Her eyes fell closed for a second at his touch. Her hand felt like bones inside thin paper. Too small, too thin, too lifeless to be Leanne's vibrant fingers. After an instant she opened them again and found his face, as if she were creeping toward him through the fog of her illness. "I'm right here and I'm not leaving until you waltz out of this hospital on my arm." A foolish, overdramatic statement.

She knew it, too. Even in her distress, Leanne could see through his facade. It took her a moment to find the energy to speak again, but she wore the vaguest hint of a smile as she did.

"I'm dying, aren't I?" The words came in simple innocence, childlike in its fearlessness. Or its faithfulness—he couldn't tell.

"You most certainly are not," he said sharply, despising and needing the deception at the same time. He wanted to say something else, something confident and hopeful, but couldn't manage it.

A fit of coughing seemed to snatch away what little energy she had. "So much pain."

"It will pass." But would it? Was he selfish enough to wish her lingering if all it meant was more suffering for Leanne? His greedy answer showed him for the faulty man he was, not the hero others thought him to be.

"I'm not afraid." The clear statement seemed as if it could not possibly come from the frail body beside him.

"That's because you're not going to die, so there's no reason for fear." Panic lodged a cold finger in John's spine and began to follow along his ribs, squeezing. He clasped her hand instead.

"No." She shut her eyes, reaching for words. "Faith."

"God can't have you yet." The petulant demand of a child's tantrum, but it was how he felt.

"And you should choose?"

He adjusted the flimsy pillow, thinking of all the fine linens he had at home and what he would give to couch her in them at this moment. "You said it yourself, I'm accustomed to getting my way and in no mind to tolerate obstacles."

"God's will is no obstacle. He is the only path."

"Then I shall insist He carve that path back to life and health."

She made to turn, and he helped her shift to her side, hating the way her thinness now shaved cruel angles into the curves he'd once so admired. She fell asleep for a second, drifting in and out of slumber the way she did lately. John took the moment's respite to lean against the wall, his head falling back to stare at the ceiling.

You cannot have her, he declared to Heaven, as if Leanne were ever his to possess in any case. The foolishness of his thoughts did nothing to stem the strength of his feeling. *I'll not let You take her from me.* Followed, almost instantly, with the more truthful, more disturbing, *I fear what I'll be if You do.*

He looked down to find her staring at him. "So much fear," she whispered. It made John wonder if his silent shouts at God had really found their way into spoken words. "There's no need."

The tear he saw wind its way down her ashen cheek was his undoing. "Do not leave me, Leanne."

"You'll not be alone. Not now."

John did not want to hear about God's comfort in loss. He'd heard Leanne give the speech too many times not to know the words nearly by heart, but such belief wasn't his. Not yet, perhaps not ever. "I've not the faith to believe without you beside me."

She smiled, and he saw the first glimpse of the Leanne he knew under the waxen figure before him. "Silly John. Still thinking faith is something you've earned."

"I sought it. You pointed me toward it." He was delighted to see her talking, engaging, coming back to him from the brink of wherever she was.

"Yes, but God gives us…" her breath seemed to falter "…our faith." Another fit of coughing seemed to steal all the progress she'd made toward life, vaulting her back to the limp slip of a thing that seemed to melt into the sheets. John reached out for the bowl and wiped her drained face. Every touch seemed precious, fleeting, and he refused to let his mind caution him that this might be their last time together. She seemed to have left this world already, as if she were more spirit and less solid than even an hour ago. John was somehow sure that if he failed to keep touching her, talking to her, anchoring her to this place, she would slip away to hide from the pain under God's wings. Colton came by to say that he was needed elsewhere, but John refused. Seeing Leanne's precarious state, Colton pressed it no further. John would have gone to fists if it had come to it: no duty was more important than the vigil before him.

He was only vaguely aware of the daylight slipping away around him. At some point he must have slept, for he woke to the feeble whisper of her voice in the lightless room. "John? John?"

"Beside you, my love." There, in the dark, the endearment slipped out of him unchecked. The shadows and disease seemed like beasts waiting to devour this woman who had stolen in to become the center of his heart. John realized he wanted her to know of his feelings, and he was too tired and too anxious to resist the urge. Calling her his love was the truth, after all, for he did love her. "And I do love you, Leanne." He looked for a response, but she seemed to be slipping away from his very fingertips, as if his next touch of her would pass his hand through her ghostly image to touch an empty bed. "I tried not to, you know. It seemed irrational, painful even, to love you, but in the end I had no defenses to resist. I love you." He pressed a kiss to her fevered cheek.

She tried to say something, but it left her lips as not much more than a struggling sigh. Had she understood what he'd just said? She seemed to be in so much pain, it almost seemed cruel to wish her awake and aware. Could not God grant her a peaceful end if she must leave him? Must it be in anguish, without the most important words he would ever speak to her? "I love you," he whispered close to her ear, even while hating the heat of her fever radiating against his face. "Come back to me so I can tell you properly. Stay with us, Leanne, please."

Her only reply was a thin, wheezing cough. A better man wouldn't be so greedy for her response, but he could not help himself. John selfishly yearned to see the look in her eyes when she heard he loved her. He craved a life with her too much to surrender her, even to her eternal peace. He didn't deserve her, knew the rage he felt at God right now made him no partner to a faithful woman like Leanne, but still he wanted her. For a few moments to look into her clear eyes and declare his love, John was sure he would have pulled the lethal fire consuming her onto himself. Despite a chest full of medals and the admiration of so many, John was sure of one truth: Leanne would bring far more good to the world than he ever could.

He would hold her. If she couldn't recognize his words, surely even in her state she would know the comfort of his arms. As he went to pick her up, it shocked him how light she was, how easily he slipped her delicate body from the bed to rest on his lap as he sat on the floor. Were he whole and healthy, he would carry her outside to the cool air, to the place where they'd sat in each other's arms and he'd felt the first of his heart slip away. But he wasn't whole and healthy, he could not walk with her in his arms. He could only offer what broken comfort was possible here and now. He handled her as though she were glass, some mythical vial with only the last drops of elixir left. He fought his urge to enfold her fiercely, to fend off all foes and somehow press his life into her fragile form.

In the distance he heard the ceaseless pounding of the casket crews as if they were banging down the door beside him, demanding entrance into the tiny sanctuary he shared with her. *I cannot let You have her,* he raged silently to the God she'd brought into his life. *I've not the faith to let her go.* He felt her heartbeat, light and skittish against his shirt. Her hands were cold, yet her face and chest glistened with fever. Even in the shadows, he could see the influenza's telltale blue-black imprint, stark and angry against her pale cheeks. Marred and thin as she was, Leanne was still the most beautiful woman God ever created. *Don't You love her enough to spare her?* He silently shouted the accusation to God through the helpless darkness that seemed to swallow them whole.

The answer came back to him with startling clarity: *Don't you?*

Unbidden, John's mind threw itself back in time to a stable when he was twelve. He was standing over his beloved mare, Huntress, the animal as bathed in sweat and suffering as Leanne was now. He was pleading the exact same case to his father, who had silently walked to the house and returned with a pistol. John had cried openly to his father that night—something a Gallows was never allowed to do—begging for the animal's life. He had never forgotten the sound of that pistol as it split the night, how even the sight of Huntress's final peaceful breaths had not soothed the wound of loss he carried in his chest for weeks. The memory overlaid itself on John's current pain, cinching around John's heart until he wanted to weep again, here, now. He had howled the same refusal to let Huntress go then as he had done to God tonight. It had been selfish and wrong then, it was selfish and wrong now.

John knew, then, that the memory was no accident. His father's words that night were his Holy Father's words to him tonight. It was not love to plead for more suffering. Leanne was more fit for Heaven than he could ever hope to be. "I don't know how to let You have her," he whispered to the darkness, praying as much for himself as for her. He looked into her face, limp against his arm with eyes sweetly closed. "How do I get to 'Thy will be done' as You would have me? I'm miles from being that man."

As the hours passed, the miles became a smaller and smaller distance to travel. Ida came in once, stopped to look at the sight of Leanne gathered against John's chest there on the floor, and silently let them be as she tended the other patients. As her fever soaked his shirt, as her winces of pain singed his ears and her spasms of coughing shook his own heart, John relinquished inch by inch. Broken, exhausted, perhaps already infected and in his own last days, John laid down what was left of his life. It seemed impossible that he and Leanne would wake tomorrow. Should he wake to find her gone, John felt sure he would stumble through life only as the hollow shell of a man who had loved and lost.

With what felt like his final thoughts, John surrendered to God this woman they both loved. "Take her even as I beg You not to," he whispered, a tear of his own falling onto Leanne's cheek as he held her near. He told her "I love you" over and over, hoping each of her shallow breaths was not her last. If he never heard the words from her, the hundreds of times she heard it from him would have to do.

Chapter Twenty-Nine

G_{ray.}

Vague gray and a strange coolness.

Leanne felt foreign inside her own skin, as if she were outside her body looking in from a curious distance. She felt pain, and yet the sensation wasn't nearly as sharp as before. It was a hollow ache, a dry and dusty feeling as though she'd blow away in the slightest breeze.

Papa was holding her. She was cradled in his arms, a little girl again. She could sense the steady rise and fall of his chest, feel the warm linen of his shirt against her cheek. Only her feet weren't curled onto the brown velvet of his sitting chair, they were on something cool and smooth. She thought about moving, about lifting her head to look around her because the sounds were all wrong, but her body seemed disconnected from her thoughts. She didn't seem to have any strength, not even to open her eyes. *Am I dreaming?* And then the more confusing thought: *Am I dead?* She felt like only a soul, surely, all thought and feeling but without substance. And then again, far too heavy to move.

The scent was wrong. This was not Papa, but still

familiar, still comforting. The shoulder was not Papa's, but yet strong and trustworthy. It came to her like a single candle lit in a dark room, a tiny circle of light changing the darkness.

John.

She had been sick. Blurry impressions of light and pain and struggle floated past her awareness. She had been very sick. Yes, that explained why she felt too weak and thirsty, why her skin felt as if it would crack open if she moved too quickly.

John.

This was John's shoulder against her cheek, his chin resting above her head. His arm encircling her. She wasn't sure how she knew, only that it couldn't be anyone but him.

The hospital. She remembered that much now. The image of her blood spattered on the dormitory sink came back to her. Influenza. With enormous effort she forced her cracked lips open and asked her body to breathe. Both her chest and throat felt ripped and raw, yet she could feel the air slipping in and out. She was breathing.

She was alive. Some part of her recognized the impossibility of that fact, recalled enough of her circumstance to know it shouldn't be. *Lord,* she reached out in prayer, movement still beyond her ability, *have You spared me? Do I live?* Leanne let out a small gasp, the marvel of her survival sending a surge of joy through her fragile limbs.

The sound made John shift slightly in his sleep, a soft and weary groan tickling her ears. She was alive. Leanne forced her eyes open, willed them to stay so until the swimming images before her gained clarity. Her first sight was the stubbled curve of John's chin, tilted back against the wall. Even in his rumpled state, he was without a doubt the most handsome man in all the world. They were on the floor of some small room with a handful of other beds. She remembered being here, gazing out the window and wishing for death to take away the pain. The memory returned the large ward's horrors to her mind, the rows upon rows of ill and dying, how she understood now why they begged for death. The image of Charles Holling's lifeless eyes just before she'd pulled the sheet up over his face washed over her vision, making her frightened and dizzy until she returned her gaze to John's sleeping face.

He must have taken her in his arms and held her there on the floor—for hours or minutes she couldn't say. He had been beside her, had cared for her. Fleeting images of his face and voice came back to her, blurred by fever and pain so that she could not remember the words, only the tone and how much comfort it had brought to her. She had a vague memory of him singing—which made no sense at all—but a very clear memory of him pleading for her to stay, to fight, to live.

And she had. She had survived, and she would survive. A tiny, powerful core of truth pulsed somewhere under her ribs like a heartbeat, telling her that her life was no longer in danger. Leanne wet her lips again, pulled another burning breath into her lungs, and pushed one word out into the morning air, "John."

He started, jolting to a bleary consciousness with another groan. It seemed to take him as long as it had taken her to remember where he was, to pull his head from its propped angle against the wall and look down. When he did, it was as if the sun rose in the blue sky of his wide eyes. He blinked with disbelief, his face melted into an expression of such joy and relief that Leanne felt tears sting her eyes. He pulled a hand across his eyes, as if to wipe away a dream, then looked at her again. He worked to form a word, producing only a tender sound; the eloquent John Gallows rendered speechless. Instead he bent his forehead to hers, and she felt the warmth of his tears steal between the rough stubble of his unshaven cheek. "You're here. Thank You, Lord. Thank You. Thank You." He rocked her gently, his chest heaving in a way that made her wish she had the strength to throw her arms around him. "You're here. You've lived. You're here."

Leanne closed her eyes for a moment, letting the pure joy push away the aching weakness.

He pulled back and touched every part of her face, cherishing her existence with eager fingers. "I'm not dreaming? You are really here?"

"Yes." She remembered, looking at his eyes, saying goodbye to him in her heart as she felt the darkness pulling her down. "I'm here."

"I was sure I'd lost you." His voice broke as he pulled her carefully closer. She felt her heart pound in her chest, wonderfully alive despite her still-frail state.

"I love you," he whispered close to her ear, and she felt it flood her soul like warm sunshine. "I told you over and over last night when I feared…" She was glad he didn't finish the thought. "I yelled at God that He couldn't have you because I loved you too much to lose you now that I've just found you. And then you worsened, and I couldn't ask Him to keep you in such suffering, so I…" He pulled back again and stared into her eyes. "I love you and you've survived. What else matters now?"

He was actually rambling, running words together like an excited schoolboy, and she let his joy flow over into her. John's exuberance radiated life and hope, and she gulped it in with every trembling breath. "Love?" Of course he loved her, for she loved him. She loved him. The fire in his eyes kindled the clearest truth— that she had always loved him.

"Yes." His smile was brilliant beyond anything she'd remembered. "Love. I would have suffered through loving you and losing you, but it seems God is kinder than that." He kissed her forehead, and it spread throughout her body as though it filled her with light and sparkles. "I'll thank Him every day forever, I think."

"You stayed with me. How I love you for that. How I love you." It took so much effort to lift her arm, and the thin gray hand that stroked his unshaven cheek seemed to belong to an old woman. He placed his hand atop hers, the way he had done on the hilltop back before all the darkness, and Leanne reveled in the warmth and strength of his touch. She yearned to give him grand words, to shout her feelings from the rooftops, but her body was still far weaker than her spirit. She was filled with too many emotions to hold back the tears.

"Are you all right? Do you hurt? You're still so frail."

How could she feel so weak and so alive at the same time? The room seemed to spin around her, and she was grateful for the anchor of John's embrace. "I'm terribly thirsty," she admitted. John tried to grasp something behind her—a glass, perhaps, on the small metal table she knew the hospital kept beside some of the cots— but couldn't reach it. He couldn't hope to get up with her in his arms. It would be difficult for a man with two healthy legs, much less his troublesome injury.

"You trapped yourself with me," she noted. He'd made the choice to stay no matter what happened when he'd pulled her onto his lap. There was something lovingly noble in the gesture. "My hero." Her smile was worth twice the effort it took.

"My damsel. My lovely, living damsel." He chuckled, attempting the rise they both knew was impossible. They were indeed stuck together on the floor, and while she could not manage a laugh, one bubbled forth from him. "Miss Landway!" he called, splitting the quiet dawn and waking the other patients in the room. "Madison!"

Ida burst into the room, the alarm on her face melting as she sagged against the doorway in relief and joy.

"Look what I have to contend with. Look at my splendid problem, Miss Landway!"

Ida's hands flew to her chest, then to her mouth, a tearful little whimper escaping her smiling expression. "She lives!" She rushed over to place an assessing hand on Leanne's cheek. "Her fever's broken. Mercy on us all, we've a survivor. You've survived, Leanne. You're the first one here."

"I have," Leanne said, letting her head return to the support of John's shoulder. Truly, he had the most wonderful shoulders.

"She has indeed." She felt John's jovial laugh tumble through his chest in little shakes that made her smile. "And I'd waltz her around the room...if I could get off the floor. Which I can't."

Grinning, Ida broke her own rule of quiet by shouting "Dr. Madison, come quickly!"

He must have been close by, for within seconds the doctor dashed in the door to show the same shock of pleasure Ida had. "Land sakes, she's still with us."

"No fever," Ida pronounced, stepping away as she gestured Dr. Madison over. "She's come through it, Doctor."

Madison squatted down to check her pulse, clasping a hand to John's shoulder with a smile. Something had changed between those two, Leanne could see it in the way their eyes met. The enmity between them had dissolved, replaced by what seemed to be a deep friendship. What all had God wrought while she slept?

"Not yet strong, but delightfully steady. You've turned the corner indeed, Miss Sample, and I couldn't be happier."

"I was wondering," John said with a stiff groan, "if we couldn't all be happier *off* the floor. I fear at the moment it'll be a week before I walk steady." He stole a look at Leanne, giving her a tentative squeeze, "but I'll be the happiest limping man east of Chicago."

Madison laughed. "You will at that."

It took considerable effort—and pain—to untangle Leanne from the circle of John's arms and get her laid out onto the fresh sheets Ida had managed to find and set on the bed. No one cared at the bother—it was far more celebration than anyone at the hospital had seen in too long. Every inch of Leanne felt cracked and dry, and yet still she smiled. John made glorious protests as Dr. Madison eased his stiffened body from the floor. "You'll pay for that night under her weight." He laughed, giving John's shoulder a friendly shake.

"Gladly," John said, fixing his gaze on Leanne again with dazzling warmth. She marveled again at his vigil over her. She loved him dearly, every boisterous, defiant bit of this man God had sent to her side. Surely God was laughing this morning at all doubts she'd expressed at the Almighty ever getting through to a soul the likes of John Gallows's.

Ida had managed to somehow find a second pillow, and she propped Leanne up, fussing about her like a queen's handmaiden. She brought a chair from the other side of the cot and handed John a tin mug of water. "You can tend to your damsel in distress for ten more minutes," she clucked like a proud mother hen, "then it's time for the both of you to get cleaned and rested."

There were still people in the room as John leaned over her to help her sip the water, but she forgot all of them in the depths of his eyes. "Drink, my love." His voice held a new, tender quality that spoke to the deepest parts of her heart. The water was bliss to her throat, cool and wet and wondrous. John looked at her as though he couldn't help but do so, as though she were a treasure instead of the rumpled sight she suspected she was. Still, he was doubly handsome to her in his unkempt, unshaven state, so perhaps the same was true of him as he looked at her. She felt herself blushing under the directness of his eyes, that dashing regard that had won far lovelier hearts than hers. He fingered a lock of her hair as he yawned. "Now rest."

"You, too," she replied, yawning, as well. She was so very tired, so grateful to be enduring a dull ache instead of the stabs of pain she'd known before. "Sleep well…" and with a boost of courage she added, "my love." She drifted into sleep recalling the sparkle in John's eyes that followed her words. She loved him. He loved her. They lived. Tomorrow could bring anything, and she would have enough.

Chapter Thirty

Dr. Madison looked at John from over the top of his glasses as they sat the next day in the tiny room that had become the doctor's quarters. "You've pushed yourself too far, but I suppose you don't need me to tell you that."

John leaned back against the room's single chair. It hurt to stand. It hurt to do anything anymore. "You know what I'm looking for."

Madison took off his glasses and pinched the bridge of his nose. "I've hardly the right equipment to make an assessment, especially under these circumstances."

John had given enough speeches to know propaganda when he saw it. "I'm long past pretending, Charles. Out with it."

There was a long pause before Madison answered. "No, I don't think you'll heal. Not properly. Not enough."

John felt the world tilt a bit and grabbed the arm of the chair for support. He'd prepared himself for this, had known on some level that this was coming, but it still felt like a punch to the stomach to hear it aloud. "I'm done, then."

"In service, yes. Honorable discharge, decorated I'm

sure, but—" he gave John a steady, direct look "—flying is out of the question." Madison took a deep breath before adding, "If you'd have gone…"

"Who can say what would have happened if I'd gone to Chicago and France?" John stood up and turned toward the room's only window. He hated how the sound of casket-builders' hammers still punctuated the air. "Not that I haven't turned it over in my mind a dozen times. I could have gotten what I thought I wanted." He turned and looked back at the doctor, wincing at the pang that accompanied the move. "Then again, I could have gotten what I deserved."

"Who can say what any man deserves? I've conferred with doctors from seven other bases, and I still can't explain why Leanne and the others live while hundreds more do not." Madison dropped his gaze. "We're not done here, John. Not by a long shot."

The randomness of influenza, the jarring lack of logic in who fell ill and who escaped, gave heavy weight to such questions. It was why Leanne had spent so much time talking about God's grace to her patients. To him. John returned his eyes to the window and the clear blue sky framed within. "I'm not fit to rejoin the service."

Madison came up behind him. "Do you regret it? Staying?"

"No." John didn't even have to think about it.

"You'd be all-too-human if you did." Madison tucked his hands in his pockets and rocked back on his heels. "To admit your regret doesn't belittle the act. It may even make it more heroic, if you ask me."

"I think I loved her even then," John explained, amazed at how easily the words came. "In the way I made the choice to stay so easily, with such certainty.

I knew, somehow, that my place was here. No, I don't regret it, Charles. I'm alive, and so is Leanne."

"And two more besides," Madison added. "But not enough live. We'll not be able to lift the quarantine for days, perhaps even weeks."

John managed a smile. "What matter is that? My battle and my prize are already here."

A week later Leanne sat in a chair for the first time since she'd fallen ill. Ida and Dr. Madison had contrived a room for her in a corner of an upper floor, away from the still-infected patients. Eventually the other survivors would join her when they became well enough to move, but for now Leanne enjoyed the ultimate luxury of privacy.

This afternoon as she dressed for the first time, privacy felt too lonely. She felt lost in the large room and large clothes—her blouse and skirt looked as if they belonged to someone else, hanging loose and awkward on her bony figure. She was gazing in a hand mirror Ida had brought with a hairbrush and a small length of ribbon. It was as if a stranger's reflection returned her gaze. While only shadows now, Leanne felt as if she could still see influenza's horrid dark spots on her own face. It unnerved her to know she had borne the purple blotches she'd found so ghoulish on her patients. She was a survivor, yes, but she was also a victim. Would she always see the spots, imagined in the mirror even when her face was full and flush with health? She still looked and felt so sickly. So weak and scarred.

It almost made it worse that Dr. Madison and the rest of the hospital staff reveled in her survival. She did not know how to be this wondrous "first survivor," or what that meant. John was the one at home in the spotlight, not her, and she had not done anything worthy to earn her newfound significance. John had once said his only heroism was "not dying." How funny that she now felt the same sentiment.

"I am glad to be alive, Lord," she preached to the sallow face in the mirror, "but I've not the grace to ignore how much of my hair is gone." Leanne could do nothing with the thinned and lifeless locks influenza had bequeathed her. She'd learned about hair thinning out during a high fever, but it was another, humbling thing to live with the symptom. "How vain I am despite all my reasons for gratitude." Where was the lovely, pretty-feeling Leanne who'd gazed at John from her place beside him on the magazine cover? She looked at her sunken cheeks and moaned at how far she was from that woman now. "I look old. A crone."

"You are the most beautiful woman in the world to me." John's voice came from behind her. Leanne turned, expecting to see his "charm and flattery" face, the one she'd seen him use during his speeches. Instead, she saw a precious genuine affection fill his features. He meant his words.

John's appearance was sometimes hard to bear. While pain darkened his expression more often than not, he still possessed the handsome features of his war-hero past. He hadn't really changed, whereas she felt like a walking war-wound. She leaned back against him as she considered herself again in the mirror. "I see far too much of Private Carson when I look in this mirror," she admitted, trying once again to force her limp hair to twist up artfully over her pale forehead.

"Shh." John placed a kiss on the spot where Leanne had affixed the thin curl. "Carson had lost his appetite for life. That's not something you catch like a disease.

It's something that festers inside a man until disease or wound sets it loose." He plucked the mirror from her grasp, taking both of her hands and turning her to face him. "You are a true beauty. I look at you and I see a warrior. Someone who has waged a mighty battle and earned her victory."

She turned away from him. "That's just it, John, I've earned nothing. Don't you see? You told me once you felt your medal was for nothing, that you were celebrated for merely staying alive. I feel like that. I don't know why I lived and others died. I've nothing to teach or share or contribute. I'm just *here*. It will be weeks until I'm strong enough to serve on the nursing staff again. What am I?"

"You, my love, are the most important thing we have right now—you are God's gift of hope. You and every other soul who manages to pull through." His winced as standing began to bother him, so he pulled a chair close to where she sat. It seemed like John couldn't stand for more than a few minutes lately, and while he was doing his best to gloss it over, she could tell it bothered him immensely. "Can't you feel how the atmosphere has changed since you've healed? Hopelessness doesn't sour the wards any longer. People don't come in here with a slaughterhouse fear in their eyes, because they know now that it's possible to live. Every healthy breath you take, every day you improve, is God's gift to everyone."

Leanne rested her chin in her hand. "Goodness, one would think you know how to give a speech."

"I know the power of inspiration. But yes, I do know what it's like to feel like more of a symbol than a person." John kneaded his thigh. "It wears on a soul to know others think you larger than you are. I do understand what you feel." He smiled. "God was wise to put us together, don't you think? Together. Us. The very idea still astounds me." He leaned in and kissed her.

It began as a soft and tender kiss, but deepened to a lingering, delighting, lover's kiss. The kind of rapturous kiss a handsome man would give to a beautiful woman. He made her feel so loved. His regard, the clear affection in his touch, was a balm to the sting of her unhealthiness. There they sat, sitting because neither of them were able to truly stand, but feeling they were strong together. She knew, *knew* John loved her, even now. Not in spite of her scars, but perhaps even because of them. Didn't she feel the same way about him, about his wounds? Could she have loved the unwounded John, the arrogant dashing hero too large for life? He wasn't the same man without the thorn of his lame leg. The way he coped with his injury, with her illness, was so very much a part of how she loved him now. How perfectly suited they truly were for each other. "Very wise," she whispered when she finally pulled away, breathless from his kiss.

"Oh," John said, reaching for a small bag he'd set down near his cane. "You had me so spellbound I nearly forgot. I've a gift for you. I know you've been far too idle for your liking, but I'm in no hurry to see you push yourself too soon."

"You," she teased, "preaching to me about the wisdom of respecting one's physical limitations? Perhaps the world really is coming to an end."

"You don't want to force me to take back this yarn now, do you?"

"Yarn! You brought me yarn?" She grabbed at the bag even as John held it playfully out of her reach. "I can't think of anything I'd rather do right now than to be knitting."

John leaned in, holding the bag behind him. "Anything?" His eyes sparkled with cinema-star charm.

"You're dreadful." She leaned in and kissed him, deftly snatching the bag in his resulting distraction. "Anything productive, I mean. I'm hardly well enough to do much else, and my hands have been itching for yarn and needles." The bag held the current set of socks she'd been working on. "How did you manage to get these sent over?"

"You said yourself, I'm very persuasive. Look in the bottom of the bag."

Leanne dug deeper to find two of the softest, plushest hanks of yellow cashmere she'd seen in months. An absolute decadence in wartime, much less during a quarantine. "John!"

"And as you also said yourself, I'm rather fond of breaking rules."

She fingered the luxurious fiber, soft as clouds and bright as sunshine. "Oh, John, I can't."

"You can and you ought to. My secret source says it's just enough to make a bed jacket or whatever it is you call such frilly things. And I shall have Dr. Madison write out a prescription if you refuse. You're to be pampered, and that's the end of it."

"A yellow cashmere bed jacket? It's scandalous."

John's smile was perhaps even wider than her own. "It's therapeutic. Look at you. Your color's improved already." He picked up the mirror and moved behind her as she sat on the chair. He bent so that they could both see her reflection and held one of the hanks to her neck. Its fuzzy fibers tickled her chin. "Mmm. I've always liked you in yellow."

"I trust," she nearly gasped as his murmur tingled

down the back of her neck, "you were able to secure the sock *you* were working on, as well?"

"Alas, no." His eyes suggested he hadn't even attempted to do so.

"Oh, but Captain Gallows, you promised me a sock for the charity auction." She pulled a strand of the cashmere from its twist in the hank, wrapping it around one finger with nothing short of glee. To knit something for herself, something so extravagant, something from John, filled her with a radiant energy.

"My duties as makeshift quartermaster don't allow for such luxuries." He straightened with a groan and returned himself stiffly to the chair opposite her. "I may not be able to walk far, but I'm a champion of stretching supplies for miles."

Leanne put down the yarn to lay a hand on John's knee. "How is your leg? It seems worse."

John's sigh told more than his words. "It is. Madison said…" He stopped himself. "No bother about that. What shall you knit first? The olive or yellow?"

"Yes, I *will* bother about that. What did Dr. Madison say? Has he been treating you?"

John shifted his weight, as if the leg ached more at the subject. "Nothing to treat, nor anything to treat with. Fevers need ice more than sore legs, pain medicine is more luxury than your yarn there, and…some things just…don't heal." He busied himself with the olive army sock, inspecting it with false curiosity. "Impressive heel, my dear. Such neat stitches."

The John Gallows she'd known didn't use tones of resignation. She pulled the sock from his hands. "John, stop avoiding the subject. What has Dr. Madison told you?"

John pushed up off the chair, turning away from her

and yet leaving his cane on the floor where they had sat. "There's no point in discussing it."

"There is every point in discussing it. Don't keep this from me. Not this."

John faced out the window, leaning against the sill for a long moment before he spoke. "Madison said I've abused it beyond repair. The leg is lame. Permanently. He couldn't sign off on active service for me now even if he wanted to, even if Barnes demanded it. Which I doubt Barnes will do, as I suspect the general's hunting for my head as it is."

Returning to service had been everything to John. He'd sacrificed everything, pushed himself, broken rules and called in favors to make it happen. He'd been on the brink of achieving that goal. The influenza outbreak was supposed to be a detour, not the end. "I am so sorry," she said, even though the words hardly did his pain justice. "I know how hard that is for you." And here she was pitying herself because she looked sickly. She had every chance to recover, and now John did not. It seemed unjust.

The second part of his statement struck her just then. "And why is General Barnes after your head?" John still had not moved. It dawned on her that John hadn't told her everything. "What did you do?"

Chapter Thirty-One

John avoided her gaze. "I did nothing out of character for me."

"That leaves a fair amount of room to wonder. What did you do?"

He propped his hands against the sides of the window and slowly stretched his leg, an attempt at casual movement she knew could not be true. "I suppose it's more about what I didn't do. The general doesn't take to having his direct orders disobeyed."

Leanne had seen enough to know John disobeying orders couldn't be news to the commander. This had to be larger than that. She put down the yarn and mirror on the table beside her and sat up straight. "And which disregarded orders are so important as to have General Barnes up in arms?" When John didn't respond, she added, "John, please. Whatever it is you think I ought not to hear, tell me."

John turned slowly, leaning against the wall next to the window. He spoke slowly, reluctantly. "I was supposed to have left the base the day we came to campus. Barnes knew what was coming. The base in Boston had already been hit and ships coming into Philadelphia were falling fast. He gave me a train ticket and orders to ship off to Chicago that night so I'd escape the outbreak. He said it was for promotional purposes but I knew better. I suspect it was my father's doing. Why else should I be swept out of harm's way while everyone else sits like targets?"

"Because you are valuable and important." Then the true weight of what he had said began to hit her. "You defied the order to leave? Knowing what was coming? Chicago and France were what you wanted, John. Why on earth did you stay?"

He looked surprised she needed to ask. "For you."

She felt his words like physical force. Tight and clenching. It was suffocating enough to be the survivor on which an entire hospital pinned its hopes. But to be the reason a man had forsaken his goal? Placed himself in harm's way? Destroyed his chance at achieving his dreams? Especially if it was a man she loved. The weight choked her. "Me?"

John limped over to the chair again, grabbing her hands. "You. And not you. Me. Everything. I looked at that ticket and I knew I couldn't use it. Knew I ought to be here. Beside you."

"John…"

"And not only beside you, but here, fighting this battle. I didn't choose what happened on that airship, but I could choose this. I knew whatever I was running back to France to find was already right in front of me."

"That makes no sense."

"It does to me. I don't know that I can explain it any better than that but I don't regret it. I didn't want you to know because I didn't want you to feel like this." He shook her hands, his voice fierce. "I don't regret it. Not for a second, do you hear me? I'll limp until I'm eighty and not look back."

"It's not just your leg. You knew the outbreak was coming. You could have fallen ill just as easily as I. Either or both of us could have…" She didn't want to finish that sentence, nor did she have to. Every single person in this building was aware that every cough held the possibility of death. "Could still…"

John pulled her to her feet and held her. "None of that. I'm invincible, remember?"

She wrapped her arms around him, and they wobbled a bit as if the unsteadiness confirmed that lie. "You most certainly are not." She had not, for one second, ignored the possibility that John could still fall ill. "We don't know how it's contracted. I pray every day you won't start coughing. I couldn't stand it if I'd infected you."

"You heard Madison. He thinks that those exposed either succumb or don't. I haven't yet, so I'm unlikely to." He tightened his embrace. "And I've been very close to an infected patient."

"They're only guessing, John. Dr. Madison says he still can't say why I survived. There's so much they still don't understand."

She swayed a bit, and John pulled them both back to the seats. He tipped her chin up to look at him. "Look at me. There's only one thing to understand here, and it is that we *are* here. Not altogether perfect, but alive, and with each other. This is where I am meant to be, where God means us to be. I know you know that. Have some of that faith you boasted to me about. The quarantine will be lifted soon and we'll trust God with the days after that."

Leanne let her forehead fall to touch John's. She could only marvel at how the disaster had changed him, what God had done. "When did you become such a wise and faithful soul?"

"One very long night not too long ago. You fought influenza while I did battle with…other things." He pulled back to trace what must be the shadows under her eyes. "You've been up long enough, as have I. Rest." He nodded toward the room's one bed. It made her wonder if John's leg let him sleep in any comfort at all. "Dream of fluffy yellow yarn." He yawned.

"I love you," she said, cupping his poorly shaven chin. She felt too full of emotion and fatigue to say anything less. "I am so very, desperately glad you are here."

"We may be the only two souls on earth thankful for an influenza quarantine. God certainly works in mysterious ways." He kissed her again, and she thought she could never tire of his tender touch. "I love you." He touched her face, then slowly moved to pull himself out of the chair.

Leanne pulled her own self upright, handing him his cane. "I shall buy you the grandest silver cane ever for your eightieth birthday. It will be so huge and impressive, little boys will fear it and little girls will think you a king. Dream of that."

"Goodness, no." He laughed weakly. "I prefer to dream of steak."

John offered Leanne a smile as he helped her into one of the parlor chairs at the Red Cross House. It was a victory, moving her back to Jackson. Yes, Dr. Madison approved it half for the benefit of Leanne's parents— who were coming despite numerous requests to hold off. Madison also approved it for purely practical reasons: the small "recovery ward" she'd "launched" was filling with patients. The quarantines at Jackson and the university had been lifted. An end to the calamity seemed to be in sight.

"I'm well, you know. In fact, I'm quite sure I could have walked." He'd borrowed an army wheelchair to ferry her from the transport car to the Red Cross House steps.

"Strolled up those steps *and* fended off your parents on arrival? You overstate your recuperative powers, lauded as they are." Her "recuperative powers" had become a joke of sorts between them, for doctors and nurses everywhere wanted to know how Leanne had survived. He felt an urge to protect her from such attentions, knowing how he felt when people asked him how he'd dared to go out on the stay wires of the dirigible. People wanted an answer where no answer was to be had.

Leanne arranged her skirts on the chair. She'd gained back a bit of weight, looking less like a scarecrow in her own clothes. Her color was better but still not what it had once been, and she tired easily. More than once he'd come up to her room in the dormitory to find her fast asleep with her knitting needles and what she called his "scandalous yellow yarn" still held in her fingers. She held that yarn in her lap now, and he felt the surge of satisfaction he always did when he'd found some way to please or pamper her. "Will you stay and meet them?" she asked.

"I don't think today is the day for such an introduction, and… I've a dreaded commitment."

She raised an eyebrow at his terminology. "Dreaded?"

"General Barnes." Horrific as it was, the quarantine had cocooned him and Leanne in a bubble of their own, shielded from the war, the outside world and all such consequences. In truth John was sure fear of infection was the only thing that had kept Barnes from storming onto campus the moment the quarantine had been lifted and hauling John personally into whatever punishment generals devised for valuable liabilities such as himself. Now John found himself with the daunting task of testing his new faith in the realities of ordinary life. If life ever became ordinary in love and at war.

Leanne reached for John's hand. "What will he do?" He was glad she hadn't asked the more accurate "What will he do to you?"

"God only knows." Such phrases used to annoy Leanne, but now he loved using it because now he knew he truly meant it. He ran his hand over the back of her palm delighted he could no longer trace the outline of her veins through paper-pale skin. "We've prayed over this, I ought to be calmer."

"The timing seems dreadful. How can I keep my mind on Mama and Papa knowing you're with General Barnes?"

"How can I keep my mind on General Barnes knowing you're with your mama and papa without me to protect you?"

The joke roused the laugh he'd intended. "They're my parents, John, not some angry monsters. They'll fuss and demand to take me home, I'm sure—" she took his hand in both of hers "—but I'm stronger now. So many things are different. I only hope I can make them see. I'll admit I do wish I had some of your persuasive abilities today."

John leaned in and kissed her. "There. I've transferred the lot of them, my mouth to yours. Now I wish I had your faith in unknown outcomes. I'm nothing near calm enough."

She returned his kiss. "There. I've transferred the lot of it, my mouth to yours."

John managed a smile. "If only it worked that way."

She caught his collar before he pulled back. "I love you, no matter what."

Her words managed what her kiss had not. Should all of the United States Army come crashing down around his ankles in the next hour, he had the love of a Sovereign God and the only woman that mattered. He let his fingers grace the perfect line of her chin. "Then I have all I need, my love. Be well, charm your parents and I'll come back when…when it's done."

"I'm well," Leanne repeated, trying to convince her parents' fearful eyes. "Really, I've improved a great deal, and I get stronger every day." She couldn't bear to tell them she looked much better than just a few days earlier, for Mama clutched her gauze mask in a white-knuckled fist.

"You should come home with us. Right now," Papa pronounced as he paced the room. She couldn't blame their apprehension on being inside Camp Jackson. Everyone was afraid of everything, for the air was the enemy, and the enemy was everywhere. Only the fiercest of worries could have pulled Mama and Papa from the protection of their home in such a crisis. Papa was clearly here to collect his little girl and take her home to safety.

"Dr. Madison says I'm not yet strong enough to travel." It was true, but only half the truth. She couldn't bear the thought of leaving Camp Jackson, not now. Her world had turned upside down and righted itself in a completely new way. To go back to who she was six months ago—which was exactly what would happen if she went home now—seemed terribly wrong. It made her thankful for Dr. Madison's medical excuse. She couldn't conceive of how to make Mama and Papa understand she wasn't anything close to the young woman who'd left them on the station platform just a few months ago. "It's best I stay here." After summoning her courage, she amended her statement. "And, Papa, I want to stay here."

"Nonsense. Military camps are the most dangerous places of all right now. We can easily take care of you at home where it's safe." Mama said the words as if defying the world to breach the sanctuary of the Sample family threshold.

The reality was that no place was truly "safe." The quarantine had been lifted, but cases were still coming in. The base hospital was still full to overflowing, as were both of Columbia's hospitals. Some were surviving, but many were still dying. The last report predicted that the number of cases here would peak near three thousand, and other cities were just coming under the wave of infection Columbia had crested. Safe? *Safe* couldn't mean a lack of danger anymore. *Safe* had come to mean simply wherever John was. Wherever God watched over the pair of them together. "I am safe here, Mama. I'm healing, and when I'm well enough I'll need to return to my post."

Mama's wide eyes showed she didn't believe a word of it, and that she didn't much care for her daughter's newfound independence. "You're so very thin and pale. Are you eating? Is everyone wearing masks?"

I've watched men die behind their masks, Leanne wanted to say. "Yes, they're very careful here. And now that the quarantine is lifted, the camp is eating quite well." Her words brought back the memory of John feeding her sausage on the front steps, and she hoped Mama would mistake the flush it brought to her cheeks as the radiance of health.

John stood before General Barnes's desk, at attention despite how much it hurt. The general had not invited him to sit as he normally did when they met. This was no normal meeting.

The general ran his hands down his face, the weary gesture a revelation of how difficult life under quarantine had been. "Do you know what the worst part of my job is, Gallows?"

"No, sir."

Barnes pointed to a stack of letters on his desk. "Signing these. Orders for telegrams bringing the worst possible news to some poor mother or father, or wife. I've signed nearly three hundred of these, and I'm sick to death of ugly, pointless deaths. Influenza isn't supposed to kill, Gallows, it makes no sense."

John couldn't argue with that. "It doesn't, sir."

"The last thing I need—" Barnes took off his glasses and looked at John for the first time since he'd entered the room "—is one of my best weapons doing something even more senseless. I needed you in Chicago. I tried to save you from what I knew was coming, and you disobeyed a direct order and went A.W.O.L. The thing I can't work out is why."

John gave the only answer that came to him. "I doubt you'd believe me if I told you, sir."

The general leaned back in his chair. "Try me."

John had prayed all morning that Barnes would simply reprimand him and not demand an explanation. He was sure any attempt to convey all that had happened to him recently would fail miserably. Barnes didn't look like the kind of man who'd embrace either a spiritual or a romantic motive, and John had no other explanation.

"You might as well sit down, Gallows," Barnes interjected at John's hesitation. "It looks to me like this is a long story and frankly I could use the diversion."

John wondered if God wasn't smiling somewhere. He'd prayed specifically for a short meeting, afraid that his passions would run away with his mouth if asked too many questions. Today his father was right when he called John "a man of too many words." The simplest explanation seemed the best place to start. "A woman, sir."

"I beg your pardon?"

"It wasn't hard to glean what was coming from my last visit to your office. I found I couldn't leave a particular woman to face it alone. Well, without me. Or rather, I suppose I couldn't bear the thought of her falling ill and not being here." The words sounded far more ridiculous than romantic.

General Barnes crossed his arms over his chest. "Surely you're not telling me Nurse Sample survived because of your illustrious presence?"

John raised an eyebrow. He'd hoped not to name names.

"Captain Gallows, you're anything but subtle and camp gossip is faster than the telegraph. I have one clerk drafting a list of charges to bring you up on while another is suggesting we should call *Era* magazine and give them the exclusive update."

For once, John was speechless, his wobbly smile feeling foolish. "I'd rather you did neither."

"I ought to do anything I please at the moment, rather than taking suggestions from the likes of you. How do I explain what you've done? I can't very well let a highly visible, recently publicized soldier—an officer at that—get away with disobeying direct, self-preserving orders for *love*. You've got to give me another reason."

God's smile must have broadened. There was only one other reason, and it wouldn't sit any better with the general than John's first explanation. "You'll like it less," he quipped, swallowing the feeling he was facing a firing squad.

"There's not much 'less' left in me, Gallows." He leaned forward on his elbows with the expression of a man bracing for a hit to the stomach.

Chapter Thirty-Two

John recalled the Bible passage about Paul defending his refusal to obey orders of silence to Roman officials. He felt a particular affinity, the helplessness of trying to explain the relentlessness of God to someone who'd never experienced it. He couldn't blame the general; two months ago, had someone given him the answer he was about to give Barnes, he would be balking, as well.

"Well, sir, I looked at those tickets, I knew what they represented, and all I can say is that I knew at that moment that God had led me to Columbia and I wasn't supposed to leave it."

Barnes looked understandably shocked.

"No one expected it less than me, sir. And I'll be the first to admit that it makes no sense to anyone else. But that's the honest truth. I knew, as much as I've known anything in my life—and certainly more than I knew on that dirigible—that I needed to stay. That the place I most needed to be was where God asked me to be, and that wasn't Chicago. Or France."

"God?" Barnes clearly would have preferred just about any other answer. "I ask you for a logical explanation to keep you from Courts-Martial and the best you can give me is *God* and *love?*" He squinted his eyes shut in frustration. "I don't know why I'm surprised at this nonsense. I can't fathom a *sensible* explanation for what you did." He gave John an incredulous look. "You've put me in a hard place, Gallows. Of course you're not the first soldier to have his head turned by a pretty nurse, and I suppose you're not the first man to turn to his Maker in a foxhole, but you've done so *with the press watching.* Land sakes, son, the two of you were on the cover of *Era.* I can't let it go, nor can it ever be known that you disobeyed direct orders without consequences. Miss Sample was the first South Carolinian to survive the influenza. I can't just sweep y'all under a rug."

"I understand your position, sir. I don't regret what I did, though. Not for a moment." After a pause, John asked, "Are you married, sir?"

Barnes managed an annoyed smirk. "Contrary to legend, I was young once. Your father introduced me to my wife, as a matter of fact. Mrs. Barnes was a great beauty and I made a bit of a fool of myself to catch her eye. I'm no heartless beast, John, but you're no fool, either. You know what's at stake here."

"I do." His heart and his soul were at stake, only he was sure Barnes didn't see it that way.

"I've no idea what to do. I can't honorably discharge you, but I can't give you a dishonorable discharge without setting off a press ruckus. I had hoped your explanation would save you, but you've only given me more rope to hang you, son. Only I can't hang you, and according to Madison, I can't send you back into active duty. Ever."

"I know." John kept his voice neutral even though the finality of the general's pronouncement stole the peace he'd been feeling up until a moment ago. He didn't know what to be if he couldn't be a soldier; he'd been raised to fill a uniform from his earliest days. He tried to remember God was in control, and his role wasn't to wrangle his future, but to stand firm and tell the truth. The old John could have invented twenty salable explanations for his actions, could have concocted a variety of stories to meet the public need. In every aspect of this situation, the truth seemed not only useless, but downright harmful. "I do appreciate your position, sir."

"'You appreciate my position.' Gallows, you pander like a confounded diplomat." The general froze. "You *are* a diplomat. You can talk out of both sides of your mouth better than half the fellows up in Washington." Barnes pointed at him. "Come to think of it, I can't fathom a worse punishment for you than to send you into a post dripping with rules and protocol. A protocol officer. If we don't have one, I'll find a reason to need one. It'd serve you right, if it doesn't kill you first. Why should I go through the trouble of Courts-Martialing you when I can send you someplace dreadful and force you to sit through endless speeches?"

John gulped. Should he protest, fortifying the general's appetite for punishing him? Or congratulate him on a creative solution? He settled for something in between. "Exactly how would I be discharged, then?" He wasn't even sure the general's current plan involved a discharge. Did it matter?

"I have no idea. It'll take me a month just to figure out how to set it all up through channels, so you can expect to be on base through November."

"That's fine, sir. I have a…commitment of sorts to keep in November."

Barnes looked up. "Commitment?"

"To the Red Cross, if you remember."

The general's laugh filled the room. "The socks? The auction of your Red Cross sock? Confound it, Gallows, you'll be the death of me yet." He waved John off. "Dismissed until I can fathom what to do with you."

John retrieved his cane and rose.

"John Gallows knits and gets religion. And here I thought I'd seen it all. Well, whatever you do," Barnes added, "don't tell me you'll pray for me. I'm not sure I'm ready to hear that talk coming out of your highly publicized mouth."

"I won't," John replied, but couldn't help adding, "*tell* you, that is."

Chapter Thirty-Three

❦

Charleston, South Carolina
November 1918

Mama touched Leanne's arm as the Charleston Holiday Ball was winding to a close. "You feeling all right, honey? It's been a long night."

She wasn't at full strength, but Leanne had enjoyed the evening despite so many missing people and decorations that were half as splendid as in years past. "I'm fine, Mama. Tired but fine." She sighed. "It'll be a somber sort of holiday season, don't you think?"

"Too many families have empty places around the table." Mama's sigh matched her own. "Your grandmother will be sorely missed." Nana had been in the last wave of influenza victims.

"You took good care of her," Papa said with a hand on Leanne's shoulder.

"I was glad of the chance." She had still been on medical leave, and while she wasn't strong enough to resume her hospital duties, Leanne had surprised herself by requesting two weeks' leave to come home to Charleston and tend to Nana. Besides, Dr. Madison felt she'd have further immunity to contracting influenza—unlike her parents. It seemed, like John said of his trip to the campus, that God was clearly leading her to her Nana's side. "We had so many wonderful conversations before she passed, Mama. I thank God every day for that time."

Mama smiled through brimming eyes. "She loved you especially. She was glad to see you happy."

Leanne looked at John, regal in his full dress uniform for perhaps the final time, smiling as he accepted the gushing thanks from a group of Red Cross leaders. He'd been asked by over two dozen Red Cross Chapters to give speeches in support of the knitting campaign before Armistice Day had announced the end of the war last week. Tonight at the Charleston Holiday Ball, his famous sock had brought in a record-breaking anonymous bid to raise funds for wounded soldiers. "I am dearly happy, Mama."

"I gather you told Nana so?" Papa asked.

"Of course I did." She'd told Nana all about John and what had transpired between them. Nana and Grandpappy had been a wartime romance, too, and Leanne heard many tender stories that cast the memory of her grandmother in whole new light.

"Well, now," Mama said with a mysterious smile, "that explains everything."

"Explains what?"

Papa reached into his coat. "Why your mother owns this, of course. Only we don't think I should keep it. I believe it belongs to John." To Leanne's surprise, Papa produced a hideous olive-green sock.

"I think you ought to frame it, though—it's certainly no good for wearing." She chuckled, peering at the lopsided garment. "The top isn't even the same size as the bottom from the looks of it."

Leanne felt her jaw drop. "*You* bought John's sock?"

"Actually your grandmother did. The last time we were together, she gave me money and told me to bid in secrecy." Mama's eyes brimmed over, and a single tear stole down her cheek. "Mother always did like a good surprise, and she wanted such a marvelous heirloom to stay in the family."

Leanne pulled her mother into a quick, joyous hug. "John will be thrilled. I should go tell him."

Papa stopped her as she turned. "No need, darlin', he already knows."

"You told him Mama was bidding on his sock?" John hadn't given any hints of knowing what was afoot. He'd acted as surprised as everyone else when the emcee had announced the generous anonymous winning bid.

"It seemed only fair to let him know, seeing how he's asked for your hand and all. I told you Nana wanted the sock to stay in the family."

Leanne was having trouble breathing. "Mama, I…" She turned and looked at John, who was trying hard to pry his way out of a gaggle of Red Cross spinsters to make his way toward her. The look on his face told her he'd known everything all evening. "Papa, you…"

"Go save your beau, Leanne." Papa's voice was warm and joyous.

"Oh, he can take care of himself with those old hens." Ida's voice came from over Leanne's other shoulder. "I'm gonna get my congratulations in first." Ida's fierce hug nearly sent Leanne to coughing.

"Did *everyone* know but me?" Leanne gasped, fanning her face in stunned shock.

"Only Colonel Gallows doesn't know by now, and

I expect he'll know within the hour if not sooner." Ida laughed.

Leanne wanted to shake her head and blink. God had granted her every single wish and more besides. "I'm stunned. I don't know what to do."

"I have a few ideas." John came up from her other side and took her hand. "But I hope you're not going to make me knit a second sock before you say yes."

"No! I mean yes! Rather, yes, I'll marry you but no, you won't have to knit a sock." She flew into John's arms, knocking his cane from his hand and nearly sending him reeling. "A hundred yesses!"

Ida caught the cane and tried to hand it back to John, but Leanne happily ensured the captain was otherwise occupied. "I'd rather he lean on me."

Epilogue

Era Magazine
Dateline: November 1919, Washington, DC
Headline: New Socks for Celebrated Knitting Couple

The war hero and nurse who charmed the nation's heart into more Red Cross knitting have collaborated on their finest project to date. Sources close to the Red Cross told *Era* magazine that Mrs. John Gallows, now wife of diplomatic attaché and decorated former U.S. Army Captain John Gallows, will be knitting a new type of socks: baby booties. Readers will remember last year's *Era* cover featuring Nurse Leanne Sample and Captain Gallows in the Red Cross promotion to encourage boys' participation in the "Knit Your Bit" for the war campaign. That effort, and their survival of the subsequent influenza epidemic and quarantine that hit Camp Jackson, evidently joined more than just yarn to needles and the couple married this past spring.

Pink or blue? "Anything and everything but army green," Gallows remarked with a smile when cornered by reporters last week. "We've had enough of that for a while."

Congratulations, Mr. & Mrs. Gallows! *Era* couldn't be more pleased that our little project paved the way for yours.

* * * * *

**IF YOU ENJOYED THIS BOOK
WE THINK YOU WILL ALSO LOVE**

LOVE INSPIRED

INSPIRATIONAL ROMANCE

Uplifting stories of faith, forgiveness and hope.

Fall in love with stories where faith helps
guide you through life's challenges, and discover
the promise of a new beginning.

6 NEW BOOKS AVAILABLE EVERY MONTH!

SPECIAL EXCERPT FROM

LOVE INSPIRED
INSPIRATIONAL ROMANCE

Rescuing a single mom and her triplets during a snowstorm lands rancher Finn Brightwood with temporary tenants in his vacation rental. But with his past experiences, Finn's reluctant to get too involved in Ivy Darling's chaotic life. So why does he find himself wishing this family would stick around for good?

Read on for a sneak preview of
Choosing His Family, *the final book in*
Jill Lynn's *Colorado Grooms miniseries.*

In high school, Finn had dated a girl for about six months. Once, when they'd been watching a movie, she'd fallen asleep tucked against his arm. His arm had also fallen asleep. It had been a painfully good place to be, and he hadn't moved even though he'd suffered through the end of that movie.

This time it was three little monkeys who'd taken over his personal space, and once again he was incredibly uncomfortable and strangely content at the same time.

Reese, the most cautious of the three, had snuggled against his side. She'd fallen asleep first, and her little features were so peaceful that his grinch's heart had grown three sizes.

Lola had been trying to make it to the end of the movie, fighting back heavy eyelids and extended yawns, but eventually she'd conked out.

Sage was the only one still standing, though her fidgeting from the back of the couch had lessened considerably.

Ivy returned from the bunkhouse. She'd taken a couple of trips over with laundry as the movie finished and now returned the basket to his laundry room. She walked into the living room as the movie credits rolled and turned off the TV.

LIEXP0121

"Guess I let them stay up too late." She moved to sit on the coffee table, facing him. "I'll carry Lola and Reese back. Sage, you can walk, can't you, love?"

Sage's weighted lids said the battle to stay awake had been hard fought. "I hold you, too, Mommy."

Cute. Finn wouldn't mind following that rabbit trail. Wouldn't mind making the same request of Ivy. Despite his determination not to let her burrow under his skin, tonight she'd done exactly that. He'd found himself attending the school of Ivy when she was otherwise distracted. Did she know that she made the tiniest sound popping her lips when she was lost in thought? Or that she tilted her head to the right and only the right when she was listening— and studied the speaker with so much interest that it made them feel like the most important human on the planet?

Stay on track, Brightwood. This isn't your circus. Finn had already bought a ticket to a circus back in North Dakota, and things hadn't ended well. No need to attend that show again. Especially when the price of admission had cost him so much.

"I'll help carry. I can take two if you take one."

"Thank you. That would be really great. I'd prefer to move them into their beds and keep them asleep if at all possible. If Reese gets woken up, she'll start crying, and I'm not sure I have the bandwidth for that tonight."

Ivy gathered the girls' movie and sweatshirts, then slipped Sage from the back of the couch.

Finn scooped up Reese and caught Lola with his other arm. He stood and held still, waiting for complaints. Lola fidgeted and then settled back to peaceful. Reese was so far gone that she didn't even flinch.

These girls. His dry, brittle heart cracked and healed all at the same time. They were good for the soul.

Don't miss
Choosing His Family *by Jill Lynn,*
available February 2021 wherever
Love Inspired books and ebooks are sold.

LoveInspired.com

LIEXP0121

LOVE INSPIRED
INSPIRATIONAL ROMANCE

UPLIFTING STORIES OF FAITH, FORGIVENESS AND HOPE.

Join our social communities to connect with other readers who share your love!

Sign up for the Love Inspired newsletter at **LoveInspired.com** to be the first to find out about upcoming titles, special promotions and exclusive content.

CONNECT WITH US AT:

Facebook.com/LoveInspiredBooks

Twitter.com/LoveInspiredBks

Facebook.com/groups/HarlequinConnection

LISOCIAL2020

HARLEQUIN

Heartfelt or suspenseful, inspiring or passionate, Harlequin has your happily-ever-after.

With new books published every month, you are sure to find the satisfying escape you know you deserve.